Be

BE HOME BY DINNER

A Novel

CARL FRANKE

Produced with Pressbooks.com

Published with Amazon Kindle Direct Publishing

Cover design by Carl Franke

2nd Edition

Dedicated to my Mom and Dad, for letting me blast my music as loud as I wanted.

Contents

Initial Taste

O ctober '78
    I sat on the curb at the end of the walkway, tapping my sneakers onto Redford Road, staring at the rainbow sheen of leaked motor oil. *Star Wars* figures stood propped up against the lawn edging with weapons in hand. Behind me, the walkway led to the front screen door where I saw Mom attending to my feverish sister. Dad was at a bank, cashing a check. I was 4-years-old.

My family had recently moved to Oreland, West Oreland to be exact, or White City as the original generation dubbed it. The rectangular cookie cutter homes were constructed shortly after WWII, all painted white.

The perimeter of my front lawn universe was the curb at the street, tall hedges to the right and bushes to the left. My parents allowed me to roam free within these boundaries, a realm of azaleas, scattered toys, a tall pine and skittish squirrels.

From the lawn, I could see several homes, all occupied by retired grandparents. They often worked on gardening projects with meticulous precision. Many were veterans that purchased their homes with the help of the G.I. Bill.

The Finns lived across the street. They drank cider on a fancy tree swing and waved at me as I made battle sound effects with my mouth. Mr. Finn sported a feather in his hat with a cardigan sweater. Mrs. Finn wore a bonnet with a shawl. They swung hand in hand.

"Garvey, what're ya gonna be for Halloween tomorrow?" Mr. Finn called out.

I ignored him and looked back at Mom. She was spoon feeding something to my sister, Siobhan.

The Finns stood up and walked to their front door, waving me over. Mrs. Finn shivered, rubbing her upper arms with her hands to warm up. "Do you like British biscuits?" she called out.

"What is that?" I asked.

"They're kind've like cookies. Superb. Come over and have some."

I thought about how Dad spoke of Mr. Finn as a good guy, an American war hero.

The wind whooshed through yellowing leaves, revealing their lighter colored bottoms. Clouds raced by the sun, as if someone was toggling a dimmer switch, their shadows gliding over the street. I stood up, looked both ways and leaped into the street toward the widening smiles of the Finns. Glancing back, I didn't see Mom through the screen door anymore. The glare of the TV lit up Siobhan's glum freckled face. Sweaty blond bangs laid heavy on her forehead.

Inside the Finn household, I took a seat on a stiff sofa. Mr. Finn sat on a wingback chair and turned on the TV. "Ya know, Oreland is exactly as named. A land of ore," Mr. Finn said, tapping his cane. "Iron ore. American iron ore was made into steel to make aircraft so we could bomb the Nazis."

"Oh, please," cried Mrs. Finn. "Now's not that time for that. Have some biscuits, boys."

"Well, it's true. We need to educate our youth. America produced the most in '45."

Mrs. Finn shook her head and put a tray of assorted beige delectables in front of us. I grabbed one with a jelly dot on it. Mr. Finn put on a PBS show called *All Creatures Great And Small*.

The living room decor included intricate framed paintings, plush pillows, ceramic figurines, and doilies. A variety of clocks ticked and chimed. The Finns stared at me with glazed eyes and grins, somehow comforted by my sloppy chomps and crumbs falling from my mouth. Their white fluffy cat sat on a puffy bed.

I watched the show and peered out the window, waiting to see if Mom was looking for me. I darted my eyes from television frame to window frame, back and forth.

"You're allowed over here, right?" asked Mrs. Finn.

"Yeah, I am," I said.

"Garvey Nolan, are you certain?"

Dad drove up to the side of our house in his green Volkswagen Beetle. He got out with a couple boxes of pizza. He headed up the walkway to the front door. He put the pizzas down and ran about our yard, peeking in bushes, arms out in a panic. He rushed to the curb and looked up and down the road, stroking his black mustache and adjusting his thick plastic glasses.

The excitement of doing something devastatingly wrong brought out a rush in me I had never experienced. But the sheer suffering on Dad's face was difficult to endure. I burst off the sofa and ran out of the Finn house, screaming out to Dad. He saw me, dropped to his knees and put his hands together as if he was praying.

"Look both ways first before crossing!" Dad hollered.

My feet were a couple steps into the road. A blur of a yellow car whizzed by with the horn held down, like a large lemon taffy being stretched. Leaves and dust whirled about. I looked both ways and crossed. Dad stared down the yellow car that sat idling at a stop sign in the distance. The driver side window rolled down. The sound of heavy sobbing and fists pounding on the dashboard emanated from the window. The driver said something about a wife.

"Garv, stay right here," said Dad, pointing to our walkway. He ran after the yellow car, shouting words I knew were naughty and only for grownups. The yellow car, a small sporty breed, screeched off when Dad got close.

"Couldn't get his plate numbers," said Dad, jogging back. "This is why you look both ways. Crazy cockroach. I've seen this car before. Keeps going 40 down our road."

Dad pulled out a folded Polaroid photo from his back pocket and put it in front of me. "This is him," he said. "A speeder. I'll get him someday. Oreland is not a shortcut to anything. This is no cut through town. People that live here don't drive like that." The photo had a blur of the yellow car passing by our house with an arm extended out of a partially rolled-down window. The middle finger was up like a flagpole waiting to be adorned.

Mr. Finn jogged out, holding his hat. "Tornado warning!" he cried. "It scrolled on the bottom of my TV."

Blustering wind tossed gravel at my face. I squinted. Mom raced from neighboring front yards. Her blond hair bounced as her apron flung off. "There you are! Where did you go?" she asked.

The sky was sea-foam green. "I'm sorry. I was—"

Trashcan lids whizzed along the lawn. Dad picked me up and carried me over his shoulders. I watched Mom's red painted toenails follow as we raced inside.

2.

Visible Spectrum

April '79

Amongst the intrigue of old men on my block, a kid surfaced named Kristoph. He seemed to idolize me. He'd see me playing on our walkway from up the road and tromp towards me holding a loud vowel noise. Each step would partially stutter his welcome noise, arms wide open, bopping up and down on the uneven lawns. He wore striped shirts tucked into tight shorts. His parents never lingered about. I waited for them to show up, but they never did. He always retreated to them.

Kristoph was a blond, pale, giddy infringer that rarely used words. He'd organize my action figures and cars into complex patterns I couldn't understand. "He's a kook," said Dad. "I think he's an Indigo Child. Kind've psychic type. He once stopped Mr. Finn to let him know a yellow jacket nest was forming in his backyard bush. And he was right."

If I wasn't on the front lawn, Kristoph walked to our front door and leaned his face into the screen to summon me, filling in the screen holes with his runny nose, his tongue pressed against the metal patchwork. My parents quickly addressed him so he would stop stretching the screen further.

When helping Dad pack the VW bug for a Jersey Shore trip, Kristoph was there, watching with excitement, thinking he was coming with us. He grasped the chrome rear fender and clutched the door handles, trying to squeeze his way in.

Mom eventually let me venture off to Kristoph's house for an afternoon playdate. As he lived on the same side of the road as me, I only had to cut through front lawns to get there, as we didn't have sidewalks. Mom tamed my cowlick with some of her saliva, wished me luck and waved me off. I looked back. She blew a kiss, her maize hair flowing. I then focused on Kristoph's blue house in the distance, about seven homes up the road.

After ringing the doorbell, Kristoph's Mom greeted me with an array of Otter Pops. I took one and followed her to the kitchen where Kristoph was sitting down and making bizarre noises with his mouth. We played a few rounds of Hungry Hungry Hippos at the kid table, sucking down the syrupy frost.

Kristoph got on his hands and knees and barked like his dog. He grabbed some of his dog's wet food from the bowl on the floor and handed it towards me. I jerked my face away. He knelt down to the bowl and chowed on his dog's brown glistening slop. I hoped it was a joke, but he didn't stop. He looked up. I saw the strains of meat in his teeth and lips, dripping pieces onto his shirt. I grabbed Kristoph's wrist to stop him but he grew more wild and pounced on the linoleum tiles, rubbing the moist processed food through his hair.

I walked backwards, deeper into the house. My arms shuddered. I found a side door and entered the backyard. Kristoph's Dad was trimming the hedges. I jumped up and down, trying to get his attention. I unplugged the long orange cord and waved him over.

When I got back to Kristoph, his Mom was there, forcing him to vomit into a bucket. "It's OK, Kristoph," she said, tearing up.

"You know, I think it's time for you to go, son," said Kristoph's Dad, putting his hand on my shoulder.

"I tried to stop him," I said. "I'm sorry."

"It's fine. It's not your fault."

I hurried for the exit and stood outside. Kristoph's parents argued, knocking things down. A sudden thrill of nobody knowing where I was or where I was going pulsed through my pounding heart. The vernal scents of April eased my mind. Tree shade brought out goosebumps and then sun rays flattened them.

The vantage points of Redford Road brought new perspectives of the floral gardens, pristine lawns and distinctive exterior decor. I slowly zigzagged along the grass, my head pivoting, absorbing the bliss of Oreland's unique stage.

As the dose of liberty heightened, a fancy yellow car puttered up beside me and stopped. It had glossy black tires, a black convertible top and resembled an ominous large hornet, a car that would be in a parade. I was certain it was the car that had almost hit me outside of Mr. Finn's house. Windows were up, but I saw the driver glaring at me through the passenger door. He wore a large hat, wide sunglasses and a bandanna covering most of his face. Symphony music was blaring. Smoke swelled from an ashtray.

"What?" I asked, gesturing my hands in the air as he glared at me.

The man kissed his hand, as if he was about to blow a kiss, but then extended an index finger and slowly moved it back and forth as if I had done something wrong.

"What do you want?" I asked, inching backwards. I tripped on a utility line cap that was sticking out of a yard and landed on my behind. I could not see the man from the ground. I watched the vibrating tailpipe as I struggled to get back up. The driver's side door opened with a squeak and the music intensified. Two shoes clacked on the road. He was out of the car, on the other side.

"You lost there, son?" asked the man. "Awfully young to be roaming around by yourself."

"I know where I'm at," I said.

"Sorry if I've been speeding. My mind's not quite right. My wife is leaving me."

Frightened by the faceless man, I bolted home. The yellow car sped away up Redford Road with peppy acceleration.

I found Dad on the front lawn hosing the bushes. "Back already?" he asked, stroking my messed up hair.

"Yep." I hovered behind Dad's legs, keeping an eye out for the unique yellow car that was bright enough to see through bushes and tree branches.

"You hiding from Kristoph?"

"No, he's sick. Acting odd. I think I saw the yellow speeder car. He stopped to talk. I got scared and ran off."

"Well, you did the right thing. Did you get a plate number?"

"No, nothing."

"Maybe he was just concerned. Young kid walking alone."

Hours later, Kristoph arrived at our door covered in varied colored construction paper. He had glued the paper to his clothes, hair and skin. "Do a craft?" he asked. "Craft time?"

Mom was in a cleaning frenzy, spraying woodwork with a lemon-scented spray, blasting Fleetwood Mac from the stereo that spilled out of the screen window. Kristoph danced around the lawn to the tunes, making chicken noises, flapping his wings like a deranged mascot.

"Don't let him in the house," Dad said, disappearing down the hall. "The glue doesn't seem dry yet."

We watched from the door. Kristoph was a spinning prism reflecting the scattered lights from tree branches. Mom turned up the volume.

Dad came back from the basement with tambourines and maracas. "Let's join him," said Dad, nudging Mom and grabbing her hand. "Remember these?"

I followed my parents outside as they danced to the delight of Kristoph. His strut intensified. He mouthed cock-a-doodle-doo sounds to the birds. The rainbow assortment of textured paper ripped and peeled off. Kristoph revealed his enlightened face. Mom twirled her flowing skirt like Stevie Nicks. Our freshly cut lawn transformed into a mess of crumpled gooey paper. Kristoph never looked so happy. He tossed the paper about. Finally,

Kristoph's Dad arrived, avoiding eye contact, mumbling how he'd be back over with a trash bag before carrying Kristoph back home.

"It's OK, really," said Mom, but Kristoph's Dad maintained his typical rigid retrieval of his son, void of a conversation.

The next day, I walked out in my syrup stained plaid pajamas to get the newspaper for Dad. The paper was secured with a rubber band near the curb. As I picked it up, I looked up towards Redford Road at the climbing sun's outpouring of orange warmth. Focusing my eyes on the street, I saw a car in front of Kristoph's house beneath tree shade. The headlights were on and faced me. It appeared to be the yellow car that had approached me. I cupped my hands around my brow to block the sun. Kristoph, dressed in tight pajamas, ran to the car and stood a couple feet away from the driver's side door. Bright bursts of light flashed out of the car towards Kristoph. A hand extended out of the car, holding what appeared to be a juice box.

"Down here!" I screamed as Kristoph stepped toward the drink. He glanced over and sprinted at me with arms open. I ran at him, feeling the morning dew soak through my socks. The yellow car reversed backwards at a high speed, tires spinning and squealing. The car swerved back and forth up Redford Road until it was out of sight and behind a bend. Trashcans got bumped and knocked down. Neighbors stepped out in their morning garb.

"What the heck is going on out here?" asked Dad with coffee in hand.

Kristoph was hugging me and jumping up and down.

"It was that yellow car," I said. "The speeder. Couldn't get the plate though."

Dad nodded his head and sipped his steaming coffee, uninterested in the hazy moment. "OK, well, we'll get him someday."

A week later, I was sitting on the toilet when I heard Kristoph's crazed knock on our door. He walked around the house, banging on all first-floor windows.

"Garvey, get out of the car!" he repeatedly yelled. "Car danger. Car danger."

A loud thud occurred. I ran out of the bathroom and joined Dad to see what the racket was. We found Kristoph in one of our window wells. He was bleeding from his head, laying in shattered glass. Dad, who along with Mom, was a registered nurse, pulled him out and rushed him home in his arms with calm precision. Kristoph kept shouting for me. Mom kept me inside from seeing anything further.

Weeks later, we heard nothing of Kristoph's condition. My parents knocked on his door and left a get-well card and chocolates. They allowed me to escape the perimeter of our front yard further. I think my parents hoped I would meet someone new. They let me mosey up and down our side of the block on the lawns. I passed Kristoph's house and saw a "For Sale" sign on the front lawn. Kristoph sat at a window, looking out, his bowl cut hair shining like a construction hard hat. His face still had stitches. He didn't react to my hand waves and seemed to look through me. His hands played with two Matchbox cars, smacking them together on the window. His gaze was somewhere else, watching a stage that seemed visible solely to him.

3.

Spirit Of America

September '79

Dad bought a red AMC (American Motors Corporation) Spirit, a brand new two-door subcompact car. It was cherry red, sporty with sleek lines, and economically priced for a dollar counting Dad. The green VW bug was toast.

Little metal Hot Wheels cars were a favorite toy of mine. Even better was pretending my toy chest was a vehicle itself. I'd cover my body in toys and sit in the wicker chest, making long fart noises with my mouth, driving off to imaginary towns. But now our family owned what I considered a hot rod.

Dad and I headed somewhere near home, in neighboring Flourtown. I sat in the back, taking mental notes of the area roads, amazed that Dad knew how to drive so far away and figure out how to get home.

On a winding uphill road, a bright yellow sports car convertible sped toward us in the opposite direction. Behind the sports car were two large white trucks. They traveled almost bumper to bumper. As the fleet drew nearer, the first truck in the group swerved into our lane.

"Hold on!" Dad shouted, turning out of the way.

I squinted tightly as the Spirit careened off the road and tumbled down a steep ditch, rolling over several times. We ended up positioned upside down, surrounded in a thicket of bushes, suspended by our seat belts. As the sounds of crunching metal and plastic stopped, my breath remained held. My hands braced the seat belt buckle receptacles. I thought of the yellow car and how it resembled the scary man I had seen before.

After checking if I was hurt, Dad clicked out of the seat belt and fell to the ceiling. He tried to open his door. It was jammed shut. He reached for the glove compartment and opened it. Paperwork and tools flew out. He grabbed a hammer and explained that he needed to break the glass to get us out. I looked around the tall weeds and imagined snakes jumping at me, not realizing any potential other hazard that leaking gasoline could bring. I unbuckled myself and collapsed down. Dad smacked his window. The glass ruptured into spider webs. He tapped out the shards. "It's good to have a hammer," he said, catching his breath. "In case crazies try to get in your car and you gotta defend yourself." Dad clambered out of the window. He reached his hands in and pulled me out.

Looking up toward the road in Dad's arms, I saw a few stopped cars and concerned people peering down at us. Firetrucks and police sirens grew louder as we climbed. The yellow car and two white trucks were lined up. When we reached the top, a man with a safari helmet reached for my hand and pulled me up as Dad held my waist. The man's hat had a mini buzzing fan below the brim, aimed at his forehead.

"Are you fellas OK?" the man asked. "I've got cold apple juice in my cooler if you want, sonny."

"Mr. Kova?" asked Dad. "What are you doing here? We're fine. Don't know about those truckers. One of them swerved into my lane. Seemed drunk."

"A bit fast, maybe. But they stayed in their lane. I was leading them in my car," he said, nodding towards the yellow vehicle.

"Bullcrap. They were halfway into my lane. They almost slammed into us. They are with you?"

"The caravan is mine, indeed. Sounds like a guardrail would

have suited you better. Maybe you can bring it up at the next Commissioners meeting."

Dad went into a diatribe with the man named Kratz Kova. I zoned out, staring up at Kova's little fan and moist face of patchy pink. His bright yellow sports car reflected in the sun and hurt my eyes. I sat on a cop car bumper and felt my forehead swelling. Dad later told me, countless times throughout the years, that the conversation went something like:

"I read about you in *The Philadelphia Inquirer*," Dad said to Kova. "You're moving to the White Ash Manor?"

"That's right. These trucks are filled with artwork from my uncle and I need to get them to White Ash."

"You picked the wrong road. These trucks aren't made for—"

"Disagreed. These laws are ridiculous. I can't have a truck on this road? It's the most direct route." Kova pulled out a crinkly map from his pocket. "All other routes are far-flung."

"Alright for you. I've seen you speeding on my road."

"You have no proof."

"Are you really having townhouses built on the White Ash preserve?"

"Yes, that's in the works. Why? Want to buy one—"

"I think our Founding Fathers would frown upon that development. Many of them stayed at White Ash during the war."

"Like me, our Founding Fathers were wealthy men that didn't want the burden of our riches being overtly taxed. They'd praise me for investing on my land."

"God will punish you."

Snapped out of my fog, I remembered the next part. Kova crouched down. "You know, I have a son your age," he said. "Are you about five years old?"

"Yes, I'm five," I said.

"So is my son. He is likely at a different school than you. Are you a good boy?"

I ignored the question. Kova stood back up and barked at Dad. A fireman put his arms between their squabble.

The cops appeared spellbound, staring at Kova as they wrote up paperwork. The Spirit was smoking heavily and firemen scrambled to hose it down. The EMTs positioned Dad and I into separate gurneys. They drove us in an ambulance to Chestnut Hill Hospital. We both suffered minor scratches and bruises. The nurse kept saying how lucky I was as she put an ice pack on my forehead bump.

Waiting for Mom to pick us up, Dad explained that Kova was a big shot golfer that inherited his uncle's plastic manufacturing biz. The boon of consumer gadgets was allowing him to live a life of leisure. His sporty ride was an Italian yellow sports car called an Alfa Romeo Spider. He lived on the wealthier side of the Oreland tracks and now White Ash Manor as well. His new real estate development company was blossoming.

"He's the one who keeps speeding on our road," Dad said, clenching his fists, satisfied that the mystery was solved, but still pissed. I thought of the flashing blasts that emitted from the Alfa Romeo Spider toward Kristoph.

The nursery school I attended the year prior was in the basement of a church. On one side of the church was a large field bordered on one side by an ominous thicket of woods. Through these trees was White Ash Manor, an estate once quartered by soldiers during the Revolutionary War. That's what the bronze tablet stated at the long driveway gated entrance. It all seemed boring, a mansion we couldn't step foot in and acres of private land we couldn't play in. But Dad and his friends were proud of it being on the border of Oreland.

The accident totaled the AMC Spirit. The new car smell hadn't even dissipated. Dad owned it for just a couple months but didn't have enough singular vehicle collision coverage to get it repaired. The truckers got tickets for driving on a non-truck route, but insurance agents and police deemed Kova's crew not at fault for the accident. Dad wrote letters to Kova, asking for help with payments, but he never replied. On his final attempt, Dad walked to White Ash Manor and entered the long gravel driveway. He had seen Kova's yellow Spider from the street. Kova quickly denied Dad and told him to leave immediately. Another man emerged from the garage with a rock salt shotgun. Dad retreated.

AMC discontinued the Spirit three years later, according to Dad. I rarely saw the Spirits on the road.

A blown out sun washed photo of Dad and I, looking perplexed at the scene of the accident, appeared in the local newspaper with our first names misspelled. In the photo, we looked down at the cool red car blankly, our favorite toy crushed. Neighbors didn't even realize it was us in the photo, as if it never happened.

Dad acquired his mother's old beige Dodge Dart, which smelled like burnt toast covered up with perfume and baby powder. The gooey seats looked and felt like a large used bandage.

Days after the accident, I kept having a recurring dream of Kova. He marched towards me in his safari helmet and dark large shades. He held a golf club and jerked it up and down with swift arms like a drum major with a baton. His pace increased as his perspiring face turned pinker. My legs were solid heavy weights as I lied on the grass, unable to rise. Kova aimed his club at my face and took his tee-off stance. He raised his club for a backswing.

4.

Unwritten Pact

October '79
Nursery school recess included wagons, tricycles and Big Wheel rides in the parking lot. I gravitated to the bold colors and chunky design of the pebble spewing Big Wheel. A steep declining driveway led to the main parking lot. Daredevils reached the peak, descended downwards with quick pedaling and tried to spin a 360 by clasping the brake handle and lifting at just the precise speed and moment.

I owned a Big Wheel. My parents decorated it for the Oreland 4th of July parades, allowing me to ride the streets with other pedal power enthusiasts, all leading to a glorious end of hot dogs and ice cream sandwiches at the Little League field.

My first bicycle was an all-black Huffy dirt bike with a big puffy seat, no gears, and pedal braking. I learned how to ride instantly when Dad pushed me down Redford Road and let go. I felt the immediate freedom. The sleepy town of Oreland became sped up and unexplored, all passing by in a self-created breeze.

It was a rite of passage, it seemed, to explore the town on our bikes as a kid. All the parents were cool with it. There was no required detailed explanation of where we were going.

"I'm gonna go for a ride with Willem," I'd holler, pulling the bike out of the shed. My parents signaled back with a quick shout or a wave from the porch.

As long as we were home by dinnertime to show face and exchange the day's events, everything was fine. Whatever given time, sharp on the exact minute, our feet had better be standing on the patterned linoleum with our hands already washed.

Dinner calmed and realigned us. We revealed our day as much as we were willing to share. We turned off the TV, often much to my Dad's dismay, as he liked the news blaring. We ordered out sometimes, usually pizza, but the same covenant applied.

The contract with our parents was one we didn't even establish. We biked off. Hours passed. Uncharted roads were divulged through uphill pedaling grunts. There was an underlying agreement that we didn't need a helmet, that we'd obey the sanctity of family, that someone would have a wrist watch to guide us. And if not, the twilight of dusk set us homeward like a lighthouse. We sprinted or pedaled to avoid the tales of boogeymen lurking in the night.

Returned home, our homes always seemed different. The smell of lemon-scented surface cleaners and Windex lingered amid the tangy steam of Crock-Pot meatballs. A wall-mounted shelf was installed or a coating of lacquer was applied to a piece of furniture. These projects added to the conversations through crunching Tater Tots and drying sweaty hair.

As my parents were both nurses, they spoke of bodily fluids experienced hours prior as if they were spices in the rack. I protested these topics often. Eating lasagna, I couldn't hear one utterance of blood or scabs.

Dad was a nurse at a psych ward. He often had to chase patients that escaped and tried to hide in delivery trucks and bushes. He also had to calm down burly patients with a hypnotic voice as he administered needles. He used this same tone when shoving forked lima beans into my face. "Come on. Just eat it. Pretend you're good," he'd say.

Willem was a kid in my neighborhood that was enjoying the

same bicycle freedom I was. We pedaled by each other, commented on our bikes and were soon hanging out at each other's homes. Willem was tan with long wild hair. He wore moccasins, even when biking, and often spoke about his Lenni Lenape Native American background, a tribe local to our area. He adorned an arrowhead necklace, and he was proud that I enjoyed his Mom's succotash. Willem's home was always low lit and bustling with music. I wasn't sure who lived there. His Mom was divorced and his Uncle Jay had moved in. Resembling Steve Perry of Journey, Jay always made me wait at the screen door when I knocked. He'd disappear toward a conversation of cigarette smoke and accusations about fucking idiot this and that.

To escape our parents and relax, Willem and I hung out along the Sandy Brook Creek that bordered behind the Oreland Little League field. This area was lined with weeds, poison ivy and the dreaded stinging nettle. We called it the "seven minute itch". It lasted much longer though. Along the creek we found a dirt trail opening to a beach of rocks. It was here that we put our bikes down and tried to triple-skim flat rocks, poking fun of tee-ball games we had on opposing teams. Depending on the runoff supply from a nearby drainage pipe, the creek could be bone dry or three feet high with water.

My parents had given me a geological gift of sixteen rocks and minerals glued and labeled to a piece of cardboard. It was a colorful array of sulfur, amethyst, quartz, mica, limestone. I brought it to the creek as a guide. Willem and I hoped to find diamonds. We took large pieces of quartz and smashed them with all of our might against a boulder of quartz, watching it splatter into deeper and sharper realms that were shinier. Slivers of quartz would spearhead into our calves.

We took our prized rocks into backpacks and stopped at the house of an old guy that was always asking what we were doing. He sat on his front steps, up on a steep hill, looking down at the kids, listening to Phillies games on his transistor radio. His fat belly was revealed for all, busting out of a tight t-shirt. The old man examined our rocks and ensured that we only found quartz.

Willem and I surmised that if we put our hands out flat and gently touched the surface of the calm warm creek water, it was identical to the sensation of touching a woman's breasts. We were certain.

We escaped our geological and botanical expeditions at Perkel's Drug Store, buying candy bars for a quarter. We sat out front of the store and watched high school dudes play basketball on the courts across the street. While chewing on sweets one day, I noticed Kristoph sitting in the back seat of a parked car in the Perkel's lot. He stared at us through the open window.

"Kristoph!" I blurted, rushing toward him. "What are you doing here? You still live in Oreland?"

Kristoph stared blankly at me. "Need more pills. More medicine," he said with a rare relaxed and cohesive tone.

"Gotcha. What's new? You all right?"

"Say cheese," he said, forming his thumbs and index fingers into a frame and bringing it up to his eyes.

"What? You want a picture taken?"

Kristoph held his photo frame up to his face and trembled. "The man. Say cheese now. The say cheese man."

"The man in the yellow car?"

Kristoph's Dad walked out of Perkel's with a white crinkly bag and jogged to us. "Boys, boys, leave him alone. We need to get going. He's not feeling well. I'm sorry." He jumped into the car and rolled up the windows before reversing out.

Down the street from Perkel's, Willem and I headed to the Oreland Station and put pennies on the railroad tracks, watching the regional trains flatten them and remove any trace of Abe Lincoln.

"My Dad thinks Kristoph has special powers and can see the future," I said.

"Like a prophet?" Willem asked. "My ancestors had those people. They told us to forgo the white man's booze."

I put a couple pennies on the tracks and Willem grabbed my wrist. "Not that one," he said.

I looked at the coins and saw an Indian Head cent sitting next to Honest Abe. Willem plucked it from the tracks and put it into his pocket.

"Sorry, I thought it was just a regular penny," I said.

Willem looked at me with disdain until a smile crept in and made him snort laughter. "I'm just screwing with ya," he said. "My people had nothing to do with the making of this coin."

The railroad tracks split Oreland into West and East Oreland. Each section lived peacefully in their sleepy cocoons. West was comprised of identical White City homes. East was more affluent with custom larger home designs.

A stairway at the station led to an overpass where commuters could get to each side of the tracks. A recent suicide had us peering about for pieces of skull and brain. A guy had jumped off the bridge and hung himself a minute before the train sped in, crushing his body and dragging his guts across the tracks. All that we knew about him was that he was a caddie at a local golf course. A few photos of him appeared in the newspaper. In one, Kratz Kova leaned one arm on his shoulder with a grin.

5.

Tunnel Vision

March '80
Using large stepping stones, Willem and I often crossed over Shady Brook Creek with our bikes to a mazy circuit of dirt trails. Slipping on moss was common, resulting in a sneaker filled with algae. The trails had mounds of dirt that were smooth, ideal for ramps and flying eight feet or more into the air. It baffled us who owned the land or how it came to be, unsure if we were trespassing or on public land.

One of trails led to a steep incline toward old freight railroad tracks covered with weeds. Other trails led to the top of Dead Man's Cliff, a dump site with mounds of garbage, old TVs, appliances. We rummaged through the garbage hoping to find a cool trophy, like a Cadillac hubcap. The flat land of trash ended abruptly and overlooked the Little League fields. An occasional filthy man with tattered clothes and a ragged beard would appear, asking for dimes, sending us into a frightened quick decline to the creek.

On one of our mining and rock destruction sessions, a group of older kids interrupted Willem and I. We knew our secret spot wasn't under wraps, as empty beer cans surfaced from the night before. But during the day, it was ours. The older kids asked if we wanted to join them into the Big Pipe, the name for a nearby runoff conduit that emptied into the creek. We agreed and followed them to the entrance.

The pipe diameter was just a foot taller than Willem and I. A small trickle of water was coming out. We followed the older kids in as they rattled off tales of large rats. The reverberations of the conduit made it difficult to hear. The damp concrete continued on and I grew terrified with each step, ready to leave everyone and head back to the daylight circle growing smaller behind me. There were multiple turns and manholes overhead where the sun pierced through and cars passed by, creating quick rumblings of steel on asphalt.

We followed the guffaws of the older kids as they raced ahead. In the distance, we saw them climbing up a ladder towards bright sunshine. Willem and I fumbled our way up the makeshift ladder and squirmed out onto a sidewalk of busy Paper Mill Road.

"Close up the hole," the older kids yelled at us as they dispersed.

I sat on the sidewalk, out of breath as Willem shoved the lid over the hole. To my left I noticed a couple guys in a yellow convertible gawking at us, waiting at a red light. The car headed towards us and I realized it was Kova in his Spider. Sometimes, I'd see him sputtering about Oreland from afar, causing my legs to turn to lead and hands to shake.

"Holy smokes, you boys all right?" asked Kova as he parked his car. "We saw you climbing out." Symphony music blared from his speakers. His passenger was a guy I recognized from church, a priest named Father Pal. He was sporting a clerical collar, toned down with a Phillies cap and Slurpee in hand.

"Just exploring," said Willem.

"The beauty of the world is above ground. What compelled you to hang with the rats? These boys need to go to penance, eh?" Kova nudged Father Pal in the ribs. "Trespassing private Township property, right? Ah, the mischief of men."

"I'm not Catholic," Willem piped up. "Doesn't mean a thing."

"Now stop," said Father Pal, slapping Kova on the knee. "Listen, we'd give you boys a ride home but there's no room in the back of the Spider. Don't let its size fool ya. It has the torque of the devil. You fellas live around here?"

Father Pal was a priest at Divine Miracles, a Catholic church and grade school down the street from my house. He was the fun priest. He'd wear tie dye socks and sported a variety of multi-colored shades. Opposed to standing at the podium microphone during homilies, he roamed the outskirts of the altar with a lapel mic clipped on his garb. He'd pick people by name out of the crowd and involve them in his pious narrative. He even trademarked his speeches with an ending tagline of: "Remember, I'm not Paul. I'm Pal. *Your* pal. Here to serve you and the Lord. Peace."

Willem and I moved backwards slightly, knowing we shouldn't tell strangers where we lived.

"You look familiar," Kova said, straining his neck to examine me.

"We've met," I mustered, backing further away. A bumper sticker came into vision. It stated: GOLF GOD. "Me and my Dad crashed into a ditch. You were there. You—"

"Oh, for heaven's sake. That's right. An Oreland boy." Kova straightened himself up, his face getting redder. "Your father waltzed through my private property and tried to get *me* to pay for his American car that *he* destroyed on his own. Right?"

I thought about the yellow car that had stopped for Kristoph, realizing that it was surely Kova's ride. An uneasy sensation made my biceps quiver. I feared Kova would find out where we lived and rat us out for being in the pipes.

"Your Daddy is a piece of work. Never mind that," said Kova. "I live in Oreland too." He paused for a while. "I don't tell many people this, but my upbringing was in Finland."

"Fun Land?" I asked.

"Fin-land. A Scandinavian country. My Uncle Heikki came to America when I was four, after the War. He built Kova Plastics from the ground up, a man with grit and vision. Sisu we call it in

Finland. He trained me early on. I didn't waste time in the mud like you boys."

"A bit harshy marshy, there," said Father Pal. "You boys want an Irish potato? Gotta whole box here. Tomorrow's St. Patty's Day." Pal dangled a brown cinnamon ball with his fingers.

"Come on," I commanded to Willem, patting his back before dashing off. My heaving breath and clomping sneakers muffled all sounds as I sprinted down a side street. After a couple blocks, I looked back and was glad to see Willem trailing close behind. We reached the Little League field. Kova followed us in his Spider for a while, but pulled over and remained parked. Over my shoulder, I saw him standing upright in his car, peering through a telescope. Willem gave the middle finger at them. I smiled through stomach cramps. We reached my front lawn and collapsed on dandelions.

"You guys look like you're up to something," Dad said, hosing down the Dodge.

I looked at Willem. We both squinted. "Just some Capture The Flag," I said.

"I'm lighting up the grill soon. Cheeseburgers will be ready in a jiffy. Don't go too far. Garv, come here a sec."

I walked over as Dad dug in his pocket. "Stick out your left arm," he said.

I put my arm out. He wrapped a gray rubber watch around my wrist. I looked down at the thick chunky face. The jagged digital time ticked the seconds. :57, :58, :59, :00. Time escalated to each minute, a backwards time bomb.

"A button lights up the display for when it's dark," said Dad. "Now, you'll always get back on time."

6.

The Quip

April '80

Willem and I hung out nonstop for months. Even when it rained, we chilled inside and played games like *Pitfall* on Intellivision or watched reruns. Our excursion through the tunnels gave us the exploring kick. We biked the uncharted areas of both East and West Oreland, trying to purposely get lost. Worst-case scenario, we'd knock on someone's door and ask to use the phone to call our parents, we thought.

Willem was always a few steps ahead of me with milestones in life. His Uncle Jay had already let him look at bare boobs in a magazine, lick the top of a fresh-opened beer, listen to a stereo cranked all the way up, grow his hair out and sit on the back of a moving Harley-Davidson motorcycle.

Willem's proudest activity was being able to push the gas-powered lawn mower for a few rows during Jay's lawn mowing sessions. I watched from the sidelines, envying the satisfaction on Willem's face of pushing a deafening massive piece of machinery that brought the yard to baseball field perfection.

I explained to Willem about Kova and the car accident that Dad and I endured.

"I know about that guy," blurted Willem. "He fired my Uncle

Jay from his factory gig, up in Berks County somewhere. Jay lost his mind."

"Why was he fired?" I asked.

"You know that piece of shit?" Jay asked, strutting towards us with biceps flexed.

"Me and my Dad met him before," I said.

"His team busted me with cocaine in my locker. You know what coke is?"

"Not sure."

"It's a drug. Terrible stuff. You guys are too young to hear about this. I've never done it. Kova had someone place a baggy in my locker. He must of. I never locked it. Had nothing worth stealing. They didn't give me a urine test or anything. Just a random locker check and boom. I'm fired. Told to get my stuff and leave."

Jay stumbled off, lighting a cigarette. He swiveled back to us, holding in the smoke. "It's because I spoke of the Lenape," said Jay. "Loud and proud." Jay pounded his chest, walking off.

"You said Kova is a golfer?" asked Willem.

"Yeah, a big shot pro," I said.

"We're surrounded by golf courses," said Jay. "It's lame. Walking around a man-made forest with chemicals sprayed everywhere. There used to be farms where the courses are."

"I've never been in one," I said.

Days later, a loud crunch occurred beneath the circular blades as Willem mowed the lawn. I sat on a tree stump, massaging a stack of Uno cards. A slew of brown and white pieces flew out the mower's side shoot. Willem let go of the handle. Silence crept over as we all inched toward the reddening mess. A nest of bunnies, slaughtered before our eyes, oozed blood on clipped grass as our sweat dripped down on their remains. Willem raised his arms over his head, his bare ankles covered in guts.

Jay shook his head as Willem stood paralyzed. I tried to console him the best I could by brushing his hair back with my hand and letting him know that it wasn't his fault. Willem's arm quaked, eyes fixated on the disaster.

"At least you didn't accidentally kill the Easter Bunny," I said.

Willem looked over at me and opened his mouth as if he was about to eat a donut from a string. He digged into his nearby bucket of quartz and threw one at my chest. It thumped into my t-shirt and collapsed at my feet. My chest throbbed in pain. I walked backwards towards Allison Road.

"I don't believe in your stupid fairy tale," he said through his teeth, eyes wide. "I may have just slaughtered The Great Hare, the Algonquian spirit. And you think this is a joke?"

Willem followed me as I ran off. He grabbed the rope handle of his wagon full of quartz and chased me down the middle of the street. Down at my sneakers, Willem's catapulted quartz splattered into fragments as his attack ensued. I looked back and his wagon was empty. He kept screaming something about my presence no longer being worthy.

I turned right up Redford Road and found Siobhan on our front lawn with a yellow dress on and red juicy blotches all over the front of her body. Her eyes were watering and her hands extended outward. Dad stormed out of the front door with an angry mustachioed sneer. "I'll take care of it," he said.

Mom guided Siobhan as she uncomfortably wobbled into the house. Dad walked down our entrance pavement, picked up a few crushed tomatoes off the grass, and went to the street where a rabid Willem appeared. They stared at each other for a moment. Willem ran up the road, his rage silenced.

Dad headed to a house down the street where some new snotty older boys lived. He knocked on the door and talked to another Dad, bickering about the bruised produce. I watched from our lawn.

A few days later, I called Willem. His mom answered and gave Willem the phone. I told him I was sorry for the Easter Bunny joke. He breathed heavily and hung up. I biked by his house and he clenched a fist at me as he pulled weeds. I headed to our creek-side beach and found older kids lingering about. They had claimed the land and asked me to leave, organized milk crates seats scattered about. Our lazy water haven was no more.

Later that day, I asked Dad if he could play catch with me in the Little League field, under the lights, within the structure of perfect steel chain link fencing. My first season of baseball started in the Spring. I needed to focus, sort through my baseball cards and line up my heroes.

7.

Slippage

May '80

Siobhan and I were both June babies, born just over a year apart, three weeks shy of being Irish twins. She was older, a vibrant strawberry blond Gemini; I was a cautious dirty blond Cancer. Although we were into different toys and TV shows, we shared a deep love of our pets. Our parents always had a dog and at least one cat. Dusty was the fattest cat we ever had, an old puffy blueish gray blob with a couple white splotches. Even though he was hefty, he was speedy and sometimes darted out the front door when we'd come home.

One Friday evening, I petted Dusty as he sat on my bedroom windowsill, jerking his head at robins. I walked downstairs. I heard a pop sound, a weird meow and witnessed a dark blob fall into the azalea bushes through a living room window. I looked out the front door but saw no trace of him. I ran to Dad. He sat on the couch, digesting dinner and sitting in an awkward angle. He was working on his daily crossword puzzle from *The Philadelphia Inquirer*, a feat he typically completed in full.

"I think Dusty just fell out of my window," I said.

"Cheese and crackers. Are you serious?" asked Dad. "That fat turd must have broken through the screen. I knew we should have gotten good ole aluminum screens. Not this fiberglass bendy stuff."

"I will go look for him."

"He'll be back. He always comes back. He better. He doesn't have front claws."

I roamed around our yards and our neighbors' yards. It was legit to trespass when seeking lost pets. It perked up the neighbors as they saw you walking about with pensive footsteps. All you had to say was: "My cat is missing. I think he's back here."

I found Dusty in the backyard of a house on Allison road. He sat on a diving board, hovering above an empty pool. I made the universal "Spsss, Spsss, Spsss" sound and jiggled an index finger. He stared at me with tiny meows. I inched closer. He backed off the board and ran towards a wooden fence at full speed and flattened just enough to fit under a gap.

The next morning, Dusty was not back yet. Our other cat, Sylvester, indulged in Dusty's full bowl of Tender Vittles. I planned to search for Dusty after a big breakfast. Siobhan and I chowed down on Fruit Loops. I couldn't stand how she ate with her mouth open, so I gathered all the cereal boxes from the cupboard and formed a wall so I didn't have to stare at her. She knocked them down with the swipe of a hand. A variety of cereal fell onto the floor.

"That's enough, guys. Calm it down," said Dad, suddenly cleaning up the mess with a dustpan and brush. "Do you want ants again?" He then went out back with Mom to work on gardening.

I went to the fridge and poured a glass of Hawaiian Punch. I paced around the house, chatting with Siobhan. I stumbled as my right toe bumped into the edge of the new one-inch high oriental carpet in the living room. A few ounces of juice flew out of my cup and splattered onto the carpet.

"God, no," I said, putting down the cup.

"You're not even supposed to be drinking that for breakfast," Siobhan commented.

I ran upstairs to get a towel out of the bathroom. I reached up and jostled loose a fresh towel from the stack. On bringing it down, it bumped into a little leather bag filled with Mom's makeup. Lipstick, mascara, eyeliner and a couple others fell out and plopped into the toilet. I had forgotten to flush earlier. Beauty products became embedded with soaked toilet paper. I looked up and saw Siobhan covering her mouth. I reached in the toilet and pulled out the mess, pieces of turds mixed in with cosmetics. I tried to clean them on the tiled floor.

I heard the back door open and Dad's boisterous laugh. I grabbed the towel and ran downstairs. Dad and I entered the living room at the same time from different entrances. He stared at the bright red stains. I stared at his shocked face. He gently put down the packets of seeds and roughly knuckled his thinning hair. "Jesus CHRIST!" he said.

Mom entered. Her body shook, mouth open wide. "What did you do?" she asked. "Our new rug. Our beautiful new rug."

The rug truly was the perfect mix for the room. She found one that matched the love seat, the doilies, the paintings, the curtains, the custom stenciled trims, the baby farm decorative dolls. It was a calm collective of peach and blue, now stained with planet Mars exploding in the center of it all.

"Come here," barked Dad, walking with brisk strides towards me, one hand extended out.

I ran off, trying to escape. He followed suit, unable to catch me as I whisked around the kitchen island and then around the dining room table.

"No, just stop," cried Mom. "Stop. Please!"

I ran upstairs. Dad was close behind. I knew immediately that I shouldn't have gone upstairs, but I didn't want to create a scene on the front lawn. I ran into my room and slammed the door shut, pushing my body weight against the door and gripping the doorknob.

Mom caught up to Dad, and they grew silent in the hallway. They were clearly staring at the mess in the bathroom. Mom's voice whimpered as she sniffled through tears. The door then jounced toward me, banging my forehead. I pushed back, trying to keep Dad at bay while looking around my room. As Dad opened the door an inch or two, I pushed back with a slam, my feet extended on my bureau for support.

"No. Stop!" Mom pleaded. I kept pushing and Mom suddenly shrieked. I looked up and saw her hand sticking in the door crack, her wedding ring preventing her fingers from being crushed by my force. I let go, ran towards my bed, lifted open the screen window and jumped to the rubber black roofing above the den. I then jumped into the bushes and squirmed my way out, getting scratched. Siobhan was on the front lawn. She grabbed my hand. My parents got to the front doorway and stared at us, regaining composure.

"You two. This is it," said Mom. "Just...Just go. You're not allowed back in this house."

Siobhan and I looked at each other.

"That's right. You've done enough damage. You obviously don't know how to respect others or listen. Go find another place to live. Understood?"

Siobhan and I walked backwards and jogged off toward Allison Road. I needed a Band-Aid for one of my cuts. I cried, wishing I'd been more careful.

"They'll cool down," Siobhan said. "We just need to get away for a while."

"Where will we live?" I asked.

We spent the next couple of hours looking for Dusty. I felt confident that if we found him, my parents would let us back in. But there was no trace of him. Growing hungry, we went to Perkel's and got Creamsicles. We sat on a bench and watched gleeful kids enter with their parents and walk out with sweets.

Our next stop was the rectory across the street from Divine Miracles. Siobhan was in first grade at Divine Miracles and we went there to mass every Sunday. We knew priests lived there, and that they were tight with friendly guy Jesus. I knocked on the door but nobody answered. We walked back towards the road and heard the door squeal open. We pivoted back and saw Father Pal staring at us with a big grin, waving us back. "Children, come," he said. "Are you guys all right?"

"No, not really," I said. Siobhan grabbed my arm. I looked over and saw Dad sitting in the Dodge Dart but not looking toward us.

"What brings you here?" asked Father Pal. "Your arm is bleeding. Let me get you a bandage. Come in. You need that wound cleaned out."

"My Dad's here now," I said, confused where to go.

"Is he? But I have rubbing alcohol to disinfect it right here. You need that." Father Pal opened the screen door. "I can put on some cartoons and fix a snack."

Dad honked the horn. I looked over at him. He was smiling and looked back to normal, waving us over. We ran towards him and climbed in the backseat. He fixed up my cut with a first aid kit he kept in the glove compartment. I looked back at the rectory and saw Father Pal peering beneath a curtain. We connected eyes and he ducked back.

"Who wants to go to Friendly's for dinner?" Dad asked, driving off.

We drove passed my old nursery school and the neighboring woods which led to White Ash Manor. Dad slowed down. "Now what the hell is Kova doing?" The spring blossoms covered up the view of the house, but we heard the metallic clunking of yellow bulldozers. "Our forefathers wouldn't likely approve."

At Friendly's, I stared into my Cone Head Sundae while Siobhan was in the restroom. "It's just a rug," said Dad. "I'm sorry. I am just stressed. Work stuff. I have to work from three to eleven now. Second shift. So, when you're home from school, I'll see you for just a few minutes, if at all."

"I understand. It will be rough," I said.

"I want to help you with things, like homework, having a catch. We'll have the weekends."

Back at home, Mom was at the front door, holding Dusty. "Look who came home?" she smiled.

"We'll see if that flea collar works now," Dad laughed, kissing my Mom on the cheek.

At night, Siobhan headed out to go to a sleepover pajama party. I listened to my parents talking through the walls. I couldn't determine the words, but I could feel the remorse. Finally falling asleep, Dusty walked into my room and let out a loud squawk and then jumped on my bed. I pushed him off, but he kept jumping up. Furious, I grabbed him and tossed him into the hallway and shut my door all the way. He motioned his clawless paws against the door but couldn't budge it open. He let out a visceral moan that jolted me out of bed. It didn't even sound like Dusty and I wasn't sure if it was even him making the noise. I opened my door and saw him lying stationary on the hallway rug. Dad walked out in his bathrobe and knelt down.

"He's gone," Dad said. "He's moved on."

"What?" asked Mom. I ran to her and jumped into bed. "Oh, Garv. He was so old," said Mom. "We've had him since before you were even born, way before."

"That noise he made was scary," I said.

"I know. He wanted to say goodbye. Why don't you pet him one last time?"

I rubbed Dusty's back, his face locked in a wince. Dad adjusted his jaw so that his mouth was closed and he leveled his eyes shut. He carried him down to the kitchen and put him in his cozy wool bed with a rubber squeaky toy before laying him in a trash bag.

"We'll bury him in the yard tomorrow," said Dad. "You can help. Your sister needs to say goodbye." Dad stepped out back and came back in with a large flat rock. "This can be his tombstone. You can decorate it. I'll get the paints out."

8.

Huffy

June '80
   Luther invited me over for a day of biking and my first ever sleepover. We had attended kindergarten together and were now enjoying the summer before going to Divine Miracles.

Tall and stocky, with blond unkempt hair, Luther liked to wear formal clothes, but he donned the threads sloppily. His button-down shirts were wrinkled, collars crooked, tails untucked and clip-on ties askew.

Luther shared a large bedroom with his older brother. The brother collected beer cans and lined them on multiple parallel shelves around the room, proudly displayed with labels facing out. Transparent fishing line stabilized them. Luther and I gazed at the cans while sitting in our pajamas and then nestled back into MAD magazines strewn on the floor, folding and aligning the back covers to reveal the secret image. Luther had a Magnavox Odyssey² video game system and a TV in his room. There was no reason to leave his cool den, aside from food and bathroom breaks.

In the morning, I saw that Luther's brother had passed out on the couch after watching *The Tonight Show With Johnny Carson*, as he proudly stated. We went into the backyard, after some Mom-made pancakes, and watched his brother tee up golf balls and aim at the Route 309 expressway in the distance. He used his largest club, swinging in his bathrobe, smacking the balls closer and closer to the speeding traffic.

I pedaled my Huffy bike around the yard in disbelief, hoping Luther's mom would notice what was going on. I removed myself from the scene, feeling nervous about an impending car accident. I circled around the house.

"It can't be done," Luther's brother finally said. "Can't hit the highway from here."

Luther and I took note, staring up his big bro's pimply sweaty face. I breathed a sigh of relief that the insane attempted feat was futile.

In a connecting yard, a neighbor high school dude yelled over at me, asking to see my bike. I ignored him. He had curly brown permed hair and large blue mirror sunglasses. He hopped into his car and pumped up Van Halen, revving his engine.

"Dude's a douche," said Luther's brother. "Don't mind him."

Dad pulled up in the driveway with the Dodge Dart and helped pack my bike and backpack. The neighbor dude yelped incoherent phrases at us.

"We have to go, buddy," Dad said to him, slamming the car door after I hopped into the backseat.

The next day, I was playing "pitch and field" in my backyard with a real baseball. There was a three foot tall painted cinder block wall along one side of our backyard. I wound up and hurled the ball, aiming for a sweet spot about 2 two feet above the ground. If I hit it, the ball would bounce back as a brisk grounder for me to field. If I missed my target, the ball soared into a thicket of bushes that were another three feet high. I'd just reach in and grab the ball, if I could find it. Sometimes the ball would penetrate the bushes completely and go into the old lady's yard. I would then sneak into her backyard to grab it.

For one high pitch, I ran over, grabbed the ball and saw five girls and a boy looking at me from the big bay window that faced the backyard. They were pale, grinning and captivated by my presence, all with brown hair. I waved, grabbed the ball and ran back home. Mom explained that the old lady moved out and a big family named the O'Sullivans just moved in.

The potential of new friends had me fidgeting. I wanted to flaunt the radical air I could achieve with my bike from zooming off sloped driveway curbs. But upon opening the shed door, my Huffy bike was not there. I ran to my shirtless Dad who was watering the vegetable garden with a leaky hose. He dropped the hose and stroked his sideburns. He walked to the shed in deep thought and then peered inside.

"Go wait with your mother," said Dad. "I'll be back soon."

"Where are you going?" asked Mom.

"I know what I'm doing. No worries. I'll be back in about thirty minutes." Dad scrambled to put a t-shirt on.

I sat on the front step, sobbing. Mom handed me a cup of iced tea. I thought of Willem and how he was going to public school, opposed to the Catholic Divine Miracles with me. I hoped we'd reunite at identical schools, that he would appear one day with a smile and say: "Just kiddin'."

Through the blur of tears, an O'Sullivan sister appeared on the front lawn from behind the hedges that bordered our homes. Her brown short cropped pixie hair was about the same length as mine, but with whimsical flairs. She held a soccer ball, plopped it on the ground and kicked it with a quick thrust. The ball whooshed towards me. I caught it at my face. I held the ball, glancing around in disbelief. She sauntered towards me. I dropped the ball and dried my eyes with my palms. The two of us kicked the ball back and forth, rotating around the front lawn, racing to ensure it didn't roll into the street, diving when needed. We didn't speak a word aside from elated laughter and praise for heroic leaps.

Dad eventually came back, KYW News Radio blaring from his window. He pulled my Huffy from the trunk.

"Good Lord. Where was it?" asked Mom, walking out of the house. "Is it damaged?"

"It's all good," said Dad. "Just a punk teenager who thought he could get away with it. I've got it all under control. You won't be seeing him."

The girl and I headed toward the Huffy that Dad positioned upright via the kickstand. "Are you an O'Sullivan kiddo?" he asked, bending down to our level.

"Yep. I'm Emma," the girl said, putting her hands on her grass stained white shirt, brown streaks of dirt on her cheeks. "I love your bike," she said, pivoting toward me. "Do you think you can show my brother how to ride? Me and my sisters have tried." Emma tilted her head, squinted her brown eyes and stared through me with hands on her hips.

"I can teach him," I said.

Dad took his shirt off and tossed it over his shoulder. He went to the garden, proudly sporting his pallid gut. His Air Force dog tag dangled in his chest hair and sparkled in the sun. He turned up the news from his portable radio, adjusting the antennae to gain precise clarity.

9.

Stung

July '80
Emma and her little brother, Ernie, became quick buddies. Ernie had dozens of freckles on his face of various sizes and a little potbelly. Emma was my age and soon to join me in first grade at Divine Miracles. Their four sisters were older and feisty. The sounds of mourning doves competed with their goofy outbursts and shrieks from the screen windows.

The O'Sullivan family praised me after I taught Ernie how to ride a bike. I simply pushed him down the street with a gentle stroke, just like Dad had done with me. It baffled them that it worked.

When Ernie wandered off, Emma and I rolled around on the lawn, tickling each other. Her scent was relaxing, emanating from her hair. "This hand is mine," she'd say in a common routine, grabbing my hand and pretending to chomp it to bits. I would then grab her hand and do the same and we'd roll a little further, getting dried up pine needles on our clothes.

Emma's house was more than twice the size of mine. We played in the family room, padded with a maroon wall-to-wall rug. I pretended the grid of bay windows was the view from the Millennium Falcon cockpit. We created couch cushion forts.

They provided a haven to eat a Pop Tart, bump warm backs against each other and play footsie with clammy stinky socks.

The upstairs, where the older sisters primarily hung out, had five bedrooms. I'd catch glimpses of them putting on lipstick and took notice of the perfume exuding in the hallway.

Hanging with Emma, Dad asked if I was ready to take our dog, Freckles, for a walk. I had been test walking the dog safely in the backyard. I was eager to walk the black and white mutt up and down Redford Road. Emma joined me. We gave Freckles gentle noogies when he stopped too long at a scent.

Almost home, on the Finn's front lawn, Freckles squatted to take a poop. I looked over as Mr. and Mrs. Finn sailed on their swing.

"Oh, it's fine," said Mrs. Finn. "We've seen plenty of that before."

Nothing was coming out. Freckles struggled, starting and stopping the procedure. We watched in confusion until it finally worked and a lacy bright pink pair of panties came out. Dad trotted over to pick it up, muttering something about the damn dog sleeping in their bedroom.

"Never seen that before," smiled Mr. Finn, showing off his white chompers.

Dad was the great bonding agent for Emma and I, helping us find caterpillars for placing on our arms, allowing us to pick pumpkins from his coveted patch and eventually assisting with snowmen.

We filled the summer with frequent visits to the Oreland Swim Club. I wasn't one for doing much but wading in the three-foot section. Outside of the pool, we dried off in the playground's sun while eating frozen candy bars from the Snack Hut.

I got stung by a bee on the foot once and hobbled back, leaning on Emma for support. Mrs. O'Sullivan rushed over and spit on old cigarette ashes and then massaged them onto the stung region. I never asked how this worked, but it brought relief and then an hour of Emma joking with me on the bench.

As with Willem, I told the stories of Kova to Emma and her Dad.

"He loves that safari helmet," her Dad laughed. "The public schools think he's a hero. He donates a *lot* of money. Their naming a new gymnasium after him soon."

Rage pulsated through me in thinking about Kova and how he almost destroyed our family with his reckless trucks. Every time I sat in the back of the Dodge Dart, I thought of him as I endured the funky odor. I sensed the doldrums of the drive from Dad as well. The Dodge got us from A to B, but was a beige bore.

10.

Hidden Hero

October '80
Late at night on October 21, 1980, Philadelphia Phillies relief pitcher Tug McGraw struck out Willie Wilson of the Kansas City Royals in Game 6 of the World Series. I was barely awake but was soon out on the front lawn in my pajamas, banging pots and pans in delirium with my folks and the O'Sullivans. Even the old guys on the blocks came out cheering and performed Mummer style struts as we tried to stay warm. We did the same thing on New Year's Eve, with my Dad lighting sparklers and letting us toss them around at midnight.

Together, Emma and I thrust into the pop culture, political glories and tragedies of the early 80s. We didn't know who John Lennon was when he got shot or why it devastated our folks. We listened to Mr. O'Sullivan and his buddies scream in agony during Super Bowl XV when Eagles quarterback Ron Jaworski got intercepted three times. We watched our mothers cringe and pace in front of special news coverage after President Reagan got shot.

Our families watched in amazement as a brown plastic box with buttons on it, which we called the Clicker, brought a variety of new TV experiences. This device had a few dozen cable channel options, all set up in three rows. A toggle allowed us to select a row. The clicking occurred when selecting a channel button. Each channel had a unique number. We later added sticker logos of stations to make it simpler to navigate.

The presence of the Clicker became commonplace on household coffee tables. "Don't trip on the wire," our parents piped up. Combined with bulky video game systems and no ideal place to store them, living rooms became intertwined with a web of cords, coaxial cables, cartridges and crumbs. But the Clicker brought us together on the couch with a bag of chips and drinks on coasters. Not that Siobhan, Mom and Dad didn't hang out before, but the shows gave us scheduled relaxation hours.

The low budget local commercials brought a lot of chatter.

"We've eaten there," Dad noted about a diner.

"I've met her," Mom said about a florist.

One night, Dad and I were watching *The Dukes Of Hazzard*. Dad insisted on turning off all lights on the first floor when watching TV. The glow of the show provided just enough light to work a plated sardine sandwich, a Dad classic. Mom and Siobhan were at the O'Sullivan's for a girls' night.

A commercial came on for Kova Plastics, Inc. I didn't realize at first what the commercial was for. The voice narrating seemed somewhat familiar. Footage of guys with hard hats standing beside forklifts bored me and I focused on my sandwich. Towards the end, it revealed Kova as the narrator. He stood in front of his roadside branded signage with his entire team, blabbering about the perks of working with him. He held a cigar and pointed at a blinking toll free number for job inquiries.

"Damn it!" Dad hollered, thwacking a fist onto a bag of hard Snyder's pretzels. White crunchy crumbs flew onto the coffee table and brown rug. Dad walked towards the kitchen and slammed the top Dutch door. I straightened up on the couch and looked over. The top door fell off the hinges and barreled toward Dad. He tried to catch it but he couldn't fully clasp it. Dad yowled as it landed on his foot. He tossed it aside and stormed out the back door. Loose screws clinked on the floor. I ran to the back kitchen window and watched Dad as he hobbled to the shed. He pulled out a fold-up chair and sat on it, head in his knees.

The commercials ended, and the show returned. I wanted to watch it as it wasn't a rerun. I watched a couple minutes and grew scared and confused. I stepped out into the backyard. I could hear the girls get-together next door as they chased fireflies and blew bubbles. The O'Sullivan backyard was lit up with floodlights, allowing them to extend daytime for as long as they desired. When I reached Dad, he was holding an unopened pack of cigarettes.

"How those Duke boys doing?" asked Dad.

"I dunno. You all right?" I asked.

"Sorry, Garvey." Dad stared into the lawn. "I just want to watch a show and not be reminded of... And my job. The hours are not good. Now I have to work Saturdays. Time with you and your sister has dwindled."

"I didn't know you smoked."

Dad finally looked up at me, into my eyes. "I don't. Haven't had one since the day you were born."

"Well, what's that?" I nodded at the pack.

"This here is the last pack I ever bought. The day you were born in '74. Never opened it. Realized that if I wanted to see you live to get married someday, I needed to stop. I was two packs a day. And the cost of them? I've smoked a BMW. Wouldn't be here right now if I didn't go cold turkey."

I put another chair next to Dad. I looked over and could see the heads of the older O'Sullivan girls bobbing up and down over the hedges as they took turns on a trampoline. Their long straight hair swirled over their glittering faces of overstated makeup.

"I better go clean up the mess before your mother gets back," said Dad.

"I'll get the pretzels with the DustBuster," I said. "I'll clean the living room."

"You know, I'm glad I quit the smokes, that I'm here today.

Sometimes you have to just listen to your intuition and follow through, not second guess it."

"Like you could see the future?"

"Not quite, but my body and mind gave me a direct order to stop smoking."

I looked into the shed and saw a little battery-powered lantern lit up in the corner. Stacks of books were on the floor.

"Do you read out here?" I asked.

"Sometimes, at night on the hammock. The cool breeze is nice."

A newspaper article was nailed to one of the particle board walls. The photo was of a young man with a military peaked cap.

"Who's that guy?" I asked, pointing to the yellowed article.

"That's me, back in the Force," said Dad, laughing. "My face filled out a lot. I'm only 19 there. I saved a guy, a General. His plane crashed into a marsh. Flames were everywhere. So, I ran to help him out. He was unconscious, knocked out, bleeding. That's the gut instinct I mentioned. It tells you when to run toward the fire. Or run from it. I knew I had to save him. Military sure will change you."

"You should hang this up in the living room," I said, lost for any words of praise. I looked up at the sky and spotted a couple jets with their blinking lights.

"The plane wasn't a big one. Just a two-seater. But I enjoy watching those 747s up there. Kind've relaxing from the hammock, wondering where they're going and who's on them."

I already thought of Dad as a hero. He had given the Heimlich Maneuver to two different choking victims in restaurants, saving their lives to the delight of onlookers who clapped and clinked their glasses with silverware. Dad and I stared at the back of our house. Through the windows, the TV set flickered inside the dark house, lighting up the vanilla walls with blinking colors as if the house had silent fireworks bursting inside.

From that day on, I knew to change the channel if the Kova Plastics, Inc. commercial came on. I knew the goofy intro music and had it vanished within two seconds via a quick draw of the

Clicker. I knew the precise time to click back to our show. It became second nature.

11.

Divine Carnival

August '82

Divine Miracles was just a few blocks away, a little stroll through the neighborhood. The church was on the first floor and the school on the second floor. Each grade had about twenty-five kids, all primarily of white Western European descent. A statue of Mary guarded one end of the hallway; on the other end, Joseph stood tall. Both watched over us with raised arms, instilling a guilty conscience that slowly eroded as you got older and let your shirt tails hang out.

The gravelly church parking lot was our playground. We played games of Alien, dodge ball, bounce ball and wall ball. We used tennis balls for everything but tennis. Priests cut through our playground to get to church, waving at us, as unlucky ones of poor agility got pegged in the back and butt. Knowing how to catch, throw and hit a tennis ball with a duct-taped Wiffle ball bat was key.

When time was up and the recess yard nun rang the bell, we froze in place for five seconds, waited for the bell again, and then formed silent lines by grade. We'd walk through the doors where the scent of incense rushed over us and strengthened our frizzled halos, urging us to tie our shoelaces and dip our fingers in the holy water.

Carl Franke

The school had other excitement. Twice a year was McDonald's Day, allowing us to eat lukewarm cheeseburgers and French fries in the basement. Daily, we had Philly soft pretzels available or Lance crackers as a snack. If pretzels were soggy, we crisped them on the furnace covers.

An annual Christmas Bazaar filled the basement with crafts, games and cookies. There were school plays. I performed one year as Shermy from *A Charlie Brown Christmas*. I had one line: "Every Christmas it's the same. I always end up playing a shepherd."

The biggest annual attraction of Divine Miracles was the summer carnival. We cheered when the large trucks showed up with the disassembled pieces of exhilarating rides and games.

Old enough to skip the kiddie rides and roam free without our parents, the large dazzling lit up rides were ready for the taking, all with various doses of nausea and screams. I was willing to be jerked around on the Tempest, take in the peaks of the Ferris Wheel, feel my face peel back on the Swinger, risk pissing my pants in the Haunted House and have my organs shifted on the Zodiac.

But the one ride I could barely even watch was The Star. I'm sure it had other names, but that's what we called it because of the blinking star lights all over it. Although it was like a Ferris Wheel in how it cycled, you didn't sit and relax to stare at the unseen horizons. You sat in a cage and rocked the seated chamber back and forth with a horizontal bar until you spun around like a washing machine spin basket. It's the one ride I didn't go on with Emma. I held her cyan cotton candy for her as she stood in line solo. The operator placed her in The Star with a boy in our class named Aengus. He entered the line stag. I watched them circle around, screaming and laughing. At the end, they bounced out of the rickety caged door with their clothes disheveled, hair messed, smiles askew, looking transformed. They gave each other celebratory hugs. Aengus bolted away. Emma had a dazed permagrin, her head angled off to one side.

To prove that I was a man, or at least a boy seeking to be a worthy man, I lured Emma toward the gaming section where the carnies provoked passersby to step up and perform simple tasks like tossing rings on sticks, popping balloons with darts and hurling basketballs into wooden baskets. I headed to the Whack-A-Mole game and handed the man some tickets. All that I had to do was smack 30 moles in 60 seconds to win a massive teddy bear. I gripped the mallet and the loud DING rang out. I felt strangers over my shoulder watching as I slammed down the cute creatures with a vengeance. A grinning Aengus, with his dog bite facial scar and scraggly hair, remained etched in my mind. Far from my goal, I scored a lower end prize: a 4″ x 6″ wooden framed drawing of E.T. sticking out his red pulsating finger. Glitter and sequins were mixed in, but it lacked the excitement of a life-size stuffed animal.

Emma and I shared the cotton candy and headed to the far end of the carnival near our homes. This area was not lit up as much and had community business vendors handing out pamphlets. We watched kids humiliate Father Pal, perched on the Dunk Tank. Pal dressed like a clown, far removed from his black Daffy Duck priest outfit. He welcomed the kids to get a photo with him after he got soused.

Emma grew tired and wanted to go home. She tossed her bare cotton candy stem into the trash can and licked her fingers clean. I assumed she wanted to be alone, so I waved goodbye and headed back into the screams of the carnival. I looked up at the spotlight pointing and turning aimlessly in the night sky, gripping my fragile lame prize. From the loudspeaker, the song "I Can't Go For That (No Can Do)" played, a big hit from Hall & Oates. The uplifting hypnotic sounds instantly broke the vision of Aengus from my mind and made me giddy, as if a spell was cast that provided temporary extreme confidence, like Pac-Man after he gobbled up the invincible dot and was on a ghost chomping tear. I briskly walked out of the carnival and went down Allison Road, treelines preventing the moonlight from shining through. Emma was in sight, her white Sea Isle City sweatshirt visible from blocks away.

"Emma!" I called out, jogging towards her. She turned as I reached her. "I wanted to get you that big teddy bear. But, here, I want you to have this."

Emma took the frame and held it. I gave her a peck on the cheek, close to her lips, tasting the crusted-over cotton candy. She lunged at me and kissed my lips with one quick thrust. My head bobbed back. I wobbled. "Thank you," she said. "I love it. I will hang it in my room."

We walked home side-by-side with languid steps, stopping to sit on random curbs and squash our shoulders together, pointing up at the sky and arguing over which star was Polaris.

12.

Confession

March '83
During recess, the guys in my grade circled around, picked me up and carried me over to Emma. She was sitting on the porch of the Convent, reading a Judy Blume book.

The guys clumsily kept me afloat, chanting: "Garvey and Emma sitting in a tree. K-I-S-S-I-N-G." I didn't stop them. Emma and I were publicly affectionate, opting to walk home together, perch on bike racks at recess and drink an extra chocolate milk together. Plopped down beside her, she nodded and covered her face with the pages of her book. A drizzle came down. I shrugged off the guys as they resorted back to their game of kickball.

The rain came on thick. A nun blew a whistle from the school, waving us to get back inside. Emma and I dashed hand-in-hand back, our uniforms getting soaked.

Because of the rain, they held our gym class in a large basement room. We played dodge ball. Emma was on my team. I dialed up my heroic dives when the ball headed my way, trying to catch it so the opposing team's thrower got eliminated. A certain dive had me flying knee first into a lead pipe at the base of a cinderblock wall. I laid on the ground, writhing in pain and limped to the sidelines. The pain never subsided. At night, a doctor explained that I had bursitis. The lump that formed would never go away.

\#

A new arcade opened in Oreland called Piggy's Palace. Mom scored a coupon for four free tokens and ice cream. Mom drove Emma and I there and waited in the parking lot as we played Centipede, Pac-Man and Asteroids and pounded soft serve ice cream. We were on a date, I thought, as we stood on milk crates, slapping plastic buttons and jerking joysticks.

Emma grabbed onto the joystick when I was messing up. "Come on, I'll show you how to do it," she said.

"This is my quarter, my game," I said, pushing her off the stool with my hips. She tickled my sides, forcing me to squirm off. My spaceship got destroyed.

Awesome date aside, Emma and I hung out in a dwindling fashion. Our schedules no longer seemed aligned due to organized and gender based civil tribes. Basketball, piano lessons, and Cub Scouts filled up much of my days along with having to visit a math tutor and take on house chores. Swim team, gymnastics, the choir, a karate stint and Girl Scouts absorbed her time. Homework became more excruciating and required us to read and focus after dinner. Desks and reading lamps became fixtures in our bedrooms.

\#

Emma's family routinely had backyard parties with a slew of relatives. I stared beneath slivers of window blinds from my bedroom, amazed at the kids, tables of food and boisterous conversations. Everyone seemed to get along and have common ties. Emma had multiple similarly aged cousins, all local, all excited to be together and joking around. I wished to join them.

On Sundays, I saw Emma at her typical section of the pews during my duty as an altar boy. I got eye contact and occasional smiles. But by the time I disrobed and tidied up the candles, she was gone. We didn't walk to school anymore as she was now on the Safety Committee and needed to be near the bus drop off early in the morning, donned in an orange vest.

I wanted to confess my love and utter devotion to Emma, so I wrote a letter and put it in an envelope, hoping to hand deliver it. I secured it thoroughly with gauze tape I found in the bathroom medicine cabinet. I made certain that no one should open it but Emma by scrawling her name on it with a black magic marker. As I walked over to her house, Emma's older sisters danced through the window. Madonna blasted from the speakers. Their parents were out.

"Hey, Garv," they chimed in unison through the screen. "Looking for Emma?" They giggled.

I freaked out and threw the letter into a sewer, pretending it was trash. Back home, I panicked, wondering if the sisters had seen Emma's name on the letter. I pictured them scooping it out and reading it aloud. I retrieved Dad's yard rake and tried to sift it out, but I couldn't even scratch the bottom. I then stole a two liter bottle of soda from our fridge and poured it into the sewer, hoping to destroy the evidence so it was unreadable, remembering how Dad said soda could take the paint off a car. My heart rate dipped down.

On my porch, a calming drizzle tapped on the roof. Globules of water glistened on the hedges that separated Emma's yard from mine. My bursitis ached. I focused on my desire to marry my cool tomboy neighbor, to settle down at a prepubescent age of 9-years-old, to escape our daily agendas now prepacked and marred by societal norms.

13.

Upon The Bridge

February '85

In the middle of 5th grade, a new girl joined our class named Farrah. Her unique qualities struck the guys. For starters, she had boobs. Even girls in 6th grade didn't have them. Her hair was a mix of various browns. Her lips were large and glistened as she gnawed gum and popped bubbles. Her stance was tall and confident. She wasn't eager to make friends and appeared quietly pissed off. The nuns told her she couldn't wear her black Ron Jon Surf Shop sweatshirt in class. "Whatever," she said, rolling her eyes and tossing it on the floor.

A rumor spread that Farrah had to repeat first grade due to a combo of bad grades and behavior. They assigned her to sit next to me during afternoon classes. We hardly talked but would connect eyes and nod in disgust when the nuns tried to be funny. I tried to figure her out through occasional quick questions. She had no hobbies, clubs, places to be at 10am on a Saturday like the rest of us.

As Valentine's Day grew closer, I huddled with the guys, shivering in the cold during recess and asked if anyone liked Farrah. They admitted that she was cute, but I was the only one smitten with her, allured by her resistance of rules.

Once the big V-Day came, a Thursday, we all exchanged pink

and lavender colored envelopes with cards for each other. For Farrah, I found a Garbage Pail Kids card of Feline Farrah. It had a girl covered with cats. I watched her open it as I ate my pink frosted cupcake. She smiled and searched for me. We connected. She nodded approvingly.

Back home, I got out of my uniform and asked Dad for a few quarters for the Piggy's Palace arcade. He slid me eight from his tall bureau that was always brimming with coins and cologne. He then gave me five dollar bill. "Don't tell your mother."

The loot jangled in my pants as I headed out the door. I ran into Emma on the road. "Where you headed?" she asked.

"I'm going to the post office for my Dad. Need to get stamps."

"You OK? You seem frazzled."

"I'm fine. Let's go to Piggy's Palace soon. OK?"

"Thanks for your card today." She reached in for a hug. I squeezed her tight.

I paused for a moment. "Want to hang out tonight after dinner?" I asked.

"Can't. My brother has a gymnastics performance. He promised epic floor routines. We're all going."

Onward I walked to Perkel's. I bought a mini heart-shaped box of Whitman's chocolate sampler. I tucked the box in my coat and headed to Park Avenue, right next to the Oreland Train Station. I found Farrah's house and saw her sitting at the dining room table, rubbing her hands on her forehead. I walked to the door and knocked. Farrah's little sister answered. "Hi, is your sister here?" I asked.

"Who are you?" she asked.

"Garvey. I'm in her class."

"She's not here right now."

"Ah. Are you sure?" I hoped Farrah would hear me and correct her.

"Yep. She's out."

"Can you give this to her?" I presented the heart with both hands, palms up.

Farrah's sister took the chocolates and walked away, leaving the door open.

I waved goodbye and headed for the street. I heard Farrah yell out: "I don't want it! Just put it with the other one."

I looked over and heard the side door open as the sister tossed the chocolates into a trash can. I walked further, looking over my shoulder. Farrah danced around her yard with her dog, a joyous display of denim legs teasing the dog with a large bone.

Trudging onwards, I moped around the neighborhood, noticing many cupid decorations in house windows. I popped into Rosario's Pizzeria. Aengus sat dazed in a booth by himself, slurping up soda with a straw. I ordered a slice and sat across from him. I rarely saw Aengus, let alone hung out with him. He preferred to be solo, cursing and spitting on the outskirts during recess. Many found him irritating. Stories loomed about him starting fist fights with his Dad and attacking his Mom with a wire hanger. I had written him off.

"Farrah's a bitch," Aengus said.

"What happened?" I asked.

"I got her a little Teddy Bear, the kind that is holding a chocolate bar—"

"Wait, when did you give it to her?"

"Less than an hour ago. Her sis threw it in the garbage. Then her Pops reamed her out about something."

"Weird. Same thing just happened with me."

"Seriously, dude?"

"Yeah. She's cute, I guess. Exciting. I didn't know you liked her too."

"Hell yeah. I played stupid when you asked us all."

I nodded, dousing my pizza with extra helpings of red pepper flakes and garlic powder. The intense fluorescent lights brought everything to vivid clarity. "She's older than us anyway," I said.

"Whatever. I'd love to grab those titties. We gave it a shot, right? Everyone else was too chickenshit to try and convert her?"

"Say what?"

Aengus shook his head. "Nevermind, man."

As I walked home in the dark night, I saw Farrah in her blue plaid winter coat as she waited for her dog who squatted against a telephone pole. We connected eyes. She raised a mitten.

"I'm so sorry, Garvey," she said as her pooch looked up at me, panting. "You came over on the wrong day."

"Why? It's Valentine's Day."

"No, not that. It's just. My Dad and I. We had a big fight. He's not accepting me for who I am. And you. You don't seem to get it."

"Get what?"

"I'm not sure what I like more. Get it now?"

My face blushed from embarrassment.

"I'm really confused," she said. "I've never talked to him about it." She smiled and gave me a hug. "Sitting next to you at school is so much fun."

We sauntered towards her house. She put the dog back into the yard through a gate in the fence. "You ever been on the bridge when a train goes by?"

The wind howled. The dog scratched at the side door and her sister let him into the amber glow of the warm house. A few homes down, Park Avenue ended and a path led to the Oreland Train Station bridge. Farrah looked at her vibrant Swatch watch. "Just a few minutes to go, if it's on time."

As we climbed up the steel perforated stairs to the overpass, Farrah spoke of the suicide from years ago. I recalled the days when Willem and I flattened pennies on the tracks and searched for pieces of skull.

"You should call him," Farrah said. "Sounded like a cool guy."

"I see him sometimes. I bike by his house and he's out on the lawn doing gardening stuff. But he really spazzed out and hates me now."

A white sphere of light appeared on the tracks in the distance.

"Oh, it's the express," said Farrah. "I can tell by the speed. Even better."

The glow grew larger. Streaks expanded into a cross formation. Reflections soared on the cables above. Blue sparks gyrated at the top of each car. Farrah leaned against the tall transparent plexiglass and spread her arms out. The electric charges writhed and crackled as the horn tooted two deep phrases. When the express passed beneath, a train from the other direction eased to a stop.

"A double train," Farrah moaned as the bridge rattled.

I watched passengers exit the train and scatter towards their cars. One of them appeared to be Kova. His blotchy face made it clear. He wore a trench coat and a wide-brim fedora, carrying a few long cardboard tubes with white caps on the ends. I scanned around and saw his yellow Spider.

"You know someone down there?" Farrah asked.

"I know of him. That guy," I said pointing. "If it's who I think it is, he's getting into that yellow car. It has a bumper sticker that says GOLF GOD."

"He's got a lot of wrapping paper with him. Wait, you know his bumper sticker?"

"Shhhh," I said, putting an index finger against her lips.

The man approached the Spider and opened the car while holding the tubes under one arm. The tubes had bright blue cross markings on them. A couple other men approached him and handed him more tubes. The man put the tubes in the passenger section, tipped his hat goodbye to the men and started to get into his car. He shifted his head slowly towards us. Exposed, Farrah and I were lit up from the bridge lights. I grabbed Farrah's shoulders and crouched her down below the plexiglass where a three foot steel partition covered us.

"You in trouble with this guy?" Farrah asked.

"Kind've," I said. My inner thighs braced the sides of her breasts.

"You better be."

I slinked upwards and saw the yellow car pull out of the spot and chug off toward the road. The GOLF GOD bumper sticker was visible.

"Sorry," I said, standing up. "It's who I thought it was. He's a weirdo. He stalked Willem and I years ago. Took pictures of my neighbor. Just creepy. Not sure if he saw us."

"Doubt it. I yelled to my dipshit Dad once when he got off and he said he couldn't see me. Oh, and don't worry. I won't tell Emma that you just spooned me."

"Me and Emma go way back. We're next-door neighbors. It's been hard to see each other. So much going on."

"So I'm your #2? You really are a Cancer," said Farrah, smiling into my face. "A romeo boy."

"Cancers are romantic?"

"And they love their mommies. I'm a Sag. Fire sign, baby. Even if I was straight, we wouldn't work out. Cancer and Sagittarius is a disaster mix."

"I do like Emma a lot. I don't know why I did this today. I hardly know you and—"

"You better get her something, like now. There's still time. She's a Taurus, I think. That's what you need."

I was soon back in Rosario's, buying their annual Valentine's Day special: a large heart sculpted pizza with heart-shaped pepperoni. I walked several blocks to Emma's house, keeping an eye out for Kova's car, trying to keep the pie straight.

"I'm in the middle of dinner," said Emma, after I knocked on her door. "You brought a pizza?"

"I figured we could share it," I said, opening the lid. Cheese stuck to the roof of the box lid and formed long gooey strings. The greasy pie was lopsided and no longer shaped like a heart, let alone a traditional round.

"Rosario's," said Emma. "You walked so far. Is that a calzone?"

"It was a heart. I figured we could have our own dinner."

Emma looked back at her Mom who was barking at her to return to her seat. "I need to go. We're not supposed to answer the doorbell during dinner. Let's get a slice this weekend."

We stared at each other as the clanking of silverware on plates grew intense. Her closed lip smile instilled calm into me. I tilted in and gave a dry peck.

"Come back now," commanded Emma's Mom. "Nobody leaves the table until we're all done."

I walked home with the pizza. Through a window, I saw Mom plating microwaved stuffed shells while Dad walked out the back door and screamed for me. I saw the jitters overcome Dad's face after I didn't answer. I dumped the slimy box of tepid pizza into a trash can on the side of the house and walked inside.

14.

Scout's Honor

May '85

As if the plaid green Divine Miracles uniform wasn't enough formality, my classmate buds and I enrolled in Cub Scouts. The navy button down Scout shirt featured multiple sections including a pocket for strung beads, a yellow handkerchief, gold and silver arrow point patches and the animal rank classification which started with Bobcat. Combined with Little League uniforms, parents had critical laundry cycles.

Mom volunteered to be a Den Mother and had our Troop work on projects in our half-finished basement. I'd wait out front for the guys to arrive, sporting my Scout duds to lure Emma over for a quick chat or to see her momentary smile and shy wave.

The Scouts door-to-door fundraising effort was the tough sell of bulk incandescent light bulbs. Dad waited a few houses down the street as I knocked door-to-door with a clipboard and presented the dream of having a supply closet stocked with bulbs of various wattages.

"Bulbs?" protested Mr. Finn, across the street. "They sell them at Oreland Hardware."

"Yes, but these are up to 30% off, depending on which package you buy."

Mr. Finn shook his head in confusion. "Where the devil am I

going to put them all? Your neighbor Emma sells Thin Mints and Tagalongs with her tribe. Delicious rare treats that come around just once a year. Is this a joke?"

Charity sales aside, the Scouts tightened my classmate friendships and created a competitive spirit through events like the Pinewood Derby, where Dad and I worked on creating the most aerodynamic car with just enough pennies glued to the bottom, and the Dog Sled Run, in which we camped in cabins overnight in the snow and formed teams to race huskies along trails.

A three-night camping trip at Treasure Island, a Scout reservation in New Jersey's Manasquan River was the highlight of the year. The Scoutmaster had touted how amazing it would be for months beforehand, preparing us by showing a slideshow of photos from past trips. We camped with our Dads in cloth tents, canoed, fished for flukes, played hoops and volleyball, dove into the deep end of the pool to retrieve bricks, and prodded at the campfires with large branches. Every hour of each day was jam-packed with scheduled activities. We confirmed each completed event with a heavy penciled X.

An event for the last evening was "Golf Basics With A Local Pro". I asked Dad about who this mentor could be on our drive to Treasure Island.

"It might very well be Kova," Dad said, immediately knowing who I was referencing. "He does stuff like this a lot. Maybe he'll buy me a new car."

"I think I saw him on Valentine's Day. On the bridge over the tracks."

"What the hell were you doing near the tracks?"

"It's how I was going to Rosario's."

"We have Oreland Pizza down the street. Why were you going all the way over there?"

"I was at Piggy's Palace. It's nearby."

"What the heck did Kova say to you on the bridge?"

"Nothing. I saw him getting off the train with a bunch of tube things. Must have been thirty of them."

"Sounds like they were golf balls. He probably gets weighted illegal balls that go further. I betcha that's what they were. He's a cheater."

As the golf training hour approached, we walked to the mapped grassy clearing with our Dads and found Kova sitting on a picnic table. He adjusted his yellow and green socks which matched his identical colored outfit and Jeff cap.

"Circle round," Kova said, waving us closer. "Dads, hang back."

We gathered around as Kova held a pitching wedge and stared blankly through big bug-eyed black shades. I figured he might recognize me from five years ago, outside the tunnel with Willem, but I was much taller and a Scout cap shadowed half my face. Dad looked different as well, sporting a full beard.

"Welcome, boys," said Kova. "Raise your hand if you've ever golfed before."

Nobody raised their hand.

"None, eh? Dads, you sure are slacking. Get it together."

The Dads eyed each other and shrugged.

"You boys are lucky. My father left me when I was four. I came to the States and was raised by my Uncle Heikki. Now golf is a gentleman's game. You're never too young to be a gentleman. It's a difficult game, sure. But it's all about trust, trusting yourself to believe in your skill set, knowing you've mastered the swing, assuring your body." Kova hopped off the picnic table and held the face of his wedge in a fist, pointing the black grip at us. "Golf is strength of mind. Not strength of body. I've seen men half my size drive the ball further than I ever could. So true. It's a game of patience and endurance. And walking. For the love of God, walking!" Kova affixed white leather gloves to his hands. "You know, some able-bodied men prefer to take a golf cart, but these men are not playing the game. They are cheating and cheating themselves. Trudging through the elements and steep contours, building up a sweat that drips down onto your gloves as you swing. That's all part of the game. You don't see the pros on TV carting around. They use caddies."

Kova squatted down to our eye level. "You know, I have a stepson who's around the age of you boys. He refuses to join the Scouts because he thinks it's stupid. Maybe he'll come around. For now, he's a disgrace to the tradition you uphold, an American tradition from 1930. You all, you are solid young men. I thank you for the opportunity to teach you this game, this societal tool, this business meeting in the sun, this pastime that will help you climb the rungs towards golden opportunities. Golf isn't going anywhere. It's here to stay. Look at all the courses back home near your Oreland troop headquarters. Toss away any negative thoughts on golf. Maybe you think it's boring. Where's the cheerleaders? Where's the Phillie Phanatic, the junk food? Where's the loud music, the lights? I tell ya, I've never hired an executive or salesman at Kova Plastics that wasn't a golfer. Wouldn't trust such a man. Golf proves you can be a team of one, a shark. You can take three clients out on the course and sell them my brand and what makes our plastic parts more superior. Boys, if you're not excited yet about golf, I don't know if you ever will be. Everyone, please take a wedge from the box over there, line up, spread apart and let me show the key fundamentals of a stroke."

As we connected with the balls in browning clipped grass, Kova walked around and corrected our grips. He shadowed over us and encased us with his arms to better align our fingers. He smoothed our jerky back swings with test strokes, cupping his hands around ours, adjusting our alignments. When it worked, the satisfaction achieved from connecting and tapping the ball to a perfect trajectory was soothing, but we mainly tore up the grass with divots. We retreated to the shade for bug juice and chalkboard lessons on golf basics, scoring, hazards and club explanations. At the end of the session, Kova provided us with four new golf balls, each with the Kova Plastics logo on them.

"See," Dad nudged at me. "That's probably what was in those cases you saw."

Later at night while roasting marshmallows by the campfire, I heard a familiar laugh from a neighboring troop. I walked closer towards it and saw Willem's Uncle Jay telling jokes with a bunch of dads. Perched on a boulder and looking down at the fire was Willem. He looked miffed, his hair much longer and in a ponytail. I called out to him at the base of the rock. He smiled and leapt off, landing on all fours.

"I heard your Uncle's voice," I said. "Figured you might be here."

"He's embarrassing me. He's great, but not when hitting his flask. He's so loud."

"Yep, you liking Scouts?"

"Not really. I think I'm done with it. I don't need this circus to learn how to use a canoe."

"I getcha. It's fun at times. I'm right next to ya," I said, pointing to our fire. "Did you have Golf Lessons today?"

"Yep. Early this morning in the dew. That guy still creeps me out. I see him on the road sometimes. He's here ya know."

"Kova is at a campsite?"

"There's a visitor's cabin over by that bright light over there. It's right on the river. Jay saw his car there and figured it out."

Jay stumbled towards us, burying his flask in his jacket. "You still being all moody on this rock?" he said, looking up.

"I'm down here," said Willem.

"Ah. Well, I'm gonna pay my respects to my old boss." Jay patted my head and formed his own trail through bushes toward the bright light on a telephone pole in the distance.

"We better follow this," said Willem.

Jay maneuvered quickly through the campsite perimeters toward the light, finally reaching a clearing. Willem and I stayed in the woods as Jay walked into the heavily lighted grass and to a gravel driveway where Kova's Spider was parked. Jay looked around while unzipping his fly and then urinated on the driver's side seat. He swayed back and forth, positioning onto the dashboard, floor and head rest. "Idiot left his top down. Here's the piss test you never gave me."

Willem and I covered our mouths to seal off laughter. Jay slithered back through the woods to the campsite. "I gotta see this," Willem said. We tiptoed on the grass toward the driveway. No lights were on inside the cabin. We looked into the car and saw the piss shimmering and dropping from the steering wheel.

"Let's go over there and get out of this light." Willem motioned to the side of the cabin that was not lit up, facing the river. We trotted over and saw Kova teeing up a ball. He smacked it with his driver, sailing the ball into the river with a plop. He teed up another ball and kept repeating.

"We better get back," I said. "My Dad is probably looking for me."

Suddenly something smacked into the side of my head. I yipped in pain, falling onto the grass. I looked up and saw Willem catching a falling camera on a tripod. He bobbled it and affixed it back upright. The lens appeared aimed at our campsite.

Kova heard the racket and looked over. "Can I assist you boys with something?" he called out, walking towards us with his driver.

Willem and I galloped back to the echoing laughter and crackling fires of the camp area, disappearing into the woods. We stopped to look back and saw Kova working on his camera.

I tugged on Dad's shirt and he bent down on one knee. "I think Kova is taking photos or video of us," I explained. "He has a camera aimed at us." I pointed toward the lights of the visitor's cabin and they turned off. "I bumped into it."

"What were you doing over there? I thought you were here."

"Just wanted to see the river up close. The stars."

Dad stood up slowly, mouth open, eyes connected to mine. He walked towards the visitor's cabin and stopped at the sound of footsteps on twigs. Kova surfaced from the periphery with a smile.

"Any chance you boys are making s'mores?" Kova asked. "I'd love a nightcap treat. Or is that just a Girl Scout thing?"

Dad put a hand on Kova's shoulder and walked him aside, talking quietly a few paces.

"Recording? Why, yes," Kova exclaimed. "With this moonlight on the river, I wanted to get a nice long shot of teeing off. My stroke needs realigning sometimes. Video doesn't lie."

15.

West Oreland Blues

June '85

On the drive home from Treasure Island, I pondered if Kova's camera was aimed at our campsite. My head hit it, possibly swiveling it around. Willem wasn't sure of its position when caught. The tug-of-war thoughts came to a halt and zapped from existence by a bomb dropped by Dad. My family and I were moving to East Oreland.

"It all happened fast," Dad said, turning the Dodge into a roadside ice cream shop. "The new house is bigger. It has a family room and a den that can be used as a guest room. A second bathroom too. No more waiting to take a leak." Dad nudged at my shoulder.

We stepped out onto the stone parking lot, got ice cream and sat at a picnic table. Although the new house was just a mile away from Redford Road, it seemed like Emma and I would be in different atmospheres.

"We looked at the house when you guys were in school," said Dad. "Got a buyer right away. Didn't even have to list it. Your mother knew someone."

On moving day, the O'Sullivans joined us on our front lawn while the movers piled up the truck. Our parents talked specifics. Emma talked about her summer which included an overnight camp for most of July and three weeks at Long Beach Island. She was evaporating from my side like the hose puddles we created and splashed in years ago. Hours lounging in her presence was no longer a humid highlight of summer. Her new outfit and fresh longer hairstyle appeared foreign in the roar of cicadas and heavy cardboard boxes plopping in the truck. In an awkward embrace goodbye, a floral perfume masked her scent and her chunky bracelets felt odd against my back.

"Follow me," Emma whispered as we hugged. She walked toward her front yard. I followed suit and slunk through the hedges to her dandelion plucking smiles. I hugged her again. She grabbed my hand and ran around her house as I held on. We ducked beneath branches and headed behind her shed. "You're not going *too* far away," she said. "We barely see each other anyway, right?"

I leaned in to kiss her lips and noticed a hornets nest hanging beneath a rafter, just a few feet away. It resembled a large grey football. Emma turned to it and shrieked at the multiple hovering hornets. Off we ran to another corner of her yard toward a neighbor's connecting backyard, sprinting until we reached the asphalt of Garth Road. We sat at the curb, arms around each other, letting our sweaty cheeks rest into each other, skull to skull.

"Oh, Garvey!" bellowed Dad. It was his last siren call of Redford Road, a voice that had retrieved me from many nooks in the past, stronger than ever.

Emma poked at my bare legs, teasing me with tickles and imitating Dad's boisterous alert.

"Well, this is it," I said, grabbing her knuckle cracking fingers. I positioned my fingers into a tight interlocked grasp, kneading her hands with my thumbs.

16.

Bored Pyro

June '85

I immediately explored East Oreland with my bike, getting to know the sloped driveway curbs perfect for ramps and getting major pop-a-wheelie height.

Down the street from where I lived, I noticed a bowl cut red headed kid sitting on his bike and eyeing me up every time I passed. He wasn't riding his bike. He perched like a top heavy mushroom, surveying me.

I eventually pulled up alongside him and introduced myself. His name was Conner and turned out to be the same age as me. He went to a private school that was an academy where he had to wear a fancier uniform than I did.

Conner pointed out that his parents were at the mall and asked if I wanted to burn golf balls with him. I pointed out I wanted to explore the town, but he drably stated there was nothing to see in "Boreland". We angled our bikes aside, and I followed his giddy mischievous cackle to a large pine tree on the side of his house. His certainty and elated facial expressions drew me in.

We entered a flap of branches and sat near the base of the pine tree, outstretched on a bed of tan dry needles. Conner took a golf ball out of his pocket and put it on the ground. "I collect these," he said. "Golfers hit them out of the course and onto Twining

Road." He put a butane lighter up to it and we waited and watched the flame burn through the dimpled mould cover that filled our coniferous cave with a toxic stench.

Conner's large toothy grin grew wider as I waved away the smoke and coughed. Flames hit the core of the ball and revealed what looked like hundreds of rubber bands. One-by-one, the bands zipped off into various directions. Half of the golf ball was destroyed. He pulled the flame away. The surrounding needles burned up and spread into a black smoldering circle. Conner burst out of the cave. I fumbled and followed him out. A stream of flowing water greeted my face. Conner held a hose, his mouth agape with joyous laughter. I dove out of the way onto the grass, giggling at the catastrophe diverted.

"Gotta have the hose nearby," said Conner. "I almost forgot."

Back at the base of the pine, Conner pulled out another ball. There was a logo on one side of the ball, facing me.

"Kova Plastics," I said.

"Yeah, the owner is a local. Hot shit golfer millionaire." Conner's thumb reddened as he held the plastic gas button. The ball burned slowly, reaching up and melting the logo.

I went home that night with Conner's phone number. We blossomed into a strange duo of 11-year-old pubescent punks. I questioned whether we were friends or just two kids with a mutual desire to play out shenanigans.

Conner's house had a climbable tree next to it that easily allowed us to hop onto the shingled gable roof. We'd then palm the textured shingles and make our way to the top and saddle up on the ridge board. We ripped off shingles and hurled them into the street at passing cars. The shingles left our hands like erratic fruit bats, never reaching our targets. This rooftop ruin only lasted a few sessions. Conner's Dad put a quick end to it, asking me to leave so he could set Conner straight, whatever that entailed.

Conner's Mom, Holly, was a gardening angel that brought us refreshments and entertained our sugar high theatrics. She was

BE HOME BY DINNER

evenly tan and wore pastel polo shirts tucked into taut shorts, even when handling fertilizer. Conner's Dad seemed disengaged and moped around the house with a tool belt and a beer, disappearing behind draped plastic to work on home improvement projects. I never knew his name. He single-handedly added a den and glass sunroom to their home in two years. Holly pointed out all the details of their expanding home, but his Dad had little words. He seemed possessed, as if he had no choice but to vanish to hardware stores and require us to be a safe distance from the sparks emitting from his sawhorses or the meats sizzling on the charcoal grill. "What sport do you play?" he asked me once. That's about it. He retreated to his den to watch Phillies games in between building, looking pissed at the world, as if forced into his role.

On summer weekends, my parents and sister were usually in bed by 11:30pm. I'd stay up late to watch baseball highlights or try to rig our cable to view Cinemax soft-core porn. The scrambled horizontal stripes seemed to get weaker at night. On lucky nights, I could see full scenes of *Lady Chatterly's Lover* and other T&A flicks. My folks kept a big plastic container in the TV room filled with a variety of chips and I'd make a sodium packed chip salad, while the roar of crickets poured through the window screens.

During these late nights, Conner and I often snuck out of our homes to meet at a particular block at a set time, usually around 1:00am. It was tricky to open the back screen door without making noise, but I eventually mastered it. Once out, I'd dart from shrubbery to bush, hiding from the occasional high beams of cars. Cops would likely question what I was doing out so late.

The goal was quick destruction of something with fireworks: lighting a round of ladyfingers, a ten pack of black snakes or launching a mysterious rocket, wondering what it would do. Shaking up beer cans and tossing them as far as we could was a favorite. Upon impact with the street, the cans would splatter and spin around crazily, like they were breakdancing, leaving us to run for our lives back home. Sometimes Dad would come downstairs right after I came back in and we'd meet in the kitchen to discuss the assholes making noise so late at night. "Did you see anything?" he'd ask.

Eggs, pumpkins, watermelons. We hurled them high and far, just to hear the thumps and see the guck spill out. We took pride in the results.

17.

I Love A Parade

July '85

Destruction aside, Conner and I educated ourselves on the anatomy of women. His brother was rarely home and had an attic bedroom with an abundance of fireworks. We snuck up one afternoon to see if any firecrackers were lying around and noticed mangled flesh glistening from the sides of the askew single bed mattress. Glossy porn magazines oozed out like grape jelly from a PB&J sandwich. Conner and I pushed up the mattress and found dozens of scattered zines. It was a cornucopia of *Playboy*, *Penthouse*, *Hustler*, *Cherry*, a gigantic leap forward from the Sears catalog bra models we ogled. We picked out some and paged through, eyes peering out the window, ready to bolt downstairs if his brother pulled into the driveway.

Days later, on the morning of July 4th, I awoke to the sounds of classic 1930s car horns. I looked out my bedroom window and saw an army tank sitting on a flatbed truck. Fire trucks were parked together. A clown on stilts practiced. A marching band hit random notes, warming up. For a large stretch of Garden Road and side roads, the Oreland Parade prepped and lined up, ready to delight the crowds with their annual tribute to America's freedom.

Conner was on vacation with his family. Before he left, he

explained that he'd leave his ground level window unlocked so I could jump in and snag Roman Candles or borrow his Atari 5200 system. It was about an hour before the parade started. I trotted over to Conner's house and knocked on the front door. "OK, I'll be right around!" I blurted, in case somebody was watching, and headed to Conner's window.

When my feet landed on Conner's floor, I shouted his name to make certain it was vacant. The disheveled stacks of porn crept into my mind. I figured Conner wouldn't care if I took a few. His brother's collection was too massive to notice three zines missing. I snuck up, shoved a few in my shorts and tiptoed downstairs. Upon entering Conner's room, I heard keys slide into the front door lock and jiggle. The cats rushed to the front door from under Conner's bed. I forgot that a cat sitter was visiting. As the door opened, I heaved myself over the window ledge, closed the window and backed myself up against the siding of the house. I waited until the cat sitter left and clomped down the walkway. I stood up and pretended that I was looking for a lost dog, just in case the cat sitter was still around, and moseyed down to the street.

A new float was positioned near my house, lined with purple and gold streamers. The side stated *Miss Oreland 1985*. I looked up at it and saw a girl dressed in a long turquoise dress, smiling down at me. She wore a crown, propped up on a throne, holding red roses and an American flag. "They better get here soon," she said, nodding at the empty 2nd and 3rd place stools. "You see any lost looking girls in fancy dresses?"

I stood speechless, in awe. "No," I said. "Maybe they're jealous of your beauty?"

"Aw, you're sweet. Do you want some candy? I have Tootsie Rolls and Starburst." She leaned forward to scoop the candy from a bin, revealing her cleavage in a half second frame that froze in my mind, like a slideshow carousel lighting up the image in a dark windowless room. "Come on. You know you want some," she teased.

I felt that if I had to bend down the zines might fall out.

"Oh, you're getting too old for candy at parades, right?" she asked.

"Yeah, totally. I'll be in the crowd though."

"Cool," she said, tossing me a can of soda from her cooler.

I cracked open the can.

"Can you do me a solid?" she asked. "See that guy way over there in the red Corvette?"

I followed her index finger to a bunch of guys in suits, standing with cigars and crouching down to inspect details of the car's body. They passed a flask around.

"Tell the guy in the Uncle Sam tie to come over here. That's my Dad. He'll know what's going on. He's in the parade too. A commissioner."

I jogged to the men as the firm porn zines chafed my thighs and abdomen. They took notice of my awkward steps as I approached. One man was Kova. I explained how Miss Oreland needed Daddy's help.

"Am I in the presence of a Scout?" asked Kova, tilting his head.

"Yep, I'm in the Scouts," I said.

"Thought so. You look familiar. Your legs hurt? You have a limp."

Drums roared down the street. We looked down and saw the tan, leggy Brazilian girls practicing in their green and orange feathers and diva headdresses. The men turned to them, pointing and hollering. I spun off to my house, walled with fire trucks. I slithered between the heavy idling engines. I looked over toward Kova but couldn't see him at all. I wondered if he recognized me from Treasure Island.

When I got to my front door, Mom was in the doorway, in a super-duper lovey-dovey mode. "Want French toast before the parade?" she asked. "And when's the last time you gave me a hug?"

"Hold on a second," I said, escaping her clutch. I jogged up the stairs. "Gotta pee bad."

In the bathroom, I heard Mom walk upstairs and go into her

bedroom. I figured that I had no choice but to hide the porn in the bottom sink cabinet. It felt wrong to put the magazines in with the plunger and Comet.

The phone rang. "Garvey, it's Emma," Mom shouted.

"I'm in the bathroom. I'll call back later."

"Oh, he's using the bathroom," I heard her tell Emma.

I put both hands over my face in embarrassment. "Great, Emma thinks I'm taking a massive dump," I muttered.

Soon, Mom and I were eating a powdered syrupy breakfast. Mom thumbed through a *Better Homes and Gardens*. "Are you finally going to have Emma come over to hang out?" she asked.

"Yeah, that would be cool. I'll call her tonight."

An hour later, I transferred the zines from the bathroom to under my mattress. Although I made my bed daily, Mom randomly washed my sheets. The chance of discovery was real, but worth the risk.

#

Within the escalating head rush that naked women provided, Conner scored a floppy disk computer game called *Leisure Suit Larry In The Land Of Lounge Lizards* for his Apple II. We controlled a dude in his forties and tried to help him buy condoms, meet chicks and score. It was as if the *Pitfall* guy fled the jungle and roamed the city.

Conner's neighbor, a lady that lived solo, asked us if we'd watch her cat for a few hours a day over the course of a four-day weekend. She was a Catholic high school teacher that was often curled on her porch wicker chair, reading. Her home had stacks of cheesy romance novels, the kind for sale in supermarket lines. On the last day, we called "976" phone sex numbers while eating Tastykakes in the lady's living room. Late night TV commercials compelled us. We pocketed a romance novel on the way out, one that had earmarks at the steamy parts. The lady later cornered us on the street and scolded us, threatening to tell our parents, holding the phone bill in her hand.

Conner and I decided we needed a fort to store our stolen

erotica. There was an old Community Center next to Shady Creek Golf Course that had a playground of rusting spring horses, slides and swings. We sat and ate candy bars, taking notice of beer caps mixed in with the safety mulch. A canopy of maple trees shaded the playground. A barb wired chain linked fence ran along one side, with the concrete Community Building to the other side.

We noticed that there were a series of breaks in a section of the fence. Pulling it apart, there was a perfect gap to sneak into the wooded area that connected to the golf course. We were in the golf course boundaries, but it was thick woods to the far right of the 16th hole that even the worst golfer couldn't get into, a buffer of land.

Walking through the weeds, a few narrow paths appeared. One led to a large stump with crushed beer cans all round it. We headed off the path towards a group of trees with low branches and slowly built a fort over several days, fastening particle board vicked from Conner's basement and tying down a plastic canopy.

No one could see us in our camouflaged realm. We'd see golfers teeing off, cars zooming by, parents pushing toddlers on swings, local caddies cutting through the fence slit to get to Shady Creek. We were prisoners of our disturbing natures, delighted, building a nest.

18.

The Lookout Man

July '85
    Conner and I spent time at Carmine's Drug Store, a mom and pop joint that housed two rotating arcade games in the store's rear by the pharmacy. Classics such as *Contra*, *Double Dragon*, *Rastan* and *Arkanoid* were installed with the volume at full capacity. Lasers whizzed and thunderous bombs exploded as adults picked up their prescription drugs.

Two other buddies, Quinn and Patrick, chilled at Carmine's. We slid in quarters, popped down Rolo chocolates and traded Topps baseball cards from the freshly opened packs, hoping that the pink stick of gum didn't adhere to an all-star card and damage it.

Carmine's was our back office. A few adults surfaced into our domain, such as Father Pal. "Don't break your fingers on those buttons. I'll see you bright and early tomorrow morning!" he'd say to Patrick and I regarding our altar boy schedules.

Patrick went to Divine Miracles with me where I now took a bus back and forth. He lived with five brothers in a house that his builder Dad kept expanding upon. The house was always in repair, plastic sheaths lining the floors and walls with unfinished wood exposed. Pat's Dad was the stoic Scoutmaster of the troop that I, along with a few others, recently quit. He wore a battered

Phillies hat with salty sweat marks of dedication. He stared you down if you accidentally said "Jesus" like I often did, leaving me to squirm into another room. Although the Scouts created wondrous memories, many of us jumped ship out of boredom at the Tenderfoot rank. Patrick stayed at it.

Pizza nights with my family resulted with slices for breakfast the next day. With Patrick, it was a fight for each remnant morsel of crust. It was an inhalation of dough and cheese in one standing session, everyone holding their oily paper plate in one hand, shoving Rosario's greasiest slice with the other.

Pat's house wasn't big, but it was exciting. If a movie was on, I found a sliver on the couch and edged my way into an awkward spot to catch a VHS movie, our hips crammed together. There was a true survivalist sensation in his house, where you had to fend off a sudden couch pillow flying at your head, or a Wet Willie when you weren't looking, or a half nelson creeping up on your spine while you stared at a poster of Christie Brinkley.

One of Patrick's older brothers, Bronson, used his deft cunning into tricking me at Carmine's. We both walked in at the same time. I bought one pack of baseball cards. He bought five. We stood outside in the heat and thumbed through the cards. Bronson got pissed by the cards dealt to him and asked to see what I scored. I rolled through them and he stopped me at Dwight Gooden of the Mets.

"I'll give you all five packs for that one Dwight Gooden card," said Bronson. He showed me Phillies players I didn't have, along with all-star guys.

I mentally freaked with excitement. I stared at the Dwight Gooden guy and Dwight stared at me. That's what he was doing in the card photo, just staring with a pissed look, nostrils flaring, like he was saying: "Take the deal!" So, I took it. Bronson scuttled off through the shade. I didn't know Gooden was Rookie of the Year and that his card was worth bucks, or that he would lead the Mets to a World Series victory the following year. I hadn't done by homework. I was just buying stocks without verifying the market.

Quinn was Pat's best friend. They lived a block away since birth, but never went to the same school. I admired their deep-rooted friendship. Quinn was a public school kid, had one older sister, Sasha, and lived in a cool mint green Cape Cod house with a large yard full of badminton games by day and lightning bug deaths by night. We'd swat at the bugs with Wiffle ball bats, trying to make them soar into a streak of gold, spreading the glowing guts onto our arms to form our initials. At the back of Quinn's yard was a split-rail fence that lined the perimeter of Shady Creek's long par 5 hole.

Quinn's parents were unruffled and often hung out on the back porch, his bearded Dad smoking a pipe and his Mom giggling and adjusting her hair in between sips of pink drinks. They sat and enjoyed the beautiful view of Shady Creek golf course, a careful selection of varied trees positioned perfectly and ascending upwards towards the massive stone clubhouse. From the porch, the view resembled a forest opposed to a fabricated enchantment. If a golfer was visible from Quinn's yard, it was because of an awful shot that landed deep in the rough near their fence. The golfer would have to deal with our fart noises and hollering to proceed.

At Carmine's, Quinn and Pat were quick to talk trash on Conner. They poked fun at his cackle, the way his eyes popped out when surprised, the restrained G-rated expletives he used when "Game Over" popped up on the video game screens. They prodded at his private school attire he proudly showed off from a wallet photo, his bowl shaped hairstyle, his pale and overtly freckled skin. With each jab came zero rebuttal from Conner. He took it and glanced at me to make sure I would not pile it on. "All right, that's enough guys," I'd repeat, smiting the words that permeated with soda belches.

\#

Alongside the Community Center was a weed laced field that neighbors used so their dogs could take discreet dumps. It was also our Nerf football arena for some three on three touch or expanded tackle bruise fests, recruiting kids walking by for an even more dense game.

I brought Conner to the field as I had spent a couple weeks with Quinn and Pat. It thrilled me to have Conner hang with us outside the joystick sugar high zone of Carmine's. I knew Conner had a fierce edge and could handle his own. Bronson joined us as steady quarterback. The game was a delicate balance of football and dodging dogshit that nobody had picked up. Even though Conner was on my team, he was a target of brutal late tackles and elbow jabs. "Ease up on him," I whispered to Quinn and Pat.

In between a play, Bronson walked up to the barbed wire fence that separated our game from the 16th hole tee off area of Shady Creek. "It's him," he announced with stern conviction, grabbing a crab apple from the ground.

"Who is it?" I asked Pat.

"My Dad won a contract to build at Shady Creek," said Pat. "The halfway house, the maintenance center, the parking garages. This douche here influenced the Board to use his cookie cutter development company."

Bronson eyed up the perfect trajectory and then lobbed the apple over the fence and trees. It landed next to the golfer who was teeing off mid-stroke. The golfer looked around in confusion. From afar and through bushes, the golfer had a familiar look and gait. Bronson loaded up again and fired. I held my breath as one apple hit the golfer in the head. They immediately spotted us. The attacked golfer was Kova, as his uproarious commanding voice made certain.

"Kova did this to your Dad?" I asked Pat. "The guy from Treasure Island?"

"Yep, same guy," said Pat, walking to pick up a crab apple.

Conner cried out in protest, muttering about how his Dad golfs at Shady Creek sometimes as a visitor. He walked off backwards toward the road, shaking his head. Conner glared at me, waving me to join him. I gave him a two-fingered salute goodbye. He slunk down the slope to the street and jogged home.

Dozens of crab apples were scattered at our feet. The golfers had nothing but an awkward escape. Two of the golfers ducked into a golf cart and drove off to their shanked shots, descending into the pines of the thick rough. Kova and another golfer stood their ground. Quinn and Pat picked up the sour firm fruit and heaved them.

With Conner off into the sunset, I backed off slowly towards the road where I stood positioned in transparent observatory mode on the outskirts, able to see a good half mile of sidewalk and street traffic. I saw Conner walking alone in the distance. He dragged a large stick as the asphalt tore it into white fragments. The golfers teed up balls and slammed them into the fence, rattling the steel. The balls dropped dead alongside the fence, except for one that got embedded in the fence links.

"Come on. Hop on over," Kova teased. He walked closer with his driver in hand and clenched the fence links, revealing a ruby and gold ring.

Bronson instructed me to stay towards the road and let him know if anyone was coming. I pivoted by head calmly. "My Dad had that renovation job," said Bronson. "Then you swooped down and paid the Board off, right?"

"Son, do you know why you're standing on that field, next to that basketball court, next to that playground? Because I donated eighty percent to get it built. Three years ago, this was just tall weeds. So, you're welcome." Kova spit on the ground and walked back.

A man approached blocks away, jogging with his yellow lab. I was glad to see him. I gave a quick warning holler to the crew, using a bassy sound from the bowels that climbed up to a high pitch whine within two seconds. The crew turned and meandered toward me, dropping their apples and getting back into football formation. "Nice looking out," said Bronson, putting his arm around my shoulder.

The golfers disappeared. We headed to the fence to shout further obscenities, to have the last jab, even though they were

300 yards out. The stuck golf ball had a Kova Plastics logo on it. We tried to smack it out, but it remained wedged between a chain link and a line post, beaming at us. We sat on a picnic table. Pat explained that his Dad broke down after losing the renovation bid. I wanted to share how Kova forced Dad and I off the road and how he chased Willem and I through the streets of West Oreland. I figured it would be a good bonding moment. But I kept it locked away, hoping it would dissolve and become dismissed from my mind.

"Everyone has a chalkboard in their brain and there's only so much you can have written on it," Dad said often. "Some people have a bigger chalkboard than others. But when it's full, you need to erase things as you learn more. It's up to you what you store."

19.

Backyard Network

August '85

After dinner, Pat and I met at Quinn's house and filled up two blue recycling buckets with range golf balls. These were white golf balls with no branding and a red stripe equator. Quinn pocketed them for the past couple years from the driving range. I had no clue what the plan was. Quinn and Pat giggled to themselves and nodded with affirmation to a rhythm I couldn't figure out.

They let me know that Quinn's next-door neighbors were on vacation. I looked up at Quinn's Dad on the porch as he packed his pipe, sipped beer and pecked his wife proudly on the cheek with kisses. His work van still radiated heat, crackling nearby. He saluted us as Pat and Quinn each carried a bucket. I waved at him and smiled. I followed along to the back of Quinn's house.

Pat and Quinn jumped the fence to the neighbor's property. I heaved the buckets over and they tiptoed with them to the edge of a pool. The reckless duo of buddies walked along the pool, dumping the balls evenly throughout the cool water. I perched at the top of the six-foot fence. The balls plopped in and sank to the bottom. I looked around, holding my thumb up, adjusting my glasses. All remained clear.

Quinn's Dad walked out onto the yard, looking towards the

sunset. "Fine job, boys. He's on vacation for a week, so you might as well take a dip."

"Is he an asshole?" I asked.

"He's the definition," said Quinn's Dad. "For the past couple of months, he's been mowing his lawn every Saturday morning at 8:30 on the dot. That's not considerate. I would never do that. Sasha don't like it either. She sleeps in these days. Needs her beauty sleep."

"She doesn't really," I said. "I mean, we all do."

"Besides, the dew is still prominent. He's an idiot. His blades are probably caked up with moldy gunk. Idiot."

Sasha was a few years older than me, a high school student. I often passed by her in Quinn's house and she would exchange a quick phrase, like, "Hey, little man." And then tap me on the head. She had long black hair kept flat and straight and white coconut milky skin, often passing by Quinn's open bedroom door in just a towel. She was a red lipsticked beauty queen with a punk rock attitude, slowed to a chilled out minimalist, a sizzling saute of uncertain spice. A tight black shirt and jeans was her uniform.

The mischief continued.

At the Twining Deli, Quinn and Pat filled their pants with candy bars while I chatted up the Russian lady that owned the place with complicated hoagie orders. She kept her head to the order slip, scribbling out my requests until I changed my mind. We darted off with mini pecan pies and BBQ potato chips.

In broad daylight, I stood lookout at the edge of a driveway as Quinn and Pat tiptoed into an open garage to yank fireworks from some kid they knew that had a stash. They hobbled out with rockets shoved down the side of their pants. I trusted the process.

#

We camped in Pat's backyard, the three of us crammed in a one-man tent. He had an above-ground pool, about four feet deep, that wore us out. Late at night, we unzipped the tent and headed out with flathead screwdrivers to pry off car emblems. The fancier the car, the better. Pat and Quinn noticed that I wasn't partaking. I shrugged it off and knelt down to unscrew coveted chromies from tire valves. I was content with being the eye seeking danger.

VW and Mercedes had large emblems that came off quickly. Saab cars had a colorful logo with a griffin wearing a crown, but it was small. We plotted our courses ahead of time, knowing a Porsche 944 was under a black cover on a winding driveway on Bala Avenue, knowing the beloved crest featured a galloping stallion. The Jaguar hood ornament was the most prized. It was a sculptural work of art, a brilliant trophy secured tight. We never got one but Pat scraped up a hood and cut his hand.

Although Jaguar was the most difficult prize to pry off, Kova's Italian Alfa Romeo featured a round shiny emblem that was the most precious. The logo included what appeared to be a serpent eating a stick figure man.

Pat psyched himself up. He wanted to gouge Kova's emblem. He snagged one of his Dad's beers, opened it and pounded a few swigs. He held out the can with a wince. Quinn took a chug and passed it to me. I took a sip and swirled it in my mouth before discreetly spitting it out, my first taste of any booze.

We took brown empty ACME bags that were in the recycling bin and cut through the yards, hopping the little three foot fences and budging past tight hedges. We were shirtless from the pool, reeking of chlorine and spotted with mosquito bites. The wind aided us in our trespassing shortcuts, adding a steady whir of tree branch rustles.

We stopped at a garden and filled the bags with bulbous red tomatoes, plucking them off the vines with ease. The owner of the garden was an old couple. We could see them watching TV through a sliding glass door. A motion detector light popped on, either from us or the wind, but it hardly shown in our direction.

We reached the end of yards to Apel Avenue and saw Kova's Alfa Romeo, reversed into the rear of the driveway. Quinn and I stayed back as Pat approached the car and released the emblem, revealing a dull gray circle.

Another car was in front of the Alfa Romeo. I recognized the

Walter Mondale election bumper sticker and backwards tennis visor in the rear window. "That's Conner's car," I said. "His Mom's car. Shelle."

"No way," said Pat.

"Definitely."

"She's getting busy with mighty Kova? Damn."

"Maybe they're just friends?"

"It's like 2am."

"I hope she's O.K."

"Looks like she's doing fine. Time to wake her up."

We reached into the brown bags and launched the tomatoes at Kova's house and his diminished sports car. The red ripe fruit splattered with vicious thuds, dousing the hood of his car with sudden sauce. The wind masked our sounds and elongated the attack. The small round windows of Kova's newly built house made for a challenging target, but Pat scored a fastball green tomato right through one. Glass shattered, interior lights turned on and we retreated through the yards back to the tent. The owner of the tomato garden was still using the clicker and flicking through the channels, oblivious to our trespassing. Our chest and arms were covered with dripping seeds and red fleshy tomato tissue. Back at the tent, we turned on the hose and rinsed off.

#

At the Community Center fort, we kept the stolen car emblems and nudie mags in a milk crate tied tight with a trash bag. Conner seemed fine with letting Quinn and Pat share the fort, but he wanted to join in the tent nights.

"It's just a one-man tent and we barely fit in there," said Pat. "Do you have a tent?"

"No. I think my brother does though."

"We're probably done, anyway. I don't think my Dad wants us back there. School's starting soon."

"Yeah, it's cool."

"So, what's up with your Mom? Is she happy? All good at home with—"

I nudged Pat in the ribs. Conner may have heard the question but said nothing and just looked at his sneakers and then our sneakers, comparing.

#

Cutting through yards, we realized that many homes had pools. As a competition, we tried to pool hop as many as we could in one hour. The frightening part was being underwater and not knowing if the owners were running out the door.

Underwater for a while, I popped up to see Quinn and Pat scaling the fence as flood lights shown down from the house. I heaved myself out of the pool, ran through a bed of flowers with my bare feet and hurled my sneakers over the fence. The growls of a ferocious doberman pinscher, galloping my way, had me clawing toward the top of the fence. The dog chomped down on my stomach as I cleared the fence, leaving four bite marks.

I picked at the scabs the next day while eating dinner. As I stood up to scoop some Turkey Hill ice cream, I saw that the blood penetrated through my white shirt. Mom shrieked. I was soon laying on the couch as Mom dabbed triple antibiotic ointment on the wound. I blamed it on a wild dog that attacked me on the way home from school, a dog that I kicked in the face and never saw again.

20.

The Locked Tabernacle

August '85

In sixth grade, becoming an altar boy was like joining a theatre company in which everyone you knew watched your performance weekly. Opposed to sitting in pews with old folks that sang hymns out of key, it made more sense to join the production. Becoming part of the holy spectacle let us escape from the clutches of our parents and let us be free, robed, and owning the parish's undivided attention.

As altar boys, the priests assigned us a specific schedule that spread everyone with equal service time. We'd each get a share of brutal 6:00am weekday masses, when just a cluster of people showed up, and prime time Sunday showdowns at 10:00 am when the packed house upped the pressure. The nuns set up the scheduling with just the initials of each altar boy. Priests never called us by name or knew of our names. They just nodded and expected us to be properly trained by the elders.

Easter Sunday and Christmas Day were electrifying. So many people showed up that the pews overflowed and many had to stand in the back. They threw rare devices into the mix, like the solar monstrance and evergreen advent wreaths. The most stellar event was Christmas Eve midnight mass. Most altar boys weren't allowed to stay up that late, let alone celebrate the birth of Jesus.

The sacristy was like the locker room before the big game, a chamber reserved for priests, altar boys, and those guys that collected money in straw baskets attached to a long handle. I showed up early, put my robe over my clothes and tied it tight at the waist with whatever colored rope belt was on the schedule. The priests sat in a meditative state, deep in thought, twiddling thumbs in a special wooden chair. They'd run over any special mass events, such as guest singer cues.

Father Pal maintained his reputation as the jolly priest of the clergy. He gave out free *Boys' Life* magazines, as he thought they were perfect guides. "I used to give out soft pretzels and mustard," he said. "But these magazines just fill your mind with wonder."

Also in the sacristy was a low-lit closet of boxed wine and plastic packaged Eucharists. Altar boys couldn't enter. Father Pal loomed in this dark room with a permagrin, a musty odor spilling out and a singular light bulb swaying. "Gotta check the inventory to make sure there is an ample supply," he'd say. "The future blood of Christ is in demand."

Once fully robed, I'd strike a match and light a three foot candle lighter, that had a large wick encased in brass, and walk the forty yards to the altar, all the while cupping the flame with my hand. Legions of faithful were in the pews, staring as I clambered up the carpeted steps toward the altar to light the series of candles. My parents didn't trust me with a matchbook, let alone a lighter. Serving the Lord, I was fractions away from torching the altar cloth. The flame blew out at times. I'd then walk back to the sacristy to start all over, hoping Emma didn't see my error.

On Sundays, there were two or three altar boys per mass. Weekdays were usually just one. At the start of mass, we lined up at the sacristy door and the priest nodded to the organist to play. The tunes barreled out and everyone turned towards us and stood. One altar boy carried a large wooden staff with a crucifix on top, leading the way. I hated this role as my feet would hit the staff or I'd pounce it into the floor after a false step. At the altar, we lined up and genuflected. The altar boy carrying the staff smoothly placed it on a wall-mounted brace that never seemed to have a firm grasp. The staff swayed in the groove, leaving me in utter horror. It appeared as if Jesus was trying to wiggle free.

The rest of the mass was a series of adrenaline rushing maneuvers based on perfect timing and not dozing off. I acted as a human desk to hold a padded bible while facing the priest as he read the Gospel. I rang bells at just the right moment while kneeling and pretending the carpeted concrete wasn't tearing my kneecaps apart. I held the shiny Communion plates at perfect spots for everyone that came forth, especially old timers that preferred to receive it by closing their eyes and having the priest stick it on their tongue.

One day, after lighting the candles, I forgot to check that the tabernacle key was on the altar. The tabernacle was a decorative lock box behind the altar. Priests stored leftover wafer hosts in it after Communion. I was trying to stay awake, sitting on the firm altar boy chair. Father Pal stared. He made hand motions as if turning a key. I didn't know how to communicate with him. He was a good twenty yards away. We never talked during mass. I extended my hands from my hips and pointed toward the sacristy. I could run to the sacristy and get the key, I thought, but I didn't know where the key was located. It was always just sitting on the altar. Father Pal made a gesture with his hands, brushing me aside, nodding while looking at the mound of crispy wafers.

I wasn't aware the priest had to put unused hosts back during the mass. He couldn't leave the altar to get the key either. Procedure trapped him on the elevated concrete island of gold carpet. I think he had to remain on this multi-platformed zone or suffer a violation.

Father Pal stuck his hand into the communion chalice and munched on the leftover hosts. It was as if someone had dumped a bag of potato chips in there. The lapel microphone on his robe captured the crunchy ultra dry Communion feast as the crowd looked on in puzzlement. I kept thinking about Dad telling me to "Eat 'em up, yum yum! Pretend you like it!" Dad said that when I stared at a plate of tepid lima beans. "Come on, Garv, eat 'em up. Pretend you're a good boy."

I sat as time stood still, robbing everyone of about two minutes, biting my bottom lip to hold in jolts of laughter, bobbing about like a detached buoy floating away. Luckily, it was Father Pal, smiling through it all. He was cool with it, a holy pop star dealing with the technical difficulties and sacrament malfunctions with ease.

"Well, that's a first," he said after mass as we disrobed.

"I'm so sorry," I said. "I must have forgotten about the key. It's usually on the altar."

"No worries at all. How's your friend doing? You both were coming out of a manhole a few years ago I believe."

"Wow, you remember that?"

"Kind've. I realized today it was you. You've grown. Your face looks the same. You're growing into a young man but have boyish qualities."

"I haven't seen Willem in a while. I saw him camping a couple months ago."

"Friends are important. I hope you both remain that way."

"So, you're good friends with Mr. Kova?"

The organist delved into dramatic procession outro music and a crackling noise emitted from the speakers.

"Oh, that didn't sound good," said Father Pal. "Need to check on that." He wobbled off in his black clerical clothes, leaving me in the doorway of the unlocked sacristy.

I wasn't sure if Father Pal wanted me to stay put. I floated around the sacristy, touching surfaces, paneling, obscure devices. I noticed the wine closet door was ajar. I peaked in and saw the hanging bulb haloing nearby bottles. The glass shimmered reflections of crosses that changed shaped and waned as I drew closer. Drips of wine from corked bottles stained the cardboard cases like dried blood that ran down a leg from a wound. A spiral notebook sat on a dusty unopened case. I thumbed through it and landed on a page with the initials of each altar boy. A numerical value was next to each initials. Mine had a question mark next to it. I scurried out of the closet to the sun shining through venetian blinds. I exited, leaving the sacristy door open.

21.

The Instaphoto

August '85

In the evenings, we hung out on the 15th hole behind Quinn's house, putting on the green. I didn't have clubs or even care to play. I watched Quinn and stood guard. Most golfers completed the 15th hole by sunset, leaving it open for us.

There weren't official security guards or watchmen at Shady Creek. There was a chubby Greenskeeper named Louie that snuck up on us in his electric cart. The quiet hum of the cart couldn't be heard until it was almost too late. He wore tie-dye socks, red bandanas and blue tinted sunglasses. We usually spotted him through trees ahead of time. Louie rode his bike to work from miles away. He looked like Jerry Garcia, but with ginger hair and a pissy pout.

After a session of night putting, Quinn removed the pin and unhooked the blue Shady Creek flag. He shoved it in his pocket. I looked around for Louie or a late golfer. Quinn knelt down and put two M-80s in the cup. He lit the green fuses, and we dashed off, running backwards to view the flash and booms that shredded the cup and green, pockets of dirt hurled about. The domino effect of dogs woofing spread all along the 15th hole homes. Quinn kept me on my toes with unplanned events.

The next afternoon we saw that Louie had repaired the green, but it was hardly of seamless perfection. We listened as golfers raised their hands in confusion and linked their awful putts to greens distorted with cleat marks.

The 15th hole was a 565 yard par 5. Most legit golfers smashed their tee-offs and then rolled on the green with their second shot. One day, we took advantage of this knowledge and hid by the 15th green pines. We saw a couple shots roll towards the pin, one from Kova. His safari hat and stance made it clear it was him. Both golfers were easily a putt away from earning the beloved Eagle score. We noticed Kova paused and showed his group a device wrapped around his neck.

Quinn and I bolted out into the daylight, yanked a ball and dashed to the fences. Instead of jumping directly over, we ran along the fence within the course and hopped into Quinn's yard. We glanced back and saw the golfers sprinting towards us with irons in their hands. Kova's buddy had a tennis visor fly off his head. He got disoriented and collapsed into his jumbled legs.

We headed towards Wischman Avenue. We didn't want to go into Quinn's house and reveal where he lived. Looking back, we saw Kova hurdle the fence.

"He's in my yard," fumed Quinn.

We crossed the street and ran into the backyard of an old lady's house. We hid in a narrow nook behind her shed, cornered by adjoining fences. The click clack of Kova's cleats drew louder, leaving us unblinking. Kova appeared and turned towards us, his chest heaving and shadowed face dripping sweat.

"Hand over the balls," Kova said, sticking out a hand.

Quinn and I scanned around for any escape route.

"If you try anything, I will smack the balls out of your pocket with this three iron."

We chucked the balls at his feet, squatted down, and curled into a ball in the thistle and broadleaf weeds. I winced, covering my face and peeking through fingers.

"If you fuck with my rounds again, your ass is grass," said Kova. "Both of ya. Stand up and look at me."

We stood up straight as Kova took the Kodak instant camera from around his neck and aimed it towards us.

"Look right towards me," Kova said, crouching. "I need to preserve your mugs so I remember you punks."

Quinn jumped toward the sloped gable roof of the shed. The click and whirring of the camera unfolded. Quinn pawed at the mossy shingles of the shed, his feet dangling as he tried to heave his way up. He slid down the roof and fell on his back, bringing a clogged gutter down with him. The plastic fractured and leaked brown water onto his chest. He moaned on the ground as Kova waited for the photo to process and spew out. I knelt by Quinn to see if he was all right. Kova grabbed the white-framed photo with two fingers.

"Your little stunt there," said Kova to Quinn. "Well, you're a blur. You look like a ghost. Let's try again."

Cleats tapped on the street with quick strides towards us. Kova stepped backwards and pointed to us. "Don't let it happen again, boys," he said. He walked off towards the road to his disoriented group.

I helped Quinn up. He put his arm around my shoulder, hobbling back to the road. The old lady made tsk tsk hand gestures at us from a window.

As Kova's foursome cut through Quinn's yard back to the course, Sasha stepped out with an iced tea and a straw. "Uh, hello?" she said at their flagrant trespass. One golfer gave a cat call and whistle at Sasha. She took an ice cube from her glass and threw it at them.

Sasha saw us quivering across the street. Quinn covered his lips with an index finger to signal silence. Sasha nodded and sat down. Quinn and I walked a few blocks out of the way, just in case Kova was watching us. We didn't want him to know where any of us lived.

"If you made it up that shed, were you gonna leave me there?" I asked.

"No way," said Quinn. "Seriously? I was gonna grab a branch from the dead tree and try to scare him off. Pounce on him."

"Sorry to question it. Just felt so trapped."

22.

Lifeguards

September '85
During Labor Day weekend, I went to Carmine's and pumped quarters into *Rastan*. Aengus walked in with a new hairdo of spiked blond hair. He sported a scar under his chin because his doberman pinscher, Ike, bit him during rough play. He had been out of town for the whole summer. We played for an hour straight.

Aengus invited me to his house to check out his pool. I smirked when I saw his house, realizing I had pool hopped there before. We stopped in his kitchen to get Doritos and cans of Coke. His parents were both out. He cranked up "Big Balls" by AC/DC, which was music I had never heard before. The stereo blasted through the house and out of poolside speakers. We laid on inflatable rafts as I didn't have my bathing suit with me and Aengus didn't want to get changed. The sun brought calm toasty elation, a mid-70 degree day where a steady breeze made sure you didn't sweat.

"I saw you with Farrah on the bridge that night," said Aengus. "You went back to her after we had pizza."

"I saw her on the way home," I said. "We talked for a while."

"Does Emma know that?"

"Well, no. Why would she?"

We both had our hands behind our heads, floating slowly. Our rafts bumped into the concrete edges, sending us in another direction.

"Maybe she should know," said Aengus.

"Dude, I'm with Emma," I said. "Have been for a while. I was confused." The view of cumulus clouds calmed me, padding my thoughts of Emma. I had seen her only a few times over the summer. The move to East Oreland may have done us in, I thought.

A hawk glided into view like a kite with no string.

Aengus got out of the pool to use the bathroom. He told me not to go near Ike, who was sitting in a cage on the lawn, panting. I pictured Aengus looking up Emma's number in the White Pages. I heard rustling noises and saw Aengus climbing a tree on the side yard. He put a bottle rocket into a cardboard paper towel tube and aimed it at me. "I really liked Farrah," said Aengus. "I meant what I said in my card to her. And you run off and kiss her on the bridge?"

"That was eons ago," I said. I paddled with my hands from the middle of the pool towards the nearest concrete edge. Aengus cackled and lit the bottle rocket, aiming it at me.

I lost control and flipped over into the pool. Underwater, I heard the muffled screeching whistle of the rocket and explosion. I stuck my head out and saw the charred white float deflating. I swam toward the edge and climbed out as Aengus reloaded. His second rocket blasted near my feet and flared up my left calf with a sting. Ike barked ferociously. Aengus fired one at Ike in his cage and then another at me as I clambered out the backyard gate. I headed straight for Wischman Avenue and jogged up the hill, leaving my Huffy Pro Thunder bike poolside and in the clutches of Aengus.

I got to Quinn's house and saw Sasha sitting on the front porch smoking a cigarette, her legs up on the wicker ottoman. I walked up to the porch and stared down at her. She smiled and tried to hold in a laugh but it puffed out of her mouth with smoke and blew up strands of hair.

"Dude, you're fucking dripping on my feet," said Sasha.

I looked down at her ghost white legs and black polished toenails. "Sorry. Is Quinn here? I need to—"

"What the hell happened? You're soaked. You look insane."

"Aengus. This guy in my grade. He seemed rad but then started shooting—"

"You don't know about him? His parents make him go to military school summer camp, like in that movie *Taps*. He duct taped his Mom's foot to a chair once, and she fell and broke her hand. He's demented."

"I left my bike there. Gotta go back and get it."

Sasha inhaled deeply and shook her head. "That little shit."

It thrilled me to talk with Sasha, to take her in with my eyes.

"Did you go in our neighbor's pool?" asked Quinn walking with Pat from the street.

I explained that I stranded my Huffy at Aengus's pool. Quinn thought for a moment and then ran into his garage. He came back with three large trash can lids.

"Let's go," said Pat.

I looked back at Sasha. She was standing, watching us, putting her Sony Walkman headphones over her ears.

When we entered the pool gate, Aengus was sitting on my bike. He saw us and attempted to roll my bike into the deep section of the pool. It fell short by a foot. We walked towards him and he loaded up a bottle rocket. We formed a barrier with the lids. The rocket whizzed over our heads and blasted in a pepper garden. I ran for the bike. Aengus ran around the pool away from us, loading up his cardboard tube again. Pat put a finger down his throat and vomited a recently eaten snack into the pool. Quinn and I smiled with delight as we exited stage left. Aengus screamed. Ike barked. Aengus's parents pulled into the driveway looking perplexed.

Back at Quinn's porch, it felt like we were on the other side of a turbulent river. Sasha was back to being too cool for school, listening to us relay the story with rolling eyes. But I didn't mind. I was blissed out on how my buds had my back, how I had earned true friends.

23.

The Golf Cart

October '85

Influenced by the film *Back To The Future*, I bought a Nash Executioner skateboard with pink wheels and a fluorescent green deck. It had a dragon on the top and another large dragon on the bottom that was standing on a pile of skulls. The only tricks I could do was an ollie and shred a 360 degree spin. The skateboard was ideal for careening through Oreland and visiting friends. It made me feel like a self contained regulated menace. The quiet hum of the wheels allowed me to traverse block to block with phantom precision, perking up the eyes and ears of neighbors as they mulched their mums. My arms balanced the glide, facial emotions hidden by a painter's cap and green framed sunglasses.

Coasting to Quinn's house, Conner ran alongside me. His pockets bulged with pink glow in the dark golf balls. Daylight savings was in effect and we hung out in the dark for a while before dinner. On the 15th hole, we crushed the balls, all taking turns with Quinn's driver.

"Conner is worth hanging out with tonight," Quinn said under his breath.

"Come on. He's a cool guy," I said as Conner pretended the driver was a horse and galloped to his ball.

"Really? What the hell is he doing?"

Through the whirring sounds of the neon novelties, Pat ran towards us and revealed that he had stolen a golf cart. He had been digging a hole near our fort for weeks, using a shovel he hid there. We headed to the secret location. Pat picked up a large piece of ground which turned out to be a few fishing nets with twigs, weeds and leaves glued all over it. Beneath that was a brown king sized bed sheet. He moved a couple large pieces of particleboard. It unveiled a steep dirt ramp, leading to a gas powered roofless cart.

"Damn, when did you do all of this?" Quinn asked.

"On and off for the past few weeks," said Pat. "I had to spread the dirt all over the place to hide it. You guys didn't want to help. Remember?"

"Yeah," we all said.

"Let's go for a joyride," said Pat. "The course is dark enough now. I've adjusted the governor switch to make it faster."

Quinn sat in the passenger seat while Conner and I stood on the rear bag racks. Pat inserted the key and gunned it up the ramp. "Gas carts are faster," Pat shouted as the cart wobbled out of the fringe of the woods.

We descended to the 8th hole, a short 80 yard par 3. All that you had to do was chip over a quarry that was wide as it was deep. It reminded me of the Sarlacc Pit from *Return of the Jedi*.

Conner jumped off and simulated masturbation with the ball washer, jerking the plastic grip up and down.

"See?" whispered Quinn into my ear. "What the hell is this shit?"

"He's just having fun," I said. "He's a goof. Give him a break. We all act that way sometimes."

"I don't."

We looked down the quarry and saw Louie at the bottom of the stone steps, descending with a headlamp and a chainsaw in hand. He reached the bottom and cut large branches that had fallen in a recent storm. Pat unzipped his shorts and took a piss, muttering about how Shady Creek should've never dissed his Dad. The long stream cascaded down, a pitter-patter on thick ivy.

Louie looked up. "Who's up there?" he hollered.

"Lose a cart, douchebag?" Pat asked with a shaky voice. "Might lose your job over that, right?"

We jumped on the cart and headed back to the fort. I clenched on and yanked my head down from sudden branches. "Louie didn't do anything!" I yelled. "He's not on the Board."

"Fuck him," said Pat, flooring the pedal.

The following days, Louie searched for the cart. We sat on Quinn's split-rail fence and watched him drive around at dusk, investigating nearby pines. He pulled up close to us and asked if we had seen a missing golf cart. Pat pretended to speak in a different language, sputtering gibberish.

"I'll take that as a no," said Louie. "Look, I should be with family now. My Mom is ill. So, let me know if you see it. Okie dokie?"

Pat laughed and emulated a monkey. I slapped him on the back to stop. Louie drove off.

Sasha sauntered over in a plum bathrobe, smelling like a soapy bouquet. "What are you dweebs up to?" she asked. "Fall into any pools lately, Garv?"

I gave a crooked closed lip smile, looking down at the grass. "Do you think Louie drives around at night too?" I asked, changing the subject.

"Yep," said Quinn. "I could see his flashlights moving around last night as he went up and down the fairway. 10pm."

Sasha lit a cigarette. "You guys are gonna get him canned," she said.

"That's what I think," I said, hoping the concern would sink in. Sasha put her hand out for a high five. I slapped it amidst an abrupt coughing fit.

Days later, Pat was ready to give up the cart, but not before one last send off. I watched from the Community Center basketball court, practicing my ollies on my skateboard. I bowed out. I felt safe on the pedestrian side of the barbed wire fence.

Pat, Quinn and Conner adjusted the cart on the 16th hole

fairway and rigged the steering wheel with twine so the tires wouldn't move. They duct taped a bushel of Black Cat firecrackers to the seat, aimed the cart towards the quarry, lit the fuses and leaned a cinder block on the gas pedal. The cart sped off and the cream vanilla seat roared into orange flames. The cart angled off near the quarry and landed with a thud into a sand trap, tires whirring and the destruction muffled.

I nodded my head in disapproval and skated down Wischman Avenue, fireflies slapping onto my chest, gnats flying into my mouth. I hoped Sasha was chilling on the porch so I could show off my confident coasting.

A small hard object smacked the side of my head. I lost balance, teetered and fell to my butt. The skateboard zoomed onwards and approached the steep decline down Wischman Avenue. An acorn plucked my head and landed at my side. A little boy tossed the nuts at me from the sidewalk. I made eye contact with him. He grabbed several at a time and winged them at me.

"Stop!" I demanded, slowly getting up off the road. "You don't want to do this. You can hurt someone."

"Poo-poo head! Poo-poo head!" he repeated. The boy's eyes were glossed over with a devilry high, a moment in the chamber of freedom, void of parents, using pointed seeds as a weapon.

A car in the distance coasted over my skateboard, clearing it. The car pulled up as I limped out of the way. "Are you OK?" a lady asked from behind the wheel.

"Yeah, I wiped out. Just a few scrapes on my back I think."

The lady got out and walked over. "Oh, poor dear."

The boy peppered the lady with acorns, smacking them against her white pantyhose. He kept throwing and swooping down to snatch the bountiful acorns from the oaks on his lawn. The lady hobbled on her high heels and we ducked behind her car.

"You better stop all of this," the lady called out. "Where are your parents?"

"He's possessed," I said to myself. "He's slipped into a different world."

A man and a woman, jogging in unison, approached the boy and stopped beside him. They continued to jog in place as he flung handfuls of acorns at their swooshing polyester track suits of matching red. The woman put her hands on her hips and stretched as the man picked up the boy at the waist and put him over his shoulder. The boy pounded the man's back with fists, spitting white foamy saliva onto his shoulders. The woman jogged over to her garage, grabbed a broom and swept acorns off the sidewalk and onto her lawn.

"Did you ever jog on an acorn?" the woman called out to us. "You'll wipe out for sure. Got to get rid of these."

"I think your son needs to be taught manners," the lady from the car said, walking back to get in. "My son is his age and would've never done such a thing." The lady drove off.

I massaged a scrape on my hand that was bleeding. The woman in the track suit caught eyes with me and bawled before briskly walking inside. A breeze knocked down several acorns into erratic bounces on the street. Car tires crushed them, streaking their pale cores onto the black asphalt.

I headed down Wischman Avenue to find my board. The sides of the roads were lined with raked leaves, awaiting the leaf sucking truck to vacuum them. Across from Quinn's house, I spotted two pink wheels sticking out of the leaves. I yanked out my board to examine and saw nothing wrong.

"What are you doing there, Garvey?" asked Sasha.

I turned to her house and saw her ivory face from behind the screen of Quinn's room.

Sasha opened the screen and leaned out. Her hair was soaking wet. Her cleavage, almost down to the nipple, hovered above the window box of petunias.

"Oh, hey," I said, trying to just stare at her eyes. "Some kid knocked me on my ass. He's like possessed or something. Throwing acorns at everything."

"Are you for real?" asked Sasha, choking on a laugh. "You better watch out for those kindergartner killers."

"Believe me. He was a rabid dog."

"You've clearly hit your head."

"Maybe, yeah. Were you just in the shower?"

"Bath actually. Super perceptive you are."

"What are you doing in Quinn's room?"

"Is he out here?" she asked, looking around.

"Nah, he's out on the course. I needed a break from it all."

"Well, I'm doing a prank on some stuff in his bedroom. Putting Vaseline under all his bureau handles, joysticks, door knobs. You name it."

"Damn," I said, smiling, looking to make sure he wasn't approaching.

"You better not tell him or else I'm gonna toss pine cones at you."

"It was acorns. And he was like a Phillies pitcher."

"Whatever," she laughed, whisking back into the dark room. "See you soon."

24.

Salt & Pepper

O ctober '85
        We sat on spring coiled seahorses at the playground of my old nursery school, sipping on soda, all facing each other. The woodchip floored tot lot was vacant. We stared across the field at the wall of orange and crimson leaves. Many had already fallen, providing a glimpse of White Ash Manor.

"You really want to do this now?" I asked. "Can't we lie low for a while?"

Quinn and Pat sneered.

"If they see us, we'll say we got lost," said Pat.

The three of us trekked across the field, walking over the shadow of the church steeple. We tiptoed into the woods, crunching onto the ground of twigs and brittle browning leaves. The curtain of the church closed behind us. We moved forward about fifty feet. A shallow creek greeted us with a low wire staked along the edge.

"A booby trap?" Quinn asked.

"Probably triggers an alarm," said Pat.

We took high steps over the wire and frog hopped a few big rocks to cross the creek, continuing to walk deeper. Vague painted colored markings were on trees.

A wide attached garage with an open door was visible, along

with a yellow utility cart. We heard a familiar voice talking on a loudspeaker. We realized it was the play-by-play of an Eagles game. A man in overalls and a respirator mask on his face walked out of the garage. He held the handles of two large plastic buckets. He put them on a utility cart flatbed and then adjusted large white papers hung on a clothesline. Bare backs of the papers faced us. Grey blobs is all we could make out. The man disappeared into the garage and returned with Kova and Father Pal at his side. They were both drinking wine.

"Let's head back," I said.

"Keep your voice down," Pat whispered, pulling out a smoke bomb from his pocket. He lit it and threw it hard to our far right.

"Dude, you said nothing about fireworks," I said.

"Just distracting them," said Pat.

Kova and company pointed at the fizzing pink smoke. Pat pulled out a laser pointer pen and positioned the red dot on Kova's chest. Father Pal took notice and gasped. Kova downed the rest of his wine and tossed the glass. Pat raised the dot toward Kova's eyes.

"That's enough, man," I pleaded.

"Didn't this guy almost kill you and your Dad in a car accident?"

"Yeah, but—"

We all turned to the flames emerging by the smoke bomb. An orange ball of fire crackled.

"Put out this fucking fire," Kova commanded. The man in the overalls scrambled toward a long hose and sprayed a stream toward the fire. Kova entered the garage and returned with a shotgun. He aimed in the general direction of us.

A couple Doberman Pinschers ran out of the garage, sprinting towards us, kicking up dirt clouds. We ran back. The dogs struggled in the creek, enabling us to gain ground. I saw the sparkling stained glass of the church through perforated leaves, giving me bursts of hope. I prayed to Jesus for my safety. Shots were fired, rattling through the branches. One shot hit a tree in front of me, exploding into white crystal.

"It's just rock salt," said Pat.

One blast nabbed the heel of Quinn's sneakers. Back on the grass of the church field, I wanted to ditch my crew. The dogs stood on the outskirts of the woods, no longer chasing us.

"Gotta take a piss," I said, rounding the corner of the church and entering the main door.

I dipped my fingers into the holy water, made a sign of the cross and genuflected. Even though it wasn't my church, I felt safe, in a vacuum, protected. The stillness calmed me as I panted and brought my heart rate down. A woman knelt in a rear pew, head down, shaking. She turned around. "You're an early bird too," she said, dabbing a tissue into the corners of her eyes. "Why, you dress just like him. So lively."

From a side entrance, two men rolled in a casket and placed it near the altar.

"Were you good friends with him?" asked the lady.

I looked at the main door and saw Pat's and Quinn's calves and sneakers pacing back and forth, waiting. "I stopped in to pray," I said. "Sorry. I shouldn't be here."

"Those scratches on your arm," said the lady, standing up. "You're bleeding. Are you in trouble?"

I strode to the door and opened it. A family dressed in black approached. They struggled with photo collages and easels. One of them had a boombox. I held the door for them. "Thank you," they each said. A woman collapsed when she saw the casket. Her bulletin board of images fell and photos became misaligned, detached. I knelt down to help.

Quinn opened the door. A breeze entered. The photos scurried down the aisle toward the altar, photos of a boy in a backyard, on a tree, eating cookies, hugging his Mom, shaking dice.

25.

Snowmen

December '85

In early December, five inches of snow came down. Pat's brother looped us in on a hill for sledding in Shady Creek called "The Pipeline". It was off the 6th hole in a remote region partially owned by the Township. The only way to get there was to cut through the course. The decline was steep, long and ended with a ramp that lined the bottom of the hill, created by a 5 foot pipe sticking halfway out of the ground. Trick was, after getting air, we had to slow down or risk falling into the frozen creek. We all took turns on plastic toboggans. Older kids stayed late, lit a fire and drank beers.

On snow days, Shady Creek was open game for anyone that lived along the perimeter or knew how to sneak in. We'd see couples cross country skiing, parents out with their little ones on saucer sleds and innocent snow battles around the greens. Golfers and Louie's maintenance crew weren't around until mid-March when they had to clean up what mother nature had done to the manmade prestige and pump the fairways with chemicals after proper aeration.

After sledding, we headed to a tree along the 16th hole that overlooked Twining Road. I created the snowballs on the ground and tossed them up to Quinn and Pat who sat perched on a branch ten feet above the ground. A small clearing allowed them to see cars zooming past. Most cars kept going after getting pegged. Some slowed down. We hadn't engaged in mischief since getting rock salt fired at us. We enjoyed a board game phase for weeks at Quinn's house, logging in hours of Trivial Pursuit, dabbling in Earl Grey tea sophistication. Sasha and Quinn's parents joined us too. The lore of a lawless, snow draped golf course brought out impish impulses.

One driver slammed on the brakes after two snowballs pummeled the windshield. Pat tossed another and it bent the radio antenna, setting it to recoil.

"Hold on. I think that's Conner," said Pat.

An argument with busy hand gestures ensued from beyond the salt and snow streaked windows. Kova appeared from the driver's side door. "Come on out, you little shits," he said, walking towards us.

Conner's Mom, Holly, stepped out of the passenger side door. "I've had enough," she said. "I can get home from here."

"Get back in the car," ordered Kova. "Stop making a scene."

"No, this is it. I've tried to be nice about this."

Cars passed around them, honking.

"You're tired. Sassy. I like it," said Kova. "Now get that ass back in the car."

Quinn and Pat jumped from the tree to my side with a thud. Holly turned to our direction. "Whoever is watching, please know I don't want this man in my car," she said. "Can you hear me?"

Holly scurried to her car and slid behind the steering wheel. She struggled to close the door as Kova held it, trying to get a kiss. "Enough!" she screamed. She floored the gas, leaving Kova in the middle of the road, alone.

Kova caught a glimpse of our brightly colored jackets and accessories and walked towards us. "You think you can get away with this?" he asked, cupping his leather gloves over his mouth.

We backed away from the fence and hid in a sand bunker,

peering up above the lip. Kova whipped out a switchblade and opened it. He put the handle in his mouth and jumped onto the chain-link fence. His heavy frame rattled the fence, his big white Chicklet teeth contrasting heavily with his dark glasses. His slicked back blonde hair was the same color of his summer hats. As he reached the barbed wire, he brought a boot on top, squashing down the spiny deterrents.

Off we bolted, leaving our sleds behind. The sounds of Kova hurling off the barbed wire and plopping to the ground with a grunt made us split up like billiard balls being broke. We were in disguise with hats, gloves, scarves and baggy jackets. "All that he knows for certain is that we're white kids," I thought as I tried to run in heavy black boots.

Pat headed deeper into the course toward the clubhouse. Quinn headed straight across. I ducked a sharp left toward the 15th street homes where I knew of backyard escape routes. Kova followed me. I cut through the nearest backyard where a black lab greeted me. He bit my hand and pulled off a Freezy Freakies glove, destroying it as I slinked off.

When arrived at my street, I looked back. There was no sign of Kova. I dashed from tree to tree until I made it to my backyard. Inside the house, I spent fifteen minutes explaining to my parents that some kids had attacked me and stole my sled.

I called Quinn in my bedroom. Sasha answered. "No, dork. He's not here. I thought he was with you?"

"He was. We had to split up. Kova was chasing us. Long story, but Quinn should be home soon. I think I got Kova to disappear."

"You're a real sweetheart, ya know?"

"Huh?"

"Checking in on Quinn like that."

"Just on Tuesdays," I said.

Sasha laughed. "Later gator."

"Wait. Listen, can you make sure Quinn calls back? We need to get our stories straight."

"Hold on. He's on the porch now."

I explained to Quinn about the chase with the knife and the level of lunacy Kova had reached. "Let's stop all this mischief," I said. "He would've stabbed me. Any of us. He's a maniac. The shit with Conner's Mom?"

"Yeah, all right. But we can't tattle," said Quinn. "He may trace everything back to other stuff. We can't tell our folks anything."

Sitting at the dining room table, I had a nervous lump in my throat and a difficult time swallowing the raviolis. I dipped buttered bread into the sauce and looked out the window as the dusk light made the snow look purple. The automatic Christmas lights on the front yard bushes turned on. "See. They work," Dad said, aiming his fork. I looked out and saw Kova walking by in the street, pumping his arms as if he was doing an aerobic workout. Realizing he could easily see me in the bright dining room, I ducked down to the floor.

"Sorry. Just need to stretch out," I said. "Feel cramped up."

That night, I had nightmares about Kova breaking into the house and chasing me with his knife. I felt uncertain whether he would recognize me. He had followed me, but I resembled a running blob of polyester and wool.

#

The next day, the temperature reached the 50s and melted most of the snow. I retrieved the Alfa Romeo emblem from the fort and took it back home to wash it in the sink to remove any fingerprints. I biked over to Kova's house with the dishwasher gloves still on. His car wasn't there. I tossed the emblem onto the driveway. It rolled all the way down and landed upright against the garage door.

A couple weeks later, during a Sunday before Christmas, I served as an altar boy and extended the communion paten below the folded hands of each individual stepping forward. Father Pal phrased "The body of Christ" repeatedly in the exact manner as recipients replied with "Amen". Kova appeared. He curled out his tongue as Father Pal placed the host onto it. For lack of saliva or a sudden movement, the host fell down and landed onto my paten.

I had never experienced this before and wasn't sure what to do. Father Pal reached for the host and consumed it. He took a fresh one and tried again. Kova walked back off to his pew.

After mass, I went down to the X-Mas Bazaar in the basement to get cookies, hoping to bump into Emma. I lurked about, shoving sweets into my face. "Nice catch," a voice said. I turned around and saw Kova sipping on hot chocolate. "You were the altar boy, right?"

"Yes," I said.

"I thought so," said Kova, drowning his marshmallows with a spoon. "Have we met before? You seem familiar."

"No. I mean, yeah, from church I guess."

"That would have been a scene if you didn't catch that."

"Right. I did what I could."

"I have a son your age. But his mother has him at a public school. He doesn't have the fear of the Lord in him."

Father Pal shimmied over to us with his Jeff cap and wool Phillies jacket. "There's the star catcher," he said. "How are those cookies?"

"Good. Snowman cookies. I need to find chocolate chip ones."

"Oh, we have those at the rectory. A couple trays. I made a few batches myself. You're welcome to stop over."

Between the crossed arms of Kova and Father Pal, I saw Emma in the distance checking out knitted hats. I wished them a good day and headed over to her. "I need to get my wallet out of the car," said Emma. "Come with me. My Dad gave me the keys."

We grabbed free hot cocoa and took them to the parking lot. We sat on the steps of an outdoor stairwell, halfway down, hidden from everyone. I longed to live back next door to her, back to Norman Rockwell flavored shenanigans and more innocent sunsets, void of sleepless paranoid nights wondering if Kova had linked me to mischief.

"How's your new neighbors?" I asked.

"They're a couple with two babies, so kind've boring. I hear them screaming sometimes."

"I miss it over there. Was so much simpler. My new friends are so into destruction. I'm doing it too. But I'd rather just chill out. Some of it crosses the line. I bowed out on some stuff before, but they thought it was lame."

Emma put her arm around my back and swished it up and down.

"Sorry," I said. "Just so much going on."

"There's dumb drama with me too. My older sisters got bitchy. Perfectionists. The catty girls in my class are so shallow."

We sat in silence and stared at the drain at the bottom of the stairs. Leaves, dried grass and black slush covered the grate. We walked to her Dad's car to get her wallet. "Gotta do some Christmas shopping," she said, leaning into the car to grab her wallet. I noticed a familiar framed piece of art sitting in the top of a cardboard box.

"Is that the *E.T.* thing I got you at the carnival, like six years ago?" I asked.

"Oh, yeah. It fell. The glass broke. I was gonna chuck it but figured I could donate it to a thrift store."

"Wow, that thing sure was ugly."

"Let's reenact it," Emma said, leaping out of the car with it. She closed the door with her foot. "Let's pretend you're giving it again."

She placed the framed Made In China art into my hands. I tipped forward towards her and pecked her closed lips. She opened her mouth. The warm membrane of her inner lips latched onto mine. "Fuck," she said pulling away with the framed art. She pulled up on the door handle. "I locked the keys in the car."

"Do you have one under the car? My Dad does that."

"No clue."

I got down under the car and slithered past the muffler. "Yep, there's a key soldered under here. I can snatch it off."

The boisterous laughs of Kova and Father Pal were heard exiting the church. Emma kicked my foot. I moved to the center of the car, curling in my limbs, as their voices approached.

"Young girl, is your friend still with you?" asked Kova.

"No, he went for a walk," said Emma. "Needed air. Wasn't feeling great."

"Ah, well tell him to stop by the rectory for some refreshments. He saved the day and deserves a special treat."

I stared at Kova's brown oxfords and hemmed, creased pants until they walked off. I stuck my hand out with the key. Emma grabbed it, opened the door and retrieved her Dad's keys. "Don't know what kind of trouble you're in with that guy, but you need some new friends," said Emma.

I wormed out and sat slouched against the fender.

26.

Manger Shepherds

D ecember '85
On Christmas Night, Conner and I planned to meet outside at 11:30pm to test out his new walkie talkie system. I waited at Dog Poopy Island, our rendezvous point, but he never showed. I headed toward his house and saw that all the lights were on downstairs. His family had hosted a dinner. I watched from behind a tree as Holly gave a boozy loud goodbye to a lady that just wouldn't leave. The bay window curtains were open and no other guests were visible.

After the lady drove off, I watched the windows for a minute. All was clear. I jogged to Conner's side yard, sidled to the backyard and peaked in the sunroom. The TV was on but nobody was around. Conner told me he always exited from the sunroom door. So, I waited.

Holly came into view at the kitchen window. She washed dishes. Holiday tunes blared from the stereo. It didn't seem like Conner could sneak out soon. I was about to dash over to Conner's bedroom window. Someone with a tight Rudolph The Red-Nosed Reindeer mask tiptoed behind Holly and raised black-gloved hands over her eyes. Rudolph wore black clothes, with a stocking over the head. Holly squirmed and tried to escape as one hand moved over her mouth.

The fluorescent lighting of the kitchen made her struggles vivid. With her free hand, Holly grabbed a plate from the drying rack and slammed it at the intruder's head repeatedly. The plate didn't break. She tossed it like a Frisbee into the adjoining sunroom. Rudolph forced her left hand onto the counter and tried to swipe off her wedding ring, wrestling with her ring finger. Able to breathe again, Holly gasped and bellowed for help.

I remained rigid, sinking into the ground dampened from melted snow. I thought of how Dad saved a General in the Air Force. I became induced with inspirational gallantry and sprung toward the sunroom door. I jiggled on the glass doorknob and pushed the door open. A safety chain, locked from the inside, brought the door open a few inches. The steel chain rattled. I swung the door back and forth, trying to break the chain loose. I slammed the door shut, hoping to break the glass panels. The intruder looked in my direction. Holly grabbed a silver cheese grater from the drying rack, the kind with multiple shredding angles, and slammed the grater into the back of his bare neck. She gripped the handle and rubbed back and forth against the flesh. The intruder escaped the sharp metal and backed off, feeling the blood of multiple lacerations soak through his gloves. They stood in silence staring at each other.

"You've lost your fucking mind!" said Holly, holding the grater up at his face. "I told you it was over!" She whacked him under his chin, grinding in a few strokes. He swatted at her hand. The grater tumbled to the floor. Holly grabbed a fire extinguisher and sprayed it towards Kova, screaming and kicking the drywall.

I let go of the doorknob and ran to Conner's first-floor bedroom window. Through the venetian blinds, I saw Conner adjusting a set of headphones, bobbing his head to the tunes. His Dad busted through the door with a pistol aimed toward the ground. He commanded Conner to stay in his bedroom and then rushed to the living room. I tapped on the window. Conner lifted it up.

"Your Mom's being attacked," I said. "Someone broke in. A guy with a mask. I was by the sunroom. I'm sure it's Kova. I heard his voice. They were—"

"What? Shit. Is she OK?"

"Think so. Where's your brother? Maybe he can help your Dad. Call 911 now."

"He's out with friends," he said, picking up his R2-D2 phone. He dialed. "He left a while ago." Conner conveyed his address to the operator, trembling, uncertain whether to jump out and join me.

The sound of a gunshot pierced our thoughts. Our eyes widened and heads pivoted.

"What do I do?" asked Conner. He ran to lock his bedroom door and came back to the window. "Did my Dad shoot him?"

"I gotta get out've here," I whispered. "I tried to help your Mom but—"

The distinctive squeal of the sunroom door opening silenced me. The squish of slow aimless footsteps in the mushy muddy snow grew louder. "Hide in your closet," I breathed to Conner before running off.

I paced homeward, in the street's middle. My sneakers squished and tapped as street lights guided me. I glanced over and saw Kova hobbling a block back. At the rate he was gaining, he'd be within arm's reach at my driveway. I swerved onto front lawns, out of sight from the road.

Kova's heavy panting grew closer. I took cover amid the lawn of the most festive neighbor on my street. Plastic reindeer, elves and snowmen were lit up with floodlights. The house was lined with strands of green and red bulbs around every framework. I sat behind a life size wooden nativity scene, peering out between the panels of shepherds. It was a corner street house, and I knew the network of connected backyards well, in case he approached.

Kova's breathing came to a stop in front of the house. He didn't seek me out. He walked to the other side of the street and ripped off a baggy breakaway sweatsuit and tossed it in a sewer. His newly revealed outfit was a magenta t-shirt and white jogging shorts. He took off the Rudolph mask and tight black stockings and emptied the costume into the sewer. His blond hair was damp with sweat. His chin and neck glistened with blood. He removed something small from a sock and fiddled with it. He made a sign of the cross and snorted whatever it was, muttering a lyrical melody in something other than English. Kova then jogged in place, stretching out his arms. He spotted a melted blob of a snowman, yanked a Philadelphia Flyers scarf off of it and wrapped it around his wounded neck. To my left, in the distance, I saw the fake candle decoration shimmering in my bedroom window. I wished that I had never sneaked out. I longed to be resting in bed with an extra handful of snickerdoodle cookies as the scents of holly berry candles and cinnamon coaxed me to slumber.

Repositioning, I stepped on a fallen tree branch and it snapped.

"Who's there?" barked Kova, walking over with careful steps, scanning the large ornamental displays. "Someone there?"

Police sirens shrilled in the distance, growing closer. Kova walked towards my general direction. I crouched down and pulled out a white spotlight that was spiked in the lawn, and carefully swung it from being pointed at baby Jesus and toward Kova.

"Put down that light this instant," said Kova, squinting, raising his hands over his eyes. "Were you the one at the back door?" He paced back and forth, trying to escape his reveal. I remained fitted into a ball, panning the light as he edged closer.

"B-B-B-Back off," I stammered. "E-n-n-n-nough." I had never stuttered words before, reduced to shaking limbs.

Kova stopped and tilted his head. "You little shit," he said, jabbing an index finger towards me. "You're not supposed to be out this late. Are you? Just you wait. If you say one goddamn thing about what you saw, I'll hunt you down and destroy you and your family. I'll make you disappear. You don't think I know where you live, do ya? I do." He swooped an index finger in the general direction of my house. I hoped he was bluffing his alleged knowledge. He then smiled. "Well, ta ta for now. Don't screw up."

Kova jogged off toward Wischman Avenue, transformed into a

late night jogger out to burn calories. Red and blue cop car lights, looking like electric wiggling gelatin molds, crept up Garden Road's hill to Conner's home. I stayed put for a while, figuring Kova was back at his house, but wondered if he was waiting to tackle me in the darkness. I focused on the sound of a mechanical waving Santa as my heart pounded.

Back at home, I sneaked into my bedroom after repeatedly checking that I had locked the back door. In my bed, I warmed up beneath the blankets. I bawled and crammed my face into my pillow. My gasps of breath woke up Mom. She sat at the edge of my bed. I told her I had bad dreams.

"Do you need new pajamas?" asked Mom. "You can't be sleeping in your clothes like this."

I called Conner the next day, early. His Mom picked up and explained that her family was going through tough times. I wanted to say I know, but I said nothing and listened to the clatter of her washing the dishes as she spoke. "Conner won't be coming out today," she said. "I'm sorry, Garvey."

I scanned Dad's newspaper in the Police Reports section. It stated nothing. This continued for days.

"Where's Conner been?" Mom asked, sitting on my bed upright, patting the firmly made bed for me to join her.

"Family stuff," I said. "Working on an issue, I think."

"Sometimes us grownups talk about things. There's sad and unfortunate news I learned through the grapevine. Some grownups shouldn't marry in the first place and they seek another mate, which is not nice. Pretty sure it's true, but one of them was not faithful."

Mom explained what I had known for months. She adjusted unruly strands of my hair. "It'll never happen to your father and I," she said. "Don't you worry."

With a knock on my door, Conner emerged ten days after Christmas. He explained that his Dad was testing the new walkie talkie in the basement rec room when the attack occurred. Neither of them had heard a thing until Holly screamed.

"My Dad knew she was cheating," he said. "But not with whom and—"

"Did Kova want to kill her?" I asked.

"I don't know. You said you saw it?"

"Yeah. Seemed more of a violent fight. You can't tell a soul. He threatened me, my whole family. He's reached a new level."

"You talked to him?"

"A bit, hidden in the dark. I saw nothing in the news. Didn't the cops report it? There's petty vandalism in there. I figured this would be in there."

"She's not pressing charges. Said it was a long story and that it's best to settle out of court. She got a lot of cash, I think. My Dad fired twice but didn't get him."

By late January, Conner was back in full hangout mode but was lethargic and withdrawn. We spent the cold days playing his brand new Nintendo Entertainment System, which had incredible graphics and sound. We cranked the volume and indulged in the bouncy and colorful *Super Mario Bros.* and got happily lost in *The Legend Of Zelda*. The 8-bit crunchy soundscapes and melodic themes drowned out his arguing parents. Occasional door slams jolted us out of our fantasy worlds. The cartridge games helped ease my fear of Kova. I wanted nothing to do with him and didn't want to reveal what I had seen to anyone, not willing to test whether his ultimatum was a fraud.

Later in the month, teachers wheeled an A/V cabinet into our classroom with a TV mounted at the top. We were being treated to a live event and early lunch with the Space Shuttle *Challenger* launch. Nibbling on bagels with cream cheese, we watched the shuttle explode. We gazed at each other in confusion. The teachers and nuns moaned and teared up.

"I don't see parachutes," one teacher stated over and over. "Where's the parachutes?"

The catastrophe saddened the teachers. Unable to continue with their lectures, they dismissed us for the day. The buses weren't ready, so I walked home, as my parents were both working. Halfway home, Conner's Dad pulled up next to me in his car and told me to get in the back. Conner's school had the dismissal as well. We ended up on our road, dressed in our uniquely different uniforms, sitting on the curb.

We watched Conner's Dad bring out packed cardboard boxes to his sedan, one at a time. He dragged his feet, pausing often. He lit up a cigarette and leaned against the car. Conner cried. He ran over to his Dad and clutched him.

"I can still lift you over my head," Conner's Dad said, raising his son to the heavens. Conner kicked his legs.

The house of steady home improvements came to a pause, and whatever compelled Holly to cheat lingered like a dense, ambiguous specter that followed and weighed me down, a fraught humid aura.

27.

Hiding In Tall Grass

April '86
After Kova's attack on Holly, I wanted to hibernate in a world of video games, sugar and salt, nestled in a room of bikini model posters. Quinn's bedroom provided this enclave escape, lit solely by a blue lava lamp. Quinn and I agreed to focus our time on making money, eager for cash beyond our weekly allowance. We embraced snowstorms and went door-to-door in the aftermath with shovels in hand, no matter how deep the accumulation.

Pat and Conner had vanished. Pat was busy with carpentry training, tuba lessons and indoor rugby that bled into outdoor rugby. Conner was in a depressed state, visiting a psychiatrist regularly, not wanting to leave his room.

In mid-March, Quinn and I embraced a lawn mowing business. We scrawled our phone number on a few cardboard signs with a black marker and stapled them to telephone poles throughout Oreland. By the end of April, we had five clients. We borrowed our Dads' mowers and walked them together to our destinations. I felt tough, pushing the mower through the street, wearing a red bandanna, Sony Walkman clipped to my shorts.

One of our clients was a retired old man named Dutch who seemed to magically appear on the lawn as we mowed. I would swing around to finish another row and see Dutch squatting and moving his hands in a formation, trying to realign me, dissatisfied with my curved patterns. At the end of mowing, Dutch talked our ears off before giving us the $20, holding the crisp bill firm in his hand as he spouted out opinions on local news.

Next door to Dutch's house lived a girl who was in Quinn's class. She sunbathed on her back deck, reading magazines. If Quinn saw her, he would stop his engine and signal at me to stop mine so we could toss a few words with her and wave. Quinn seemed smooth with this girl even though she was way out of our league.

"Man, she's in your grade?" I said as we wheeled back home. "She looks older, more mature."

"Our school has tons of chicks like that," said Quinn. "You would dig it. No plaid uniforms either."

Sometimes, the girl would take in some rays in her bikini as we mowed, trying to make us falter. I played it cool and just nodded at her, walking taller than usual, trying to glimpse just enough of her lotion application.

Like many kids, Quinn got a Nintendo Entertainment System. The console was gaining intense popularity. After earning lawn loot, we lounged in his room playing *Donkey Kong* and *Popeye*, chugging iced tea and taking turns standing bare chested in front of Quinn's window unit air conditioner.

"I'll kick both of your asses in *Super Mario Bros.*," said Sasha.

"Step up to the challenge," I said.

"Your combined B.O. would knock me out before I finish World 1-1."

I prayed for rainy days when overheating the NES was all that we could do. Relaxing in front of the video games, with their soulless yet fun challenges, is where I felt safe and content, void of confrontations and mischief. The anthem styled melodies of the games stuck with me all day and I played them in my head, adding string sections and tympani to intensify them. I was reprogrammed, dulled, excited to count cash on the floor and think of the next game to buy.

28.

Blue Crosses

May '86
As our bus approached Divine Miracles, we saw police cars with flashing lights and news vans parked near the rectory. We figured there was a big car accident. The bus driver nodded and talked to someone on his CB radio.

We exited the bus to the recess lot. Reporters and cops loomed about. Helicopters approached and hovered over us. The thunderous chopper blades made it difficult to talk. We pointed and hollered possible scenarios. The nuns and teachers stated nothing, just as uncertain as the kids. Investigators walked in and out of the rectory with gloves on, carrying various items to their cars.

At dismissal, our teachers handed us a paper for our parents with details about a meeting that same night in the church basement. At home, Mom was on the phone with Dad at work, muttering. She escaped to the furthest room in the house when she saw me, walking with the cordless phone.

Against Mom's wishes, Siobhan and I watched the 5pm news on Siobhan's tiny black-and-white TV. We saw Father Pal's smiling face framed in the top right corner of the screen with an overlapping graphic of handcuffs. It was the top story. The anchor stated that Pal owned volumes of indecent photos of children.

Pal had the packages delivered to an address at an apartment community where there was a public mailroom. Too large for mail slots, delivery men placed the packages on the floor. Detectives had spied and watched Pal enter the mailroom, exit with the packages and drive back to the rectory. Pal hid the photos in the drop ceiling, behind a large mirror and in slitted drywall.

"He's a nutcase," Mom said, slapping a dishrag on the counter. "A mentally ill perverted man, no longer holy. He better see jail time. Was he ever—strange around you?"

"No. Not like that," I said.

"But he was strange in other ways?"

"Just silly, I guess."

The apartment address of the photo deliveries was Louie's, the greenskeeper at Shady Creek. In video clips, Louie's chubby face look bewildered as they questioned him after biking home from work. His beard, brow and tie-dye shirt were a sweaty mess. He admitted he had seen weird packages, but never opened them. They weren't addressed to his name.

"I get all kinds of junk mail catalogs delivered to my unit. But I don't have anything delivered here due to this mess of a mailroom," Louie said, cuffed and escorted to a squad car. "Don't trust it. Packages disappear. I gotta P.O. Box in Glenside. Figured whoever needed them was taking them. I'm just a Wharf Rat living the simple life. Clean and sober."

Footage showed detectives walking out with cylindrical tubes with cross markings, similar to the ones I had seen Kova piling into his car, back with Farrah on the bridge over the tracks.

"We've seen this delivery method before," said the detective. "It's always Class C apartments with no security. Always from Scandinavian countries. There's a pattern here."

At night, I snuck downstairs shortly before 11pm and set the VCR to record the news. It revealed even more footage, including overhead shots of Oreland from the helicopters. Police had searched Louie's apartment and found no evidence of the packages or illegal photography. I watched the footage, rewound it and watched it again, pausing on new snippets of investigators walking out with the cylindrical tubes. The cross markings were blue, more evident on the color TV. Dad walked in as I stood in the glow.

"What're you doing up?" Dad whispered, flopping on the La-Z-Boy recliner.

"I taped the news," I said with an exhausted breath. "I've seen these packages before."

"You've seen what's inside them?"

"No. The tubes with the blue crosses. Kova had a bunch. Last Valentine's Day at the train station."

"Yeah, you brought that up on the way to Treasure Island. Weren't they for the golf balls he gave out?"

"Maybe. I guess so. These just look exactly like the ones I saw."

Dad chuckled, took his glasses off and rubbed his eyes. "Some say the devil has gotten a hold of Father Pal. I think he was born that way. But, look. Those blue things are postal markings. Looks like a flag of some sort. What would Kova have to do with Pal?"

I explained that Kova and Pal followed Willem and I after we ascended the drainage pipe.

"Did they touch you?" asked Dad, jolting up with his Tastykake snack.

"They asked questions."

"First, you shouldn't have been in the drainage pipe. I'm not gonna tell your mother about this. She'll have a conniption. Second, they were probably just making sure you were headed home safely."

"I guess so," I said with a cracked voice. "There was also a yellow car." My breath felt strangled, unable to shape words with my lips or create sounds. "It stopped in front of Kristoph's house. I swear Kova was taking photos of him. I saw flashes, but the car drove away quickly. It was sunny though. I had just woken up."

"Did you see a camera?"

"No. It was early. I was staring into the sun."

I turned off the TV. The blue glow vanished. My eyes teared as

Dad chomped on the final morsels of his late night treat. I thought back to the previous Christmas. The image of a barking, bleeding Kova threatening my family shivered through my torso.

In my room, I took up Dad's thought on thinking the blue markings were flags. I opened the proper "F" encyclopedia book and found an identical marking in the Flags of the World section. It was Finland. I heard Dad get up to use the bathroom in the middle of the night. I ran to him with a flashlight aimed on the page.

"This is the same one," I said, pointing to the flag.

"Kova is Finnish, ya know. Probably has business ties there."

"Right. And the cops traced it to the Scandinavian region."

"You need to get sleep. The police will figure this out."

29.

Chopping Block

August '86

The revelations of Father Pal led my parents to forgo enrolling Siobhan and I at Divine Miracles further. They registered us to start at Stony Stream Middle School, a National Blue Ribbon school, in September. It was tuition free with better curriculums, teachers and facilities. My folks would save a bundle. Quinn attended Stony Stream, so I was excited that I had a friend to guide me.

Quinn talked about his many friends at Stony Stream as we played Nintendo in his room. Someone pounded on the downstairs aluminum screen door. We ignored it, not expecting anyone. The door opened and slammed. Lumbering footsteps pounded through the living room and up the carpeted stairs. Quinn and I dropped the controllers. We grabbed old soccer trophies and held the miniature golden men, ready to slam the marble bases into whoever entered Quinn's bedroom.

Conner appeared. "Hey guys," he said with a cheery disposition. "Sasha let me in."

"Jesus fuck," said Quinn, tossing the trophy into a milk crate.

"Sorry. Did I scare ya?"

Quinn ignored Conner and unpaused the game.

Conner was on the mend, yearning to hang out. He had never

147

knocked on Quinn's door before. I smiled at his new take charge approach.

"Figured you guys might be here. You guys reek. Just finish a lawn?" asked Conner.

"Yeah," I said. "We're doing a lot of them. All the way through October I figure. Good dough."

"Man, is Sasha hot," Conner whispered into my ear.

Quinn turned up the TV volume.

"Yeah. She's so cool," I said. "She's probably lounging in the backyard right now."

"Really?" Conner stepped a few paces into the hallway and looked out the window. "Holy shit," he mouthed without stating the words.

The next day, Conner knocked on my door. He wore the Cub Scout binoculars I used for a bird watching merit badge.

"Oh, you had those," I said. "You can keep them."

"Want to check out some rare doves?" asked Conner, with a frothy grin. He unfurled his plan to spy on Sasha from the golf course. I was equally excited and appalled.

We headed to the 15th hole that lined Quinn's backyard, sneaked to the base of a pine tree and climbed as high as we felt safe. A browned out limp section of branches made for a small window towards the yard. We waited.

"This is insane," I said of our lame mission. "Has Kova returned to your house?" I asked.

"Nah. Drama is over," said Conner. "It's been calm. My Dad picks me up sometimes and I stay at his apartment."

Sasha popped out of the porch door and sauntered down the stairs. She headed to the shade with a black one-piece swimsuit and dark shades, her skin China doll white. She held a small radio that was playing the synth sounds of Human League. Sasha sat facing us on a lounge beach chair. Conner and I passed the binoculars back and forth, nodding in approval. It was as if she was staring at us, summoning us to her anti-sunlight meditative discotheque. One moment, she walked towards us, maneuvering behind the shed to smoke a cigarette.

The view was beautiful, fulfilling a longing of mine, to just eye her up. I couldn't do this passing her by at Quinn's house. I became transfixed by her curling toes of purple nail polish and the rustling branches above; the wind created a sound barrier. I studied the sunset and wondered about the girls of Stony Stream. I thought of Emma and our childhood romance, knowing rekindling it was beyond grasp.

The following day at dusk, Conner knocked on my door with his Mom's video camera so he could zoom in on Sasha and preserve it. "We can watch it later in my room," he said.

"Just got off the phone with Quinn," I said. "Told him I was watching a movie with my Dad. That's my plan, man."

"Push it back thirty minutes. We won't be long."

The camera was huge compared to the binoculars, but Conner kept it steady, ready to tap the red record button, poised like a sniper. Sasha stepped out of the house in jeans and a t-shirt. She grabbed stuff from the garage and rinsed her black Honda Prelude with a garden hose.

"I like it," Conner confirmed as he zoomed in and captured the moment. "I'll let you see it later, Garv. Gotta keep this going. I'm in close."

An abrupt feeling of disgust swept through me. Our lame plight tainted the visuals. I didn't want to be in the golf course, locked into more devilry.

"I'm gonna head out," I said.

"Well, I'm staying put," said Conner. "She sprayed her shirt by accident. Killer."

"You're gonna stay here by yourself?"

"Yeah, man. I'm doing you a favor. Trust me."

Later at night, Conner called to explain how amazing the footage was. It pumped him to get more. He wanted to learn how to create slow motion.

The following Saturday afternoon, I hung out with Quinn in

his side yard as he pointed out edible mint leaves. I noticed a red blinking light coming from the pines. I couldn't see anybody, but I knew it was Conner peering down at Sasha who was sniffing the tomatoes and peppers in the garden, close to the pines. She was wearing a cleavage heavy bikini top and stirrup pants.

Abruptly, Conner dropped the camera. It smacked several branches before plunging to the ground, like a Plinko chip descending on *The Price Is Right*. I heard the faint repeating ding sound of the VHS cassette door being open.

Quinn and Sasha turned their heads in unison toward the pine, staring it down in a motionless panic. Conner emerged and picked up the camera.

"Were you recording me?" Sasha yelled. "You creeper!" She stormed back to the house, giving the middle finger behind her back. "Your friend Conner is a little stalker," she spat.

Conner dashed off with his camera, along the perimeter of the course.

"Let's get him," said Quinn, dashing toward the street. I followed suit.

The only way out of the course towards home was to cut through a yard or squeeze through the Community Center fence. We saw Conner slink through the chain links and run through the playground. Sprinting, I rooted for Conner to get a clean escape. But as Quinn and I reached Dog Poopy Island, we had gained on him. At his front lawn, we were a few feet behind him. Conner stopped and stood next to Holly who was face down on her knees, pulling weeds. Conner turned to us, about to burst into tears. I connected eyes with him, knowing he could oust me and ruin my friendship with Quinn.

"You better fucking stop!" said Quinn.

The three of us wheezed, catching our breaths.

"What's going on here?" asked Holly, holding a spade with black gloves.

I noticed the video recorder had the VHS cassette door open with nothing inside. I looked at Quinn, but he didn't seem to notice the missing evidence. He backed off, staring at Holly as she cried.

"I don't understand," said Holly. "Conner is your friend, Garvey. Are you guys fighting?"

I shrugged, restraining tears.

"You crossed the line," said Quinn, sticking out an index finger toward Conner. "Don't do it again. Don't come anywhere near my house."

Conner ran inside. Holly stepped toward us, pointing the muddy spade at me. We walked backwards as she berated us with slow paces toward the road. "We've gone through a *lot*," Holly said. "The last thing Conner needs is threats. Garvey, I expected more. You both let my son be."

At night, I sneaked out with a flashlight to the tree where Conner had dropped the camera. Nobody was around in Quinn's yard or back porch. The white reel hubs of the VHS tape stood out. I grabbed the cassette. It was labeled: *Cape May Family Vacation – 1981*. I then heard sounds of whooshing water. I tiptoed to the fence behind Quinn's neighbor's yard and saw Sasha sitting in a raft, floating in the moonlight through the sounds of katydids. She was sucking on a green Otter Pop, one leg wading in the water. I watched for a moment.

Blocks from my house, I pulled out the shimmering tape from the VHS cassette and ripped it up. I put the cassette on a curb and stomped on it, shattering the plastic shell. I scooped up the plastic shards and tossed them into a trash can on the side of the road.

30.

Public Offering

S eptember '86
   On the first day of 7th grade, Quinn and I met at the Community Center so we could walk together. Our homes were a mile away from the school, but there was no bus service for the small range. Quinn strode with vigor, always a step or two in front of me as he mouthed out names and attributes of hot girls in our grade. I was pumped to not be wearing a uniform. I sported Ocean Pacific pants, a bright button-down shirt with funky patchwork and Adidas sneakers. I felt confident in new threads and a Jansport backpack, my hairstyle tweaked with mousse.

   As we walked, several buses cruised by with faces sticking out of the windows. Some yelled out Quinn's name with praise. He raised his fist, keeping his face stoic. At the entrance of school were two tennis courts and a bridge over a creek. From there lied multi-use sports fields and ramps leading up to the school's main entrance. It was an airport compared to Divine Miracles. I went from a realm of 30 kids per grade to 400.

   In the extended homeroom session, I stared at the school map. I realized that if I was in the wrong wing of the school, it would take several minutes to get to where I needed to be. Walking through hallways, the diverse ethnicities of kids stood out. It was refreshing yet intense, plunged deep into unfamiliar patterns. But any sensation of unity was void as cliques mushroomed together with high fives. Nicknames were hollered at fluctuating intensities. I skirted around their volcanic chatter, in the way of their nests.

At lunch I took my tray of hand-selected cafeteria food (Fiesta Sticks, french fries, vanilla pudding and chocolate milk) and headed to the vast region of tables. I found Quinn at a group of tables that had no empty chairs. I sat as close to him as possible, tossing him a wave. He nodded. His crew was a boastful bunch, pointing to people from afar and barking out compliments as if they were star sluggers walking up to home plate.

I chomped on my food, eyeing up outfits. My new duds fit in with what Quinn's crew was wearing. Many of them had athletic builds and roared about lifting weights and signing up for football. They glanced at me but none of them introduced themselves. I figured they had a lot to catch up on from their summer apart. The guys at my table seemed nervous, deep in whispered conversations. I nodded hello at everyone I made eye contact with.

After lunch, everyone poured outside to linger in the sunshine. The girls hung out on the patio and Quinn's crew hung out by a field goal post. The guys hollered to the girls by name, pointing out those with endowed T&A. I ambled about this crew, opposed to the guys I ate with. I stood beside Quinn, mirroring him for a few minutes, hoping he'd introduce me.

"Stop following me," said Quinn.

"What's wrong? What did I do?" I asked.

"Just stop following me."

I headed off towards the dumpsters where some guys were poking lard with a big stick. They looked nervous and filled with dread, grunting. I walked on. In the shade of the pillared bus terminal, I introduced myself to another group. They said hello but instantly diverted back to argumentative conversations of sports stats.

I wanted to be with Quinn's crew. They appeared energized,

eagerly poised to flirt with cute girls. I dubbed them the Gold Chainers because of their confident dynamo and adorned shimmering gold chain necklaces.

The next day at school, I wore white canvas pants with a thick rope drawstring and a lime green polo shirt. I called Quinn the night before to see what the big deal was but nobody answered. Unable to find Quinn in the morning, I walked to school solo. Siobhan walked separately. We were just too cool for each other. While I was embracing surfwear and the California look, she was into New Jersey's high crimped hair and acid washed denim outfits with sewn on patches of big hair bands.

I approached Conner's house and saw Holly walking out with him, holding his hand. Conner wore a tie, button-down shirt and blazer. I stopped to catch eyes with him and waved. "Please, Garvey," said Holly. "Just keep walking. Haven't you done enough?"

Conner let go of Holly's palm, ran ahead of her and jumped into their car.

"Seriously, Garvey," said Holly, clacking in high heels. "Take another road next time."

"I'm sorry we chased him. Ditched him. All of it," I pleaded. "It was a big mistake."

Holly glared at me and got into her car. I waited, not wanting to go to school. I watched the rear window defroster melt the cold moisture and reveal Conner's face. The reverse lights came on and I scurried off.

At lunch, I saw an empty chair next to Quinn from afar. I headed towards it and the whole table turned towards me and chanted "FAG-GOT! FAG-GOT!" in unison, pointing their fingers in time with the syllables. I approached them closer, in disbelief of their gestures. Quinn kept his head down, focusing on his food. The majority of the cafeteria turned toward me as the chant continued. I assumed a guy named Wolfgang orchestrated the smearing chorus. His eyes bulged out more than the others. Veins stuck out of his forehead. They restrained him from trying to attack me. The chorus continued until I found a spot to sit. There were a variety of cliques, all at the exact tables as the day prior. I joined the first table that had a free seat. They didn't make eye contact. "Screw those guys," one of them said, once it resumed to normal.

Back home, I collapsed on the floor, my backpack of textbooks weighing me down. When my parents arrived, I begged them to enroll me back at Divine Miracles. I didn't give them details of what happened. I wanted to be back with the old crew. My parents insisted that I wait a couple more weeks. I bawled into the couch cushions, trying to mute the sounds from Siobhan. They pointed out how Stony Stream's education would be more fruitful.

Day three at lunch, I sat at a table of jaded looking dudes. Towards the end of recess, I tried to approach Quinn, but he scattered off. The bell rung to come back inside. Wolfgang approached with a smile. "Hey, new guy. What's your favorite show?" he asked.

"Oh, well. There's many," I said. "I like *Who's The Boss?* a lot. Alyssa Milano is cute."

"Good one." Wolfgang placed his palm on my chest and pushed lightly. My calves brushed up against something firm and I tipped backwards. I tried to break the fall but landed on my back. I looked up and saw one of Wolf's buddies leap in front of me from his squatted position.

"We don't want you hanging around, faggot," said Wolf. "Stop trying to chill with us." He held a packet of chewing tobacco. A logo of a Native American chief was on the package. His friend jerked around like a gyrating cake batter mixer, a ball of flailing limbs and giggles, reenacting my fall.

I started to get up.

"Nah, not yet," Wolfgang said. He spat a hunk of moist tobacco at my face. "Damn, I got aim."

I stayed on the ground until they walked away and were inside. The chew residue soaked into my pores. I wiped it off. A bald man with a tie and blazer poked his head out the door, looked around and locked up the cafeteria. The breeze shook the grass and weeds against my ears. I stared up at the chalky sliver of a daytime moon. Just weeks prior, I laid on the ground, shoulder to shoulder with Quinn and Sasha, watching a late morning crescent moon vanish while we tried to whistle with a blade of grass.

I stood up. Mud stain streaks were on my white pants. I was alone on the football field and thought for a moment about sprinting home.

"Do they really think I'm gay?" I pondered.

The bald man headed my way with unswerving strides, his open blazer flapping. "Hey, space cadet. You want a special invitation? Inside. Now."

31.

Dealt Dis

October '86

Aside from the Gold Chainers, there were other lunch groups: the Jaded Jedis, the Sport Statisticians, the Smart Asians, the Awfully Dressed With Bad Hygiene. I squeezed in at their tables, hoping my suave threads masked my crumpling confidence. Quinn and the Gold Chainers remained defiant against letting me join them. The second time they brought me down to the ground, I landed on a concrete path. My shirt ripped. An elbow got grazed, leaking blood onto a later pop quiz.

The Gold Chainers seemed collectively synced into the same rationale of what was cool. I hoped that I was enduring a hazing and needed to prove that I was thick skinned. But the pat on the back didn't happen. They never hoisted me up in celebration.

I got my Mom to buy me an 18 karat gold herringbone necklace to help boost my esteem. I felt cool in the mirror at home, like a smooth snake was shifting around my neck, popping out of my sweaters, ready to bite.

Walking to school, I dreaded seeing the buses as drive-by chants of "FAG-GOT" and "DORK" were lanced at me. When the roar of buses shifting gears drew near, I hid behind trees and ducked behind cars.

To make it easier on myself, I cut through Shady Creek. The

slitted barbed wire fence was in use again. In the early morning hours, the sole danger on the course was the automated sprinklers positioned on the fairways. They popped up with random precision, requiring a quick sprint to escape.

Although no golfers were present on the teen holes of the course, Louie lurked about. I hadn't seen him since he was on the news and figured he was innocent. Father Pal had disappeared and not him. When he first saw me, he hollered out and cruised up to my side in his cart. "You realize this is a private property right?" he asked, taking off his shades and cleaning them with his t-shirt.

"Sorry," I said. "The woods at the 18th hole connects to my school. I get picked on in the streets. Labeled something I'm not. It sucks. Can I just cut through?"

Louie didn't look at me. His head turned like a weathervane in a slow breeze, a stout rooster. He paused, mouth agape. "Roger that. I can relate to that shit," he said. He pressed play on a boombox fastened to the cart with duct tape. Led Zeppelin's "Custard Pie" played. "Remember, I didn't see you out here, all right? You didn't see me. Capeesh?"

"Sure, no prob."

"And, kid, stand up for yourself."

I walked on. I looked back and saw Louie sitting Indian style in a meditative state, sitting on the top lip of a bunker, inattentive to his job.

After that, Louie saluted me when he saw me from a distance. I remained uncertain of him and figured he might bury me alive in a sand trap. I carried a pocket knife with me, hiding it in a jacket sleeve and leaning the open blade up against my wrist, ready to stab.

At the 18th hole woods, I tossed my backpack over the fence and climbed to the other side, landing in the middle of Stony Stream's Maintenance Center. Piles of mulch, salt and sand barricaded my presence. I slinked toward the school's main entrance with ease, unscathed every time.

Throughout the day, I dreaded free time in between classes. It was ten minutes of intense chatter and connections being made. No one spoke to me, but I wouldn't speak to anyone either. Quinn and I ignored each other. My prime concern was being elbow slammed into the lockers by one of Wolfgang's buddies.

The twenty minutes before Homeroom began was tolerable. Most people hung out in the lawless hallways, but I sat on a long metal heater casing with a kid named Zakk and his open collective of followers. Zakk resembled a latter stage Jim Morrison mixed with a short hockey brute. If he wasn't wearing a Flyers jersey, he wore band shirts. He always sat in the middle, jacked up on jellied toast and orange juice. He reenacted the best parts of sitcoms and movies and performed play-by-plays of WWF matches, emulating the likes of Ricky Steamboat and Bill Cosby. He provided a guaranteed laugh session before a day of tiptoeing through landmines. I admired Zakk's exclamations at things he glorified and despised. His words were pure, unfiltered, all steering us toward amusement that bolstered us for hours.

On weekends, I mowed lawns with Quinn, but we didn't talk. We met at our clients' homes opposed to walking there together. Quinn fled the lawns solo after getting the cash. My lawn loot went towards J. Crew sweaters, ordered from a catalog mailed to our house. The models in the photos gleamed happiness, with perfect skin, entrenched in autumn festivities.

I continued to serve as an altar boy. The scent of the hallways reminded me of calmer simple times. I hoped to bump into old friends and morph back into being a Catholic schoolboy, donned in the Divine Miracles v-neck sweater and uniform, settled back in the trademark spruce green and resolute brotherhood.

32.

Feet Out Of The Batter's Box

March '87

Come springtime, I was ready to stand up for myself. I tried out for the 7th grade baseball team. Tryouts were comprised of each kid trying to hit about 25 pitches from the Coach while he assessed everyone taking turns fielding.

Coach had hair like Peter Tork of the Monkees and he wore a red track suit. He reeked of Noxema and Ben-Gay. At the plate, I smacked several line drives deep into the outfield. Coach nodded in appreciation. After each swing, I adjusted my new thick brown glasses. For my second round at the plate, the fielders moved back. I walloped the ball again, my lanky body making that aluminum bat clink with ease. One ball soared out of the park and into Twining Road. It smacked a passing garbage truck, almost hitting a trash collector standing on the back. He waved his cap at me. In the field, I bobbled grounders, dropped pop-ups and couldn't always reach the cutoff man.

The offensive strides worked in my favor. Coach posted my name on the list outside the gym. I made the team, a third baseman with the crew I longed to befriend. Quinn didn't make the team. I was hoping we'd both make it and forge a new foundation.

Wolfgang didn't make the team either. "Congrats, gay boy," he said in the hallway. "I'm gonna do tennis anyhow. More my thing."

From the onset of practice, teammates pounced me with dead arms, elevated me with wedgies and slicked me down with wet willies in the locker room. In the shower, they slapped me in the nuts and shoved me into tiled walls. The brazen hatred of my presence on the team dismantled my morale. Even though it was only a few teammates doing it, they set the tone for the others.

I was the second string third baseman and never started a game. Coach reduced my role to pity pinch hitting. For away games, I sat as close to the bus driver as possible, pretending to read our playbook.

At daily practices, each player took turns carrying the heavy canvas duffel bags of bats and balls from the locker room to the field. When it was my turn, I lagged way behind the already assembled team. My teammates stood at second base, ready to practice full sprints to home plate. As I dropped the gear by our bench, they all chanted "FAG-GOT, FAG-GOT" as Coach patted the air with hands, silently trying to calm them. "Come over here and start us off, Garvey," said Coach. "Remember, just slide before the puddle."

Due to heavy rain, home plate and the batters' boxes were engulfed in a large puddle. The rest of the dirt on the field and the pitcher's mound was dry.

"No, you have to slide into the puddle," a teammate said.

Coach rolled his eyes and leaned down with his hands on his knees to analyze my base running.

"That's right, go into the puddle. That's it," said the teammate. Everyone roared with laughter.

I crouched down with my left foot on second base and tore off towards third base.

"Pud-dle, pud-dle, pud-dle!" the team cried.

I pressed onward towards home plate and intentionally slid smack dab in the middle of the four foot wide puddle. My light gray sweatsuit absorbed the cool April brown water. The gooey gunk reached the skin of my legs and back. I winced as the sludge caked my face. My body laid in the puddle for a few seconds. I took off my glasses and stood in the puddle, looking at the crew that were pointing, high-fiving, and gyrating limbs. Coach buried his face in a hand, nodding in disgust. At that moment, I succumbed completely to becoming a freak, taking immediate ownership of the new role, doused in the moist Earth and smiling back at my teammates as they jeered at me. Self assured, I wanted to scare them, to perplex them. I lost total respect and admiration of the Gold Chainers.

For the rest of practice, the mud on my clothes slowly dried. It soaked into my pores. The first string third baseman and I took turns fielding balls. "Why don't you go home?" he asked.

"Why? I'm having fun," I said. "Gotta support the team."

He spit at my feet and uttered something under his breath. When practice was over, I headed toward the duffel bags to carry them. Coach ran over. "I got this," he said. "Just head home from here. You're a walker right? Come back fresh tomorrow."

I walked home with my glove, getting odd looks from drivers passing by. I entered my backyard and smelled the dinner that Mom was making. I stripped down naked. Even my cup had mud on it. I turned on the hose and stood shivering as I rinsed off the sweats and put them on the clothesline. I rinsed my body and entered the back door. I cupped my penis and saw Dad on the couch with a newspaper covering his face. "Your mother is on the QVC," he said. "She's live on the air again." I looked at the TV in front of Dad and heard Mom talking about an exercise bike. I glanced toward the kitchen and saw the telephone cord headed towards the den. On the stove, red flat strips of Steak-umm meat sizzled and turned gray in a skillet. Nobody knew I was naked and dripping water. I showered. The smell of a cinnamon Yankee candle burned in the hallway and put me at ease.

The next day in homeroom, I sat with Zakk. People came in and out and looked at me. "You really slid into that puddle?" they asked, one by one. They responded by saying I was a freak before stammering off.

I enjoyed the *freak* classification better than *faggot*, comfortable in being an outcast. The rejection of my desired peers left me jaded, uncertain, unwilling to trust the male gender. I wanted to coast through school days with minimal friction, conversation or spotlights. I wanted to blend into the background like a dull mannequin, exerting zero emotion. I took part in class only when called upon by the teachers. I hid behind *Rolling Stone* magazines at lunch recess, sitting in a nook of the hallway that led to the janitor's closet, waiting it all out.

33.

Sega Master / Caddie Master

June '87
For my 13th, my parents bought me Nintendo's rival, the
Sega Master System. Everyone was getting a Nintendo. But Sega's
TV commercials lured me and I requested it. The ads featured
cryptic text in sand that revealed "Now, there are no limits." They
priced it the same as Nintendo but it had a darker edge with a
sinister black console and controllers. As the Dad said at the end
of the commercial, holding a light phaser gun after killing ducks:
"Sega. It's the one."

Even though Sega had limited games and simple grid
packaging, I wanted to enter an untrodden gaming realm. The
more arduous the games, the better. From side scrolling action
adventure to weekend absorbing role-playing games, I delighted
in its escape. *Aztec Adventure, Alex Kidd In Miracle World, Miracle
Warriors*. Enraptured by the digital sagas, I stalled my hygiene.
I ignored cries from my folks to join them for dinner until
pounding fists against drywall shook me free.

Mom stormed to my side with the cordless phone. It was Pat,
asking if I wanted to become a caddie with him at Shady Creek.
He heard the pay was good, all under the table. "It's tax free like

your lawn money," said Pat. "Way bigger bucks. And you can do it every day."

"Is Quinn in on this?" I asked.

"Nah, he doesn't wanna deal with the sun. Wants a job at the mall."

"I don't know anything about golf though."

"My bro used to do it. He says you figure it out."

The next Saturday morning, I met up with Pat at the Community Center and we cut through the slitted entrance of the barbed wire fence. I didn't explain that I walked through the course to get to school. We carried hand towels with us, wrapped over our shoulders. The dew of the course soaked our sneakers and socks. I had become adept at evading the automated sprinklers and guided us to dry terrains. I was eager to make cash. Even though running into Kova was a possibility, I had grown taller since I saw him back in '85. I looked different. I kept my cap low over my eyes. Kova's ultimatums seemed vaporized. I was no longer the boy hiding. I was ready to mingle among cigar smoke and pretend to care about the rich man's game.

Louie's maintenance crew was spread out, patching up greens and using gas powered trimmers and blowers to tidy up unruly sections. The drone buzz of the machines made me yawn, aching to be back in bed. "Only if they knew the damage we did here," Pat said.

We passed the new Halfway House, built by Kova's developers. "Probably was a rush job," said Pat. "Shitty framing. Uneven flooring." Pat spat at the structure and filled me in on golf basics: the ladies vs. men tee off areas, the yardage markers on the sprinkler heads, the divot repairing methods, the need to clean dirt off clubs with a towel, identifying irons for each distance.

We took a wooden bridge over a creek towards the first hole fairway. A blue heron rose from a pond and glided low to the ground before us. The stone country club and first hole tee off area were a couple stories up. I had seen this building in the distance from Quinn's yard. To escalate, we walked up a sloped asphalt path and headed around groomed shrubbery and black wrought iron fencing that bordered the tee off area. Uproarious caddies hung out by the caddie shack. They seemed antsy, looking around. Some sat on benches and meditated towards the distant treelines. They eyed us with a slow raise of their chins.

We looked for the Caddie Master, a guy named Merv. We walked towards the Pro Shop and saw a pagoda of similar-aged kids as us. They told us to sit tight. "He drives a white Mitsubishi Eclipse," said one kid. "You can't miss it. He's not here yet."

"That's a chick car," said an older caddie, passing by. "Strippers drive those."

The kids pointed out that we were at the Soda Pagoda, a place where golfers grabbed a can before tee-off. The sodas sat in a trash can full of ice.

Merv sauntered down the stairs from the lot. He positioned a series of bags along the fence, grouping them into an order that made sense to him. He walked towards the Soda Pagoda and nodded affirmatively, smiling wide, his large gold chain entangled in greying chest hair, his tumbleweed bushel of hair hanging onto his balding head.

"Boys," he said, approaching us. "Some new faces, I see. I'm Merv. Welcome aboard."

Pat and I spouted out our names and shook his hand.

"Since you're both new, you can put bags on the carts down below for the all-cart foursomes," said Merv. "We call it Running The Hill. You walk back up, ka-ching, you get a buck or two."

Pat and I observed Merv and his constant handshakes and one-off jokes to the golfers. They gave Merv tips with subtle maneuvers like a secondary handshake, an awkward high five or a scrunched up bill handed over with two fingers like a dangling piece of licorice.

"Gary!" Merv called out.

Nobody got up.

"Gary, I'm talking to you baby." Merv squatted to my level. "It's time to shine."

"It's actually Garvey," I said, following Merv and his clipboard.

"All right, Gary, my boy. Take these two bags. Walk them down and strap these bad boys on tight."

"Gotcha. It's Garvey, though."

Merv didn't hear me. Maybe he didn't care.

"Good luck, Gary," a kid said.

I put a bag onto each shoulder and stretched out my arms over the clubs to balance the weight. I felt like the horses that clomped through Wissahickon Park and left massive turds amid the paths of joggers. It was simple work. I had to watch out for the mossy bordering trim of the asphalt steps. At the bottom, I dropped the bags and bolted over toward a row of carts, ensuring the golfers weren't in mid-stroke. I drove the carts over to the bags, fastened them and climbed up the hill. Shanked shots crackled through the branches above, causing me to scrunch into a ball and cover my head with my hands. After the golfers teed off, I met them while hiking back up to hill. They held dollar bills at me, their metal golf spikes scraping like marching robots. A precision grab of the cash, void of small talk, was key.

Pat and I went home with about $30 each after spending two hours at Shady Creek, all under the table. I rolled with being called Gary, enjoying an escape from being Garvey and the mischief that name took part in. There was no W-2 form, liability waivers or job application, just a slow cooking loyalty to Merv. Gary it was.

At Shady Creek, golfers had to either walk with a caddie or take a cart. They couldn't carry their own bag or use push carts with the bicycle tires. These methods were too low brow, unmatched for the prestige of Shady Creek.

After a couple weeks, Merv assigned me to caddie. I carried one bag and fantasized about the next Sega game to buy. I was already selling my baseball cards to buy more games.

The best days to caddie were the weekends as the traffic was higher. From the first tee off at 7:30am, there was a steady flow of golfers. If assigned early enough, I went out again after a couple cans of Gatorade. Each completion of an outing was called a loop. Some caddies called themselves "loopers".

After a month of running the hill and single bagging, Merv assigned Pat and I to caddie together in a foursome with two bags each. Merv mentioned that the group was a bunch of high handicappers, so we'd be in the rough often. I nodded and faked full acknowledgement of what was going on.

The golfers teed off from the plateau of the first hole. I didn't know where the balls went. I saw them soar into the blue sky and then hook left towards a massive pine. I felt embarrassed for the golfers. They were nice and easy on me, but I couldn't find every shot. Many times, I dropped the bags down and examined the bases of trees and thickets of bushes. I captured balls from the creek with a fold up retrieval tool. I pretended not to see the golfers reposition balls with bad lies.

Pat and I rarely talked. We were to lend advice, but they knew we were caddie virgins. On the greens, when all four balls were on, we handed out the putters and avoided stepping in front of the imaginary line from the ball to cup. Our thin frames had enough weight to make footprints in the green. Pat and I took turns holding the pin before they putted, ensuring we wrapped the vinyl flag around the pin in case any sudden wind moved the flag and caused distractions. After a golfer hit a ball out of the sand trap, we smoothed out their footprints. Carpenter bees often hovered around the trap.

The Halfway House was after the 11th Hole. The caddies had a separate area partitioned off. We sat and munched on pretzels dipped in Grey Poupon, waiting for the golfers to finish their orders. If we had time, we got free hotdogs and a drink.

At the end of the 18th hole, the golfers gave out the tip, the sole payment. We were to never look at the money or count it in front of them. We then took the clubs to the Pro Shop to wash them and count the bills. We dipped the clubs in buckets filled with water and towel dried the clubs while staring up at a wall-mounted TV playing ESPN. If Merv was around, he gave his signature slow handshake. His hand pointed toward us from afar, advancing like a shark with a quick thrust. "My man, Gary," he'd say. "How'd it go out there? All good in the hood?" Other times Merv left early, and I trotted off with my dough.

Merv never assigned work schedules. We showed up and Merv worked with what he had. The more you showed up, the less that you had to wait.

A typical loop took about 4.5 hours, depending on course traffic. The worst events were Shotguns. These were tournaments where every crappy golfer seemed to be able to attend. They put two foursomes on each hole of the entire course. When the shotgun blast sounded from the clubhouse, golfers teed off at their assigned holes and finished all 18 in unique orders. The rounds were so backed up though that it took almost 6 hours.

The optimum set up was a "cart and caddie" foursome with professional level players. With this angle, the two walking golfers were commonly hitting par and in the fairway. The guys in the cart tipped also. We just had to wipe crud from their balls, rake their bunker blasts and smile. Three $20 bills was the result, sometimes more.

The caddie shack had a round table with a couple decks of cards. It was the last place you wanted to be as it meant that you were waiting for rain to stop or waiting during a sluggish period.

Merv smiled, chatted me up and chose me often if I arrived Saturdays and Sundays and a couple weekdays. With no schedule, I could show up once a week, as some caddies did, but waiting hours was the punishment of sparse loyalty.

Since attending public school, my family's attendance of Sunday mass at Divine Miracles dropped to once a month. I saw Emma from afar with her family that always secured the same pew. She looked unfamiliar. I was excited to see her walk to receive Communion, just to check her out. We talked after mass a few times but caddying took over Sunday mornings. Dad muttered about "being an atheist anyway" as he lounged in his bathrobe. The thick Sunday *Philadelphia Inquirer* covered his body as he sipped caffeine and crinkled his way through the news.

"You caddie for Kova yet?" asked Dad.

"Not yet," I said. "He's still a member. I've seen him. He trains golfers at the range."

#

Once 8th grade started in September, Pat stopped caddying because of rugby and opting to work with his Dad. The solace of caddying was parallel with my school days. I was in the golf course daily, walking to school or work. The slitted fence was a mouth and anus, absorbing me with the dream of crisp $20s, leaking me out sunburnt and sore, caked sweat on my shirts and hat brim, exhausted, jealous of the wealthy. The fence was no longer an entry to enduring friendships and mischievous highs. The fort remained, unattended. The money seduced me. I made the best of the land I had tattered and destroyed. I kowtowed to the golfers I once took aim at.

My shoes turned green around the borders. My shoulders became red, leathery, often breaking out in zits from the mix of sweaty t-shirts and bag straps leaning on skin. I always put the heavier bag on my left shoulder and felt bent, misaligned.

The days were a haze of caddying, avoiding friendships and spending hours alone playing the Sega Master System in my bedroom. Dad knocked on my door during a long RPG game bout. "You still alive in there?" he asked.

"Yep," I said, pausing the game. "Just trying to rid the world of evil. I keep dying in this tough section."

"You can't cheat taxes and death," said Dad, sticking his head in and looking down. "Well, not for long at least. Just remember, friends come and go. Family is forever, if you're lucky. Let's go. Shrimp scampi time."

A general disdain for brotherhood and school spirit kept me lingering as a farouche recluse. I stayed on the perimeter of events and walked without eye contact, hopping class to class with ghost like measures. In classrooms, I was captive to getting Dead Arms that left my shoulder sore for days. Although I loved hooded sweatshirts, they were bait for the Hoodie Yank. A sudden hand would appear and yank a hood string toward the ground, leaving me to fall with one long string threaded incorrectly.

I didn't hang out with my parents much, aside from trips out to eat and watching funny shows like *The Simpsons, Perfect Strangers, Alf, Mr. Belvedere* and *Saturday Night Live*. We all mutually loved SNL. Mom made popcorn or baked a snack and we lounged in front of the TV. I positioned myself on the thick brown carpet, stretching out any kinks from hours of using a joystick to save a princess.

With video games, I assumed the roles of a sorcerer, barbarian, ninja, soldier—all trying to find secret maneuvers, hidden tablets and treasured tunnels that led to a final round and cinegraphic ending that only victors viewed. Finales included closing melodies and scrolling credits of the Japanese programmers and designers. The games then reset and I twitched, aching to smell the plastic packaging and finger through the stiff manual of the next game.

34.

Rotten Eggs

J uly '88
Younger neighborhood kids that didn't know my dork status at school were potential friends. One of them lived across the street, named Aberelli. I called him Abe. He was two years younger than me and went to Divine Miracles. Abe and I traded baseball cards and played catch with hard balls in the street. We never scheduled hangouts. He was always there, a body that could follow me around, laugh at my jokes and obsess over baseball stats. At age 13, it felt odd to hang out with an 11-year-old, but he was always game when I phoned him. He never called me once, ever. It was always me plucking him from his pristine home.

Abe's parents were a spectacle, walking the twilight hand in hand while licking Fudgsicles, unaware their son didn't have buddies. His Dad looked like Burt Reynolds and enjoyed reapplying asphalt to his driveway every year. His Mom sat curled in the living room, reading detective novels. Every time I called Abe or knocked on his door, his Mom answered. She was a gatekeeper to size up the situation. I always got approved.

I had a box of fireworks leftover from when Quinn stole them while I was the lookout man. I lit a slew of them off on the 4th of July in front of my house, the one day when they seemed legal and nobody cared that Oreland sounded under attack. Some kids about three years younger than me found out I had extra rockets. They knocked on my door, asking if they could buy some. Bored with them, I sold the rest for just a couple bucks.

Days later, Abe and I walked past the Community Center and saw the kids I had sold the rockets to. They were setting them up to launch, waving with lax, inane gestures.

"It's broad daylight," I said.

"Don't they know they're illegal?" asked Abe.

Mauve billows of smoke were in the air from their previous launches. The kids laughed aloud, uncertain whether a fuse was lit. A rocket fell out of the soda bottle launchpad and whisked toward the edge of the field where piles of brown lawn clippings sat. The dead grass ignited and spread down the perimeter of the fence.

"Just keep walking," I told Abe. "Don't look over."

As we passed them, a police car roared by us, drove up the curb and onto the lawn. A cop got out and chased the running kids.

Abe and I got Cool Ranch Doritos and iced teas at Carmine's. We stood outside and heard a fire truck approaching and turn on Bala Avenue.

"I might be in deep shit, Abe," I said.

Abe chimed in with innocent thoughts of how I wasn't there to light the fuse.

Walking back, we saw firemen hosing down the toasted smoldering lawn remnants. Golfers looked aghast through the fence, just feet away from their man made forest of perfection.

At dinner, there was a knock at the door. Through a window, I recognized that it was a mother of one of the kids that got busted lighting the fireworks. I sat and forked in mashed potatoes while Mom perked up. Dad walked to the door.

"*Your* son sold *my* son illegal fireworks," said the mom. "My boy is innocent. He's only 11. The police found him lighting them. Who taught him how to do this? He doesn't even know how to use a lighter."

"Well, maybe he used a match?" asked Dad.

"My boy is crying in his bed, ashamed. The town pyro!"

"Look, we're in the middle of dinner right now. I'm sorry this happened, but my son is not responsible for what your kid did and—"

"Bullcrap."

Dad nodded and slowly closed the door on the panicked mom. He walked back over, still chewing his London broil. "Garv, no more fireworks, OK? I'll dispose of them tonight."

"They're all gone," I said.

"Good," said Dad. "Just stay away from those kiddos."

From my chair, I watched through the window as the woman walked off our front lawn, shaking her head in defiance.

#

Abe had a next-door neighbor that was three years younger than me, a husky guy named Deion. He was the same height as me, but heftier, almost obese. After chatting with him, we used Abe's side yard to toss a football between the three of us. Deion performed fake falls when he couldn't catch the ball, collapsing after putting a knee down for support. "Too high," cried Deion, face to the ground. "I think I'm hurt." Tears crept down his red cheeks as he moaned about grass stains.

Deion's Dad, who let us call him Blake, came out of the garage where he reorganized boxes of gear, many of it piled on the driveway. He always told us to play nice and for Deion to pull himself together. Blake was unemployed and rumored to sleep in a cot in the garage. He often brought a four foot tall orange and white robot to the playground, named MettoTron. It appeared to be built with LEGO-like bricks and wires. A big black eye sported a camera lens. Parents got pissed because their kids swarmed over to watch MettoTron do things like dance on command, speak Spanish and give high fives, leaving kids to sit motionless in awe opposed to working off sugar highs.

Leaving Carmine's one day with Abe, I went to the payphone and put in a quarter. I called Deion's house, punching in the digits with careful presses, using a ripped out section from the White

Pages for the phone number. When Blake answered, I pretended to be a miffed Chinese Restaurant manager.

"You no show," I said. "And you have reservation? Come now! Who does this thing?"

"Who is this?" asked Blake. "I'll find out where you are."

The calls to Deion's house continued for a couple weeks, all from the same payphone. Finally, I got Deion to answer the phone and not Blake. The kids I sold fireworks to hung near the phone booth, eating candy on milk crates. They paused and listened to my performance. I acted as the owner of the 309 Cinema who was cracking down on ticket stub littering. I suggested that Deion was recently in attendance at a film. The kids cracked up as I savored the comedic role. Abe brought an index finger to his lips to hush them. Deion apologized, sniffling. He admitted that he had just seen *Crocodile Dundee II* and likely left his stub on the floor.

"Well, you better get over here with a flashlight and find it," I demanded. The kids pounded their fists against the painted brick of Carmine's. I smiled in delight with the joy I had created. My dismal ranking shattered and produced a coaxed euphoria, as if a slow comb was repeatedly stroking out the dweeb filaments of who I was. Perhaps I could be a tormentor, leader of the East Oreland Youth, I thought.

A car sped down Bala Avenue toward us and slammed on the brakes. The driver parked crooked and the younger kids ran away. I stood with the phone in hand and saw Blake hobble out of the car in a Philadelphia Eagles bathrobe and tan sandals. Abe stayed nearby, peering around a parking bollard near the corner of Carmine's.

"Head home," I mouthed to Abe. He nodded at my signal and dashed off. I put the phone back on the receiver.

"So, it *is* you," said Blake. "The guy that sells fireworks to young kids and roughs up my son."

"What are you talking about?" I asked, looking down at his sandals and white tube socks.

"Don't play stupid. I traced your call. Guess what? You're

busted. With proof. I used to work for a police tech company and got to test out gear at home. They let me keep a few units. Professional grade."

"Oh, man. I'm so sorry. I was just having fun. This really isn't me."

"What? Calling at various times of the day? My wife works 3 to 11. You woke her up a couple days ago. You call that fun?" Blake blocked the phone booth door, hands straddling the exit, his body shadowing me.

"I'm such an idiot, sir. Please, I really don't want to be this guy."

"Yeah, well." Blake looked away. "You made my son cry. You ruined our dinner tonight. Here's the thing. I know you're up to something. I've seen you and that red-headed kid down the street walking around at night. I have a camera aimed at our walkway."

"Conner? I'm not friends with him anymore. We used to be. Haven't seen him in a couple years."

"Your friends just disappear on you, huh? Where are they now?" he asked, backing away from the phone booth and looking at the cars zooming by Pennsylvania Avenue. "Looks like they all ran home and left you stranded. Aren't they a bit young for ya?"

"Yes, they are," I said under my breath, scouring for the best direction to dart to.

"I was bullied as a kid. I'll be damned if my son is gonna go through the same shit."

"I'm not a bully, man," I said, staring at the back of his balding head. He then stood in silence, rubbing his temples.

"I know. I just got to get my shit together. Did you know his mom?"

"Whose mom?"

"Conner's."

"Yeah, I was there a lot. Holly."

"She's such a nice lady, a sweetheart. I don't know why we did it. But, my wife. She finds out everything."

"What did you do?"

"Oh, come on." Blake sat on a milk crate. "So, is she still with Kova? I know he's got money and all."

"I wouldn't know. Like I said, Conner and me aren't buddies."

Blake stared up at me, scratching his balding head. "You ever meet him before?"

"A while back, with my Dad," I said, wondering if Blake was a spy.

"Stay away from him. You see this?" Blake revealed his hairy chest. "These scars here. I wrote an op-ed piece in *The Sun* about his real estate shenanigans, his overdevelopment with shitty condos. I got off at Oreland Station and was walking home. Men popped out of a van and slice me good. Kova was there staring me down, letting me know I've been warned."

The helpless fear that overcame me years ago, when I hid in the manger scene on Christmas night, raced back like a spiked boomerang that someone forced me to catch. I nodded in understanding.

The incessant warning chimes of Blake's engine running and his door left open pulsated my mind.

"Whatever," said Blake. "This phone stuff ends now." His voice changed from assertive barking to inaudible. "I need to get a job. My wife is not happy with that either." Blake stood up. "You want a soda? I'm sorry."

"Nah, I'm gonna head home."

"You all right? Didn't mean to be so harsh."

"I am. Just scared of him."

"Tarnish his image or disrupt what he's proud of and you're screwed. Whatever antics you got going in that mind, end it now."

For the rest of July, I refrained from hanging out with Abe or Deion. I often saw Blake working in his garage, gear scattered on his lawn, never satisfied with his stacks of cardboard boxes. He labeled the boxes with a black marker, his wife never in sight. It seemed Blake was no longer allowed inside the house.

If Blake saw me, he gave me a thumbs up, as if I was in rehab, under surveillance. He had a hammock fastened to two dogwood trees and slept in it overnight, ditching the garage cot. Sometimes I'd see him mowing his lawn in a bathrobe, his beard getting thicker, grass flying all over the street.

As I biked by one day, Blake's garage door was fully open. It was vacant inside, just a cinder block box with dark stains on the cement floor. Chalk scrawlings were on the wall. "Deion, I Will Always Love You" the biggest one said. A landscaping crew descended on the lawn. They edged, bagged, mulched, flowered, weeded and beautified the lawn. Trash cans sat overflowing on the side of the road. MettoTron stuck out of one, his head broken, an eye missing, strangled with Blake's discarded rope hammock.

35.

Gallery Installation

August '88

The Shady Creek golf course was closed to golfers every Monday, allowing Louie and his team to work on lengthy repairs. Monday was also Caddie Day, a day that allowed loopers to golf for free. Night putting on the 15th hole one Caddie Day evening, I saw the familiar trot of Quinn creep out of the pines. My hands shook and my face quivered. Quinn paused for a moment when he saw me and continued toward me. We nodded.

"Finally got yourself some clubs?" Quinn asked, flopping his golf bag on the outer rim of the green.

"A cheap-o set. Nothing special," I said. "Just odd numbered irons and woods. You're no caddie. What are you doing here?"

"You gonna tell on me?"

We smiled and scattered a few balls on the green. We took turns putting, keeping our faces down, let alone making eye contact.

"So, what's up, man?" I asked. "It's been a long time."

"It has. Been busy," said Quinn.

"Doing what? Dicking over friends?"

"Look, I'm sorry man, but shit got weird."

"Whatever, dude."

"No, seriously. Remember that night when Kova chased us?" Quinn asked, leaning onto his club.

"When we hid behind your neighbor's shed?"

"Right. That photo he took of us. I saw it. A bunch of them. Enlarged on a wall."

"Where?"

"At White Ash. Kova was on a trip Labor Day weekend before school started. Wolf had a big party. I was looking for a bathroom. Had to take a mean shit, so I was trying to find one deep in the mansion. I stumbled into a series of doors that led to a big office. There were the photos of us, hanging on the wall. I was totally blurred out, but you were crystal clear. I moved at just the right moment."

"You joshing me?"

"Nope. They were bigger than posters. A sloppy gallery in the works. They were treated with different shades of color, like a Warhol. Glitter sprinkled on them. Wolf came in and saw me. He cursed at me to get out. He grabbed a mug and smashed it on your head and scribbled all over your face with a marker. He went berserk."

"Why's he pissed at me? It's not my fault his dad is a sicko."

"Don't know, man. Kova must think he's an artist."

"Well, good for you for being blurred. Lucky you. You could've helped me out, ya know. Those first days of 7th grade. Why was I a punching bag?"

"You don't get it. I did stick up for ya. On that first day. I told them you were cool, but Wolf told my lunch table that you were gay, a homo, a dweeb. He bashed you right off. He set the tone."

"Fuck him. He's just as bad as his Dad."

"Stepdad. Look. This crew. I've known these guys longer than you. Some are new to me, like Wolf. Everyone digs him with his access to liquor and parties. He's got this untouchable power, tons of dough. But I don't call the shots. I'm short, thin. Can't play sports well enough anymore to make teams. I'm just funny enough to make them laugh. I need these guys. Some girls I had crushes on last year are now taller than me. I'm sorry, man."

I paused for a moment. "Did you see any, like, mailing tubes lying around in there?"

"A few, I think. Why?"

"Did they have any blue crosses on them?"

"Like the insurance company?"

"No, like the flag of Finland. Nordic cross."

"Can't remember. I was buzzed. What's that about?"

"I think Kova is mailing photos out...of kids."

"There were other blown up photos. Kids on a nude beach. Europe, I guess. It's weird to think Kova would be into this shit. He seemed like a stud, a Don Juan lady killer type. That night we saw Holly at his house and all."

I stared at Quinn and nodded in appreciation for the details. My lips trembled. I looked in the distance and watched bats joggling around the pines as Quinn putted. I nibbled on my fingernails which were already red and sore. The sunset morphed the peach wisps of cirrus clouds with jet chemtrails. The beauty dissolved into a Picasso of Kova's bloody neck from that Christmas night, a night I wished I had stayed home amongst the safety of cookies, TV specials and rooms strewn with sparkling tinsel, far from the ogres.

36.

Increase In Wages

September '88

Merv assigned me to caddie for Kova and three others. I took the bags and propped them upright by the first tee, standing at attention. Kova appeared first, wearing a seagrass gambler hat with his initials on the ribbon. His signature mini battery powered fan whirred into his pink, sunburnt face. He shook my hand and held it as if he was testing whether an avocado was firm. I stopped breathing and saw the panic in my face from his mirrored sunglasses.

"You're late," Kova announced, letting go of my hand as Wolf appeared.

"Whatever," said Wolf, sizing me up. My Phillies baseball cap covered most of my face. "Oh, wow. You're carrying my bag?"

I nodded and stared at Wolf's clutched wooden tee.

"I'd rather take a cart," said Wolf.

Kova walked over to Wolf and I, putting a hand on each of our shoulders. "Real golfers walk," Kova whispered through clenched teeth. "Traversing the course is part of the game. Toy carts destroy the course and are visual distractions. If you can't walk, sit it out. You're not made for this game. Carts are for disabled men, a war hero with a bullet lodged in his femur."

Wolf pulled out a round tin of tobacco from his pocket, pinched a few strands and shoved it into his mouth.

"And quit that disgusting habit," said Kova, bringing a cigar to his mouth. "This is how you relish tobacco leaves. Not with a trail of drooled slime."

The other two golfers taking the cart appeared, slabbing sunblock on.

While forecaddying in the middle of the 6th hole, a steep par 3, Kova teed off and immediately yelled: "FORE!" I saw nothing but the white overcast sky, no inkling of a careening ball. I stood Kova's bag upright to shield myself behind it. I scrunched into a ball, holding the sides of the bag to keep it steady. The ball pounced on the bag's buckle and ricocheted towards Kova. I peeked to the side of the bag and saw the ball fly back about 50 yards. It landed on an asphalt path and rolled onto the rough.

"Great shot," said Wolf, clapping his hands.

Kova tossed his 4-iron club into the creek in front of the tee off box, raising his hands in disappointment. The foursome crossed the bridge and marched towards me. The typical jolly banter towards stroke two was nonexistent.

"You had one job," Kova said as he approached me. "To watch the ball and get out of the fucking way. I should be on the green. Now go down there and get my club out of the water." He grabbed an iron and continued.

I raced down to find Kova's club. I had seen where it splashed but the water was at least a murky two feet, far from reach. I removed my sneakers and socks and eased off the embankment into the creek. My bare feet embraced the mossy stone floor, and I slipped. I reached for some tall weeds and straightened out. I looked up at the foursome and saw they were all putting. My toes found the graphite shaft. I gripped it and plucked it out. On retreating the creek, something sharp pierced the sole of my left foot. I tossed the 4-iron onto the grass and lugged myself out. A fishing hook laced in algae dangled through my skin. I tried to thread it out, but the barb had it locked in place. At the green, Kova was down to his final stroke as the other golfers stood relaxed and cross-legged. I closed my eyes and ripped the hook out. I shoved my face into the ground to muffle screams. Blood trickled out. Biting pain endured. I put my socks and sneaks back on and raced with the club to Kova's bag. The foursome were already at the 7th hole. With each step, the tender wound twinged.

"I'll ask them for a handkerchief or bandage," I thought to myself.

Kova stood with his hand out, awaiting his 4-iron. I placed it in his hand.

"It's still dripping wet," he said. "Can you wipe it down, please? Or do I have to flag down a cart and get Merv to replace you?"

I dried the club with my towel and decided to just deal with the pain.

At the 10th tee off, gray overcast skies mutated into plum colored clouds and drizzle. Lightning flashed in the distance. By the time we reached the green, the rain was steady. The wind picked up, flapping the pin flag. The slender branches of a nearby willow writhed about like an enchanted beast trying to break free. Thin yellowing leaves broke off and speckled the green, creating obstacles for final putts.

The golfers putted in the downpour with quick sloppy strokes and then ran into the adjacent Halfway House. Kova took his time. I stood with him, getting drenched, as he crouched down to examine the lie. Droplets poured off his hat and splattered his sunglasses. Lightning intensified. I wanted to run inside but waited, holding the pin steadily.

Entering the Halfway House, the others stared up at the TV as a warning scrolled over *The Price Is Right* about heavy storms in the area for the next couple hours. I entered the partitioned off caddie area and waited for the lady to come my way with a free hot dog. Louie ran in soaking wet. The screen door slammed. He walked over to me.

"Fuck me. This thing came on fast," he said, waddling back and forth. "I should've came over here when it started spittin'. Waited too long."

The heavy rain beat on the roof and created a steady loud drone. I usually heard the golfers' conversations, but could barely hear Louie talk. We chowed on hard crunchy pretzels dipped in mustard and stared out the window at the squirming branches.

"Ah, you're that morning cut through kid," said Louie, realizing who I was. "Where you at now?"

"Yeah. Thanks for letting me do that," I said. "I'm a freshman now. Take the bus."

"Gotcha. Well, don't take any shit from anybody in high school."

"So far so good. Just a week in."

"Damn, I'm gonna have a lot of work to do tomorrow," said Louie. "Mother Nature gives me job security at least."

I explained to Louie that I used to attend Divine Miracles before public school.

"So, were you there for the big Father Pal thing?" asked Louie.

"Yeah, I saw you on TV."

"Luckily they kept my job here. Whole thing was bullshit. My apartment address was just a random target. Had no idea what was in those deliveries. Only saw them a couple times. Pal picked them up as fast as the mailman dropped them off. Damn news crew pointing cameras at me and shit. Worst part is Pal is back in action."

"How is that possible? At Divine Miracles?"

"Nah, some parish in Jersey. Got relocated."

Kova came over to our area and called Louie over to him. They walked to a back room. Minutes later, they came out. Louie stifled tears with an index finger as Kova patted his back.

"Guys, do you want a beer?" asked Kova. "You too, kid. You want one? We're done at 10 holes today. I'm sorry, but you're only getting paid for 10 holes. But it's Miller Time."

"I'm only 14," I smiled. "I'm in Wolfgang's grade."

"Oh, I know. He's at the bar phone now calling his Mommy to

come pick him up. He chose to be a little shit today. He's scared of rain. Doesn't respect me. He'd rather play shuffleboard with Mommy. He's not a tough cookie like you."

I nodded yes and Louie nudged me in the ribcage. "There you go, buddy boy."

Kova brought over a couple beers and a non-alcoholic brew for Louie.

Louie took a big swig and then burped into a fist. "Gotta take a piss. Be right back," he said.

I cracked open the beer and smelled it. I stuck a finger in the can and slurped up a trace amount. I dumped it down the cement floor drain.

"Did ya pound that thing?" asked Louie when he returned.

I grinned and tried to look loose. I stared at the ceiling beams up above. Kova popped over. "Nice design, huh?" he said.

"Really cool," I said, thinking of Pat's Dad and how he could have been the one that built it.

"Look, about today. You screwed up on that 6th hole, but you know what? I'll let it slide. I won't tell Merv. I mean, normally I would. I'm a stickler. This game is my life, and it's not just a game. It's a negotiation table. A four hour long mental massage. You'll understand someday. You play. You talk. You build relationships out here."

A car pulled up outside. "Your Mommy's here," Kova barked.

Wolf walked over to us and gave us both the middle finger before walking out, a large wad of tobacco lodged into one cheek.

Kova slapped a hand firmly on a beam. He walked over to the screen door. "You get in that car and no dinner tonight. No fancy meal! No Bookbinders or DiNardos."

The other two guys in the group quieted. Louie sipped his drink. I crushed my beer can and tossed it in the trash. I looked out the window and saw the orange backboard of the playground in the distance.

"Y'all want another hot dog?" asked the counter lady, coming out of the basement.

"No, I'm good," I said. "I'm gonna head home."

"You're leaving?" asked Kova. "Back in my day, if a gentleman offers a drink you relax, play a round of pinochle or paskahousu. You don't have to leave. Where are you headed? We're far from the parking lot."

"I parked near the 15th hole," I lied. "And cut through someone's yard to get to the course today. Barely made it in on time."

"What? Why would you do that?"

"Car issues. Engine light came. Some weird noise. It's not even my car. It's my Mom's."

"So, you live in Oreland?"

"Erdenheim. Anyway, I'm drenched already. It's not stopping. Buh-Buh-Buh-Buh—"

"Cat got your tongue there?" Kova squatted down and stroked his chin while gazing at my stutters.

"Buh-Buh-Bye bye."

I waved and jogged home. As I crossed the 12th and 15th holes, a voice screamed out. I turned and saw Kova running full speed towards me. Instant paranoia swept through me. I ran as fast as I could towards the slitted fence exit, but the fishing hook injury made it difficult to stay ahead.

Kova's breath heaved close behind. "Your money!" he said.

I stopped and put my hands on my knees to catch my breath. I looked up. He held out a fist. I opened a hand. He put in a few crumpled bills.

"This is from me and the guys in the cart. Your payment for ten holes." Kova closed my fingers together to protect the cash from the rain. "Why are you running?"

"You looked mad. The 6th hole thing. The beer maybe. I just don't feel guh-guh-guh-good."

Kova held my clenched fist with the money and put his other hand on top. "It's you, isn't it?"

"What do you mean?"

"Christmas night. 1985. You were there, snooping."

"I'm not sure what you're—"

"You live beyond these woods."

"No. Erdenheim, off Bethlehem Pike."

"You've done good so far." Kova rubbed his thumbs over my knuckles. His slow buttery words reeked of booze. "Just keep staying mum. It makes no sense what you saw. Little chap like you should've been snug in bed. But the moonlight lured you out. Right? The freedom of the still night. I know how it is."

"You're confusing me with some other dude that—"

"Me and you. We're both out there together. Should've been home. You'll be driven mad someday. It was a mutual fight, me and that lady. Damn husband had to get involved."

"Seriously," I said, yanking my hands back. "I don't know what any of this is about."

"Well, maybe. You better drive back home to Erdenheim then, right? Driving at 14-years-old. Isn't that illegal?"

"Yeah, it's just to work. Sometimes."

Kova's drenched clothes clung to his plump frame. I put the cash in my pocket and walked backwards several steps, pissed that I had told him my real age and botched by tale. Kova stayed in place, waving me off. I jogged to the dirt trail and made it through the fence. I moved to the basketball court where crab apples were scattered. I peered through the fence and saw Kova standing in the rain, watching me. A large bare tree branch hovered high above him, swaying like an elephant trunk. I imagined it falling and crushing him. I wished it so, focusing on the action in my mind. I waved at him and approached the few cars parked by the courts. Kova waved back. I grabbed my keys and fumbled with them, dropping them on purpose. Kova stayed put. I picked the least expensive looking car and went to the driver side door. I took my t-shirt off and wrung it to buy more time, as if I didn't want to get the seat soaked. I looked up again. Kova was gone, but I didn't see him heading down the fairway and back to the Halfway House. I hightailed home.

Inside my house, I peered through the door keyhole, between

the blinds and through slits on the curtains, dripping all over the house. Nobody was home. I locked the doors and windows. I pulled the squashed damp bills from my pocket and unfolded them on the carpet. Opposed to the typical three $20 bills, there were five Ben Franklins staring at me.

37.

Facemask

November '88

With my high school being several towns away, I had to take the bus. I was glad to no longer cut through Shady Creek to get to school and trudge through the elements. While the bus stop was a social delight for most, I enjoyed my continuing fading presence and hid on the outskirts of the bus stop with my headphones on and expanding long hair. Once on the bus, I sat with the marching band kids. Now that my grade was diluted with three other older classes in an even bigger building, I drifted from Algebra to World History to Study Hall, untethered by previous bullies. The Gold Chainers were preoccupied with status, extracurricular activities and the blossoming beauties. An occasional hockey check against the lockers occurred if I was alone and face to face with a bully. But it was almost like it didn't count if just a handful saw it.

Soon after figuring out the school layout without the need of the provided map, my first zits blossomed. The year prior, Siobhan suffered from occasional zits. I poked fun at her while she cried in the bathroom as Mom applied hot wash cloths to her face. It seemed like something solely divvied out to girls, due to overuse of cosmetics.

But no. Dime sized cysts and pimples formed on my forehead

and chin overnight, leaving me to scramble for pricey tubes of Benzoyl Peroxide based creams. Some of these brands offered "skin tone" ointments ideal for the average white dude. These pastes acted as medicine and cover-up. But I was so pale and Irish-white that these foundations looked like dark orange blotches on my face.

Each day, I awoke and stared at my face in the mirror while holding a stainless steel dental tartar scraper, pondering what to pop and release. Along with a sewing needle and sharp thumbtack, I found these tools to be ideal pimple poppers. Not all zits were worthy of popping. It was a game of what was better off being left alone. A gigantic whitehead seemed worthy of lancing, but would cause what looked like a gunshot wound hours later.

I had a whole routine down. If a whitehead had formed, or even a trace of one, I'd pop it and squeeze the infected area until my two pressured fingers were shaking. As long as I released pus and blood, I felt like I accomplished something. The next day, it would be a scab, but I'd cover it up with foundation cream and hope no one really knew what I looked like. Gym class was like ice held to a burning candle with whatever was on my face, revealing what was truly there, melting any chance of maintaining a mask.

If it wasn't for zits, I would have attempted to ask girls out to standard social offerings, like the Coronation Ball. But the zits were radiant manifestations of the loser status I felt entrapped in, aiding me in giving up all hope for normality. Oozing pus in the classroom's corner, I rarely raised my hand to draw attention to myself.

Popular high school students sprouted random zits, but they were freakish events and odd accessories that vanished quickly.

Some zits were more tolerable, like the ones on the scalp hidden within the hairline. The worst were dead center ones: on the tip of the nose (The Rudolph), the philtrum above the upper lip (The Chaplin) and in the forehead's middle (The Hindu).

The gritty caddying experience was not ideal for pores either, combined with the stress of Kova paying me to be quiet. Merv assigned me to caddie for Kova twice more since he had figured me out. Each time, he hardly said a word and presented me the same outlandish $500.00 tip. "Nice job, Gary," he'd say. I kept his cash in an envelope in an encyclopedia, afraid to spend it.

The Kova qualm was likely the culprit of my zits, combined with genetics, my age and sudden tense eating habits. Gobbling down three packs of Tastykakes in one session after school was common.

On one of my last Saturday loops of the season, I cut through the course in the early morning and saw Quinn sleeping upright on a bench with a girl in his lap, surrounded by beer cans. I snapped my caddie towel at the air as I walked, making loud cracking noises. I startled Quinn. He perked up, saw me and put his hand on the girl's hair, petting her like a cat. I didn't say hello.

The only lawn mowing client that I kept was Dutch. I felt bad for the guy, as if he relied on reciting local news babble to a teenager to survive. I walked by Quinn's house to get there. It was out of the way, but I was eager to see if Sasha was on the porch. On the last mow of November, I saw her sitting on the Cape Cod porch chairs with her legs folded up towards her body, her arms around her shins. She rocked back and forth in an oversized sweatsuit. "Jackpot," I thought.

"Hey, you. Where've you been?" Sasha asked.

I felt like I suddenly had a megaphone to all of Quinn's family. "Just busy," I shrugged.

"Did you and Quinn break up or something?"

"Nah. Just busy."

"Don't worry. Nobody's here. I got locked out after stepping out to talk to some Jehovah's Witness. Luckily, my mom had this in the garage," she said, bunching up the bulging sweatshirt fabric with her hands. "Hot look, right?"

"Looks cozy." I walked a few steps onto her lawn.

"Ah, don't get too close," she said, covering her face with her hands. "I'm hideous. Was in the middle of giving myself a facial. I'm like a slug."

"I'm struggling with this," I said with a nervous laugh, framing my zit laden face.

"It's not too bad. I've been there. You need a hobby, a stress reliever. Do you have one?"

"Video games."

"That's not what I mean. Something fulfilling, physically. Karate, sculpting, dance. Doing something meaningful with your hands opposed to just jerking off a joystick."

I laughed. "Yeah, I'm good with the control pads."

"All right, dork. You better go mow your lawn. I'll tell Quinn you said hello."

"We're not talking right now. Long story."

"Do you want a hug?" Sasha stood up and jumped off the chair. She held out her arms. The long sleeves hung off her hands.

"On the first day of school, he—"

"Jesus, I don't care. Do you want a special invitation? Get over here."

Confused, I walked off with a wave. "Gotta run."

Over my shoulder, Sasha crammed herself back into her Jack in the Box pose. I thought of the smell of her house, a steady mix of fabric softener sheets and Chef Boyardee.

38.

Soundtrack

March '89
Technically, the first album I ever owned was *No Jacket Required* by Phil Collins on cassette. I requested it for Christmas in '86. He was exploding on MTV with music videos and I felt it was a good safe entrance into music ownership. Although he was a balding guy that wore blazers and sang divorce themed lyrics, he seemed like a loner that I could relate to. Maybe it was because his face was always floating alone, deep in thought, on his album covers.

Although Siobhan had albums of music going back to the early 80s, I had never purchased cassette tapes or vinyl records. I listened to whatever was on Eagle 106.1 or whatever Siobhan was cranking, which was a lot of Bon Jovi. I took a chance with the Columbia House Record and Tape Club and got *any 12 cassette tapes for a penny*. I played it safe with family friendly albums like Billy Joel's *Greatest Hits Volume I & Volume II*, listening with my headphones in bed until I fell asleep.

A few caddies were heavy into music and touted bands I had to invest in. Most were 70s albums from Pink Floyd, Neil Young, Yes and Led Zeppelin. I soon went to the Wall To Wall Sound and Video Superstore in the Willow Grove Mall. The rows of alphabetized bands and groups was overwhelming. I went straight to "P" and found Pink Floyd's *The Wall*.

Upon first listen, Pink Floyd struck a chord with me. The anger and frustration of *The Wall*, lyrics aside, was a raw and welcome tonality I already was on the level with. From the sheer intensity of the opening progression of "In The Flesh?" to the delicate piano tinkering of "Nobody Home", the album felt like a parallel struggle of the human condition that I was immersed in. The isolationism in the lyrics, although I barely understood them, was almost a celebration. The songs brought tears, goosebumps and left me holding the accordion-folded lyrics with the jitters. The saccharine pop hits of the day were not for me. I soon bought every Pink Floyd album, slowly but surely. Although each album was very different, there was a dark frolic of freakdom to them that stepped outside the realm of typical good-time ditties. In school, I drew the characters from *The Wall* onto my paper bag textbook covers, tattooing the bags that once held groceries.

Dad tested my motives by setting up a ladder outside of my window. He climbed up it and shined flashlights around. Hours later, I asked what he was doing. I figured he was trying to eradicate a wasp nest.

"Oh, I wasn't out on the ladder today," said Dad.

"What?" I laughed. "I saw you. You were tapping your fingers on my window."

"Wasn't me. Are you experimenting with the wacky weedy?"

"Did Mom make you do this? I don't even like beer."

"Whatever it is you're listening to. It's all due to Elvis. He paved the way."

"OK, thanks. Trust me. I'm not doped up."

Although I wore headphones on the bus rides, I was now an active member of the music community and wanted to showcase the progressive bands I respected by wearing t-shirts. The Willow Grove Mall became my home base for new threads. My psychedelic King Crimson shirt clashed with Siobhan's Whitesnake patches on her jean jacket.

I kept an empty cassette in my stereo with both the pause and record buttons pressed down. Through continual recommendations from the caddies, I blasted classic rock from 93.3 WMMR. If the first few seconds sounded enticing, I deselected the pause button to record the gem.

With my bedroom door shut and music cranked up, I drowned out Siobhan's stereo and Dad's AM news radio. I knew everyone in the house heard my songs. Although I still tapped plastic Sega Master System buttons, I did it with the TV muted and a morphing soundscape of heady sexual desire and bluesy rage that rattled the floorboards. The soundtracks and sound effects of video games no longer mattered.

To alert me of dinners, Dad banged his fist three times on the stairwell wall that connected to my room. As long as I was clutching silverware in thirty seconds, my parents were fine. It was as if I deserved to make a racket after many seasons of withering on a floor of wires and instruction manuals, striving to get to the next level.

39.

Stalling

May '89

I preferred the solace of the Township Library, as soon as it opened, for weekend research. The school library was an option, but I didn't want to run into bullies that might sucker punch me in the dim-lit aisles.

One Saturday, while studying in a second-floor workstation, I had the urge to use the Men's Room. Two granola bars, a banana and cinnamon toast for breakfast wasn't a good idea. While sitting in a stall, someone entered the room. "Now hurry and don't lollygag," a man said. "I'll meet you down the hall."

Someone scurried into a stall two down from mine. I heard poops plop into the water and a sloppy wrangling with thin toilet paper. Although I finished, I sat and waited for the rushed guy to leave. I heard something flick open, followed by a scraping metal-on-metal noise spinning around on the guy's wobbly stall door. The guy grunted and swirled what I figured was a tornado pattern. It continued for several seconds, shaking the connected framework of the stalls, rattling my door. My twist lock vibrated and turned toward the open position. I grabbed it with two fingers and locked it. The scraping ceased. A scrawling then occurred on the door. I pictured a penknife or a switchblade. I glanced at the goofy etchings in my stall. Band names. Girl names. Wanna have a good time? Meet me here at 7pm on Saturdays. Swastikas. Crucifixes. Scribbles. Phone numbers. Individuals called out as assholes.

Suddenly, the guy ran out and exited without washing his hands.

I got out and opened the decorated stall door. The tornado drawing was there with "Stop Mr. Kova" written at the top. I ran out of the bathroom. At the end of a long hall, a boy with longish blond hair walked down the curved stairs, holding one hand onto the railing. His hair bobbed like hay bale processing, revealing fragments of a face that looked familiar.

"Kristoph!" I shouted through a cupped hand.

The boy stopped and stared up at me as I leaned on the balcony railing. I jogged over to him. "It's me. It's Garvey. Remember me?" I asked. "Were you just in the Men's Room? I read it. What did he do to you?"

Kristoph looked at his feet and clenched his hands. "You get what you get and you don't get upset," he said.

"What are you getting? What has he done to you?"

"You get what you get and you don't get upset."

"Does your Dad know? Nevermind. Come with me. I can get you help," I said, looking through the window at the rows of police cars lined up at the Township Department next door.

"There you are," said a voice up from the balcony.

I looked up and saw Kristoph's Dad pointing at us.

"I told you to stay right outside the door." Kristoph's Dad kept his hand on the railing and walked toward the stairs. "Just where do you think you're going? We have your session in a few minutes."

"I used to live down the street from you. On Redford Road," I whispered into Kristoph's ear. He stood upright and faced me. His eyes grew wide. I tugged on my shirt in the same manner that he did when he followed me around my yard.

"Time to go now, bud," his Dad said, placing his hands on Kristoph's shoulders.

Kristoph screamed and ran past me toward the white glow of the exit doors in the distance. His Dad chased him down the stairs, tackling him at the bottom. Librarians with carts of books moved in, uncertain what to do. I looked through the large oval decorative window. Cops joked around and got into their squad cars, ready to start their days. I wanted to run over to them and bring them to Kristoph, thinking he might open a spiral of evidence against Kova. Proof was locked in the damaged psyche of Kristoph's mind and my own, both of us dealing with the demon in the yellow car, confined by threats.

40.

Korean Cowboy

April '90

I had a crush on my 10th grade Spanish II substitute teacher. She was tall, slender with brown hair and wore tight fitted suits with white pantyhose. She was our teacher for a couple months while our original teacher recovered from surgery.

The chance of dialogue with the sub incentivized me to study more than usual. I wanted to know the answers and raise my hand. I created an index card system of memorizing words and phrases. I studied them until the minute before a quiz and then zipped them away in my bookbag. One day, I accidentally placed the cards in a sloppy pile on top of my bag. The sub came over, grabbed my test and ripped it in half.

"Automatic F," she said. "Get those cards out of my sight."

I looked down and couldn't muster a sound.

After class, I approached the teacher.

"You've been doing so well," she said. "Did you really need those cards?"

"Please, can I retake the test? A different version?" I asked. "I totally forgot to put them in my bag."

"It's too late, Garvey. It's just one quiz. You can bounce back."

I looked behind me and saw a guy in my class, Jinwoo, wading back and forth by the door. Jinwoo was a muscular Korean guy with spiked hair and a popped collar. He was a gum chewer, lathered in Drakkar Noir cologne. He didn't sit with other Koreans at lunch, bouncing around tables, seemingly wanting to be solo. He walked with ease, flexing his chest, able to hold his own from a Gold Chainer attack.

"Aw, come on. He wasn't cheating," said Jinwoo. "He always has those cards."

"This matter is not in your court to decide, now is it?" asked the sub.

I turned red in the face. "It's fine."

Jinwoo and I walked off slowly down the hall to our study hall class. We talked about how cute the sub was which segued into how Jewish girls are the hottest and have the best asses because they wear Guess jeans to shape their cheeks to perfection. In the library, we hunkered down at two study desks and talked with textbooks open. Jinwoo asked if I wanted to hang out later that night, as it was Friday. I was game.

"It's Spring, man. Chicks are everywhere," said Jinwoo. "Even the ones from other schools."

Typically, I watched *Perfect Strangers* alone in my bedroom on Friday nights. I was thrilled to leave Balki Bartokomous and Cousin Larry in the dark.

Jinwoo showed up in my driveway with a black '88 Lincoln Town Car Signature Series, a beast ride gifted from his Dad. He blared the love ballad "Nothing Compares 2 U" by Sinéad O'Connor. My parents peered through the screen door as I jumped in the car.

"Stay warm," shouted Dad.

"Why's your Dad want you to stay warm?" asked Jinwoo. "It's like 80 degrees."

I shook my head and flicked a hand at the air, just wanting to feel the car go in reverse and move far from my tree house of a bedroom. "Just go," I said.

We arrived at the Montgomery Mall parking lot. When Jinwoo

found a spot that satisfied him, he eased the car in and crashed into a parked car on the right.

"Do you see anyone?" Jinwoo asked.

"What? Where?"

"Anywhere."

As Jinwoo backed out, I saw the large gash that the jagged decorative front panel of the Town Car had caused. Jinwoo maneuvered out of the lot and back onto Route 309 toward Fort Washington and then towards Dresher. I got a tour of Upper Dublin Township. "Let's get some Wendy's Superbar," he insisted.

After tacos and vanilla pudding, we sized up the Town Car one more time and couldn't find one scratch on it. It sliced through the mall car like a can opener.

Cruising through Ambler in a carb coma, Jinwoo made a sudden left into a long dirt driveway next to a traffic light. Tall arborvitaes stood along the sides, all leading to a house.

Instead of watching *Perfect Strangers* in my room, I watched it in Jinwoo's large family room. His Aunt sat and sewed calmly in between angry Korean bursts with Jinwoo. A couple rice cookers were in the room.

Jinwoo's Dad showed up with a white tank top and sweaty brow. He sold produce in Philly and had a long shutdown procedure and drive back. He looked at me with disgust and barked something at Jinwoo while pointing at a back room. They bickered, slapping magazines around. Jinwoo emerged and rushed toward me. "You need to take your sneakers off, Garv. Put them by the door."

"Why?" I asked.

"Well, I don't know *why*. This is just a stupid tradition."

"Oh, it's OK. I can do it."

"No. It's dumb. Nobody else does this."

"It's cool."

"Let's get out of here."

After a quick wrestling match with his younger brother and

watching Jinwoo do a set of curls, we were back on the road. "Time to find some girls," I thought.

Jinwoo drove around Maple Glen, explaining Korean traditions and how his Dad was a tight ass. We ogled new McMansions, salivating over their sizes. Moments later, a cop pulled up behind us with some beeps and lights. "Shit," Jinwoo whispered. "Mall cops must've taken my plate number."

"I've been following you for a few blocks," the cop said. "Can't find the party, huh?"

"Party? What do you mean?" asked Jinwoo.

"Don't play stupid. We know there's a kegger. Random cars are parked crooked all over. What side yard is the cut-through?"

"Uh, we're just hanging out."

"In a luxury housing community?"

"Yeah. We had Wendy's earlier." Jinwoo showed the crumpled empty bag.

The cop aimed his flashlight at me. "Yep," I muttered. "Just admiring the houses. Nothing like this in Oreland."

"All right, fellas," the cop said, banging the hood with his hand. "You should join Town Watch. Make better use of your time. Help us find hooligans." He handed Jinwoo a flier.

Onward, Jinwoo cruised as I took mental notes of the neighborhoods, leaning my head out into the cool air. Dance music cranked as we blurted out the names of hot girls, back and forth, nodding appreciatively. Jinwoo stated a name I wasn't on board with and he tried to convince me otherwise.

The high beams shown upon two guys sucking down large sodas with straws, walking on a road with no shoulder.

"Get out of the road, you doofuses," Jinwoo barked at them, slowing down beside them.

It was two guys from our grade, Blue and Rusty.

"What're you doing walking around in the dark?" asked Jinwoo.

"Getting some air," said Rusty, brushing his blond hair from his eyebrows. "Was playing some *Might And Magic*. You steal this car from an old folks' home?"

"Whatever. You got a better car?"

"Donger need food?" Rusty quipped, quoting *Sixteen Candles*.

"Get in the back, fellas."

Blue laughed, stuck in a coughing fit. He took long drags of his Marlboro Reds and exhaled praise about specific bands, junk food and shows. "Oh, you've gotta try it," tail-ended his many comments. Blue was short, chubby with a mullet and a steady rotating black t-shirt collection of heavy metal bands. He recited obscure *Star Wars* film quotes at random.

Rusty was lanky, about 6'5" tall. He bragged about how he excelled in math and sciences without having to study, allowing more time for arduous role-playing games. He preferred to play the games while cranking raunchy west coast rap.

We spoke with ease, all ganging up on Jinwoo's choice of pop bliss and sappy ballads. Jinwoo responded by increasing the volume, serenading jogging mothers at red lights.

Blue's chain smoking, combined with the scent of honeysuckles and new mown grass, served as ceremonial incense of our aimless mission.

We ended up at Dairy Queen in Glenside where we mouthed down soft serve twirls and pumped quarters into *Tetris*. The fluorescent lights glared from above as we sat across from each other at a booth. Every pore, scar and trait of poor hygiene was on display. I regretted getting a cone and tried to lick the melting mint chocolate chip in the coolest manner possible. A stream of garrulous middle school girls poured into the store in pink and lavender hoodies. They didn't size up one inch of us.

Out the window, we noted a guy making out with a girl in an adjacent vacant parking lot. The couple, entwined, leaned against a red Mazda Miata. A beer can sat on the hood. Moths circled an exterior light above them. We observed the guy's exploratory hands, our eyes pivoting towards him in one second blips, magnetized by a crazed desire. Nobody said a word. The dirtiest Led Zeppelin lyrics came to life before us, a welcome tutorial.

The couple shifted, stumbling in their interlocked sway. The light revealed the guy to be Wolf.

"Oh, fuck that guy," said Jinwoo.

We mouthed obscenities, a fierce equal disdain for Wolf. We stewed in the drab high caloric achievement of the night as personal stories of strife unfolded, all of us dissed by Wolf at some point. A swift bond sealed between us, a comforting, as brainstormed tactics of revenge seeped out and molded our foundation.

41.

Payback Payment

May '90

Jinwoo was proud to drive us around in his Lincoln Town Car, which we nicknamed The Tank. Rusty, Blue and I had permits but no license to drive yet. It delighted us to offer gas money to roam the night. We dealt with Jinwoo's affinity for romantic power ballads.

After dinner with our parents, Jinwoo swung by our homes in The Tank. We'd get a second dinner at the likes of Taco Bell, the Willow Grove Mall Food Court or Old Country Buffet.

In the school cafeteria, we ate together and hung in the courtyard. I felt safe with them and we talked down the Gold Chainers with ease.

Quinn was around but we never talked to each other. We'd see each other in the hallway or piss in urinals next to each other, only to nod after a brief connection of eyes.

Cruising in The Tank, Jinwoo pointed out he owed Wolfgang $15.00 due to a Phillies game bet he made with him during Biology. "He's at his Mom's apartment in Ambler. I think he splits up his weeks with her. I need to drop off his cash."

"Can we stop at my house first?" I asked. "I've got an idea."

In my room, I had multiple shoe boxes of coins, a couple

hundred bucks worth. I emptied fifteen one dollar rolls of pennies into another shoe box.

"I like it," said Jinwoo, hitting up Wolf's pager with my house phone. Wolf phoned. We were on our way to deliver the loot.

A cocktail of *Saturday Night Live* and borrowed booming Metallica cassettes from Blue instilled a defiance. It swept through my soul and bloodstream, boosting me with gusto.

Jinwoo and I pulled into the apartment community and found Wolf sitting in his red Mazda Miata convertible with the top down, thumbing on his Nintendo Game Boy. We sat in The Tank. I waved Wolf over. He hopped out of his car. "What's up, caddie?" asked Wolf. "Figure out how to golf yet?"

I presented Wolf with the lidded shoe box and stared in envy at his red sporty car. Thoughts of my Dad's old red AMC Spirit flooded my mind.

"Not quite, but I'm still learning," I said. "Maybe one day I'll be as perfect as you."

"What did you say? And what the hell is in this box?"

"It's your fifteen bucks that Jinwoo owed you."

Wolf shook the box. "Coins?"

"Maybe. I forget what we put in there."

Ripping off the rubber band, Wolf scowled at me. "There better be cash." He flung the lid onto the ground and fumbled with the box. "Pennies? I want cash yo."

"It's legal tender!" I yelled out the window as Jinwoo floored it.

In the side-view mirror, I saw Wolf heave the box toward us. An arch of glistening copper sparkled in the sun, only to plummet onto the parking lot and spread down the sloped asphalt.

Jinwoo stopped the car. We got out and looked back and saw Wolf amid the russet mess beneath his feet, his middle finger jabbing towards us with futile stabs.

42.

Love-Love

June '90
 While talking with Jinwoo at his locker, Wolf approached us with a trash bag.

"I want cash," said Wolf. "Here's your coin collection back." He dropped the bag on Jinwoo's sneakers. The pennies plopped with a quick clang and a foul stench. Wolf talked to a girl named Steffi who tapped him on the shoulder.

Jinwoo opened the bag. We peeked in. The pennies were slimy and mixed with pungent garbage. Jinwoo sealed the bag and looked over at Wolf, listening intently to the blossoming couple's tennis date plans.

After school, we ambled about a store in the mall called Spencer's that sold gag gifts and smutty fun. As I rotated through the framed poster collection of slutty looking models, Jinwoo bought something at the checkout. I walked over to him. "Wolf is playing tennis with Steffi tonight at 7," he said. "High school courts. This will help his game, right?"

Back in The Tank, we opened the new device of retaliation: a gigantic three-person slingshot. We headed to a party store and got special rugged water balloons. We then picked up Rusty and swung over to Blue's house to fill them up in his backyard.

"Blue, do you have any cologne you don't like?" asked Jinwoo.

"God, yes," said Blue. "I have some unopened ones sitting in a box from my Bar Mitzvah."

"Bring 'em on down. Gotta spruce up these babies."

I hoped we'd come to our senses and realize that the plan was brash. Having seen Kova scold Wolf in public at Shady Creek, I empathized with Wolf a bit. I imagined that his personal time with Kova led to punched drywall and the taste of blood in his throat.

It was almost time for the attack. I microwaved a Hot Pocket with Blue. Jinwoo was on the back deck trying to piss into a balloon.

"This is all too crazy, right?" I softly asked Blue.

Blue was in a wide-eyed state of bliss. "Wait a second. I have red food coloring dye," he said, undaunted by my question.

Shortly before 9pm, we pulled into the vacant main parking lot of the school. The tennis players parked at a separate lot near the courts which were lit up with towering bright lights. Rusty and I got out and grabbed separate ends of the launcher while Jinwoo brought out the bag of balloons. He put one on the launch pad and carefully leaned back with it until his ass was on the ground. Blue eyed up the trajectory. The new rubber smell lingered as we tested the tension. Jinwoo let go. The balloon propelled into the dark night sky, only to land outside of the court gates and into some bushes, about 30 feet off. Nobody noticed the sound or spotted us.

After a few more attempts, a balloon finally entered the court and exploded near Wolf's feet, splashing water on his socks and calves. He stopped and looked around. He cupped his eyes to see through the beaming court lights.

"Even easier now," Jinwoo said with confidence as Wolf stood still. "Time for red dye."

The next one slapped Wolf on the left cheek. It looked like a wobbly gelatin mould exploded on his face. His date ditched him and ran off the court. Wolfgang threw his racquet at the fence.

We jumped into The Tank and headed to Blue's back deck to revel in the victory. Blue offered us Miller Lite bottles as we recapped the story, imitating Wolf's reaction. I held the beer but drank none. I dumped ounces into the kitchen sink when nobody was looking and pretended to loosen up.

The new crew brought me out of a degenerative funk. I had grown accustomed to never leaving my house, accepting my craven role in high school's stage. But now our oppressors were dangling from tightropes themselves and just needed a shove. Sure, the crew and I ripped into each other and busted balls but it was not with the vile permanent smear of our oppressors.

43.

Returns & Exchanges

June '90

Rusty and I yearned to play Sega Master System role-playing games. Opposed to buying each game at $50 a pop, we bought one, completed the game, returned it for another and continued the cycle. We did this without having a receipt or the proper packaging. Rusty's knack for conning the clerks with tall tales produced steady results.

A typical scenario:

"I want to exchange this *Miracle Warriors* game," said Rusty as I stood beside him at Electronics Boutique. "I got it for my cousin. He opened it, even though he already owns it. Got confused. He banged his head on the monkey bars earlier that day."

"We don't allow for returns unless it's unopened," said the clerk. "And you need a receipt."

"That's the thing. The gift receipt got lost in the wrapping paper. His uncle kept grabbing the paper and tossed it the garbage. He's a clean freak."

Rusty leaned on the counter and detailed the con job further while I nibbled on my bottom gums, trying to maintain composure, pacing on the floor and trying to appear downcast. "Right, Bruce?" Rusty asked me.

"Yep. It's all a shame," I said. "We know which one he wants though."

"OK. Well, pick a game then," the clerk said, pointing to the wall of games. "I'll get you a receipt for the new one."

If I couldn't maintain composure, I stormed out and watched from a bench outside the store, panicking as mall security guards approached. For the price of one game, we temporarily owned, played and mastered ten games. Although rentals became available at West Coast Video, the high of the swindle was downright fun, and the "Made In China" cartridge smell was more superior.

After a successful exchange, we often headed back to Rusty's house with a victory bag of 7-11 junk food. His Dad knew of our efforts, roaming outside and wearing his gardening garb: an old The Cure t-shirt from a thrift store. "You guys scored again, huh?" he'd mutter, wiping soil on Robert Smith's pale face on his chest.

"Of course," said Rusty.

"Well, that's their own damn fault."

Enthralled in video games, I felt a certain peace and ease, transfixed in the progressing unveiled levels and storyline. No matter how ridiculous the premise, the games allowed me to mentally check out.

Sometimes we took the new game to Blue's house. He lived with his single step-mom, Shelle, who was seldom home. She was an ultrasound tech at a hospital and worked late shifts. A couple years prior, Shelle came home early from a work conference to find her husband in the hot tub with Blue's old babysitter. Blue was sleeping. Breaking vases and screams jolted Blue out of bed. He walked out of his bedroom to see a drenched naked girl struggle down the carpeted steps.

Blue's home was ultra modern, sterile, cleaned by a Mexican maid that said nothing. A black grand piano stood in the living room, never played. The family room had a large screen TV, hooked up to 3' tall Bose speakers, and a red leather sectional that could seat a dozen people. It was a video game and movie viewing heaven. Blue had his favorite corner spot with an armrest. The sectional surrounded a thick square glass coffee table with mirrored borders. Architectural photo books sat visible beneath the glass. The table looked like a movie prop from a 70s cocaine scene but we used it for spreading out dipping sauces for Chicken McNuggets. Fading photos of Shelle and her husband, clad in bell bottoms, hung on the wall.

If Shelle was home, she'd enter the family room and have constrained arguments with Blue, a glass of wine in hand. Blue never aimed his face toward her, let alone look into her eyes. She paced like a llama over us. "Get your feet off the coffee table, Blue. Do you see Rusty and Garvey doing that? No, they're good young men. They're not scarfing food down their mouths all day."

"Yes, they do," said Blue. "They eat just like I do."

Once the bickering began, Rusty and I paused the game and headed to the back deck. Blue would try to outshine her progressing bitch status, clutching his mullet. If it got bad, Blue turned off the game, ejected the cartridge and handed it to us. Rusty and I would take the game to one of our dingy bedrooms to continue play on inferior TVs.

#

Knocking on Blue's door with a new game in hand, Shelle answered the door. "My two favorite guys. Come on in. I'll fix ya a snack."

"Is Blue here?" I asked, stepping in.

"Yep. I got him a personal trainer. They're finishing up in the basement. He needs to lose twenty pounds. At least."

We entered the kitchen. Shelle leaned on a blender full of greens and tapped an orange button. The machine pulverized the ice cubes and veggies into a smoothie. "Don't worry," said Shelle. "This is for Blue. Have a seat. I've got to tell you something."

We sat down at the small round table.

"I found a beer bottle in Blue's room. Half drunken. And that's fine. I get it. I was in high school before. But if you're gonna party in this house, you're gonna party with *me*." Shelle bent into the fridge, swaying her booty, rooting around plastic bags of vegetables.

Rusty and I looked at each other. "Not bad," Rusty whispered, shaking a flattened hand.

"Here we are," said Shelle, pulling out three bottles of beer. "Nobody's going anywhere. No DUIs. Just a beer, right? You guys deserve this."

"What did we do?" I asked.

"Exactly. Nothing," she said, twisting off the caps. "You're both perfect specimens. Thin, in shape. Smart. Although, Garvey, no offense, but you're hair is getting meshuga."

I rolled my eyes. "When's Blue coming up?"

"He's got another twenty-five minutes down there at least."

Blue grunted from the basement.

"That was him," said Shelle. "I'll put the MTV on." Shelle fiddled with a micro TV.

"Thanks for the beer," said Rusty. "Very cool of you."

"No problem boys. And your parents. God bless them. They're still together. Divorce is rough. Do you know where I go on Friday nights?"

"Dance clubs?" I asked, yet to take a swig of beer.

"Fucking divorce support groups. Yep. I sit in a circle with a bunch of women, all different ages. At least I'm making friends. One of them lives nearby. Her boy is your age." Shelle seemed buzzed, slurring her words. Her chunky bracelets and necklaces rattled on the table. Her opal earrings wobbled. "Wolfgang. That's his name. His mom calls him Wolfie. Know him? Cute kid. Nasty chewing tobacco habit. Maybe you guys can help him? Add him to your posse?"

I closed my eyes and stroked my brows with rigid presses. I went to the powder room and dumped half of the beer down the drain. When I got out, Shelle was slobbering beer from laughter. She slapped Rusty's thigh and leaned toward him to deliver a secret through cupped hands. Her knee banged on a table leg and her bottle fell. Rusty grabbed it, diverting a spill. He held his hands over the mouth of the bottle as it foamed out through his fingers.

Blue entered the kitchen in a baggy gray sweatsuit and headband, sweat seeping out of his face. "Jesus Christ, Mom!" cried Blue. He panned his eyes from Rusty to me as I stood in the powder room doorway. "Screw this. I'm fat. This is who I am."

Rusty pounded his beer. I went to the sink and dumped the rest of mine out.

"See," said Shelle. "I am a cool mom. I can hang with the guys."

I got paper towels to clean up the spill. I leaned into Shelle's ear. "Wolf is no friend of ours."

44.

Prank Chorus

J uly '90
My parents let me use their video camera to record goofy improvised skits. Even after I accidentally recorded over vacation footage of Dad climbing the Aztec pyramids, they were cool with it. This mishap led me to label tapes with utmost accuracy.

I directed and recorded semi-scripted *Saturday Night Live* influenced skits, creating scripts and plots on the spot, maneuvering my crew into gangster or bizarre goblin roles. I purchased an audio mixer from Radio Shack and added post production music and narration.

Sometimes a unique location spurred a scene, like the Oreland quarry or a mansion that served as a backdrop for mobster renditions. I brought the camera wherever I went, batteries fully charged, ready to capture.

At the Twining Deli, we pretended to be a local news team and interviewed the Russian owner about whether the hoagie rolls were truly "delivered fresh daily", as the sign read. We stated a rumor had surfaced of their bakery deliveries occurring infrequently.

"Oh, no," the deli owner objected, pointing to the camera lens. "Five o'clock in the morning. All fresh, all the time, every day!"

Jinwoo grew fatigued from my directives. "Enough of this, Garv," he said, putting his hand on the lens. "It's getting cheesy."

"Whatever, dude," I said. "You're the one that likes Milli Vanilli."

Jinwoo smiled and clutched my cranium, pretending to crush my skull. "I know of a place where we can make money *and* meet chicas."

Rusty, Blue and I hopped into The Tank. Jinwoo drove us to one of the many summer carnivals. We were too old for the rides, games and cotton candy, but this one had casino style table games and dancing. Jinwoo and Rusty scrambled together a sack of quarters, hoping to win big.

Upon entering, we learned that we had to be 18-years-old to take part in the gambling arena. Jinwoo looked the oldest with his patchy mustache and muscular build, so we let him approach the most susceptible looking dealer. I grew bored and eyed the girls gyrating on a portable dance floor to a rockabilly band.

After a failure to understand craps and bad luck at roulette and blackjack, Jinwoo lost all of the money. We walked out to the grassy field, used as a makeshift parking lot. As we got into The Tank, Jinwoo noticed a couple dollar bills crumpled up under a cassette in a car with all of the windows down.

"Guys, look. What an idiot. Why would you leave that exposed?" Jinwoo asked.

"Don't know. Nobody around if you want it," said Rusty.

The guys looked around for anyone approaching. I scanned around in horror, hoping to find a cop lingering that would fizzle out the notion of theft. I thought of how I had broken into Conner's house, stolen porno mags and eventually threw him under the bus. I wondered why certain wrongdoings made me want to evaporate, while others, like crank calls, brought righteous delight.

Jinwoo snagged the cash with deft hands and stuffed it into his pocket. Opposed to getting in his car, he walked on slowly, checking out more cars. Rusty joined and then Blue.

"I'll be the lookout," I said.

Jinwoo saluted me. I fantasized about walking out to the main road, Route 63, and disappearing. I wanted to shuffle down the tight shoulder of the road toward something safe.

Some cars in the lot had their windows down all the way, others just enough to reach in and grab coins. After about 20 minutes, we had over ten bucks and an unopened pack of Certs.

Days later, the crew wanted to try it again. I declined and waited solo at a pizzeria, playing pinball. Jinwoo dubbed the heist method "Car Scooping". My crew was digging the theft game, but I had zero interest and hoped it would phase out.

When they picked me back up, they flicked the many dollar bills in my face, fanning me with the filth of past fingertips. We headed to the orange traffic cones of a quiet section in Fort Washington, where a big project had construction in progress for months. We jumped out and took cones and a couple blinking barricade lights and shoved them into The Tank's trunk. We took them to a sleepy part of Ambler and lined them up at an intersection of minimal traffic. This provided us time to install them in the dark with no one seeing. We parked nearby and sat cowered in the dark. Cars approached and screeched quick u-turns. Perturbed drivers got out of their cars in disbelief, cursing and baffled at how to get home. Nobody got out to move the obstacles of orange safety, trusting their legitimacy.

45.

Technical
Difficulties

August '90

The crew and I overheard that Wolf was having a big party at Kova's Oreland house. Kova was on a business trip. We drove by the house, chomping on burritos and sizing up the increasing parked cars that extended down Apel Avenue. We were in Blue's new ride, a white Plymouth Horizon Hatchback.

Wolf's Miata was parked with the top down on the driveway. Around 10:30pm, way past my curfew, we pulled out a few blinking barricade lights and blocked off the main entrance to Apel Avenue. Jinwoo crouched in the shadows and made it to Wolf's Miata as Blue, Rusty and I waited in the Plymouth. Jinwoo reached in and grabbed the detachable cassette player and ran back to us. He bumped into a parked car and an alarm beeped. A digitized voice stated: "Protected by Viper. Stand back!" Jinwoo dove into the back of the hatchback and clung unto the backseat.

Blue tore out of Oreland and headed towards Ambler. We passed the trophy cassette player around.

"Hey, there's a cassette in here," said Rusty.

"What band?" asked Jinwoo.

"Don't know. It's a blank Memorex."

"Let's have a listen. Maybe Wolf makes a good mix tape."

Blue was sitting at a red light about to make a left turn onto Fort Washington Ave. The light turned green while Blue fidgeted with the car cigarette lighter. The car behind us honked.

"Alright, alright," Blue said with a Marlboro Red in his mouth. He floored the left turn. His left hand held the lighter and the steering wheel. He bent his head down so the cigarette tip could reach the hot orange glow of the lighter. His right hand fidgeted with the cassette, stabbing into his console and seeking the insert dock.

"Jesus, dude! What the fuck?" blurted Jinwoo.

The left turn went off track and the Plymouth hopped a curb with a loud thud, Blue's foot still on the accelerator pedal, stuck. He steered with his left hand, tearing up a lawn, dodging a roadside mailbox. The turn sharpened left further. The car swooped back into the street across two lanes of empty traffic and over another curb. The car knocked over a large black man lawn jockey holding a lantern. Blue adjusted his body and found the brake pedal. The car skidded. We got out and saw the jockey laying in between two tire marks that unearthed dirt on the lawn. The cassette slunk into the console and played. A series of coughs and throat clearings rattled out of the speakers. The volume was up. Wolf's voice blasted out: "Testing... 1, 2, 3... Um, so... Hi, Steffi. It's me. Wolfgang. Your Wolfie. I wanted to know if you wanted to go... I think it's time that... We've reached a great point to go steady. Damn't. Ummm..."

The four of us connected eyes upon hearing the treasured recording. It transcended the car accident. Jinwoo ran into the car and ejected the cassette. He grabbed the stolen cassette deck and concealed it in a pocket of his baggy Randall Cunningham jersey.

"We're making copies of this," said Jinwoo, dancing. "Gotta protect this. Cops will be here soon."

The whirring of an automatic garage door opening broke our daze. Shimmering speckled light emitted from the growing clearance. The opening slowly revealed a girl and her outfit. Two black Chuck Taylor sneakers. Slender legs wearing fishnet stockings beneath denim cutoff jeans. A chunky belt. A Dinosaur Jr. t-shirt on top of a white thermal undershirt. A pink electric guitar strapped on her shoulder. Purple dyed hair, shaved on the sides and back. The girl seemed boyish. I wasn't sure if I was more attracted or intimidated by her presence. A lighted mirror ball spun the funky lights.

"Goody gumdrops," said the girl.

"Hi," I said. "We're so sorry. We lost control and—"

"You guys knocked down Jim," she said with a half smile.

"Who?"

"That stupid racist thing on our lawn. My Dad is gonna freak. You guys get hurt?"

"Not sure. You guys all OK?" I piped up.

The crew examined the car. Blue kicked the rims and bumper, cursing the moment. All four tires were flat.

"My parents are away for the weekend," the girl said. "I was just practicing chord progressions. I thought I heard something. Damn."

Blue called Shelle. She soon pulled up in her BMW.

"For the love of God. I buy you a car and you bust it up in *two* days," said Shelle. "You are such a fuckup."

I stepped away from the argument and chatted with the girl. "I'm Veronica," she said.

"Ah, like The Kinks song," I said.

"No. That's Victoria."

"Oh. Well, they have one called Monica. I was thinking of that *onica* sound, I guess. Sorry."

"Nice," she said, nudging the tuning pegs of her guitar into my shoulder.

After the police arrived and made a report, Veronica headed back into the garage of effects pedals and whirling electric radiance. I gave her a high five goodbye.

"Sweetie, hold on," Shelle called out, holding a card of insurance info. "I'm sorry my son did this to your beautiful lawn."

"It's fine by me," said Veronica, massaging the shaved sides of her head.

"What's going on with your hair?" asked Shelle. "A stylist did that?"

"I did it."

Shelle sneered and walked backwards towards her Beemer. "Get in the cars, boys. I'll take you home. Blue needs to wait for the tow truck."

At home, I immediately saw Dad in his bathrobe, peeping through the window. "This can't happen again," said Dad. "Understood? Way too late. Your mother and I haven't slept at all yet. It's 1:30 in the morning." He shined a flashlight into my eyes.

"I'm fine," I said.

The following days, we listened to the Wolf cassette often. Jinwoo made his own copy and listened to it at school with his Sony Walkman, sometimes purposely walking by Wolf while it played. The recorded material was twenty minutes of Wolf practicing methods of asking Steffi to go steady. He wasn't the natural smooth guy we thought he was. He was vulnerable, scared shitless of failure.

Wolf appeared bleak in the hallways. No suave threads or slick haircut could reinforce him. We sat tables away in the cafeteria, noticing how he shifted his eyes and sized up his buddies. Even when he elbowed me into a row of lockers, I smiled with tight lips, knowing paranoia consumed him. At lunch, he chewed tobacco at a heavier clip, slobbering on the periphery, far from the center of his scene.

46.

House Party Hideout

April '91

On a rare balmy Friday evening, Siobhan had a house party. My parents were on a cruise, gone for five days. I wanted nothing to do with the party and hid in my bedroom. I couldn't relate to her cheery super positive friends that had the same energy as the marching band or color guard they belonged to. I despised Siobhan's glam rock choice of music. That alone was reason to hide. I still didn't partake in beer, liquor or cigarettes either. The smoke clouds, clanking bottles and hollering after drained shot glasses made me antsy.

In my room, I read the backs of my baseball cards and memorized team stats. I kept my door locked from the inside with a simple door latch. A few times, couples looking for a make-out chamber tried to burst through the door.

"It's occupied," I said.

After an hour, I headed downstairs and grabbed a can of beer out of the fridge. The revelers tainted the house with spilled drinks. Nobody said anything to me. I believe no one knew who I was. I pictured my parents on their large cruise boat headed to Bermuda.

Back in my room, I stared at the intricate red and white design of the beer can, with its sophisticated fonts and detailed descriptions. I cracked open the can. The foam rose to greet me. I thought back to when Kova gave me a can at the Halfway House. I took a sip and swooshed it around in my mouth. After swallowing, I felt the immediate urge to vomit but also felt the effects of the alcohol in my bloodstream. I pounded the remaining ounces of the can as quickly as possible. I instantly wanted to listen to my music. I played a cassette of *Synchronicity* by The Police, one of my Columbia House selections. I paged through my binders of baseball cards, held together and protected by plastic sheets. I laughed at the many anal retentive hours I had spent coming up with the perfect presentation of them. Suddenly, the heavy bass of the downstairs stereo stopped and the crowd noise diminished. I turned off my stereo and peeked my head into the hallway.

"Cops are out front," a guy said, sitting on my hamper.

I looked out of my window and saw a squad car sitting in the driveway with no lights on. I ran downstairs to look for Siobhan, but everyone had fled out the back door. I followed suit and hurled over our backyard fence into the property of a house on Twining Road. I was soon on the street, watching as revelers split up into different directions in the darkness. I didn't know where to go. I realized that I had a quarter in my pocket and felt the urge to give Emma a call. There were only a few numbers I had ever memorized. She was one of them. As horrible as the beer tasted, the result was an abrupt sweeping of courage. I went to the payphone at the Community Center and called Emma.

"No, she's not here," said Emma's brother. "May I take a message?"

"No, that's OK, Ernie," I said.

"Wait, who is this?"

"It's Garvey. Your old neighbor."

"Oh, wow. Haven't seen you in, like years."

"I know. I moved over here. My life changed. I really miss you guys. You guys were so much fun."

I hung up and wondered if Emma was dealing with the same

parties with her Catholic School friends, whether she was safeguarding her friends' vandalism.

I proceeded to the slitted fence entrance into Shady Creek. A heavy refreshing breeze blew through the trees. I found my way to the old fort, wondering if it was still standing. When I arrived, a man was laying in a hammock. He heard my feet crunching on fallen branches and opened his eyes. The high beams of passing cars provided temporary light into the darkness. The man put his glasses on and sat up. We both smiled at each other. It was an older caddie I worked with named Bill. We called him Billy From Philly.

"Hey, there," said Billy. "What the heck. Is this your hangout?"

"No. Not anymore," I said. "Just stopping by. Cops are at my house."

"What? Old man problems?"

"Nah, a house party."

"Oh, Jesus Christ. Sorry to hear. Guess you're wondering why I'm here?"

"Don't you live in Flourtown?"

"Yeah, a rooming-house. A shit show. But I don't drive, so I have to walk there. It's just too far sometimes. I like it here in Oreland. I can grab a few drinks at Dutch's Tavern and just crash somewhere. I was sleeping in various backyard gazebos, but I got busted and got a hose sprayed on me by some crazed woman in a bathrobe. So, I found this little place. You still use it?"

"Nah, not at all. You can use it all you want."

"Nice job setting it up. Keeps me dry if there's rain. Don't worry, I still get showers. A few houses down from the course, there's this huge ass mansion owned by an old guy. He's got an outdoor shower, like at a beach house. I get squeaky clean there before arriving to loop."

"Ah, that's why your hair is wet when I see ya in the morning."

"Yes sir, that's right."

"Are there *Playboy* magazines still here?"

"Yeah. Saw them in the trash bags wound up tight. Want a shot of bourbon?"

"I'm OK. Just had a beer."

"Oh, you gotta try this though. Evan Williams. It's cheaper than Jack Daniel's. Just as good." Billy gave me the bottle.

I took a sip. The liquor spilled out of my mouth, dribbling down my chin and onto my shirt. The trace amount I ingested gave me a buzz.

"So, you saving your caddie dough?" asked Billy.

"Kind've. Well, not much."

"You gotta save, man. Don't wanna end up like me. I'm 39 now and let me tell ya, I'm feeling it. My back is permanently bent, fucked up. And the chemicals they use on the grass? Can't be good for ya. No way. Not long term."

I kept nodding my head, trying to keep it together and not vomit. Billy went on about how when it gets cold in Pennsylvania, he takes a bus to Florida to caddie with alligators. "If you think carpenter bees in sand traps are scary, try dodging a gator by water hazards. Holy shit, man!"

I fell into a daze and saw something glistening, wrapped in cellophane. "Twizzlers?" I interjected.

"Huh? Yeah, why. Want some? You can have the whole thing if ya want. I'm the one in your fort. Tear it up."

"Thanks," I said, ripping into the strawberry twisted goodness.

"Didn't ya eat supper?"

"Not today. Just never happened I guess. I had a big lunch. Siobhan was taking over the kitchen, getting ready for the party."

"Yeah, enjoy your dinner," he laughed. "Did I ever tell ya 'bout the time I caddied for Dan Quayle?"

"Who's that?"

"That's your Vice President, boy."

"Ah, gotcha." I told Billy it was unlikely that I'd see him at the course the next day and shook his hand.

"No prob here. One less caddie to compete with. You all right, man?"

"Yeah, just feeling nostalgic. I miss this girl I used to know. Simpler days. I'm living in the past and thinking of the future."

"You gotta get grounded. I'm not one to give advice but this is it, man. Right here with me. This is where you be standing. You got me?"

I got within a few houses of my home and didn't see the cop car anymore. My house lights were dimmed. I walked to the backyard and saw Siobhan smoking cigarettes with her friends, discreetly sipping beers.

"Garvey!" they all chimed. "Man, you smell like a bar."

"Oh, I had bourbon," I said.

"Where?" Siobhan asked.

"In the woods. It was my dinner. Some candy too."

"You're such a freak, dude."

47.

Chants & Congas

May '91
When I got my driver's license, my parents let me borrow their car on weekends to go caddie. This saved time as I didn't have to hike the full length of the course and arrive in a sweaty mess.

While caddying, I thought about Emma often. I headed to West Oreland after looping, hoping to bump into her at Oreland Pizza or Perkel's Drug Store, wondering what she looked like.

At the Oreland Market, I bumped into someone while soaking in the air conditioner, not paying attention. I fell onto a closed pickle barrel, my back piercing the curved top edge. I looked up and saw a guy covering his nose and mouth.

"Are you OK?" he asked

"I think so. Sorry about that," I said.

"No, I'm sorry. These aisles are tight and I was in a hurry for no reason."

The guy had a beaded necklace, rainbow crow t-shirt and a familiar cheeky smile. I realized that this patchily bearded dude was my old friend Willem. He extended a hand, helping me straighten up.

"Wait. Garv? For real? What are you doing in these parts, man?" asked Willem, slapping my shoulder.

I shook his hand firmly, laughing. "I'm from here. Love it here. Come on now. Was hoping to run into this girl. Emma."

"Ah, I've heard about you two. Old flames."

"Barely."

We ordered hoagies from the in-store deli and sat outside on a bench. Willem had given up on Boy Scouts as well. He invested his time in studying and researching his ancestral Lenni Lenape tribe. I explained that I was a caddie at Shady Creek.

"Don't tell me that," said Willem. "You're like those natives that stayed in the Skippack area and hauled grain for money for the white man."

"I'm a white man hauling for the white man," I said. "Money is good. I'm sick of it, anyway. It's just until I get to college."

"Kova still a member there?"

"Indeed."

Willem explained that Kova was looking to start a new development project in Skippack. Upon examining the soil of the site, an excavator found over fifty pieces of Lenni Lenape artifacts. Willem's Uncle Jay thought there might be fieldstone markers and possible grave sites. But Kova wouldn't let any historical societies research the area. Supporters of the Lenni Lenape protested outside White Ash Manor's newly gated entrance. The road was busy, too dangerous to try again. At Kova Plastics, security had them removed from the lot. Jay later met a Kova Plastics bookkeeper at a bar. She explained that Kova only entered the building twice a week, walking around the office with a putter and tapping it on desks. The biz was in cruise control, ready for Wolf to be the third generation.

"We need to get him where it hurts, the place he loves the most," said Willem.

"At Shady Creek Country Club?" I asked.

"Yep. If we know he's there, we can make noise at the exit and wait for him to leave. Everyone will see our signs, hear our chants. He'll be chastised before his peers. All monsters have a weak spot."

"Like the big boss at the end of a video game. How will you know when he's leaving?"

"We don't know. Can you alert us when he's golfing? We'll race over."

"Everyone loves him there. He's a hero. But, yeah, there's a way."

"You can weaken him too. I know you're leaving Oreland soon and he'll be gone from your life."

"He won't be. That's just it. He's threatened me and my family for things I shouldn't have seen. I shouldn't even be talking about this."

The next Saturday, I kept a steady eye on Merv and his scheduling clipboard which contained the tee off times and names of each member. He usually walked around with it, but sometimes he put it down on the cement border of the soda pagoda. When I had my chance, I sifted through the soda cans, pretending to look for something they didn't have.

"I know there's a Dr. Pepper in here," I said to the younger caddies while staring down at Merv's crazed handwriting. I discerned that Kova was not teeing off at any point through 10:30am, but needed to flip over to the next page.

Merv later put the clipboard down outside the Pro Shop on a bench as he smooth talked a golfer. The wind picked up. I thought of Willem and how this needed to happen. The page flipped over, leaving the rest of the morning's schedule. I walked toward the unveiled agenda and pretended to have issues with my shoelaces and saw what I needed: an 11:50am tee off time for Kova.

At the payphone outside of the Pro Shop, I called Willem.

"Making a call to the ladies?" asked Merv.

"Yeah, you know," I said. "Late night last night. Making sure she's out of my place."

"I hear ya, baby. I like it."

My foursome teed off around 11:30am. Kova's group was behind me. By the time I got to the 3rd hole green, I heard the chanting protests. I couldn't hear the exact words but there were drums and a steady beat. My foursome became irked and blamed poor putting on the distractive hollering.

"Is that a drum circle? Who is doing that?" one asked.

I shrugged.

At the 4th green, I looked towards the 3rd hole and saw Kova seething. He raised his hands and paced, unwilling to attempt a stroke with the ongoing disturbance. A golf cart zipped towards Kova from the 2nd hole pines. It was an assistant from the Pro Shop. He hopped out and waved Kova to come and join him on the cart. Kova took a club from his caddie and pounded it repeatedly into a sprinkler head. Plastic and metal fragments whirred about. The Pro Shop assistant crouched behind the golf cart, covering his eyes. With a roar, Kova tossed his club high into a tree. It got stuck in some branches, sparkling in the sunlight. Eventually Kova joined the assistant and they cruised back to the clubhouse.

After my loop, I called Willem. He explained that Kova met with them at the parking lot exit but offered nothing. Kova spat at their feet and mocked their demands. The police arrived and the Lenni Lenape dispersed in peace.

I later met with Willem at our old creek-side hangout. We skimmed stones and nibbled jerky. "We're grateful for your help," Willem said. "I felt the fear in that man. It emanated around him. Although he declined, I feel he will give in. We got a local newspaper guy to come out. He took photos and is writing a story for *The Times Herald*."

"I hope it works out for you," I said. "His son is in my grade, ya know. It's like I can't escape him."

"You'll escape him when you go to college. You mentioned Emma. I can return the favor and check in on her. Don't know her, but I see her with her flock of Catholic school girlfriends. They keep the uniforms on and hang out, get slices."

"Nah. It's been too long. There are other girls."

"Why did you ask about her then?"

"I miss her. I'm caught up in some stupid shit. Mischief night is every night. Just miss the old days."

"Once you get out of Oreland, Kova will disappear," Willem said, whittling a perfect found branch. "Don't worry."

48.

Aboard With The Con Artist

September '91
Autumn was the best time of the year to caddie. It was crisp, cool, and the foliage was stunning. Golfers relaxed about losing their balls, hidden in leaves. Greens were riddled with tree branches and pieces of scattered bark. The wind was a bigger factor for club choice, but made the loops void of sweaty brows.

A newer caddie, Francis, started in the summer and was an instant hit with Merv. Unlike myself, Francis showed up every single day, weekends too. He wore golf polo shirts and Titleist brand hats. If I didn't know him, I'd think he was a young member. He sat in the soda pagoda or paced eagerly near the caddie shack, gripping his clean white towel, grinning and looking available. He faced the first tee area seeking eye contact, branding himself as ready and hungry. His daily commitment ascended him to the top of the ranks. He didn't have to wait two hours for a loop like I often did. I had seen him cut through the course to get to work and found out he lived near Quinn and had a 15th hole house too.

"It's all bull," he said as we downed sodas. "I'm not into this whole golf thing."

"Really?" I asked. "You look like a pro yourself."

"Screw that. This is just good money. I'm brown nosing, playing the part."

"I'm just not committed, even though I've been doing it for years."

"Yep. Merv don't like it. Look, you have a ponytail tucked in that Pink Floyd cap. We all know that. The members can see that. You gotta dress for the part you want, right?"

Francis and I got assigned to the same foursome. Our conversation continued throughout the day. He was one grade below me and a sponge to new music. As we walked through the course, his over inducing kiss assery was the stark opposite of my mute monitoring of golf strokes.

"Great shot, Mr. Walker," said Francis. "You played the wind perfectly. Right at the pin."

All that I ever dished out was occasional yardage readings from the sprinkler heads. Francis strode about his golfers with quick feet, hustling to rake the trap for one golfer and pull the pin for the other seconds later.

"Wipe down?" he called out on the green, sticking his hands out. The golfers put their markers down and tossed the balls to Francis so he could remove the slightest trace of grass stain or debris that would disrupt their putts.

"You're showboating out here," I said as we approached forecaddie mode at the next hole.

"Gotta work it. In turn, they tell Merv how great you are and then you don't have to wait around so much for a loop. You got to get on board. You're wearing shredded jeans shorts. You look like you wanna be a roadie."

"I would! And I'm fine with a C average."

After the round, Francis invited me to a gathering at his house and offered to drive me to school in the mornings. "If you didn't live in Oreland, I would be like, go fuck yourself. But I can pick ya up. Got my license. Got a used '85 Toyota Supra."

As an 11th grader, I was delighted to be rid of the school bus and the eight different stops that took 45 minutes to get to school.

I waited at my front door and saw Francis pull up in his white Supra.

"Damn, this is like a Porsche," I said, getting in the passenger side.

"More like an eighth of a Porsche," said Francis. He put in a cassette and the album *Bossanova* played by the Pixies. We cruised to school, talking about his get-together. He named off two girls that would be there.

"Oh, I've met a Veronica before. Purple haired guitarist chick?" I asked calmly.

"Yep, that's her. I'm sorry. It's not really a party, I guess. Just the four of us. Bring a friend."

"Should I bring some snacks?"

"No. You serious? We'll likely just get high and listen to music, paint pumpkins, smash pumpkins. Who knows?"

After two thundering Pixies songs, he popped out the cassette and put in the hypnotic dance music of Deee-Lite.

As with me, Francis didn't partake in after school extra-curricular activities. He gave me rides home. We even had time to stop at 7-11 and get cigarettes. I got junk food and enjoyed the unceasing second hand smoke.

I brought Blue to the gathering because he enjoyed getting high. I figured he'd take my place. I was just into sugar and still didn't even like beer. We got out of my Mom's car and walked along the side of the house to the backyard where Francis said they'd be. A chiminea fire was burning at the far end. The flames lit up Veronica as she swayed to a boombox laying on the grass. She wore chunky black boots, that made her seem much taller, black leggings beneath Daisy Duke blue jeans and a fisherman cabled sweater cut just enough to show off her navel ring.

"Oh, man. *You* guys," said Veronica, covering her face with her hands, leaving just enough room for her eyes to peak over her fingers.

"He's not driving tonight. Don't worry," I said.

"Come on," Blue gushed. "Cut me some slack."

"Have a seat, boys," she said, pointing to beach chairs surrounding the fire. "Francis is trying to quell the storm. His Dad came out and gave him shit for the fire." She glanced up at the kitchen windows where we could see the conversation fizzling out. "Guess he wasn't supposed to use it."

Blue babbled on with intense hand gestures about the accident that ended up on Veronica's front lawn. He weaved in the ramifications with his insurance company and the grounding he suffered. I sat and nodded, trying to catch Veronica's eyes darkened with plum eyeshadow. Blue and I appeared to be an oddball novelty act brought to entertain her.

Moments later, Francis came out of the back door. "Hey guys," he said jogging over. "I have some bad news."

"We can't have the fire?" asked Veronica.

"No, my Dad's finally cool with it. I gotta put it out though if we leave. But Olivia isn't feeling well and is staying home. She's the only one with weed."

I breathed a quiet sigh of relief.

"Well, I got something with me," said Blue, reaching into his army jacket pocket. "But that depends on what kind of night you wanna have." He pulled out a small transparent plastic bottle and shook it.

"What are they?" I asked. "Sunflower seeds?"

"Seeds they are. They're Woodrose seeds, straight from Hawaii. I got them mailed to my house."

Francis and Veronica leaned towards Blue.

"What do they do?" whispered Veronica. "I think I saw these in the back of *High Times*."

"Never done them before," said Blue. "They're like a natural LSD, but lasts only six hours. It depends on what you had to eat. I skipped dinner tonight. The more empty your stomach, the better. We won't feel anything full tilt until three hours in."

"Let's go under the stars and do this," insisted Veronica. "You want to?" she asked, looking at Francis and lightly touching his wrist with both hands. Her shoulder length hair formed a shimmering tunnel over her face, revealed only to Francis.

"I'm in," said Francis. "Come on. To the golf course."

We hopped over the split-rail fence and sat Indian style on the 15th green. Blue gave the proper dosage of seeds to Veronica and Francis. They eyed each other as they swallowed and hopped into a steep sand trap of giggles. I grew jealous of their sudden reciprocated public display of affection. I imagined they would remember the day forever as their hallucinogenic journey that started by making out in trespassed damp sands. Although Veronica dressed like a rock star, Francis's non-caddie look was simple blue jeans and a white shirt. With his slicked back hair, he appeared more 1950s than modern, as if he was protesting grunge fashion.

Blue looked at me. I cut the air with a flat hand. "I good, man," I said.

"Here you go," he said, rattling the seeds and pretending to put some in my hand, respecting my decision to exit stage left from the ensuing phantasm.

"Have fun," I whispered. "I'll keep an eye on you tonight."

Back at the fire, Francis freaked out that his Dad was visible in the window, pacing back and forth and opening endless envelopes of mail. "Why won't he close the curtains?"

Francis ran to a hose, dragged it out to the fire and put it out. Veronica grew mesmerized with the rising swirls of smoke. We walked to the playground next to the Community Center and positioned ourselves on the roundabout spinner, each laying on a unique color. Wind rustled through the trees.

"What was that noise?" Veronica asked, sitting up.

"Just crab apples falling," I said, pointing to the tree, recalling the day I became a lookout man. "And now I'm a chaperone for drug testers," I thought.

A white work truck drove by and slammed on the brakes. It sat idling for a moment.

"Uh, do you guys know who this is?" asked Francis.

The work truck reversed a few feet and drove off. The eyes of a fawn appeared where the truck had stopped. It looked towards us, hobbling about, scratching hooves against the leaf-strewn curb.

"It's still alive," said Blue, taking out yet another Marlboro red and standing up. "You guys seeing this?"

"Yep," Veronica and I said at the same time.

Blood oozed out of the fawn's mouth under the yellow streetlight.

"I'm gonna be sick," said Francis. He ran off and puked by the fence. "It's the seeds!" he assured.

"They make some a little uneasy," said Blue after a big cigarette drag.

"This is a buzzkill before the buzz even happened," said Veronica, leaning her arm on my shoulder. "There's a girl in my Bio class that drives around and picks up roadkill to give them proper burials. She says the Township doesn't do such a good job with it. I'll give her a page."

Veronica went to the Community Center phone booth. Her friend called within a minute

"He stopped moving," said Blue. "He's a goner. Poor guy must've been lost. God, I hate seeing this. It's a bad omen. Gotta walk this out. I'll be back."

"Dude," I said. "Come on, you gotta stay here. I'm watching out for you."

"Damn't. Now I have to hurl," said Blue. He walked off to vomit with the prompt precision of pausing a movie and going to the bathroom.

Veronica checked up on Francis. I sat on the swing, gripping the metal chain, unable to stop staring at the dead deer's open eyes looking into me.

"Can I braid your hair?" Veronica asked, walking up behind me, putting her hands into my locks. "You can probably dread pretty easy. It's so wavy."

"Never thought of that," I said as she dug her fingertips into my scalp and rubbed, gently scratching with black polished nails.

I kept staring at the fawn. The grazing at my scalp put me at ease and drowned out the retching sounds of Blue and Francis. "So, when is that girl going to show up?" I asked.

"Soon. She lives in Oreland."

"Cool. How's Francis?"

"He's seeing visions. Just laying down and staring at the stars."

I wanted to glance over at Blue to see if he was fine but didn't want to stop the massage. It reminded me of the one time I went to a hair stylist and got my hair shampooed.

"I'm feeling it now," she said. "You feeling it yet?"

"A minor bit," I said. "Not really. Maybe I got some dull ones."

"You gotta give it time." Veronica let go of my hair and walked in front of me. She blocked the sight of the fawn, squatting down to my face with a full toothy smile. "You're so cute," she said, grabbing the metal chains. She leaned in and I moved. Her lips connected onto my forehead. When she pulled back, her smile was wider. Her top and bottom rows of teeth separated further. I stared into her mouth at the glistening dark soft palate, the uncertain fibrous realm of a French kiss.

"We need to see some bands together," she said. "Your taste in music is right on. Do you watch *120 Minutes* on MTV?" She grabbed my knees and pushed me back on the swing. I returned toward her. She pushed again as if she was a mother pushing her son. I glanced at Blue and saw him on his knees. Veronica ran off toward the Community Center stairwell which led to a basement entrance. She threw up onto the concrete steps.

A little black car showed up and the back trunk popped open. A girl got out with long black hair. She wore a black gown and white surgical gloves. She positioned a large trash bag onto the sidewalk and transferred the fawn onto it. I walked toward her to help. She hauled the animal into her trunk. Veronica remained bent over on the railing, her face aimed down. The black car disappeared. I headed to where the fawn was. Remnant blood sat pooled on the street. I looked at my nauseous friends, awaiting their elation.

49.

A Mosquito

September '91
Francis picked up Veronica in the morning as well. On the way to school, I slouched in shotgun. Heading home, I sat in the back where I rummaged through tossed cassettes and avoided greasy fast food wrappers. Veronica rubbed her hands on Francis's corduroy knees. They made eyes at each other at red lights and shouted conversations. I only heard the blared tunes and watched their lips move. Francis gunned it at green lights, igniting instant queasiness.

In the courtyard during lunch, Veronica played with my hair in front of Francis, as if I was a doll prop. I wondered if she recalled lunging her lips at me during the Woodrose seed night.

My hair was long. I hadn't trimmed it in over a year. I never combed it or applied product. I positioned the strands into clumps, parting down the middle, draping it around my temples and cheeks. This natural tunnel vision blocked out peripheral irritating menaces, allowing me to focus on what was in front of me.

On Sunday nights at midnight, technically Monday, I watched *120 Minutes* on MTV. It became a favorite two hours of the week. The show featured "alternative" rock videos. These rare snippets were a trove of bands that had sounds and anthems that I was in agreement with. I recorded the shows with the VCR and watched them again after school in my room.

Although I consumed FM classic rock, *120 Minutes* was my Sunday gospel. The ritual of discovery and adding modern psalms to my life became more important than homework. I scribbled the morose band names on notepads for further sonic research: Alice In Chains, My Bloody Valentine, Mudhoney. I bought Spin magazines from B. Dalton Bookseller, thirsty for band tidbits. I cut out photos of the groups and taped them to my bedroom walls.

I also discovered 103.3 WPRB, Princeton University's radio station. A slight hiss or fuzz was heard, but reception to my boom box was good enough with the antennae extended fully, aimed at just the precise angle. The noise rock, avant garde instrumentals and poetry slams were foreign to me. My palate expanded to the mesosphere as I swayed through the minimal mile radius of my Oreland home.

Song gems led to cassette or CD purchases, allowing me to crank the tunes in my room. Framed photos in the hallway became misaligned from the bass. Nearby neighbors working on their front lawns were privy to the new sounds as I blasted them with the window open. Joggers and dog walkers all got a taste.

On September 29th, *120 Minutes* aired a video for "Smells Like Teen Spirit" by Nirvana . Outside of being a great song, the video was an enhanced fantasy of mine. A loud band took over a gymnasium while tattooed cheerleaders, branded with anarchist emblems, gyrated to the rhythm, culminating into a bleacher clearing riot and destruction of gear.

My hair was of similar length to Nirvana's singer. I felt a kinship with him although I couldn't play a single chord on the guitar, yet alone know how to strap one on. I didn't know what the lyrics were getting at, but sensed profound poetry to dissect.

The dynamics of "Smells Like Teen Spirit", from mumble speak to head vein popping howls, was a wavelength I endured. From coasting in the calm to gripping on for dear life with the flick of a drum pounding fill, my psyche felt matched to the song. The torment of the guitar solo and throaty vocals was something I'd never heard before.

Monday, after school, I watched the video repeatedly, rewinding back to the beginning as soon as it ended.

"You like this song, huh?" Siobhan asked, peeking her head into the living room.

"It's awesome. Just came out. You like it?"

She made a grimace. "I don't know. What is he singing about?"

"It's not a candy-coated love song or T&A crap."

Siobhan rolled her eyes. "I don't think it's my thing."

On Tuesday after school, I called my parents on a payphone and left a message on the answering machine. "Gonna hang out with Blue after school," I said. "I did my homework in study hall. Gonna get hoagies, so I'll see ya this evening."

I searched for Blue and his car in the parking lot. We had plans to watch my VHS cassette of *120 Minutes* at his house. After the lot cleared, there was no sign of him. I walked to his house, several blocks away. His car wasn't there. I pressed the amber doorbell button. Shelle opened the door dressed in a fuzzy headband and pink leotards. "I'm in the middle of aerobics," she said. "Working four to midnight today."

"Sorry. Is Blue here?" I asked. "Was supposed to meet him at his car."

"He tells me nothing, Garvey. I'm the last to know where he is. Do you want to come in and wait?"

Shelle's workout video blared. Her breath smelled of wine and her mascara was running. "No, he's probably at Rusty's. I'll head there."

"Do you want a drink? Come on in. I don't need to workout. Do I? What do you think?"

"I'm good. Maybe I misunderstood the plan. I should find him."

"Do me a favor. Can you get him a job? Do you think he can be a caddie?"

I cringed. "Don't think he wants to. It's grueling. He'd hate it."

"He needs a fucking job. You're out there like a mule in the sun."

"I hate it, really."

"I see. Why don't you boys hang out with Wolfgang, the boy I told you about?" Shelle stepped outside. "His mother says he's depressed."

"Yeah, right. He's the toast of the town."

"He's got something wrong with his gums. You know? Pain in his jaw. Blood here and there. He's getting it examined soon. Could be serious."

I shook my head. "I've tried being his friend. Trust me. Gotta go."

Rusty's house was a few blocks away, but Blue's egg white car wasn't there. Jinwoo, Rusty and Blue were "Car Scooping" for loot at a progressive pace. I knew they were slithering in the autumn twilight, sidling up to unlocked cars. They stopped asking me to join them, knowing I had zero interest.

I walked to Veronica's house. Her parents were still at work. Francis and Veronica were eating a sleeve of Chips Deluxe on the front lawn, examining fallen leaves. Blue's auto mishap was still evident. The grass was patchy where the tire marks were.

In Veronica's big sloppy bedroom, we sat on white bean bag chairs, thumbing through expensive art magazines. Clothes were strewn all over her orange carpet of brown blotchy stains. Lighting was low.

Halfway through a CD, Francis and Veronica retreated up to the attic to smoke weed. I declined. I waited to hear Veronica's Dr. Marten combat boots clunking down the ladder. But their giggles, directly above her bedroom, segued into scuffling and moans. I stood on a desk chair to get my ear close to the ceiling. A repetitive thump ensued. I touched the ceiling at the exact spot. The pressure of thrusts pulsated through my fingers.

Back on the carpet, I roamed around Veronica's room, waiting it out. Deep cuts of the CD played. Clouds of floral body oils shifted through my nostrils. A lilac bra was draped over a lampshade. The intricate laces were a perplexing entangled trap. The soft cups begged to be explored. I brought one to my nose and inhaled whatever fragrance of Veronica still lingered on the polyester.

I thumbed through a *Philadelphia Weekly*. I saw that a band named Nirvana was playing in a few hours at a Philly venue called JC Dobbs. I used Veronica's phone and called the club, asking if it was the band that released "Smells Like Teen Spirit".

"Yeah, that's them," said the man. "Doors open at 7. But it's sold out, so, unless you know someone..."

Veronica and Francis returned disheveled, tickling hips. Francis called out some bands I liked as too mainstream. "Ya know, you really need to listen to Inside Out, Operation Ivy, Bad Brains," said Francis in a stoned rant. "Shit is more raw, real—"

"Guys, Nirvana is playing Philly *tonight*. South Street," I said, pointing to the ad. "Totally. No tickets left though."

"Fuck it, let's head down there," said Veronica, snatching the paper from my hands. She leaped onto her bed and laid on her stomach to analyze the ad. "It's with the Melvins too. Good find, Garv." Veronica bent her knees and swayed her feet back and forth, toes peeking through ripped black stockings.

Francis and I looked at her and then at each other. His crooked grin flattened. "I've got major homework to do tonight. I'm so behind," said Francis. "It's supposed to pour soon too."

Veronica twirled onto her back and stared at the ceiling. "Francis, it's fucking Nirvana. We gotta at least try." She jetted outwards and put on a hoodie. "Garv sounds like he's ready to go."

At Francis's car, Veronica let me sit shotgun. As we exited the suburbs and snaked through Lincoln Drive along the dark woods of Wissahickon Park, I wondered what I'd tell my parents. Maybe I'd be home in time, I thought. I had been to Center City just a few times. Parades and museums were previous destinations, alongside my parents or the Scouts.

"Garv, can you grab *Bleach* and put it on?" asked Francis. "It's back there somewhere."

I reached into the backseat floor, grabbed a few cassettes and eyed them up. It wasn't there. I reached back to scoop a few more. Veronica snagged my hand. "I'll help you find it," she said. I looked back. She leaned forward, rooting through cassettes with her right hand and holding my palm with her left hand. She dabbed my index finger with her tongue, tasting it. I kept my arm still. I looked at Francis. His hands were at 10 and 2 as he traversed through meandering Kelly Drive. Puddle splashes squished. My finger became consumed within Veronica's mouth, her tongue lapping my knuckle like a caged serpent. She released her tight grip, my fingertips fumbling with her lips.

"Here it is," said Veronica. She slapped the plastic casing onto my moist hand. I popped in the cassette. I brought the sucked finger to my nose and whiffed her saliva laced with clove cigarette smoke.

Veronica recommended that we get a drink at Dirty Franks, a dive bar on 13th Street covered with paintings and photos of famous Franks. After a minute on the stool, a bartender came over with a rag and wiped the bar down. She threw coasters at each of us and looked up. "Honey," the bartender said to Veronica. "It's not that I don't like ya. But you and your friends need to get the fuck out." The bartender nodded to the door.

"I blame your baby face," Veronica said to Francis, elbowing him into a jukebox.

We ran across the street through drizzling rain to The Last Drop Coffee House. We ordered slices of iced lemon pound cake and banana chocolate muffins, a dinner of desserts. We got coffees in to-go cups and drove closer to JC Dobbs. I never had coffee before. It was scorching hot. I burnt my tongue on my first sip, spitting it out. The sprinkled in cinnamon and nutmeg steamed into my face as I tried not to let any spill out of the sip hole.

At JC Dobbs, a line was formed outside. Entry wasn't allowed yet. The drizzle wasn't enough for an umbrella. "When I give the signal, follow me," said Veronica. "Gonna smooth talk the bouncer."

Francis and I watched as Veronica cut to the front of the line and talked with a large guy on a stool. We clutched our coffees, still unable to drink them. The bouncer listened to Veronica but didn't budge a slight smile or slacken his folded arms. He scratched an ear and pointed for her to step away. From inside the venue, a bass drum was pounded while one guitar chord was strummed clean and then distorted.

Veronica paced up and down the line, asking if extra tickets were available. Francis had to take a piss and gave me his coffee to hold. He ran off to find a restaurant bathroom, unable to get into JC Dobbs. I shadowed Veronica as she worked her charm.

At the end of the line, Veronica hit it off with a pony-tailed solo guy. He stroked her purple hair, talking with glittery eyes. He wore a tight white t-shirt with a black vest, showing off his biceps. He had one extra ticket and wanted her to join him. Veronica shrugged it off, stating she needed three. The guy grabbed her hand and yanked her to his side. She tried to wiggle free, jerking back. Some in line glanced at the commotion.

"Never saw a couple argue before?" the guy asked.

Veronica went boneless and collapsed onto the sidewalk, scraping her elbow. Her body writhed around like a freshly hooked fish. The guy held her with one calm hand. I squinted through the dark blue drizzle, recognizing a logo on his vest.

"You a member of Shady Creek?" I asked.

"What? Who are you, barista boy?" asked the guy.

"That insignia on your vest." I moved closer.

"Who knows? I got it at a thrift store. Back off. I only have one extra ticket." The guy flicked a finger at my forehead. I flinched too late. Sizzling drops of coffee leaked out of both cups, onto my hands.

"Enough!" I screamed and exerted a coffee cup up toward the guy. The brown steaming liquid splashed onto his face. I dropped the empty cup. The guy screamed, contorting his jaw. Veronica wiggled free. The guy buckled and fell into a large planter of prickly junipers. I tossed the other coffee at his stomach. The crowd cheered. My chest heaved.

I ran off with Veronica. "I have a key to the car," she blurted. We looked around before entering the car. There was no sign of the burnt brute monster. We hid in the backseat, cheek to cheek under a large plaid shawl.

Several minutes passed as we kept our eyes peered out for Francis.

"I guess I'll have to try coffee some other time," I said.

Veronica cracked up and tickled my stomach.

"We're not in the clear yet," I smiled, removing her hand.

"That was kind've brave, what you did."

"Well, I couldn't fight him. Had to do something."

We turned to each other. "Why won't you kiss me?" she asked.

"You're with Francis. Come on."

"I am?"

"You have a copy of his car key."

"So?"

"And I heard you guys. In the attic. There's a girl I dig too. Emma. She's so—"

Veronica laughed through her nose. "I am..."

"You're what?"

"I am...where I am," she said, leaning towards me. "Right now, I am here. Where are you?" She dabbed her tongue against the lobe and folds of my ear. The pulpy wet sounds and warm breath shivered my core. My tense shoulders dropped. I closed my eyes, focusing on the sensory tingling. My mind felt massaged. A tranquil glazed coating smeared over all concerns, immersed in a warm weightless gelatin, a deep cleansing of doubts within my skull. "That's nice," I managed. Veronica chuckled. Her voice reverberated down my spine.

I opened my eyes and saw Francis walk into frame. I sat back up. Veronica faced forward. I tapped on the glass, waving Francis over. "What the?" he asked, getting in.

"Just sit down and drive," said Veronica. "Unless you want your ass kicked."

"Can you at least tell me what you're both doing under there?"

"Hiding. Just go!"

Francis dropped me off at my house around 10:30pm. Dad walked out the door, fumbling with keys. "Oh, you got a ride," he said. "Did Blue get home?"

"I ended up with other friends. Couldn't find him earlier."

Dad smiled. "Well, thank the Lord."

Francis spun back around after a u-turn. Veronica remained hunkered in the backseat. She blew a kiss at me.

"Blue's Mom called from her job," said Dad. "Asked if I could pick him up from the Abington Police Department. She said you were with him."

I turned away. "Damn. I think I know what happened."

"Are you involved in this at all?"

"Once," I nodded. "Couldn't do it further."

"Do what?" asked Dad, crouching down. "Drugs?"

"No. Just stupid shit. Thieving."

When we pulled up to the Police Department, Blue sat at the top of the steps. Rusty and Jinwoo were already headed home with their parents. We walked to the bottom of the steps. Dad tapped his wedding band on the black railing.

"My Mom's gonna kill me," Blue said, tearing up. "She's gonna take my car way. Ground me for months." He banged his head on the railing. "Fucking idiot! I am so screwed."

Dad and I ran up to stop him. He turned to us. Red sore marks throbbed on his forehead. "OK, enough of that," said Dad. "Let's get you home."

"I gotta do community service."

"You 18 yet?" asked Dad.

"No. But I might have to go to juvey."

Blue sat in the backseat.

"You guys know this shit ends now, right?" asked Dad.

"Yeah," said Blue.

Dad put on KYW and drove off. We zoned out to the news and the Teletype machine. Blue fidgeted with a prescription bottle, rattling it like a rumba shaker. He popped the cap. Dad pulled over to the shoulder and slammed on the brakes. He stormed out and snagged Blue out of the car, grabbing the bottle. He examined it. "How many did you swallow?" Dad asked.

"None yet," Blue mumbled.

"Spit 'em out." Dad slapped the back of his head a couple times. "All of it."

I jumped out of the car. Blue slobbered out several pink pills.

"Bupropion? Why are you taking this?" asked Dad.

"Depression. Obesity. Nicotine addiction. My Mom says it's a cure-all for my fat fuck life."

Dad pierced his eyes into mine, tucking the bottle into his inside coat pocket. "Did you know he was on this?"

"No clue," I said.

Blue connected eyes with me, unblinking. "Sorry. I just don't care," he said. "Fucked up getting into college too. Got nothing but that nagging bitch."

"Once you're 18, you can move out," said Dad. "Do whatever you want. Get a job at Wawa. I lived on beer and chocolate for a couple years. Slept on a wooden floor with cockroaches. Makes ya think about what you really want. Does your family have a business?"

"Uh, no," said Blue.

"You gotta work your ass off then."

Dad escorted Blue into the backseat.

Back in the car, Dad rested his head on the steering wheel. "Sorry to smack you," he said. "Had a brother once, older than me. Never met him. He died in the big one. Saved lives. But got shot up in the chest. I have one photo of him. It's on my bureau. Always there."

At Blue's house, Dad pointed to the backyard. He insisted we wait for Blue's Mom to arrive. We laid on the cushioned chaise lounges. The auto sensor flood lights turned on and off as we moved. Dad talked of brotherhood until he noticed Venus. "Remember, stars flicker. Planets don't." We nodded off until headlights came up the driveway, accentuating the pink Bupropion streaks on Blue's chin.

Days later at dinner, I ate fish sticks and fries with the family. We had MTV on in the background, acting as a radio. Gerardo's slimy "Rico Suave" ended and segued into the intro chords of "Smells Like Teen Spirit". I dropped my fork and coasted to the TV, in awe that the video was in prime time rotation. When Siobhan fled the dinner table, it was for a Bon Jovi video. They made her bang her head, rock with fists clenched and adorn band patches to her jean jacket. She even had an ankle tattoo. Her allegiance was proven. And Bon Jovi was still omnipresent. But a switch seemed to be flipped. Jarring abrasive anthems grew commonplace, a heavier new ingredient was laid thick, bookending pop perfection, the vice tightening on sugar-coated earworms.

50.

Lunar Eclipse

April '92

Francis introduced me to a hardcore and punk band venue called The Fiesta, located nearby in Willow Grove. The place hosted inexpensive wedding receptions and was a hangout for local drunks. Monday nights, it transformed into a dim-lit home of sweaty mosh pits. Friends and strangers slammed together to the abrasive rhythms, pushing on backs, trying to stay upright. We dodged windmill arms with clenched fists, respecting the need to wind them. We honored crowd-surfing bodies, heaving them afloat above the six feet of bones and flesh. It was a dance, but we resembled spirits trying to escape an exorcism. The torment of the songs bound us into a singular body of flailing limbs, trying not to fall.

Before The Fiesta, the only place I whipped my hair about was in my locked bedroom, where I frothed and imitated lead singers. I performed in front of my mirror, pretending a street hockey stick was a microphone.

One evening, I ventured to The Fiesta by myself. Francis and Veronica opted to watch a movie. I didn't mind, bored by being their bungling third wheel. During the final song of the night, I stood on the outskirts, exhausted. I watched the band perform, which was impossible to do while moshing. I noticed a girl with a euphoric smile bumping shoulders. She spiraled toward me, got tripped up and took a bad tumble. I grabbed her forearm as she descended, just before her head slammed onto the tiled floor. I pulled her out of the crowd with one firm yank and positioned her to my side. She had scarlet streaked pigtails, a nose ring and leather wristbands. Seconds later, through the flashing lights and smoke, I realized it was Emma. We hugged for a long moment, my mouth buried in her hair, our sweaty shirts bunching up. Too loud to have a conversation, we whisked off down a long corridor toward a back room. An emergency only exit sign stood above us, stating: "Do Not Open Door Or Alarm Will Sound". We tried to figure out how many years it had been.

"Catholic school uniforms blow," said Emma. "And I can't even wear a nostril stud."

"I can wear whatever I want," I said.

"Just rub it in, why don't ya." She tickled my rib cage and gave a light slap on my left cheek. "It's been almost six years. Just did the math."

Back in the day, Emma was a boyish cutie pie. She had flourished and was now ample where I tried not to stare. The simple smile was there but now with glossy crimson coated lipstick. Her eyes were innocent but decorated with an eyeliner that made her squints and laughs tinged with deviance.

"Been hoping to bump into you somewhere," I said. "I miss seeing you."

"Hell yeah." Emma went on a tangent and mentioned a boyfriend. She peppered in the two syllables repeatedly, a pungent ingredient mixed into a savory pie. She referred to him as Quinny.

"Is your boyfriend here?" I asked.

"He's driving around with a friend. He hates this music. Despises mosh pits. I think he's just scared. He's picking me up soon. He lives in your part of Oreland."

"Blond hair? About this high?" I put my hand down to my shoulders.

"Yep. Sounds like him. He said he didn't know you. I brought you up a few times."

I laughed. "He knows me. Where'd you both meet?"

"A kegger. A mix of schools. Never saw you at those. Was hoping to see you at one."

"I'm not into booze. Me and Quinn though. We went through some shit."

"The guy with Father Pal? Kova, right?"

"Basically."

Our eyes clamped together, heads tilted. We moved closer and leaned foreheads together, staring at the cruddy floor in silence for a minute. I squinted, holding back watering eyes. "Smoke is bugging me," I said.

Emma moved back and rummaged through her tightly strapped purse, crossed diagonally over her breasts. "Turn around," she said.

I faced the wall and she wrote on crinkly paper on my back.

"Here. It's my number. I am still on Redford Road, but in case you forgot it."

I grabbed the piece of paper. "We didn't call much back then. We showed up at each other's house."

"Times have changed."

I gave her a hug. She pecked my cheek and walked out. I crumpled the paper, the number already memorized from years ago.

I wanted to walk out with Emma, but didn't want to deal with Quinn. I waited until management flicked on the lights and waved people out.

In the parking lot, it drizzled at an increasing pace. The cold drops felt refreshing with the smell of worms. I sat in the car and let the showering rain shroud me for a moment. I turned the ignition switch and put the wipers on.

My passenger side door opened. "I thought I saw you getting into this car," a voice said.

I looked over and saw Sasha, her heaving cleavage directly in front of me. Her shirt was sopping wet and fitted tight. I looked up to her eyes.

"That's right. I'm up here," she said. She slunk into the passenger seat. She looked stunning, a pale damp curvature crawling out of the streetlights. "So, is this Mommy's car or Daddy's car?"

"Uh, both, I guess. They both drive it. My Mom more than my Dad, so I'd say it's my Mom's."

"Gotcha, Daddio. Your hair's getting long. Wasn't sure if it was you."

"So, do you need a ride home or something?"

"Yeah, I do. Please. Had Quinn drop me off."

"Sure. Were you in the pit at all tonight?"

"Nah, I like the music. It's fucking brutal. Love it. I chill in the back on the stools and smoke. I like to watch them play. I appreciate good techniques. Things happening at the right time. I want to see how they do it. The intricacies of the band. The pedals."

I turned on the headlights. The beams faced out toward Route 611. They were aimed at the left side of Quinn's face as he sat at a red light with Emma.

"Ya know, that girl you were talking to tonight is Quinn's girl," said Sasha.

"Yeah. I'm looking at them right now."

"What?" Sasha straightened up and looked forward. She dropped onto me and put her head on my lap, staring up at me. "Let me know when he's gone."

I shook my head.

"You like her, right?" asked Sasha. "I can tell."

"Yeah. Used to mainly. Haven't seen her in years. Grew up with her."

"Ah. A rekindling?"

"Are you here to just prod at me?" I snapped.

"No, I really need a ride. Just making conversation, sensitive boy."

"Quinn can drive ya. You want me to flicker my beams?"

"Screw that. His car smells like ass."

"OK, the coast is clear. He's gone."

"You sure? I don't want him to see me in here with ya. He'll spread rumors."

"About what?"

"Forget it." Sasha sat back up. "Gum?" she asked, holding out a silver wrapped stick.

I looked down at her smooth legs and black leather boots. "No, I'm good."

As we headed to her house, Sasha bitched about how most of her friends went to college and how she's stuck working at TGI Fridays. Almost at her house, she pointed at Quinn pulling into their driveway. "It's them. Pull over now," she blurted.

We watched Emma and Quinn run through the downpour and head inside.

"There they go, off to make out upstairs," Sasha remarked.

I grimaced.

"You need to chill the fuck out." Sasha grabbed my limp right hand from my side and tossed it like garbage onto a pile of cassettes. We sat for a moment in silence. She spat out her green gum and put it on the dashboard. She took my right hand again and put it onto her kneecap. "I saw you looking earlier. I know."

I turned and saw her eyes for only the second time that night. She locked me in.

"Turn off the car," she said, moving my hand up towards the shreds of her pink corduroy cut off shorts.

I turned the key. The wipers stopped their incessant whirring.

"Lights," she said.

I flicked off the exteriors as the dashboard lights faded. The engine halted. The radio commercials silenced. The rain grew more intense, windows filled with cascading falls.

Sasha eased my hand back to her knee and then back up to her shorts. She unsnapped the button of her shorts with her right hand. Her zipper instantly moved down to reveal dandelion printed panties. They seemed too innocent on her. I expected something lacy. She put her finger under the top elastic waistband and lifted.

"It's all yours," she said. She leaned the seat back a bit and spread her legs slightly.

I looked around. "But I told you about Emma."

"One more mention of her and I'm gone."

I took a handful of her warm thighs, focusing on speckled freckles I never had the chance to notice. An instant headache ensued. "Why are you doing this?" I asked.

Sasha held the liner up, refusing to answer. My finger floundered in, poking over her pubes, searching.

"Woah, gentle," she said through a slight giggle. "I'll help you."

I looked over and saw her chin raised high. The back of her head dug into the headrest, positioning my index finger into a rhythm.

"There," she said a few times. "Firm, push there. Against that."

The rain remained steady and loud, curtaining us with funneling water on glass. A shadowy figure walked by with a dog and an umbrella, but we remained undetected, the windows fogged.

For minutes, Sasha maneuvered my hand as one and then two fingers hooked and kneaded the warm wettening wonder.

I turned toward Sasha. She shoved my face. "Don't look over," she said.

I peered off to the left and watched tree branches sway. Through the leaves, I saw the shed I hid behind with Quinn, years ago, where Kova took my photo. I watched a pizza get delivered via the side-view mirror.

Unable to resist a peek, I took a glimpse of Sasha. She bit her bottom lip. Her mouth opened as if clamped in position. She was finally in my control. Her breath shortened. Her musky scent overrode her vanilla clove perfume. I kept my hand lifeless, as if it wasn't mine, as if I wasn't there, as if the moment didn't count. The more I didn't exist, the more unhinged she became. Her right hand slapped the window. A boot kicked the dashboard open, sending Dad's pay stubs and paperwork onto the floor. I wanted to lunge my other hand at her but resisted, content with being a theater prop. But in looking down, I was no longer being guided. I was making swift swirls myself.

With a stomp on the floor, Sasha clutched my fingers down, keeping them. I wasn't sure whether to retreat. Sasha opened her eyes. "Here you go," she said, slowly giving my hand back. She put the gum back in her mouth. "Nice," she said, panting back to normal. "I know you've never felt one before and wanted to know what it was like. So, now you know."

I sat speechless.

"The more you know, right?" said Sasha, making the trademark sound from a late night PSA on TV. "You've got a lot to learn."

"Sorry. It's just. I saw Emma tonight and—"

"Stop, for the love of God," she said, fixing herself back up. "Seriously, it's just some fun. You should thank me. Do you mind if I smoke?"

I paused and released frenzied chuckles. A fantasy had warped into reality, unrecognized. "That's what my Driver's Ed teacher asked me," I said. "He was a big fat guy. He turned to me and asked that same question. A couple lights later, he asked me to pull into a coffee shop and he came back with strawberry frosted donuts."

"You feeling alright there, Garv?"

I looked over at Sasha. She slid a hand under the bottom of my chin and held it.

"Just a crazy day," I said. "I just. Ya know, I've always thought you were so hot since—"

"What, I'm not anymore?"

"No, you are."

"I just want to get out of *Boreland*. There's nothing to do here."

"It's not so bad here. It's safe. No alligators or cobras or scorpions. No hurricanes or tornadoes. We get the four seasons."

"Nope, I saw a tornado once on Bridge Street. Sky turned green and a thin finger came down in the distance. It wasn't a Finger Of God sized tornado but it caused damage."

"Where would you go?"

"Portsmouth. New Hampshire. I like the cold. Cabin life. No hot ass beaches. Peaceful up there. I have to start saving. This guy I know says I can make big money at the Lucky Lounge."

"That place in the Glenside area?"

"Yeah. Just a few months of work."

"Doing what? Waiting tables?"

"No, dumbass. Dancing."

"They have a stage there?"

"You *do* know what the place is, right?"

"Sure, it's where golfers go to smoke cigars, escape their wives."

"Exactly. I'm not talking *The Electric Slide*. Haven't you noticed there's no windows?"

"I can't remember."

"There's pole dancing here in the burbs. Five golf courses around here. That place gets packed on weekends. Good money."

The rain reduced to a slight drizzle. I pictured Sasha stripping.

"I think it's time I bolt," she said, flicking her cigarette butt out the window. She leaned over, put her hand over my zipper and squeezed. "Still ready to go. Very nice," she said, taking extra juicy chomps of gum with her left molars. She fled. I sat in the car alongside overflowing trash cans.

I drove off and guided the Toyota through the quiet Oreland streets. The car smelled like her hair, as if she was still next to me. I circled back to her house and saw her in the kitchen, fixing something to eat. Her hand prints were still on the window. I brought all windows down to air out the cigarette stench. The sound of tires and moist traction against a slowly drying street, combined with crickets, put me at ease.

At stop signs, I peered toward bay windows and saw outlines of families sitting in front of their TVs in the dark. Bright parts of the shows flashed, revealing cozy couch relaxation. I circled back toward Sasha's house. She was smoking on the porch. I could only see her moonlit pale legs and an orange ember.

"Want to watch a show or something?" I asked from the car.

"What?" asked Sasha. "My parents are watching TV."

"What about your room?"

"Dude, it was a favor. I'm four years older than you."

I smiled. "Well, thanks." I drove off. A couple houses up, I heard Sasha's flimsy screen door fling open. The spring stretched with a squeak. The door pounded shut. In my rearview, I saw Emma trotting with brisk strides down Weldy Avenue toward West Oreland. I waited awhile and reversed back. "What did she say?" I asked.

"Nothing," said Sasha. "She didn't see me. Just flew outta here." Sasha lit another cigarette, her bare feet on an ottoman. "I don't want to tell ya what to do, but... My boots really stunk up my feet."

I drove alongside Emma. She was fuming, clobbering tree branches in her way. I called out to her. "Need a ride, slugger?"

"Where you coming from?" asked Emma, stationed like a linebacker ready to tackle.

"Rosario's. Just got a slice with some friends. Was starving after that show."

"I'm a big girl. Can make it back myself. But, I'll take a lift." Emma jogged over. "Sorry, just shocked to see you. Again! Twice in one day. Sorry, I'm just..."

"It's fine."

Emma climbed into the still reclined seat. "Is your seat broken?"

"Oh, just—My friend was being a goof. Left it like that," I said. "Where were you at?"

"Was at my cousin's. Second cousin. She's a bitch."

Emma and I drove around for an hour, not wanting to enter our separate front doors. We impelled laughter from each other and smacked the dashboard from observational humor. We annihilated whatever we thought or saw with lowball insults, reducing Oreland to shreds, diminishing it to just us, back together.

51.

Phat Laces Bro

April '92
The next day, I awoke to the sound of Francis laying on his horn. I scrambled from my bed sheets to the window. "Go ahead," I called out. "Overslept. See ya later on."

Veronica bent over Francis's lap and came into view. She curled her index finger and wiggled it toward her. "We can wait," she said.

"No, we can't," said Francis. He slapped her hand and sped off.

I dressed without a shower while chomping an untoasted Pop-Tart. I heard the bus roar toward the bus stop. As I locked the front door, the bus brakes squealed. I sprinted across lawns and hurled over bushes, only to see the rear red lights descending down Twining Road. A cloud of exhaust loomed. No other way to get there, I walked the five miles to school. A delightful daze carried me as I replayed Emma's embrace in my mind, looping the visual and sensation of her squeeze.

After signing in at the Admin Office at 9:45am and getting tallied tardy, I headed to class. I walked through the long glass tunnel that connected the East and West buildings. A few kids approached from the distance. One was Wolf. He extended a hand and smiled. We slapped hands and shook with tight vigor. The other kids appeared to be freshman and scuttled off. I awaited

Wolf's insult or sneak attack. Sunlight beamed through the glass, spotting the tiled floor with colors.

"My man," said Wolf. "Heard Sasha went down on ya last night."

"Say what?" I asked.

"My buddy was there. He saw her jump in your car and lay right into ya. He thought *he* had her and was waiting—"

"Nah. I mean, I gave her a ride home."

"Nothing happened? So, you're a homo?" Wolf attempted to dead arm me, but I caught it with my left hand.

"What gives, man?" I asked, dropping my bag. "What'd I ever do?" The solar warmth hit my back, guiding me forward. I bumped his chest with mine. Wolf's face twitched. He stepped back, shrugged and looked for witnesses. We stood at the tunnel's center. Nobody lingered. My hands shook. I eyed his bottom lip. A chunk the size of a pencil eraser was missing.

"Easy, there," said Wolf.

"Seriously, why do you hate me?" I knew the deal, but wanted to hear it from him.

Wolf rubbed his forehead with quick strokes as if bugs were crawling on him. "Eh, you. You're just. Ya know, Sasha's a real cutie." Wolf's demeanor melted back to normal.

"Yeah, I guess so."

"Nice orange shoelaces," Wolf said, kneeling down to inspect. "They glow in the dark?"

"Not sure. Just got them. I like the fatty style." I stared down at Wolf's mane.

"They're so bright."

I wanted to kick his head like a soccer ball. He was disarmed, teed up. The hot tunnel was void of anyone. Just one solid nose crushing punt, I thought.

Wolf rose back up.

"So, what's up with this?" I asked, pointing to my bottom lip while staring at his.

"Not sure yet," said Wolf, walking off backwards. "Doctor's looking at it today. Heading there now."

"Hope you heal up soon. It looks really—"

"You watch Pearl Jam on SNL last weekend?"

"Uh, hell yeah," I said, surprised he changed the topic.

"Cool, see ya at Study Hall. Sharon Stone too? She was smoking hot in that airport skit." Wolf talked louder with each step, imitating scenes.

Later at study hall, Wolf sat behind me. He usually sat in the back. We talked more SNL before doing homework. A half hour in, I stood up to get a magazine from the Current Events station. I tried to take a step, but a weight halted my lower body. The room turned upside down with a swift thrust and the sound of scraping metal. My head landed onto the edge of the desk next to me, occupied by a girl. I fell to the cold tiles, face down onto the canvas shoes of the girl.

"You're bleeding on my leg!" cried the girl.

My desk collapsed onto my knee, banging my bursitis. I laid stuck on the floor, watching the feet of students scurry toward me. Blood trickled down my face, creating pink blurry vision, like looking through a slice of watermelon.

I tilted my head. Wolf stood above me. He squealed in a strange ladylike high-pitched tone. "I thought you were dead," he said, pointing. He walked in and out of frame, muttering. Dreadful faces circled above me, staring at Wolf's falsetto shrieking.

"He's gonna be OK," someone said to Wolf. "Your voice, that's a different question." The crowd laughed, mocking his shrill, unable to reach the high octave.

Wolf knelt down and put his face close to mine. Salty drops fell from his eyes, plopping onto my cheeks. "I'm so sorry, man," he whispered. "Didn't think you'd fall hard." He struggled to unfasten my left laces, tied to my desk's legs.

The teacher overseeing Study Hall was in the bathroom. Wolf heaved me up. I put my arm around his shoulder, my head and knee aching. He walked me to the school nurse. I sat in a chair as she examined and sponged away the blood. "Honey, you're gonna need to go to the hospital," the nurse said. "I'll get a bandage and clean it up. You need stitches." Drops of blood dotted my orange laces and the floors.

"I'll drive him," said Wolf.

"Who did this? What happened?" asked the study hall teacher, appearing at the doorway, blocking our exit. "Did you fall? Did someone push you? Did—"

"A nasty trip," I mustered, holding a bag of ice over the bandage. "Let's go."

"Are you sure?" asked the teacher. "Nobody did anything?"

"Why would they?" I asked.

The teacher stood inert, mouth open. He got out of the way. "No reason. Just..."

Wolf assisted me to his car.

"We'll notify your guardians," said the teacher.

Wolf and I sat in silence as he drove to Abington Hospital. He sobbed, repeating apologies with a high-pitched whine, exposed. My forehead ached but my mind felt jostled, realigned.

"Assholes are out there," I said, as Wolf parked the car. "Monsters. But you don't have to be one."

We turned to each other. He nodded in consideration before guiding me to the triage. His demeanor and walk had changed, distilled to a genuine self, void of bravado. I patted his shoulder to leave.

52.

Entertainment Options

May '92

The next Saturday, I headed to Emma's house to watch my homemade videos. When I arrived, I was looking forward to saying hello to her family, but they were at a diner. We watched about twenty minutes of my goofy SNL inspired skits. Although she laughed often, we were not talking. I wondered about her and Quinn and what I was doing back in her family room with the same maroon carpet and sectional from years ago.

Eventually, Emma led me upstairs to show me her room. She sat on her bed as I examined shelf decorations and asked questions about them. I looked out her window and saw my old house. I had never seen it from that angle. The new owners had enclosed the porch and installed a fence. The stucco no longer resembled chunks of butter, painted gray. Dad's voice of tidbit advice permeated my thoughts: *Don't you know? You can't go home again.*

I wondered what my life would have been like if I hadn't gone to public school or moved to East Oreland. Emma put both of her hands on my shoulders and dug her fingers into my tense muscles. I turned to her and dove in for a kiss, just catching part of her upper lip. I landed mainly on her nostrils, a sloppy attempt. She put her head down and smiled. "Let's try again," she said, sliding a thumb over my head bandage.

On our third date out, I took Emma to Caddie Day at Shady Creek, along the 15th hole. She had asked about golf. We cut through the same hole in the fence that had been there for years and I walked my chintzy bag of clubs with her. I looked over at Quinn's house as we passed it, but she said nothing. I was hoping to get answers on where they stood.

The twilight was muggy. We sweated profusely, getting divot dirt on our hands. I impressed her with a deep drive that bounced on a sprinkler head for extra yardage. By the time we reached the green to putt, our own stink had soused our shirts. As cute as Emma looked in her barrettes and beaded perspiration mustache, I knew the date had turned grotesque. With just one hole completed, we headed back to my Mom's car. We took turns letting the air conditioning cool us down by lifting our shirts up over the vents.

"Let's get a movie at West Coast," said Emma. "I think *Edward Scissorhands* is out now. We can watch it in my room."

"I don't have a membership. Do you?"

"I have my Mom's card. There's one in Maple Glen."

"Cool. My buddy Zakk works there."

Upon entering West Coast Video, the place was empty. The A/C was intense. Emma danced around the store with arms out, releasing sighs in the frigid air. I found the movie and brought it to the checkout area. Nobody was there. On about ten different TVs scattered throughout the store, an action movie called *Showdown In Little Tokyo* was playing.

"Hello?" I shouted, looking around.

"Be with you in a minute," said a voice. I looked toward the Adult Video Room and heard the saloon style doors squeal at the entry / exit. Footsteps approached. Uniformed and branded in West Coast Video red, Quinn appeared. "Oh, hey there, Garv," he said.

"Didn't know you worked here," I said, looking around.

"Yep, for now," he said. "It's not too bad."

I saw the top of Emma's head, a few aisles over. A shootout

scene from the movie erupted. Quinn and I looked up at the TV. He scanned Emma's card and bar coded the movie with eyes fixated on the violent scene.

"All set, Garv. Have it returned no later than Friday," said Quinn in a robotic corporate voice, as if he never met me before. He slid the movie to the far end of the counter. I nodded and picked it up. He stared back up at the movie.

I bolted toward the exit where Emma was staring at a freezer of packaged ice cream and popsicles. I grabbed her hand and raced the four steps out the door with her. She gasped. "I want ice cream," she said.

"Oh, I know of an even better place," I said. "Custom custard." I tossed the movie to the sidewalk and pulled Emma close. We locked lips and swirled tongues. I didn't mind if Quinn saw us. I didn't care if they were still dating or if she purposely took me there to see him. I felt as if my intentions were being tested. I dug in and squeezed her back close.

An old man with a cane got out of his car and took notice. He waddled over. "America, baby," he said. "This is what it's all about. *This* is why I served." He stuck out his hand. I gave him a high five.

"That was much better," said Emma, getting air. "You've been practicing?"

I smiled. "Let's get ice cream."

Back at Emma's house, we sifted through the previews. At the beginning of the movie, she paused it to use the bathroom.

"So, are you still dating Quinn?" I asked, after she sat back down.

"That's abrupt," said Emma. "What do you think?"

"He was there. At West Coast Video."

"Your friend Zakk?"

"No. Quinn. I mean, Zakk was there."

"I'll meet him next time, for sure." Emma spooned some Bourbon Praline Pecan towards me and I mouthed it down. "As for Quinn, I am supposed to go to your prom with him. He asked back in March."

"Are you still going?"

"I'm feeding you ice cream in a dark room."

"Right..." I thought of how Wolf knew about Sasha getting in my car. I drifted into bits of ease and paranoia, trying to play it cool. "Maybe we shouldn't go to the prom," I said. "It might be a big rub on Quinn and—"

"Yes! Screw the prom. Totally agree. I never even got a dress."

"I'll go if you want to."

"Nope. Let's go berry picking. There's a place up in Bucks County. We can take them home and make pies. Slap some whipped cream on them."

And while most of my class huddled in the parking lot of the Post Prom Party, sneaking swigs of Mad Dog 20/20 and Peach Schnapps, I swung in Emma's backyard hammock with a belly full of tart baked berries, listening to crickets and her whispered ideas of future escapades.

53.

The Irish Goodbye

August '92

Summer was a muddled fog. Thrilling hours with Emma seeped into stagnant hours on the golf course. Exhaustion ensued.

Friends were busy. As juvenile offenders, Rusty, Blue and Jinwoo were each ordered dozens of Community Service hours. They delivered groceries to elderly neighbors and read stories to the visually impaired. Combined with their summer jobs and being grounded, I didn't bother calling them. Francis and Veronica were around, but they broke up. I didn't side with either of them.

A girlfriend was plenty.

The day before I moved to a state college in rural Berks County to major in TV Production, I went to caddie. Merv avoided selecting me all day. Lackluster SAT scores yielded minimal options for college. I sat and pondered the wasted high school hours. I regretted the lack of focus on studies and zero participation in extracurricular activities.

After four hours, I was the sole caddie left. Merv walked over. "Thank God you're still here," said Merv. "Didn't forget ya, baby. I got Kova teeing off soon. OK?"

"Sounds good," I said.

"He pulled this unscheduled shit on me. He'd kill me if I didn't have a caddie. He never carts it. So, hang tight, Gary. It's just him and a guest. Should be a quick round."

A slight drizzle arrived. I waited in the shack, rereading magazines.

I thought of a glum moment from college orientation. The Director of Telecommunications had us newbies sit in the bleachers of a basketball court. "Look to your left and then look to your right," said the Director. "One of these people will be gone by December. You know why? Because they can't focus. And let me tell you. Even if you graduate, good luck finding a job. It's slim pickings out there in this industry."

A few minutes passed. I heard the march of golf cleats coming from the Pro Shop to the path below. Left, right, left, right. Kova walked by and nodded at me. "Son," he said. "See ya at the first tee in a few."

A rush of blood went to my head. The anguish that Kova had caused Dad, Pat's Dad and Conner's family, all of his conniving and threats, his over development of Oreland—everything became reduced to a prickly sparkling pinpoint I couldn't shake. I thought of Kristoph and his etchings in the library stall. I paced with my caddie towel, swatting gnats, chest heaving. I saw Kova at the driving range, his back facing towards me. There wasn't a caddie in sight. I was it. I was his sole chance to enjoy a round of golf the only way he insisted, with a young man hauling his clubs.

I looked towards the Pro Shop and saw Merv chatting on the phone. I grabbed an iced tea from the soda pagoda and darted up the steep incline through a series of bushes to the entry drive. I peered down and saw Merv pacing with his hands up. I thought of running back down and pretending that I needed to get something from my car.

"Enough of this," I thought. I ran onwards to Dad's car, parked up on the sloped lot. I took a plastic bag from the backseat and tucked it over the license plate. I reversed out and drove towards the exit. The large wrought-iron gate started closing. I couldn't get through in time. A mix tape wheeled in my mind, a motivating guide of riffs and anthems—the best parts of my favorite songs threaded together, pushing me on.

Through my rearview, I saw a cart coming up behind me. A Pro Shop kid, a cashier, was driving it. I managed a sloppy three-point turn, driving over bordering flowers. "Hold up!" the kid yelled. I sped towards him and he chickened to the left. I knew of another exit, far off.

I approached the bag drop off area where I slowed down for a speed bump. I heard Kova demanding to Merv: "You better produce a caddie. Where *is* he?" I looked down and saw Merv walk into frame. He shrugged, twisting his confident mustache like a slug being salted.

I zoomed off around a large floral circle, going the wrong way. I passed the pool area. Ladies having post round cocktails faced me as I revved down a straightaway. They gasped in disgust as they tried to tan their white cleavage.

I connected with the Maintenance Road, an asphalt trail that careened through the course. The trail came into play for some holes. Golfers loved the bounce it gave their ball, often adding thirty yards to a tee-off. I tore through the trail, disrupting backswings. Several scratched their heads. As one golfer teed off, I continued through. His ball bounced off a hubcap and sent his mid fairway position to a shrub in the rough.

At the halfway house, three servers stood outside with their aprons and ordering pads. I honked the horn at them and saluted.

In the far straightaway distance, I saw the wide open maintenance gate which emptied onto Twining Road. I knew the hours the gate would be ajar, open for shipments of food and supplies. Louie was near the exit on his walkie-talkie, tossing his arms in the air. He sprinted toward the trail, belly fat escaping from his t-shirt and jiggling. As he intersected the trail, which became gravel, he skidded and fell to his back. I swerved around him on the grass and made it past the gates, waiting for a clearing from the cars speeding by. In my rearview, Louie slowly stood up, wiping the rocks from his thick legs. The Pro Shop boy careened into sight on his cart. He pointed a finger at me and belted a toothy holler.

I drove up Twining Road and saw a golfer deep in the rough of the 16th hole. He lined up a shot near the fence. During his back swing, I held the horn down and passed him, laying deep into the rubber center of the steering wheel. I pounded the ceiling of the car with a flat hand and screamed in key with the note of the horn. Residents working on their lawns turned toward me.

Relaxed, I cracked open the iced tea. A few instances of regret shivered through me. The manual labor job was over. I pictured Kova lambasting Merv. I ended up at a diner on route 611. It was midday and rather vacant. I sat at the counter and ordered a He-Man Special. It had two of each: eggs, bacon, sausages, pancakes, toast. The waitress was stunning, out of my league. She chewed gum blankly and refilled my water, standing beside me the entire time as I ate. I pumped quarters into the jukebox and explained how great each song was.

Outside, I leaned against the car and watched the Blue Angels perform marvelous aerobatics by the Willow Grove NAS. They appeared in the sky with booming roars. Shady Creek had nothing on me. No friends. No street address. No phone number. No tax documents. No true name. I yanked the plastic bag off the license plate. The caddie named Gary signed off.

54.

One Horse Renaissance

September '92

College was exactly what Rusty's brother said it would be, a welcome rebirth of our identities. Nobody knew I was an outcast in high school, that I was a virgin. Every person was a fresh face void of any past connection or prejudice. My dork status was erased. The fresh rural Berks County air, infiltrated with manure fertilizer, gave me energy. Everyone was the new kid that knew nothing about how it all worked.

After my parents hugged me goodbye, I hung up my band posters, awaiting my roommate to arrive. I heard a guy playing a Jane's Addiction bass line down the hall. I floated towards the plucked notes. A guy that looked similar to me nodded, glancing up from his amplifier. We hit it off immediately, name dropping songs. All throughout the dorm, quick brotherhoods formed. Athletes, artists, quirky ones, all sharing the common hell of being in the sole all male dorm on campus. Each floor brimmed with testosterone, ogling eyes out windows at the girls. Unlike the seven co-ed dorms, we were lobby to rooftop with horned up dudes. Our dorm was nicknamed The Dog Pound due to our pack mode and complimentary woofs. When a guy was lucky enough to escort a girl through the obnoxious halls of sweat and overflowing trash cans, barking occurred and heads stuck out of doorways.

My roommate, Doug, was a quiet preppy guy that was edging out with Bob Marley posters and a first ever goatee. Two girls from his Pocono Mountains high school class lived in an all-female dorm. They arrived and sat on the edge of his cot in their mini chino shorts. They spoke to Doug like southern belles, making sure he bought his proper text books and that he had enough snacks.

My professors were fun except for the one in American Government. From day one, I was not in his realm of decent folk. He openly pointed out his distaste for men with long hair, calling them hippy freaks that have done nothing good for America. I looked around the room and there were a handful of us. The prof's sunburned face and balding head glistened.

"Now, grading works like this," the professor said, gripping the podium as he swayed. "There are four exams. That's it. This syllabus here explains what chapters are covered for each exam. You need to show up for these exams, these four dates. But for lectures, you don't have to be here. Right now? You can walk right out the door. Anyone want to leave now? Go ahead. I've been teaching for over twenty years and the last thing I want to see are students that don't raise their hands, nod off, doodle, daydream. So, does anyone want to leave now? There's the exit. Anyone?"

The professor looked over at me, eyeing up my tie-dyed Jimi Hendrix t-shirt. I was far from being a bohemian subculture hippy, but I resembled one. I planned to vote for Ross Perot via absentee ballot in November. I didn't even smoke weed. The prof asked several questions about the current Bush's administration. Nobody knew the answers. "Of course not," he sighed, waddling to the blackboard. A student darted out behind his back. I wanted to exit as well, but I gave him the full class, the chance to see if he could convince me to arrive in person again.

#

Unlike high school, girls approached me. All that I did was flip the hair out of my eyes and look their way. When guys asked if I had a girlfriend, I was excited to tell them about Emma and how we were in the raw beginning stages. After a few days, I called Emma's mom and asked her to give Emma my dorm phone number. A week later, Emma called from her dorm room, just over an hour drive away at another remote Pennsylvania state college. My roommate left the room to give me some privacy. The call was bubbly although tedious to explain everything. I wanted to schedule a Saturday with her and when I finally got to that question, Emma paused.

"We can meet up at your campus if you want?" I asked. "I can take the bus there."

"Garvey, you're a sweet guy. But why?" asked Emma. "We're in college, ya know. Aren't you meeting girls?"

"Well, yeah. But I'm just talking music with them and stuff. Not getting phone numbers."

"I think you should. I should too. We should date around. We're on two different planets now."

"But we could meet in Oreland for winter break, holidays. Summertime. It can work."

"It could. But I'm probably gonna stay up here for the summer. Get a waitress gig."

I mumbled incoherent phrases, breathing heavy.

Emma sighed. Her dorm mates frolicked in the background. "Call me during winter break," she said. "After the holiday insanity. We'll both be off in January for a couple weeks."

Saddened, I realized Emma had the logical approach. The thoughts of seeing her again was something that brought me joyous confidence, meant to be together. Our first grade childhood sweetheart status had vanished but the world of local live music had realigned us at the Fiesta Motor Inn, only to fragment again.

The next day, I sobbed all over my all-you-can-eat breakfast buffet in the cafeteria, huddled in a corner booth, solo with shades on. But the glum thoughts became diluted, peppered with exchanges from meandering campus girls. Roaming about with my new buds, I took in the reciprocating long seconds of smiling eyes from girls passing by. This casual intentional communication with the opposite sex was new, exciting. I wasn't sure how to act, but I picked up the game and entered a stage of random awful make-out sessions.

The center of campus had a large grassy quad called the DMZ, filled with everyone from muscle heads tossing footballs with no shirts on to hippie drum circles. It seemed cliquish at first, but the bubbles of people weren't bound, allowing phone number exchanges. If a pen or paper was needed, we'd shout out the tool, bopping from group to group, or just scribble it on a palm.

One way to meet girls was to smoke cigarettes in abundance and hang in a populous area, like outside the library. As I watched with my vending machine bought Snapple, I envied how easy it was for a guy to offer or bum a cigarette. The result was an introduction, a conversation, a lasting moment between strangers embracing nicotine fixes in any weather. Cigs were a literal lure for the social smokers to the two-pack per day gotta-have-it-now breeds. Nobody wanted a swig of my Snapple. As Dad had quit his smoking habit for me, I knew I shouldn't be a smoker. I took a few puffs once, but ended in an embarrassing coughing fit.

I kept seeing one girl around town that smiled back and lingered slowly, but I never jumped out of my pack to talk to her, intimidated by her blond dreadlocks and proud strut. Her eyes were a rare amber and copper color, the whites glistening with her gap-toothed grin. Connecting eyes with her brought a sense of relaxation, the converse of her beaming self assurance. I imagined a prolonged stare with her would knock me into a slumber, driven by a black magic she couldn't steer or stop.

"Nice green Puma suedes," she called, eyeing my sneakers.

"Primus!" I responded, digging her band t-shirt, raising my fist to the sky.

Days later, I headed to the cafeteria for dinner and saw her sitting with her crew, smoking and eating pizza on the DMZ. I considered that she might not want to talk with a mouth full greasy mozzarella, so I just waved.

Leaving the cafeteria, I saw her sitting solo by a fountain, looking sullen. I walked over to her and sat thigh to thigh next to her. Her cosmopolitan face oozed a sophistication, but it didn't match her baggy overalls and knit cap. She seemed in disguise, downplaying her attractive qualities. A large black leather art portfolio case sat alongside her.

"Finally," she said. "I figured you would have stopped when I yelled about your kicks."

"I wanted to. Trust me," I said. I felt tense as I watched her smoke, noticing her red lipstick marking the filter. She eyed me up.

"You want one?"

"Nah, I don't smoke. I'm Garvey."

"I'm Tessa."

"Art major of some sort?" I asked, pointing at her case.

"Communication Design. I gotta haul this thing around a lot. I'm not a total sellout. I still do paintings, gothic stuff."

After exchanging numbers, we soon went to a basement keg party at the Lacrosse House. We knew no one, but they took our $2 each in exchange for plastic cups. Tessa and I chugged Milwaukee's Best in a musty cellar, lit by swaying light bulbs. Beer still tasted grotesque, but the confidence it produced made the cold urine flavor worth enduring.

I walked Tessa back to her dorm and went in for a confident kiss at her door. I had Frenched a few girls by this point, but this was the most awkward tongue jabbing yet. Tessa's kiss was of slow warm satin; Mine was a blind octopus trying to latch a tentacle.

Shattered by my performance, I roamed through the DMZ. An inflated sex doll was positioned on the statue of a donor, in the middle of a fountain. The legs of the doll straddled the wealthy donor's face. Laying in bed and dreading the 8am class, Tessa called, asking me to join her for a nightcap joint.

"Oh, I'm OK," I said. "I need to be on my A game tomorrow.

Carl Franke

Got an early class for my major and this prof pop quizzes us like crazy."

55.

Entranced By The
Wiccan

October '92
The following Friday, I slept over in Tessa's massive triple room at her Old Glory dorm. Her two roommates disappeared most weekends. We each drank a 40-ouncer of Mickey's Fine Malt Liquor and watched *Saturday Night Live* tapes on her tiny TV. While we passed out in each others' crooked sweaty limbs, I confessed that I was not only a virgin for marijuana but also for sex. She held her hand over her mouth and straddled my chest. "Oh, my god. I'm going to be your first time?"

"What, right now?" I asked.

"God, no. You need something special. I want cheese fries right now."

"Yeah, me too. Tomorrow night then?"

"OK, I'll make it special for ya."

"Shit, I'm supposed to go to The Cliffs with the guys. Some band is playing out there. I promised them."

"Don't worry. Just be here by 1:00am."

The next day, a marching band woke us, practicing outside Tessa's window. Hangover headaches throbbed. "Fuckin' football," she said.

As I stretched, I noticed an assortment of crystals and dried
flowers formed into a circle, positioned on the floor. A large star
was in the middle, made of green branches and yellow roses on the
points. White candles surrounded it. "Was that there last night?"
I asked.

"There was an hour I couldn't sleep last night. Been researching
Wicca. The magic of the universe coursed through my veins one
day and led me to it."

"Are there spells you can learn?"

"Absolutely. I cast it on you. That's why you're here," she
smiled.

"We're still on for tonight, right?" I asked.

Tessa tossed dried petals at me from a saucer. "See? So
subservient. It's working."

"Whatever. I need a breakfast burrito."

At night, I walked with my dorm buds for several blocks to
The Cliffs, a large apartment community on the outskirts of town.
The uniformly designed pads seemed identical aside from their
address numbers, serene yet identically drab. Then we saw a
couch on fire in a parking lot. A jam band played and cast its
boozy web on us. I drank beer with shots of whiskey and grooved
to the music, unaware of who lived at the house. A girl grabbed
my hand and pulled me into a black light room where several sat
around a dude rolling a joint and admiring his faux felt posters.
As the joint was passed to me, I bolted out the door and walked
solo to Old Glory. The lit up clock tower, reminiscent of an angry
chicken's face, stared at me, luring me with the promise of sex
within her nest. The eyes were analog clocks, continually
reminding all students of the time. A long stretch of the walk was
dark and tree lined. I thought of Kova and how it would be great if
he decided to move to Texas or got arrested, just to disappear for
good. I wondered if I should have trashed my caddying gig just to
piss him off.

I stopped into a pizza shop to get one slice to soak up the booze.
Fluorescent lights were a buzz kill. I bought breath mints and

sucked on a few. I then went to a 24/7 pharmacy to get condoms. More fluorescent lights hampered my mood. I figured the rubbers were up front by the cigarettes.

"Need any help?" asked a perky lady with a tall bun.

"Found it," I said, snagging a candy bar.

"Protection products are in the back by the pharmacy, if you need any."

I nodded and walked through the inescapable yacht rock blaring from the ceiling speakers. Once at the back, I slowly squatted to size up the options. I turned to the right and saw my American Government professor sitting in a waiting chair. We connected eyes briefly, his podium power reduced to nervous twitches. As I bought the chocolate and semi ribbed condoms, I wondered what he was doing up so late and suffering from.

At Old Glory, the front desk girl rang Tessa for me. Down the winding steps, Tessa appeared in a flowing dress, halter top and a beaded hemp necklace. She grabbed my hand.

"You've been smoking some ganja?" asked Tessa.

"No, no. I was around a lot of it though."

"Well, that's getting one step closer," she said while tickling my side.

On entering her room, "Gold Dust Woman" was playing by Fleetwood Mac. Several red candles were lit and sandalwood incense burned. The floors were clean. Her bed was made, with decorative pillows lined against the wall. We immediately kissed. I noticed a painting in progress on an easel.

"Is that..." I said, staring at the artwork.

"Yep, that's you. I'm so embarrassed," Tessa said, startled that I recognized the subject matter.

"It's amazing. But my biceps aren't that big, are they?"

"Oh, just shut up," she said, pushing me into her bed.

"Do you mind changing the cassette? My Mom is a big Fleetwood Mac fan."

"OK, say no more," she said. She got up and took a hit from a glass bowl, and changed the tape to a Syd Barrett solo album.

"He's so good," I said, sitting up Indian style on her bed, staring at the painting in progress.

"Oh, no you don't. Lay back down."

After I lost my virginity, Tessa and I were soon hand-in-hand walking around campus. She gave me a lifesize painting of us hugging, which I hung up on the sliver of wall I had in my dorm room. We had afternoon quickies, dates at the diner and perused her stack of VHS movies. We had future names of our kids. She begged me to partake in weekend acid trips with her local band friends, but I had no desire.

"He just likes his booze," she'd say to them.

56.

Naturally Imbalanced

November '92

After Thanksgiving break, I succumbed to marijuana. My next-door neighbor and buddy, Ricardo, was a perfectionist joint roller. I had watched him separate stem and seed and craft the perfect jay for weeks in his room while he played bootleg Grateful Dead cassettes at the precise volume. I watched his ritual of smoking a joint while incense burned and towels lined the gap beneath his door, followed by exhaling into a fabric softener sheet. He was professional grade.

Although too paranoid to try it in the dorms, I agreed to do it outside one afternoon. We walked to a nearby cemetery and crouched down beneath a gigantic headstone of a wealthy dead man. We took our tokes in the light breeze. I felt nothing. We walked. I realized how loudly I was laughing. I was no longer reserved, grounded and trying to be proper. Alcohol didn't quite produce the radiant even-keeled permagrin haze that weed instilled. The ripe smell was divine, lingering on my fingers and facial scruff.

We stayed in the cemetery for a while and sat on a gravestone that was also a bench. "Come Sit With Me" it said. I saw farms and pastoral calm for miles, routes 222 and 737 crossing between them. On the ground before us was grass, plots not ready to be dug. We watched a woman in a modest home put freshly washed clothes on a line in her yard. The wind flapped the shirtsleeves and pant legs to life. The bearded husband backed his red pickup truck into the driveway. He got out and walked in his overalls and gave his wife a kiss. A cat stretched on a picnic table. Just far enough from the college antics of Main Street seemed an inviting simple world, an American dream void of greed.

I continued to take a few tokes with Ricardo and sometimes from strangers at parties. Tessa was delighted. Sex became extended and book ended by scalp rubs and massages. In an afternoon before classes, Tessa and I met in her room for a quickie.

"Wanna smoke a bowl first?" asked Tessa, with her gap-toothed grin and tilted head.

"I shouldn't," I said. "I have my final American Government exam. I got A minuses in all the others."

"It's—not—for—two—hours," she said in a high-pitched melody, undressing.

"True. Just a puff then. I have it all in my head,"

"You need this. You'll be focused."

Tessa lit the bowl and took a hit. She passed it. The first hit knocked me to a stupendous range of fuzziness. My neck and cheeks twitched. I stared at the wall, trying to escape a dead weight that formed in the back of my head. Tessa giggled with bloodshot eyes, dancing around her room.

"Come and get me," she said, bouncing off her roommates' beds.

We were both done with one puff each. I let out a quick piercing laugh, unlike any sound I've made before. I slouched on the bed, watching my chest rise and fall with my breath, feeling like a body of rippling water. Pulsating waves traveled up and down my torso, almost electric, in perfect intervals, as if I was plugged into a motor. I moved my arms about. They floated as if in a pool. I walked around the room and the waves vibrated. Tessa grabbed me by the belt buckle and tugged me over to her. She unzipped my pants.

"No," I said. "Something's off. Do you feel it?"

Tessa giggled.

"Get your clothes on," I said. "I need air."

Outside, I felt better. I breathed deep doses of air and fixed my eyes on the blue sky.

"The sky," I said. "It's the only sight that all mankind from anywhere on Earth can share."

"What?" asked Tessa.

I walked as if in a steep creek, a current against my knees. Tessa held one hand around my hip. The temperature was the same as inside Old Glory, an eternal room temp.

I headed to American Government and saw my professor cut in front of me at an intersecting pathway. "Ah, going to join us today?" asked the prof.

"Exam day. Of course," I said.

"Great. You might have some struggles. I decided to use my lectures toward the questions. Current events."

I giggled uncontrollably and sulked, seconds apart. Emotions fluttered in my mind. Facial tics folded my cheeks.

"Look at your eyes," he said, suddenly sounding exactly like Kova. "Are you? Nevermind. Pathetic, you are. I can tell. Long-haired hippy freak."

The prof's face morphed into Kova's sneer. I looked around in panic, covering my ears. My voice sound like a Munchkin from *The Wizard Of Oz*, high pitched and sped up.

"Do I sound different?" I asked Tessa.

I stepped off the busy path and dropped to my knees on the grass. "I need you to get me to the school nurse."

"No, you can't do this. We both have classes now. Learn to control it. Steer it back to the good vibes."

"Please, I need a doctor or something."

"I can't go there. I got flagged for walking out with cough medicine there. Twice."

"What? What was in that weed? Are you hearing this? I sound like that *Chipmunks* cartoon." I wept, holding onto Tessa as if the ground would swallow me up, but wanting to push her away, certain she was trying to poison me.

Tessa walked me back to my dorm room. "He's feeling sick," Tessa said to my friends gathered outside. In the hallway, I straddled a water fountain but the water wouldn't go down my throat. I could breathe through my nose but couldn't swallow.

In my room, Tessa rubbed my forehead while I sat curled on my bottom bunk. We watched my roommate play *Tecmo Bowl*. I held onto the crisp anthems of the game, rallying me back to safety. I closed my eyes and felt like I was falling from a tower. As I opened my eyes, the sensation stopped. The free fall furor continued with every time I closed my lids.

"Is this a Wiccan spell?" I asked, gripping the steel bed frame. "For real. Tell me. I'm a good Christian boy. Don't do this to me." My mouth and tongue became numb and I blacked out.

I awoke hours later, famished. Tessa and my roommate were gone. The TV was off. I wondered if I had dreamt the whole ordeal. I sat up. Tessa walked in with a box of pizza and a gallon jug of water.

"I'm good now," I said, unwilling to look her in the eyes. "What was in that anyway?"

"It was laced a bit," she drawled after a long sigh. "With PCP. You had a bad experience with it obviously. I felt fine. *Real* good actually. Until, well, your situation."

"I'm so screwed."

"He'll let you take the exam again. He has to. Say you had the flu."

"He reminded me of Kova," I said to myself.

"Who's Kova?"

"Did you know it was laced?"

"No, not really. I mean, sometimes the guy I get it from throws me a surprise."

I chewed the pizza, primed to regain my strength.

57.

Gift Exchange

December '92

The day before Winter Break, I called Tessa at her dorm so I could give her a Christmas present of burgundy Dr. Martens boots. She walked down the stairs to escort me up. She gazed beyond me while grabbing my hand, leading me to the lobby. We sat in cozy chairs with a coffee table between us. She looked at the goofy Grinch wrapping paper and scrunched her nose as if the gift had a vile smell.

"Sorry, the wrap job is as good as I could get it," I said.

"That's not it," Tessa said. She took a deep breath. When she opened her gift, she cupped her nose and mouth with both hands. She locked eyes with me. She picked one boot up out of the tissue paper and plopped it down. Her eyes watered. "This is nice and all, but the reason I brought you here is that I need a break. Some time off. Things are just moving too fast."

I couldn't look at her eyes anymore. I noticed her hair was tossed about, socks inside out and a larger than usual flannel shirt was draped across her back, incorrectly buttoned.

"Just like that?" I asked. "You're gonna end it?"

"Let's get through the holidays. It's hard for me with my Mom and her fucking girlfriend. She's my second Mom."

Warm tears leaked down my cheeks as the girl residents entered and fled through the glass revolving door. I watched their studious strides, chins raised high, marching to achieve excellence. They resembled a squad of strength, ready to dominate.

"I want you to have this," said Tessa, holding out a clenched fist.

I reached out. She dropped a ceramic one-hitter and a dime bag into my hand. "It's not laced with anything. Don't worry. It's from the normal guy. The stuff you dig."

I swooped the weed into my pocket. Tessa stood up with her shoebox and patted my shoulder. I sat looking at the red wrapping paper and bow on the floor. I had hoped for a night of jolly rum-spiked holiday sex and vending machine cookies. Instead, I walked through the frigid winds of Main Street, listening to the carnival sounds of Tom Waits on my Sony Walkman, wondering who Tessa was banging. I headed to a keg party and drank quietly in the corner.

Outside of Old Glory, I looked up at her window and saw the dull candlelight flickering past her mandala tapestry she used as drapes. I sat back down in the same chair in the lobby, confused whether I was dumped. A girl approached me that looked familiar. I realized it was one of Tessa's roommates that was hardly around.

"Look, just move on," she said, standing across from me.

"Who's up there with her?" I asked.

She sat down, looking irritated, keeping a hand on her purse. "It's her ex."

"The guy that's five years older than her? The townie dude that lives in a barn?"

"Yep. I like you, Garv. More than I like her. I'm stuck living with her for just one more night. Hopefully she goes to his place later. Look, I'm sorry, but she treated you like shit. You look like a younger version of him. Your hair, eyes, height, clothes. You're thinner though."

"Unbelievable," I said. I thought of the paintings she had drawn, rubbing my hands through my hair. I reached over and plucked poinsettias from a large pot. "Do you want to get a drink with me?" I asked, presenting the red-leafed plant.

"God, no. You should just get some rest."

I passed out in the lobby. A security guard prodded at me hours later and told me to scram. I realized Dad would be picking me up in a few hours for the holiday break. I walked the vacant campus to my dorm, passing by the halted folly of inebriated youth as they sat fazed out, flaccid on benches.

58.

Eject Button

December '92

Days into the holiday break, my grades arrived in the mail. I ran the letter up to my room after tossing the other mail aside. I plucked off the perforated edges and pulled out the card. I circled my eyes at my bedroom walls of Scotch taped athletes, sex symbols, video game heroes and rock stars, large photos ripped out of magazines. Darren Daulton, Drew Barrymore, Shinboi, Jim Morrison, Chris Farley all looked at me in anticipation. Mom's clogs tapped louder as she walked upstairs. I glanced down, delighted to see a D+ for American Government. The other grades, Bs in everything else, saluted me until I reached Ethics. Where I expected an A, an F sneered at me with an asterisk next to it. This indicated that I had to call the Philosophy Department.

Mom's clogs drew closer. I stuffed the report card into a pillow case. Mom entered with a laundry basket. "You've been mixing your reds with your whites, haven't you?" asked Mom. "All your tighty-whiteys are pink. Maybe we should get dark earth tone boxers for—"

"Mom," I said. "I need to call the university. There's been a mixup. I was supposed to get an A but got the wrong grade."

"Did they bump you down to a B+?"

"Nope. F. I don't know how this is possible. He loved my essays. I always got As."

Mom dropped the basket and sat on a fold-up chair. "You better call them now."

Standing in the kitchen, I dialed the number while Mom hosed the flowers in the front yard. Dad was at work.

"Well, I think you know why you got an F," said the professor. "It's because you and Blaine handed in identical final papers. Word for word!"

My jaw dropped. I twirled the phone around my forearm and kicked the moulding of the kitchen floor. I wanted to scream. "What do you mean?" I asked.

"You think I'm stupid? You think by just having different fonts I wouldn't notice?"

#

Blaine was dopey. He dressed in bold multi-colored rugby shirts, acid-washed jeans and a baseball cap—trapped in 80s fashion. I didn't know what his hair looked like. He always wore a hat. His face was patchy with red continents drifting on his cheeks. He had a mucousy speech impediment and laughed at everything. Jokes made him fall to the ground, reduced to a pile of thrashing limbs. I had given my essay on Utilitarianism to Blaine. I was proud of it. I sat perched on my dorm room desk as the Brother word processor rattled out each sentence like a machine gun. I completed the paper with Mozart on my headphones while Blaine played gin rummy with Doug.

"You're really done?" asked Blaine. "Congrats. Can I read it?"

I tapped the ten papers together on the desk, stapled it and handed it to Blaine. He walked off to his room.

Five minutes later, Blaine was back. "I'm too hungover to read it," he said. "Looks good though."

#

"He must have used the copy machine in the lounge," I explained to the prof.

"You did give it to him?" asked the prof. "On purpose?"

"Yes, just to give it a quick read."

"We'll see what he says on the phone."

A couple days later, Mom drove me to meet with the Department Head. The campus was vacant, frigid. My prof greeted me in the Philosophy lounge in his wool blazer. He massaged his goatee and nursed a coffee. Mom waited in the car, listening to Rush Limbaugh bash Bill Clinton on the radio.

"Follow me," the prof said, guiding me down a hallway. "You're first. Blaine will be here later today. We're to determine if this is a collaboration or if one of you is innocent." The prof opened a door. I went in. The Department Head, Dr. Zhuk, sat at his desk stroking his gray beard, reading my paper. He pointed to a chair. I sat down. All window blinds were closed. Several fish aquariums were lit up with bright pink and yellow stones.

Dr. Zhuk looked up at me, clutching the straps of his fair isle pom hat. He had a lazy eye and a head twitch. I wasn't sure which eye to focus on. "So, did you write this paper or what?" he asked, tossing it on his desk.

"Yes. I wrote the whole thing," I said. "I have the word processor disk with my file on it as proof, here in my pocket."

"A digital file? How's that proof?"

"It has the date when I last saved it, the day I printed it out."

"That means nothing. Can you name your references? From memory?"

I pictured the library books in my head and spewed out their long titles the best I could.

"Look," said Dr. Zhuk. "I need to ask these questions. Blaine admitted fault over the phone. Why would you give him your paper? He sounds like a moron."

"I figured he'd have insight or spot a spelling error. He barely even had it."

"You're very lucky, you know. Expulsion without question would have occurred to you both at most PA state schools. Did Blaine seem off to you?"

"Kind've. Always has. We mainly eat dinner and play chess and—"

"A piece of advice. It's more survivalist than philosophical. Avoid fuck-ups. OK? Keep them out of your life. They'll bring you down. Discern bullshit from fact. Sense motives. You seem to have known he was cuckoo. Divert yourself."

"I hear ya. Loud and clear."

"It's a good paper you wrote." Dr. Zhuk lunged out of his chair and did a butterfly kick on his area rug. "Most importantly, be strong. Mentally." He sat back down. "Do you smoke herb?"

"I have," I said.

"I'm not against it. You look like you're promoting it. That's a big hemp necklace there."

"My girlfriend gave it to me. Well, we're taking a break."

Dr. Zhuk laughed. "And what is she doing on her break?"

"I don't know. Figuring things out I guess."

"With whom?"

"Likely with her ex."

"Identify venomous snakes and steer clear." Dr. Zhuk aimed both hands toward the door and snapped his fingers. "Your updated report card will be mailed out to you."

My parents were relieved. After a celebratory stromboli dinner with them, I headed solo to the mall. I walked toward Babbages to check out new games. The store was gone, replaced by a U.S. Army Recruitment Office. The buttery scent of Auntie Anne's pretzels wafted over me. I sucked on my Orange Julius drink, staring at large Victoria's Secret banners. I turned to the Recruitment Office. A man in military fatigues walked toward me. "You looking to learn how you can be all you can be, son?" asked the man, handing a brochure.

"This used to be a video game store," I said, taking the collateral.

"Was it? I've only been here a few weeks. Wouldn't know about that. You like to play the games?"

"I did. Played them daily for years."

"They're great for developing hand-eye coordination. They help enable quick responses. You in school? I'm Sergeant Sanders."

"College. First year."

"What're ya studying?"

"TV production, basically."

"How you liking it?"

"Almost got kicked out," I said, thumbing through the brochure. "Wasn't my fault."

"I understand. Video production is an integral part of the Army Training Program."

"I see that," I said, pointing to a photo of a guy in a control room.

"Sounds like you've seen some tough times. Remember, America's always your home." In the distance, a Chinese guy stood in the food court, holding a tray of samples lanced with toothpicks. "If you feel your path is set, I'll move on. But we could use video engineers."

"Yeah, maybe." I thought of how the military would be the ultimate escape from Kova. I'd be physically transformed with a shaved head and a bulked up body. I'd no longer be screwed over. I'd be void of fraternal passive mischief, secure in the Army's brotherhood, following my Dad and Pop-Pop's proud military footsteps.

"Here's my business card and application," said the Sergeant. "I served in the Persian Gulf. Artillery brigade."

I walked off in a trance, feeling the need to change my look, to prove that I was on the straight and narrow. I went to a Hair Cuttery to get a conservative doo, parted short like a Senator. The stylist washed my hair, massaging my scalp. I became relaxed, deflated. I sat with the black gown around my body, just a head peering out, forced to stare into the mirror. The stylist combed my wet hair as I contemplated the Army. My blue eyes glared back with disgust and my breath shortened. I pondered if the Sergeant had brainwashed me into curtailing my chosen direction in life.

The stylist brought the scissors up to snip a long comb-clamped section of hair.

"Hold on," I said standing up. I slithered out of the gown and explained that I wasn't ready. I handed the stylist three five-dollar bills.

After stress eating a huge chocolate chip cookie, I went to an ear piercing kiosk. I laid on my back, grinning at the rooftop flags of trapeze artists, clowns, and serenaders. The piercing gun punctured my lobes.

On a third floor bench, I caught glances of my gold studs reflecting in a store window. I watched the second floor customers with their sluggish walks and large bags. Sergeant Sanders chatted up a group of young men as they held shoe boxes. Within the mix of purchasers, a guy that appeared to be Wolf walked solo. His face had gauze around his chin and his hairstyle shortened. I jogged along the third floor balcony to catch up with him. The back of his head faced me as he stared into The Gap. He turned to the railing and leaned on it, peering down at the first floor merry-go-round, revealing his face. It was Wolf. His chin was missing a chunk and his mouth askew and ruddy, stretched apart. I stood ready to wave, but he never looked up. I called out his name. He didn't hear me. Loud carousel organ music looped. Effervescing flashback images of callow days spun in a glittery mobile in my mind, warming the back of my neck.

Stores away, the bopping head of a safari hat approached, mixed in the crowd. I wasn't sure if it was Kova, but the height seemed similar. Maybe he's here with Wolf, I thought. I ran to the parking lot, clutching the rolled up Army application like a baton ready to relay.

59.

Funneling Out

January '93

I took my parents' border collie, Fonda, for long walks. It was a simple way to use the ceramic one-hitter. Smoking weed at my parents' house was an impossible feat, so Fonda got a lot of exercise. She needed a harness around her neck because of instinctual desires to chase every squirrel, bird and car she saw.

Walking Fonda down Wischman Avenue, I passed the Community Center. A blinding, solid white vinyl fence was installed, completely blocking the view of Shady Creek. Three rows of glistening snug barbed wire lined the top. The chain link fence was gone. I made a left down Apel Avenue and saw a "For Sale" sign posted into the ground at Kova's house. I stood and stared at the house, then back at the white fence. A smiling old man strolling with both hands behind his back walked up to Fonda and petted her. He took a knee to get a slobbery kiss on the cheek.

"You interested in this house?" asked the old man.

"Is this house really for sale?" I asked. "Wasn't somebody living here?"

"Sure was. But he passed away months go. Last summer."

"He died?"

"Indeed. Don't know who he was, but he's responsible for that there eyesore." The old man nodded to the new fence. "I'm not a fan of it. Overpriced PVC made in China. I'd rather have American steel. Did you know him?"

"Wow. Uh, yeah. Kind've. He was a golfer. I caddied. He was. Well, he was unique."

Back home, I let Fonda loose. She ran to Dad who was taking a nap on the couch with newspapers draped over his legs. I asked him about Kova.

"Oh, yeah. He died last summer at Shady Creek," said Dad. "I think it was in the Clubhouse. Didn't you hear about it?"

"What? Why didn't you call me?" I asked.

"I didn't want to bother your studies. I figured the news might've messed you up with an exam. Don't you watch the news up there?"

"Yeah, but it's Berks County. We get Allentown, not Philly. I saw him the day before I moved up there. Sunday. It was the 30th of August."

"I'm sorry, Garvey. It was on the tube, in the papers. I didn't want to bother you with it. I know how much leaving Oreland meant."

I stammered out the door and took Dad's car to the Springfield Township library. I used a microfiche reader to examine archived local newspapers. I searched for summer obituaries and found Kova's half page spread. There were no details about how he passed, other than he died *doing* what he loved best at the *place* he loved best. The rest was a resume of great achievements and community involvement. They included a photo of him talking to Cub Scouts. I printed out the article and headed home. He died on the day I ditched him on the course: August 30th.

I drove to West Coast Video in a complete daze, wondering if Kova was truly dead. Quinn and I connected eyes in the store. He acted like he didn't see me and retreated to the curtained off Adult section. I chatted with Zakk at the counter.

"Wolf's Dad?" asked Zakk. "I heard a rumor he got turned into a bloody pulp while golfing."

"Like he was shot by a machine gun?" I asked.

"I don't know. Could've been. A cop I hook up free movies with told me a maintenance man witnessed it."

"For real? So it was definitely on the golf course?"

"No idea."

I headed to the Adult section and spread the velvet curtains. Quinn was sitting alone in the smut room, sitting on a stool, reading *High Times*.

"Taking a break?" I asked.

Quinn rolled his eyes. "Kind've," he said. "It's usually dead in here. Heard your fling with Emma is over."

"The whole college distance thing. She didn't want to do it. I would've tried it at least. We're supposed to hang out soon."

Quinn kept looking at his magazine. "I'm trying to get into the t-shirt biz and put an ad in here to sell them, but it looks like there's...competition."

"Sorry, man. You should still go for it. You've got mad illustration skills. So, do you know what happened?" I asked, handing over the obituary printout.

"I've heard some gory stuff."

"Did you talk to Louie?" I asked.

Quinn looked at me and gave an affirmative nod with the most minimal of maneuvers, keeping his eyes connected with mine. "I don't know if what I heard was true," said Quinn. "Who knows? Man, you go to college and Oreland truly disappeared for ya, huh?"

"We watch Bob Ross reruns up there," I smiled. "No time for news."

Quinn laughed. "It's weird Kova's gone. I know he ruined you with—"

"You know some of it, sure. But there's more. I can't even begin. I feel like he's still here and might be in the parking lot."

"Louie doesn't work at Shady Creek anymore. He had a nervous breakdown. I think he still lives in those apartments in Roslyn by the tracks. You should see him."

I reached my hand out to give Quinn a shake. He gripped it after a swooping slap. Dozens of sleazy porn titles surrounded us. The cover sleeves had faces of girls mid-orgasm, locked in ecstasy.

I drove to Louie's apartment complex parking lot. I recalled how Louie didn't have a car and commuted with his bike. I reversed into a spot that gave me a panoramic view of all entrances. I listened to 610 WIP. The host predicted the Phillies would go all the way in 1993. After two hours, Louie coasted passed me with plastic grocery bags slung on each of his handlebars. He got off the bike and fumbled with the bags. He dressed the same as he did on the golf course, with round framed sunglasses, cut-off jeans, a band tour shirt and a heavy viking beard. I jumped out of the car and approached him.

"Who the hell are you?" asked Louie.

"Garvey," I said. "Used to caddie at Shady Creek. I cut through the course often. Don't I look familiar?"

"Not particularly."

"I always had a hat on. Merv called me Gary."

"Weren't you just sitting in that car over there?"

"Yeah. I'm not gonna lie. I was looking for you."

"What the fuck you want with me?"

I pulled out the obituary. "This. What happened out there that day?"

"None of your business." Louie locked up his bike, grabbed his bags and walked up the stairs to the entrance.

"I was supposed to caddie for him that day. August 30th."

Louie stopped, turned and looked at me. "Where did you exit the course that day?"

"17th hole gate to Twining Road. Drove through the course like a lunatic, cutting through play."

Louie grinned and kicked the glass door open with his sandals. He waved me over.

In his apartment, he put the groceries away while talking about how my escape caused a shit storm. I sat down on a green leather couch and eyed framed ticket stubs from concerts and posters, carefully aligned guitars and volumes of shelved books about world history. The air conditioning was on high. Sandalwood incense lingered in the air.

"I'd offer you a beer but I'm sober," said Louie. "Been clean for 17 years now. Can't have it in my pad. How about a burrito? Gonna zap up a veggie one."

I declined. I stood and eyed the classic rock artwork on the walls. On the dining room table was a pamphlet entitled *The Four Methods Of Judicial Hangings*. I picked it up and examined it. The graphic photos inside startled me.

"Don't worry," said Louie. "I'm too chickenshit. But I've researched it. Pictured it. Thought about it. Bought the gear."

I nodded, watching the rotating burrito in the whirring microwave. The bean and sodium snack stench filled the room, eliminating the pleasant whiff of wood.

"When things were bad, I figured it'd be best to vanish and join Mama," said Louie.

The microwave beeped. I sat back on the couch.

Louie plopped down across from me in a wicker rocking chair. He had a closed lip smile with hands folded together. He gazed at me, letting his burrito cool as it steamed his beard. "So, you're the one that did it," he said.

"Did what?" I asked.

"You're the one that's given me a reason to live on."

"Because I ditched by job?"

"Yes, exactly. He ended up carrying his own bag. You found a way to break him down, to get him so irrational that his body withered and the Earth swallowed him up."

"Wait, what? This wasn't a plan. I didn't mean to hurt anyone."

Louie seesawed a hand. "You set it up."

I scratched the back of my head and eyed the door, uncertain of Louie's intentions. "I didn't kill anyone," I said.

"Because of your escape that day, you gave me freedom," Louie grunted, chomping into his heated snack.

"I'm not following."

"You used to cut through the course? You an Oreland boy? Any chance you went to Divine Miracles?"

"Yeah, I remember you. In the news."

"Lift up your shirt for a second."

"Why?"

"Real quick. Just need to know you're not secretly recording this. Pockets, out."

I revealed my skin and lint in my liners.

"Sorry, thanks. I trust ya. It's you. It really *is* you. Merv went mum after it happened. Depression. Took a sabbatical."

"Man, I'll just head out if you want me—"

"Alright, alright. Back in '86. The Father Pal thing. I was in on it."

I stood up and inched to the door.

"Relax. Sit down," said Louie. "It ain't like that. Kova made me a deal. He said secret real estate plans would be sent to my box in the Mail Room. Competitors spied on him. He didn't want them to snatch the plans from his doorstep. Someone picked them up, that being Father Pal. I never opened them. Had no idea it was really photos of kids. This went on for over a year, man. $400 a week cash. I needed the dough. The news crews did me in. Made me look demonic. My lady left and—"

"Did Kova threaten you?" I asked.

"Before the media came, he called me from a payphone. Warned me to be quiet. Said he'd have a guy suffocate me if I snitched."

"Jesus. I got caught up in some shit too. I just don't—" I waved my hand at the air, verklempt.

"You saved me brotha. He's gone. He was on the 16th hole. I was working on a nearby sand trap. I heard him cursing. He couldn't find his ball. He started making angry divots, fucking up the fairway. Then he walked down the quarry steps a bit. Paused. He turned back, holding his chest. His hat slid off. His mouth wide open. Hair all sweaty. He couldn't get back to the top. He fell backwards. I heard a bang on the railing. I ran over with his partner. Those steps are asphalt. The back of his head was busted open, arms twisted, just a pile of limbs, blood. His face got impaled by bamboo. His partner ran down. Called 911 on a cellular phone."

Louie walked over to his computer desk. He clicked his mouse around. I jumped up and walked over to him, keeping my eye on the monitor. Louie positioned the cursor over a folder. "The quarry is closed up now," said Louie. "If a ball goes in, it's treated like a water hazard. Weeks after, I found a disposable camera, about ten feet from where he ended up, stuck in some weeds. A photographer friend developed the film and sent me these." Louie clicked into the folder and revealed the scanned images: kids at convenience store parking lots, weird angled shots at carnivals, boobs, crotches, couples holding hands. One was from the inside of Kova's Spider. His distinct safari hat sat on the dashboard with Kova's reflection in the windshield. Louie leaned back in his chair and crossed his arms. "Monster predator alright."

I sat back down on the couch.

"The cash was good though," said Louie. "I paid off Mama's medical bills. But I missed her. I missed her final day."

"Her passing?" I asked.

"Merv forced me to work late to search for a missing golf cart. Some punks had stolen it. Kids come on the course and cause mayhem. Maybe it was a drunk dude at a wedding that left it in the woods. I found it with the seat charred and smoking in a sand trap." Louie laughed, thumbing away a tear.

I held a forearm up to disguise my eyes and twitching lips. I pondered whether intervening with Pat further would've prevented the cart theft.

"It's all over now though," said Louie, grabbing a photo of his Mama from a side table and kissing it. Louie picked up his Martin acoustic guitar and sang a verse of blues. I asked if it was Derek and The Dominoes and he rolled his eyes.

"Well, they covered it. Bessie Smith recorded a version in 1929.

Maybe's there's an older one. I've always wanted to check out Venice Beach, join a band or just play for tips. I think it's time."

"Can I use your phone?" I asked. "I need to let my folks know I'm not gonna make it for grub."

Louie reached for his cordless phone and tossed it.

Mom picked up and seemed upset that I wouldn't be in attendance. "I will leave a plate of chicken parm for you in the fridge," she said. "You can nuke it later. Listen, I found something on the kitchen island today. It doesn't belong to me or your father. Do you know what I'm talking about?"

"A frozen veggie burger?" I asked.

"We're not sure what it was. But we emptied it into the toilet and flushed it away."

I reached into my pocket and found my ceramic one-hitter but no dime bag. I juggled the phone and searched all of my jean pockets.

"We'll talk about it when you're back at the house," said Mom.

"Shit," I said after hanging up, covering the receiver as if Mom could still hear me. "I left a bag of weed in my parents' kitchen."

Louie cackled. "Sober is the way to go," he said. Louie walked me out of his building and through the lot. It was dark out. A dull yellow flickering light hung high above my Dad's car in the distance. After giving Louie a hug, I walked to the car and noticed white marks on the windows, each with zigzagged streaks of soap, pressed hard into the glass. Under a tree at the far end of the lot, a few young teens snickered, peeking out from behind a dumpster. I walked towards them to scare them off. They responded by popping out and pounding their chests. They took brisk strides towards me.

"You don't live here. We don't gotta listen to you. This is our home," one said, taking out a couple eggs from his cargo shorts.

I breathed through my mouth, astonished. I made a run for the car, awaiting the splat of yolk on my back. I made it in with just a marred hubcap and front windshield.

Driving off with a barrage of middle fingers in the rearview mirror, I turned on the wipers, smearing the yellow protein across the glass and mixing it with windshield fluid and flakes of soap. The windows grew heavily streaked. I pulled into a Glenside self serve power wash station. I hosed off the gunk with pressured water. A foamy lather and bubbling suds surrounded my feet.

I drove up next to the 16th hole and parked where Kova had climbed over the barbed wire to chase me in the snow. I got out of the car and gripped the chain links. Yellow tape, staked to the ground, surrounded the top of the quarry, stating: CAUTION DO NOT ENTER. The wind shook the glossy tape, tossing white sparkling moonlit reflections at me. Fervent thoughts of dodging Kova haunted me.

At home in my room, I thumbtacked Kova's crumpled obituary to the corkboard. I placed it beside the yellowed newspaper article about my Dad's car accident from '79. Dad and Kova faced each other from separate photos, both wincing into sunlight.

I called Emma. I had left a message earlier in the week, but she never phoned back. The phone rang with no pickup. I tried again minutes later. "Hello?" answered one of Emma's sisters.

"Oh, hey," I said. "Is Emma around?"

"Eh, no. Wait, is this Quinny?"

"No, it's Garvey."

"Garrrrrr-vey. Wow, you both sound alike. Good ole, Garv. I'm actually on the other line with my boyfriend."

"Gotcha. It's fine. I'll hang up."

"Listen," she said, lowering her voice to a whisper. "She's at a warehouse rave in Philly. My Mom would kill her. She wrote on a note here that she'll definitely call you tomorrow."

60.

Plan C With The Dragon

January '93

Being present for dinner was originally a deadline that assured our parents that we survived. We checked in, showed face and twisted what really happened into the expectation that matched the pristine aligned morsels of starch, protein, vegetables and beverage. Dinner was a time to comment on our faces altered through age, stress and progress. At 18, it morphed into a moment I never wanted to end, excited for a surprise dessert and awkward chats on current events. I enjoyed the satiated state when there was nothing to do but have more coffee, enjoy the music and laugh, with never a need to rush and wash the dishes or race to a calendared event.

I decided to make dinner for my parents for the first time ever. It was a fluke warm January day with the high temp at 70 degrees. As a proud vegetarian of three months, I was eager to saute some homemade falafel. It seemed more exciting than my potatoes and spaghetti dish.

Back from the supermarket, I plopped the bag onto the kitchen island. Dad took off his glasses and picked up each item to examine. "Chickpeas? Never had this before," he said. "Fava beans? Never even heard of these before. Unhulled sesame Tahini sauce? I don't even know what this means."

"It's good stuff," I said. "Trust me, once I get this fried up, you're gonna love it."

I ran upstairs to use the bathroom. When I exited, I thought of the dime bag I had left behind in the kitchen, cast aside like a gourmet bag of oregano. I received no punishment, just a few stories of lives ruined by more powerful drugs. I pivoted from the stairs and entered my parents' bedroom, knowing they were clanking ceramic mugs out of the dishwasher. I remembered how simple it was to find hidden wrapped Christmas gifts when I was younger. I slowly opened my Mom's underwear drawer, a typical stocking stuffer concealer, and saw a mess of straps, D cups and frilly satin. I reached for the top bra, torpedoes aimed at my head. I picked it up and saw the dime bag sitting in a larger transparent bag with a roach of a joint left. About half of the dime bag remained.

#

I wasn't used to cooking and having a conversation at the same time. Combined with using their mysterious electric range and too much olive oil, my lumpy constructed falafel balls became black smoke bombs and set off the detectors on the ceiling with incessant beeps. Dad opened up all the windows in the house to get the charred garbanzo bean stench out while Mom waved magazines around. I stood up on a stool and silenced the beeps.

"Looks like we're going to Juniper Palace," Dad said, rubbing his hands together and sticking his tongue over his upper lip. "Gotta get out of this smell before I puke."

"It's your father's new favorite place, over in Abington," Mom said.

"The food is outstanding," Dad said. "Best Chinese I've ever had. And there's a nice back bar I've been to a few times."

"Your father has a poker night right near the Juniper. He and his new buddies go there."

"I'll have a couple beers there some nights. Nothing crazy. Chinese pizza is great with beer. Owner's a good guy."

The Juniper Palace entrance featured a large fountain and

waiting area of red velvet chairs. Framed autographed photos of local Philly sports and news celebrities were hung on the walls. Some were comedians or musicians that performed at the nearby Keswick Theatre. In each photo, the Juniper Palace owner stood with a glistening brow, putting his arm around the VIP royalty. Deeper into the restaurant, as the hostess seated us, the framed items included signed headshots that said stuff like "Best Kung Pao Chicken Ever!" scrawled in marker. There were newspaper clippings of sporting events, snowfall totals and hurricane floods, a delightful mixture of local trivia. The Juniper featured traditional Chinese decorations as well, like detailed drawings of pagodas, dragons and pandas.

When the waitress took our order, I chose "Basket Of Steamed Vegetables". Dad put the large menu over his face and snorted aloud, trying to hold in laughter. Mom sported a large grin.

"What?" I asked. "It's so good. And healthy for you."

"I'm sorry," said Dad to the waitress. "My son is now a veg-a-mac-tarian, or whatever you call it."

"Ah, so am I," said the waitress with excitement and positioned toward me. "It's a great choice. Best thing on the menu, I think."

I looked up at the waitress and bowed at her viewpoint. She wore a red floral qípáo dress and tugged at the bun at the top of her head.

"Well, as long as it doesn't smell like whatever it is you tried to cook at the house," said Dad.

The waitress placed our orders and came back with a bowl of crunchy wonton strips and dipping sauces. "How long have you been a vegetarian?" she asked.

"Only a few months," I said. "Just exploring it out."

"Have you tried tofu yet?"

"No, is it good? Been meaning too."

"Yes, it's most excellent. It's all about what spice you cook with it. I like it firm."

Dad made a confused face. "You guys might as well be speaking Chinese," he said.

"I'll be right back with some green tea," the waitress said. She walked away.

"He's also single," said Dad through cupped hands. Mom slapped her cloth napkin at Dad's chest. The waitress stopped in her tracks with her back facing us and then walked on. I buried my face into my forearm, staring at the Chinese zodiac placemat. I pushed my hands down in the air, trying to smother any future outburst from Dad. He seemed more relaxed than usual. I was happy he gained new friends while I was at college.

"You gonna tell me why you brought your bookbag?" asked Dad.

Beneath my chair, I stored my Jansport backpack. I got it out, unzipped it and pulled out a paper. I had written an essay about Dad and his experience in the Air Force when he saved a General from a burning crashed plane.

"Remember when I interviewed you over the phone last month?" I asked. "It really worked out." I slid the paper to Dad.

"98%? Holy smokes," said Dad.

"Yeah, it's for Journalism. Had to interview a local hero."

"I'm coming for you, Elizabeth. It's the big one." Dad put a hand over his heart and pretended to be Fred from *Sanford and Son*, looking up toward the ceiling. He thumbed through the pages, back and forth, reading snippets of sentences. "Well, I'll be. I'm proud of you, Garv. Seriously, this is amazing."

Before we left, I went to the bathroom and passed the bar area that Dad was so fond of. I stared at the dozens of framed photos of frequent patrons. One photo was of Kova and Father Pal, sitting in the coveted fish tank section of the restaurant. The edges of their mouths glistened with sauce and their table was cluttered with porcelain tureens.

Back at our table, my parents and I sucked down our complimentary orange slices and read our fortune cookies aloud. Mine said: "All things come to him who goes after them."

Walking out, our waitress stood by the hostess podium with

hands crossed at her waist, smiling in our direction. "Hope you enjoyed your meal," she said. "Please come again."

"Definitely," I said, turning toward her. My parents started a conversation with the manager and stepped aside. "Just found out I'm a Tiger. What are you?"

"Chinese zodiac?" asked the waitress. "I'm a Dragon."

"That's the best one."

"How so?"

"You're the only mythical one. The rest are farm or pet animals."

"Tigers are pets?"

"Oh, and wild animals of the forest."

"And the ox?"

"Grassland regions, right?"

"Your folks are ditching you," said the waitress with a half-smile, pointing.

I looked over. My parents exited.

The hostess walked over. "Table C-13 needs help with a big spill," she said with brisk lips to the waitress.

"Gotta go," said the waitress, double-tapping a stack of menus at my chest. "Do come again." She winked and sauntered off.

I walked outside. "Who wants ice cream?" Mom asked. "There's a Baskin-Robbins two doors down."

"Sounds good," I said "Wait, I'll be right back. Forgot my backpack."

"Oh, you're gonna go talk to that waitress, eh?" asked Dad with a big smile and an arm around Mom. "He left it inside on purpose. What flavor do you want?"

"Rocky Road," I blurted, walking back. "With rainbow jimmies."

"Stay warm," said Dad.

"Why do you say that once in a while? My friends even picked up on it."

"Warm equals alive—stay alert, stay alive. Blood racing through your veins. Warm. You don't want to go cold. Got me?"

I shook off the Dad-ism and walked in. The manager saw me and made a silly face with arms out in confusion. "I forgot something," I said.

"Ah," he said, patting my back.

Bus boys were clearing our table. I squirmed through them, snatched my backpack and put it over a shoulder. I headed to the back bar. Tabletop signs on the bar stated: "Not Open Until 7:00pm". I glanced about. Nobody was around. I leaned up on my tippy toes and unhooked the framed photo of Kova and Father Pal from a nail. I put it into my bag and darted into the Men's Room. A guy was pissing into a urinal. I ducked into a stall, locked the door and waited for the man to wash up and exit. I unfastened the black cardboard from the back of the frame and removed the photo from the glass.

The Men's Room door opened. "What the hell do you think you're doing?" a gravelly voice asked.

I sat in silence and didn't answer.

"You're so busted," said the voice. Someone entered and walked towards my stall. I unlocked it. The door opened. The waitress from dinner stuck her face in the gap. "Ah-ha," she said.

"What the—nice male voice skills there," I said.

"So, what are you doing?"

"Yeah, this must look odd."

"I saw the whole thing. Saw you take it and head in here."

I heard a loud voice outside in the hall. The palm of a hand slapped onto the door and opened it an inch. The door creaked open further, the man unable to walk away from a conversation to relieve himself. The waitress freaked, jumped into the stall with me and locked the door. Her qípáo dress was no longer on. She wore a tight white t-shirt, white sweatpants and red cowboy boots with golden western swirls. She shushed me and hopped onto my lap, facing me as I sat on the toilet lid. Her knees hugged my hips as she gripped my shoulders.

"Sorry, that's my manager," she whispered into my ear. "Can't be in here. He'll be pissed."

"No prob." I looked at her boots. Her belly button ring caught my eye as her shirt crumpled up to her ribcage.

The manager continued to chat, holding the door ajar.

"Are you a Chinese cowgirl?" I asked.

"He told me last week I can never wear them again," she said. "Can't let him see my feet."

The manager ended the conversation and entered. He walked to the urinal and released a lengthy piss while moaning relief. The waitress put a hand over her mouth, applied heavy pressure and squinted, stifling herself. I eyed the black tattoos on her forearms, each arm with identical tigers and squiggly text. The manager fled after flushing.

"Gross. He didn't wash his hands," the waitress murmured, mouth open. "And what *was* that? A piss or an orgasm?"

"Don't wanna know," I smiled. "How did you see me?"

"Surveillance," she said, hopping off my lap. She smelled her armpits. "Do I stink?"

"Uh, no. Don't think so. Maybe a smidgen of wonton soup broth."

"Can't do much about that."

"I swore nobody was around."

"Ah, I wasn't around. But our cameras were. I stopped into my manager's office to tell him I was going on my break. I saw you swipe this from one of the monitors."

"Didn't think this place would have cameras."

"It's new. So, what are you doing?"

"Long story, but these two guys," I said, pointing to the photo. "They're monsters. Evil to kids in the darkest of ways. They must've ate here often but—my Dad loves this place. This guy here screwed me over. He's some Oreland hero. I mean, he's dead now."

"Why do you want to steal a dead man's photo?"

"I want to replace it." I pulled the article of Dad from when he saved the General. I had his photo and caption scanned to fit on a piece of paper, clipped to my essay. It was the same size as the photo of Kova and Father Pal. "This is my Dad. He hangs at the back bar with his buds. This would be awesome for him to see hung up."

"I remember that guy," the waitress said, pointing to Kova. "Bad tipper."

"He was known for that at the golf course. For most caddies. I used to carry his bags."

"Your Dad on the other hand. Great tipper. Speaking of, does your Dad always try to set you up with every waitress or just Asian ones?"

"Sorry about that."

"Well, I'm on my lunch break and hanging out with you in the shittiest of places, so I think we're off to a good start."

My face turned red. I couldn't see it, but I felt the heat in my cheeks.

"Let's go honor your Dad," she said.

I replaced the photo, fastening the black matte backing and locking it in place with the metal locking pins. I secured the frame beneath my belt and draped it with my shirt. I left the restroom and scouted out the hallway and around the corner towards the dining area. I ran back and stuck my head in the Men's Room door. "Coast is clear."

The waitress left the stall and trotted out. "I'll be around the corner," she said. "Gonna make sure no one is at the monitors first. If someone is coming, I'll flick the light switch on and off for these." She pointed up at the red pendant lamps hanging from the ceiling.

I leaned against a pillar close to the vacant photo. There were so many of them. It barely stuck out that it was missing.

"You're all clear," the waitress called out.

I angled myself up and hooked the frame onto the nail. I stepped back and smiled at the view. The light flickered. A mother rushed by with her son who was shouting how he had to pee. The waitress jogged around the corner. I gave her a thumbs up.

"Do you smoke?" she asked, walking over.

"No," I said.

"Join me anyway."

I followed her to a rear exit door and entered a fenced in area of dumpsters, beach chairs and an acoustic guitar. An opening to the parking lot showcased shoppers striving for prime spots. A raspberry and peach sherbet sunset competed with a red Circuit City sign atop a long metal pole.

"Are you related to anyone that works here?" I asked.

"Uh, no," she said. "I'm not even Chinese. I'm Thai. From the northern region. The pale ones. Lived there as a kid." She mouthed out smoke rings. "My boss knows. He was hard up for waitresses. I don't want to live this lie, but the money's good. Thai food is way better than this stuff. "

"Never had it before."

"It's more vibrant." She grabbed the guitar. "Spicy. Colorful. It's beautiful to just look at. Refreshing. You feel good after eating it. Haven't been to Thailand since I was 4. I knew a monster too. He lived there. A wicked man. My memory might be off, but—" She raised her eyebrows and kicked a dirty tennis ball hard against the fence. "Think I just have been blocking him out. Selective amnesia."

"Sorry. Didn't mean to stir up old demons. When's your shift end?"

"Are you coming onto me?"

"I suppose so. My parents are getting ice cream and waiting for me. I gotta split."

The waitress strummed some chords. "Gave a guy a lapdance in the Men's Room, smelling of wonton soup," she sang. "Helped him steal a photo. He's got silver earring hoops."

"A natural. Great voice."

"So, are you really hitting on me?" She pounced toward me and arched up to my face with unblinking eyes.

"Yes, I am. That's an awful phrase though, right? Hitting on you."

"I'm done at 10:30. Come to the back bar here. I'll save two stools. We can have a drink. Or at least get it in a styrofoam cup to go. The bartender hooks me up."

"I might take a break from drinks for a while. Barely got through my first semester and—"

"Even better. We'll get doughnuts here. The dipping sauce is dope."

"Cool."

"You sure you're sure? I'm not at my prettiest, if you're wondering."

"Sorry, just got distracted by that." I pointed to a person in the parking lot covered head to toe in paper. He was walking up to people getting out of cars and dancing. "Are those your takeout menus?"

"Oh, that guy," she said. "He keeps doing that. He runs in and grabs them from the breezeway. It's a riot but my boss hates it. Customers think it's a marketing campaign of ours that—"

"I know a guy that did this with paper, back when I was 4."

The paper clad man drew closer, strutting and making old folks shake their heads. He waved at us.

"A security guy will tell him to stop soon," the waitress said. "He's like a rare bird sighting."

The character beelined to us and started a tap routine with sneakers.

"Kristoph?" I asked.

The man chuckled and tilted his head back. I couldn't see an inch of his face. He danced like a chicken, fluttering his wings. He waved and walked off.

"You good?" asked the waitress. "You look spooked."

"I'm great," I said, shaking my head. "That was him. He's OK. Been wondering about him and—"

"You. Need. To. Tell me this story later. I gotta get my Chinese uniform back on. We'll Sanuk later."

"Wait, what did I sign up for?"

"Sanuk! Thai ethos. It's in my blood. Thailand. The land of smiles. It's all about striving for joy. You'll see." The waitress walked backwards, staring me down, adjusting her hair. She vanished into the sounds of a plucked guzheng.

I took in the swift clouds overriding the sunset. A shriek arose from the parking lot. Kristoph appeared running full speed, menus falling off, as a plump cart retriever boy chased him. Kristoph slunk past the automated doors of a discount clothing store and vanished.

I grabbed my ceramic one hitter and tossed it into the open dumpster. It clanked against a steel rusty wall. I walked onto the lot and circled to the front of the restaurant. My parents sat on a high curb, feet dangling in the yellow markings of the fire lane. They looked like two kids, dripping ice cream on their shirts, not having enough napkins. I stood and watched them for a moment as Dad produced a thunderous laugh at something Mom whispered.

"We got you a cup, not a cone," said Mom. "Didn't know how long you'd be."

"Did you get her number?" asked Dad.

I froze and realized that I didn't even get her name. "Kind've," I said.

Back home, I grabbed a condolences card from Mom's emergency Hallmark drawer. I picked one with a photo of flowers on the front and blank on the inside. I went to my room. I wrote: *I heard about your Dad this week. Thought you might want this. Stay strong.*

I folded up the stolen photo of Kova and Father Pal from Juniper Palace and placed it in the card. I paced about my room and opened my closet door. In the corner on the floor sat the vibrant orange laces that Wolf had used to trip me, coiled on a box of baseball cards. I unfurled a lace. Brown dried blood dotted the cotton. I put the lace in the envelope with the card and applied a stamp. I found the street address of Wolf's mother in the White Pages and wrote it on the envelope. I kept the return address blank.

At my desk, I filled out half of the crinkled Army application from the mall, wondering if I should enlist, a Plan B to the excess of college. I checked the answering machine, but there was still no callback from Emma. I headed out and gave Fonda a sober walk around town, taking deep breaths of crisp rapidly cooling air. I put the envelope for Wolf in a mailbox. Nearby, the owner of the house of extreme festive Christmas decor was disassembling the manger scene, walking with a life-size Joseph in one hand and Mary in the other.

"Love your lights," I called out. "Every year. Just beautiful."

The old man appeared stunned, struggling to hold the parents of Jesus. "Thank you, young man. When you're alone and old like me, it's what you do. My gift to you, to all of Oreland."

"And you keep them on all night. Most people turn them off at 10. It saved me one night. I hid behind that." I pointed to the spotlight I had used to blind Kova, back when fear sent a crevasse through my entitled mould, when I was a fringe accomplice that wanted to abscond into 8-bit lo-fi digital delights.

"Sounds like you shouldn't have been out that night, eh?" asked the old man, leaving the question to crystallize with frigid permanence. "Have a happy '93." He paced onward to his dark garage.

I arrived at the Juniper Palace bar early and ordered a coconut bubble tea. I sat beneath my Dad's photo. Dragon stencil art surrounded a massive mirror, perimetering patrons' reflections with red rugged scales, large claws and sharp teeth. My nameless date smiled from afar, lit up by round tasseled lanterns, serving a dessert to her final table. Her grin trailed off. I watched her work. Grey bags hung beneath her eyes at the verge of tears. I sensed a shrouded haunting, velvet theatre curtains revealing a truest self. I was eager to learn the joy that Sanuk brought forth, but felt torment encompassing her, tainting the filaments of her hope.

"What's wrong?" I asked, walking up to her at a silverware station.

She stared into my chest. "Haven't thought of him—the monster—in years," she said. "Now it's like it was yesterday." She wiped a single tear with the tip of a pinky and inhaled deeply through her nose.

"What we're about to talk about," I said. "We don't have to."

"I've never spoke of it before. Go. I'll be over soon."

At the bar, I pulled out the Army application to fill it out further. A tea candle flame flickered, extending to the top edge of page one. The paper blackened, flames racing to my first and last name. I slapped it with my hand, pressing the thick stock into the cool granite bar, smothering the accident. The scent of burnt ink drifted to my nose, unbeknownst to others amid cigarette smoke. I looked around. All of the candle flames writhed with a sudden chill in the air. Two fingertips traced down my shirt, along my spine. My date sat beside me in her tight qípáo dress. I lifted my hand. My printed name was no longer there, reduced to charred fragments. Lights dimmed. I turned to the Dragon.

"I'm starving," she said. "Can you eat again?"

"Always," I grinned.

Our shoulders kneaded together as we glanced in the bar mirror, licking appetizer glaze from our lips, hoping to lobotomize certain sudden souvenirs that seemed lodged away, forgotten, but triggered by a certain hue of metallic yellow or a squawk of a crow—nuisance reminders. We rubbed knees and spilled the heavy witnessed events of age 4, faced forward, white-knuckling the bar rail, plunging into dearest life. We maintained the arch of smiles, spirits upheaved with droll reverie. We took heavy dips into tangy chef's special sauce. Through sounds of calm woodwinds and pan flutes, we clutched onto spicy chili blend thresholds, our heads steaming with murky childhood dances.

We stayed warm.

About The Author

Carl Franke is a husband and father of two, residing in Glenside, PA. This is his first novel. Carl attended Kutztown University where he wrote an opinion column for *The Keystone Newspaper*, performed at open mic poetry readings and wrote short stories. When not immersed in fiction writing, Carl enjoys song writing with piano and keyboards, biking, discovering bands and learning new digital marketing strategies.

Learn more at: carl-franke.com

Made in the USA
Middletown, DE
10 July 2020